STAR WARS®
ORDER 66
A REPUBLIC COMMANDO™ NOVEL

By Karen Traviss

STAR WARS: REPUBLIC COMMANDO:
   Hard Contact
   Triple Zero
   True Colors
   Order 66

STAR WARS: IMPERIAL COMMANDO:
   501st

STAR WARS: LEGACY OF THE FORCE:
   Bloodlines
   Sacrifice
   Revelation

STAR WARS: Clone Wars
   No Prisoners

GEARS OF WAR: Aspho Fields

WESS'HAR WARS
   City of Pearl
   Crossing the Line
   The World Before
   Matriarch
   Ally
   Judge

STAR WARS®
ORDER 66
A REPUBLIC COMMANDO™ NOVEL

KAREN TRAVISS

BALLANTINE BOOKS · NEW YORK

Star Wars: Order 66 is a work of fiction. Names, places, and incidents either are products of the author's imagination or are used fictitiously.

2009 Del Rey Mass Market Edition

Copyright © 2008 by Lucasfilm Ltd. & ® or ™ where indicated.

All rights reserved. Used under authorization.

Excerpt from *Star Wars: The Clone Wars: No Prisoners* copyright © 2009 by Lucasfilm Ltd. & ® or ™ where indicated. All rights reserved. Used under authorization.

Published in the United States by Del Rey, an imprint of The Random House Publishing Group, a division of Random House, Inc., New York.

DEL REY is a registered trademark and the Del Rey colophon is a trademark of Random House, Inc.

Originally published in hardcover in the United States by Del Rey, an imprint of The Random House Publishing Group, a division of Random House, Inc., in 2008.

This book contains an excerpt from the forthcoming book *Star Wars: The Clone Wars: No Prisoners* by Karen Traviss. This excerpt has been set for this edition only and may not reflect the final content of the forthcoming edition.

ISBN 978-0-345-51385-4

Printed in the United States of America

www.delreybooks.com
www.starwars.com

OPM 9 8 7 6 5 4

For the British squaddie—with pride and gratitude

ACKNOWLEDGMENTS

My thanks go to editors Keith Clayton (Del Rey) and Frank Parisi (Lucasfilm); my agent Russ Galen; Bryan Boult and Jim Gilmer, for insight and unstinting support, even when I get really, *really* tedious; Mike Krahulik and Jerry Holkins of Penny Arcade, for being Mike and Jerry; Ray Ramirez, HHC 27th Brigade Combat Team, for technical advice and generous friendship; Haden Blackman, for relighting the fire; Sean, for great one-liners; Wade Scrogham, for disturbingly efficient hand weapons; and Lance, Joanne, Kevin, and everyone in the 501st Dune Sea Garrison, for practical and inspirational armor expertise, as well as being *or'aliit.*

THE STAR WARS NOVELS TIMELINE

1020 YEARS BEFORE
STAR WARS: A New Hope

Darth Bane: Path of Destruction
Darth Bane: Rule of Two

33 YEARS BEFORE
STAR WARS: A New Hope

Darth Maul: Saboteur*

32.5 YEARS BEFORE STAR WARS: A New Hope

Cloak of Deception
Darth Maul: Shadow Hunter

32 YEARS BEFORE STAR WARS: A New Hope

**STAR WARS: EPISODE I
THE PHANTOM MENACE**

29 YEARS BEFORE STAR WARS: A New Hope

Rogue Planet

27 YEARS BEFORE STAR WARS: A New Hope

Outbound Flight

22.5 YEARS BEFORE STAR WARS: A New Hope

The Approaching Storm

22-19 YEARS BEFORE STAR WARS: A New Hope

**STAR WARS: EPISODE II
ATTACK OF THE CLONES**

The Clone Wars
The Clone Wars: Wild Space

Republic Commando
  Hard Contact
  Triple Zero
  True Colors
  Order 66

Shatterpoint
The Cestus Deception
The Hive*
MedStar I: Battle Surgeons
MedStar II: Jedi Healer
Jedi Trial
Yoda: Dark Rendezvous
Labyrinth of Evil

**STAR WARS: EPISODE III
REVENGE OF THE SITH**

Dark Lord: The Rise of Darth
Vader

Coruscant Nights
  Jedi Twilight
  Street of Shadows
  Patterns of Force

10-0 YEARS BEFORE STAR WARS: A New Hope

The Han Solo Trilogy:
  The Paradise Snare
  The Hutt Gambit
  Rebel Dawn

5-2 YEARS BEFORE STAR WARS: A New Hope

*The Adventures of Lando
Calrissian*

The Han Solo Adventures

The Force Unleashed

STAR WARS: A New Hope
YEAR 0

Death Star

**STAR WARS: EPISODE IV
A NEW HOPE**

0-3 YEARS AFTER STAR WARS: A New Hope

Tales from the Mos Eisley
  Cantina
Allegiance
Galaxies: The Ruins
  of Dantooine
Splinter of the Mind's Eye

3 YEARS AFTER STAR WARS: A New Hope

**STAR WARS: EPISODE V
THE EMPIRE STRIKES BACK**

Tales of the Bounty Hunters

3.5 YEARS AFTER STAR WARS: A New Hope

Shadows of the Empire

4 YEARS AFTER STAR WARS: A New Hope

**STAR WARS: EPISODE VI
RETURN OF THE JEDI**

Tales from Jabba's Palace
Tales from the Empire
Tales from the New Republic

The Bounty Hunter Wars:
  The Mandalorian Armor
  Slave Ship
  Hard Merchandise

The Truce at Bakura

5 YEARS AFTER STAR WARS: A New Hope

Luke Skywalker and the Shadows of
Mindor

6.5-7.5 YEARS AFTER
STAR WARS: A New Hope

X-Wing:
  Rogue Squadron
  Wedge's Gamble
  The Krytos Trap
  The Bacta War
  Wraith Squadron
  Iron Fist
  Solo Command

DRAMATIS PERSONAE

Republic Commandos:
  Omega Squad:
    RC-1309 NINER
    RC-1136 DARMAN
    RC-5108/8843 CORR
    RC-3222 ATIN
  Delta Squad:
    RC-1138 BOSS
    RC-1262 SCORCH
    RC-1140 FIXER
    RC-1207 SEV
FI SKIRATA, former Republic commando
BARDAN JUSIK, former Jedi Knight, now Mandalorian
  (male human)
Sergeant KAL SKIRATA, Mandalorian mercenary (male
  human)
Sergeant WALON VAU, Mandalorian mercenary (male
  human)
Captain JALLER OBRIM, Coruscant Security Force (male
  human)
General ETAIN TUR-MUKAN, Jedi Knight (female
  human)
General ARLIGAN ZEY, Jedi Master (male human)
Null ARC troopers:
  N-7 MEREEL
  N-10 JAING
  N-11 ORDO
  N-12 A'DEN

N-5 PRUDII
N-6 KOM'RK
ARC trooper Captain A-26, MAZE
ARC trooper A-30, SULL
ARC trooper A-02, SPAR
Agent BESANY WENNEN, Republic Treasury investigator
  (female human)
JILKA ZAN ZENTIS, Treasury tax enforcement officer
  (female human)
LASEEMA, waitress (female Twi'lek)
Dr. OVOLOT QAIL UTHAN, Separatist genetics expert
  (female human)
NYREEN "NY" VOLLEN, commercial pilot (female
  human)

PROLOGUE

So that's *me*.

So that's how *I* once looked. We should all see ourselves from a stranger's perspective at least once in our lives.

There's a Jedi walking toward me, all brown robes and earnest piety; no braid, so despite his youth he's not a Padawan any longer. He'll be commanding troops. At the very least, he'll be on active service on his own. The war makes us veterans before our time.

I want to grab him by the shoulders and ask if he thinks this is a just war, a war fought honorably, but he'll panic if a Mandalorian in full armor accosts him—especially one he'll sense is a Force-user like himself. Nobody else is taking much notice of me. Mandalorians on Coruscant are just foreigners, bounty hunters, one more bunch of economic migrants out of the many thousands of species who flock to the galaxy's capital.

Ah, the Jedi's looking around the crowd. He can sense me.

I'm lost in the crowd of shoppers and sightseers. It's very strange—obscene, even—to see everyone going about their business on Coruscant as if we're not in the second year of an ugly war. And for them, of course, they're not. It's someone else's war in every sense—fought on other worlds, fought by other beings, fought by men who aren't Coruscant citizens. Clone troopers aren't *anyone's* citizens. They have no legal rights. They're objects. Chattel. Military assets.

Nobody should stand back and let that happen, least of all a Jedi.

I'm just a few meters from the Jedi now. He's so serious, so *committed*. Yes, that *was* me, just months ago.

A passerby glances his way and I sense her unease. When I walked around the city in my robes, I thought that others saw me as someone there to help them. Now I know different; they probably saw someone they didn't trust, with powers they didn't understand, someone they didn't elect but who shaped their lives behind the scenes anyway.

If they'd known how much I could shape their thoughts, too, they'd have fled from me.

The Jedi passes close by, but I still don't recognize him. He stares into the T-slit of my helmet as if I've grabbed him. I can feel his confusion as I walk on by—no, not just confusion: *fear.* A Force-using Mandalorian has to be on his list of worst nightmares.

There was a time when it was on mine, too. Funny, that.

Then I sense him turn. I feel him working his way back through the crowd toward me, burning with questions. Before he reaches out to tap my shoulder—and I have to give him credit for even trying—I turn to face him.

He flinches. What he sees doesn't match what he can *feel.* "What *are* you?"

"A man who drew the line," I say. "How about you?"

"You're General Jusik . . ."

Is it that obvious? To a Jedi, yes, it is. I used to be Bardan Jusik. Everyone in the Jedi Order knows I finally went native. It's the only response I know; complete surrender to a way of life—first Jedi, now Mandalorian—with every fiber of my being. My Jedi Masters didn't raise me to live my life by halves.

"Not any longer," I say at last.

"You walked out on us in the middle of a war—a war we *have* to fight." He's puzzled, resentful—scared. "How could you betray us like that?"

I wonder who he means by *we:* Jedi, or clones?

"I left because it's wrong." I shouldn't have to tell him that. "Because you're using a slave army to do it. Because there's no point fighting one kind of evil if you replace it with your own brand." Get specific. Get personal. Don't give him a chance to look away from his conscience. "*You,* personally. *You* make that choice each morning. A belief you suspend when it suits you isn't a belief. It's a lie."

Oh, *that* stung. I feel his soul squirm.

"I don't like it any more than you do." He seems oblivious of the stares of passersby. "But if I walk out, it won't change the Council's policy, or the course of the war."

"It'll change *your* war," I say. "But I suppose you're only following orders. Right?"

Everything that has happened in the galaxy—everything that ever *will* happen—is framework made up of countless connections of individual choices: yes or no, kill or spare, survive or die. They shape every moment for all eternity. One man's decision *matters.* One being's choices, moment by moment, connected to a network of billions of other choices, is all that existence is.

"We need every general we can muster," he says. Maybe the Jedi thinks he can appeal to my sense of guilt. "There's a terrible darkness coming. I can feel it."

So can I.

It's vague and unfathomable, but it's there, looming, like someone stalking me. "Then do something about your *own* darkness."

"Like joining a gang of mercenaries?" He looks over my armor with evident disgust. "Thugs. Savages."

"Before you choke on your own piety, Jedi, ask yourself who *you're* fighting for."

Fierfek, I called him *Jedi.* My disconnection's complete. His expression is one of quiet horror, and I walk away knowing I'll never see him again, I know that. And this war will end in grief; I know that, too.

I've made my choice. Unlike the clone troopers, I *have* one. And I choose to let the galaxy look after itself, and save those men that the rest of the civilized world relegates to the status of beasts. It's the *right* thing to do. It's what a Jedi should do.

The day of reckoning is coming. Yes, I can feel that, as well. I can't stop it, whatever it is; but I can defend those dearest to me.

Choices. I had one. I made it.

1

So, who's to know whether Jango had more than one son or not, or even how old he is? Come on now, Spar, it's time to be doing your bit for Manda'yaim. You don't have to lift a finger. Just act like Fett's heir while we sort ourselves out, so everyone knows we're still in business.
—Fenn Shysa, appealing to deserter Spar—former ARC trooper A-02—to pass himself off as Jango Fett's son and heir in the interregnum following Fett's death

Mes Cavoli, Mid Rim, approximately fifty years before the Battle of Geonosis

"**G**et up! Get up and *run,* you little *chakaar,* or I'll *drag* you up."

Falin Mattran could see the curling smoke of the mercenaries' camp a couple of hundred meters away, but it might as well have been a hundred kilometers. He couldn't get up: he couldn't go on. He knelt on all fours, struggling for breath, every muscle burning, but he refused to cry.

He was seven years old. *Nearly.* He thought it was six years and ten months, but he'd lost count in the war.

"Can't," he said.

"*Can.*" Munin Skirata was a big man with pockmarked green armor and a blaster that fired metal pellets. He loomed above, voice deafening, face invisible behind a helmet with a T-shaped visor that scared Falin the first time he saw it. "I *know* you can. You survived Surcaris on your own. And you're not strolling in your fancy Kuati park now, so shift your *shebs,* you lazy little *nibral.*"

It wasn't fair; life generally wasn't. Falin's parents were dead, and he hated the world. He wasn't sure if he hated Munin Skirata, but if he could have killed the man right then, he would have. Only exhaustion stopped him. He almost reached for the knife he'd taken from his father's body when he realized Papa was dead and was never going to wake up however hard he tried to rouse him, but he couldn't take his weight off both arms without collapsing into the dirt.

"You can do it if you want to," Munin yelled. "But you don't want to, and that makes you a *nibral.* You know what a *nibral* is? A loser. A waste of space. Deadwood. *Get up!*"

Falin wanted one thing, and that was to show that he wasn't lazy or stupid. His dad had never called him stupid. Neither had his mother; they loved him and made him feel safe, and now they were gone forever. He struggled into a kneeling position, then stood up, swaying and tottering, before breaking into a run again.

"*That's* more like it." Munin jogged alongside him. "Come on. Shift it."

Falin's legs didn't feel like part of his body anymore. He'd run so far that they wouldn't do what he wanted; he was *trying* to run, but stumbling along in small steps, unable to find a steady rhythm. His lungs screamed for a rest. But he wasn't going to stop and be a *nibral.* He didn't want to be one of those.

Ahead was as near to home as he was ever going see again, a camp that moved from place to place each day, where he sobbed himself to sleep every night with his fist crammed into his mouth so the Mandalorians wouldn't hear him and think he was a baby for crying so much.

He could see the *Mando* soldiers standing around in the camp, watching. They all wore armor. Even their women were tough soldiers, and it wasn't always easy to tell who was under that armor, male or female—or even if they were human.

Falin willed his body on, but it wasn't listening. He pitched forward flat on his face.

Every time he tried to get up, gravel and dirt cutting into

his palms, his arms gave way again. He sobbed in frustration. The finish line was still a long way off. But he *had* to get up. He *had* to finish.

I'm not lazy. I'm not a nibral. *I won't let him call me that—*

"Okay, *ad'ika*," Munin said, scooping him up in his arms. He sat Falin on one hip as if he was used to carrying kids and strode into the camp. The sudden switch from yelling to kindness was confusing. "You did okay, lad. It's all right."

Falin hit Munin as hard as he could, but his balled fist bounced off the metal breastplate. It hurt. He wasn't going to let Munin know that, though. "I *hate* you," he said, now certain at last. "When I'm bigger, I'm going to kill you."

"I bet you would," Munin said, smiling. "You already tried once."

The other Mandalorians watched, some with helmets on, some not. They'd finished fighting their war here. They were waiting for a ship to take them home.

"You trying to kill that boy?" One of the men stopped to ruffle Falin's hair. His name was Jun Hokan, and he was eating shavings of that horrible dried fish stuff, *gihaal,* carving them from a big chunk with his vibroblade and popping them into this mouth the way some folks ate fruit. "Poor *shab'ika.* Hasn't he been through enough?"

"I'm just training him."

"There's such a thing as too much."

"Come on, he's *mandokarla.* He's already managed to survive on his own. He's all guts, this one."

"Guts or not, I didn't have *my* boy do proper training runs until he was *eight.*"

Falin didn't like being talked about as if he couldn't understand what was going on. In the center of the camp—tents made of plastoid sheets strung over pits, then covered with grass and branches—a pot of stew was cooking over a crackling fire. Munin set him down and scrubbed his face and hands clean with a cold wet rag before ladling stew into a bowl and handing it to him.

"We'll have to get you some armor when we get home," Munin said. "You need to learn to live and fight in it. *Beskar'gam.* The Mandalorian's second skin."

Falin slurped from the bowl. He was always hungry. The stew was more like a broth—no lovely fat dumplings like his mother made—and he didn't like the fishy smell, but this was a banquet compared with what he'd scavenged in the ruined city for a year.

"Don't want any armor," he said.

"You can do all kinds of things when you're wearing armor that ordinary folks can't do, Kal."

Munin called him *Kal*. In the man's own language, it had something to do with knives and stabbing. Munin had nicknamed him Kal because Falin had tried to stab him with the three-sided knife when they first met; the Mandalorian seemed to think it was funny, and hadn't been angry at all. But Munin fed him, and didn't hurt him, and in the weeks since Falin had been part of the mercenary camp, he'd felt better even if he wasn't happy.

Sometimes Munin called him *Kal'ika*. The mercenaries told him it meant "little blade," and showed that Munin was fond of him.

"I'm *Falin*," he said at last. "My name's *Falin*." But he was already forgetting who Falin was. His home in Kuat City seemed like a dream mostly forgotten when he woke up, more a feeling than a memory. His family had moved to Surcaris while his father did engineering stuff on the new KDY warships there. "I don't *want* another name."

Munin ate with him. When he wasn't shouting, he was actually a kind man, but he could never take Papa's place. "Starting over can be a good thing, *Kal'ika*. You can't change the past or other folks, but you can always change yourself, and that changes your future."

The thought grabbed Falin and wouldn't let go. When you felt powerless, the idea of being able to make the bad stuff stop was the best thing in the world, and he didn't want to feel this bad ever again. He *wanted* things to change.

"But why do you make me run and carry things?" he asked. "It hurts."

"So that you can handle anything life throws at you, son. So that you never have to be afraid of anyone again. I'm going to make a soldier of you."

Falin liked the idea of being a soldier. He had a vague but long list of beings he wanted to kill for hurting his parents, and you could do things like that if you were a soldier. "Why?"

"It's a noble profession. You're tough and smart, and you'll be a great soldier. It's what Mandalorians do."

"Why didn't you kill me? You kill everyone else."

Munin chewed thoughtfully for a while. "Because you don't have parents, and me and my missus don't have a son, so it sort of makes sense that we do what Mandalorians always do—that we take you in, train you, set you up to be a soldier and a father yourself. Don't you want that?"

Falin thought about it for a long time. He didn't have an answer, other than that he was lonelier now among other beings than when he'd lived on his own in the rubble on Surcaris, because all the Mandalorians seemed to *belong*. They were close-knit, like a family. And they hadn't killed his parents; they'd just rolled into town a year later while the war was still raging. He still felt angry, though, and they'd do as a focus for his anger until the real thing came along.

"You think I'm lazy and stupid," Falin said.

"No, I just say that and shout at you to get you mad enough to push yourself to the limit." Munin watched him empty the bowl and then refilled it. "Because strength is up here." He tapped his head. "You can make your body do anything if you want to badly enough. It's called *endurance*. When you find out just how much you can do, how much you can face, you'll feel fantastic—like nobody can ever hurt you again. You'll be strong in every sense of the word."

Falin *wanted* to feel fantastic. On a full stomach, life seemed vaguely promising as long as he didn't think about his mother and father, lying there among the shattered beams of the house they'd rented on Surcaris.

It was an image he couldn't get out of his mind. He got up to wash the bowl in a pail of water and then sat down again next to the fire to look at his father's knife, as he did every day. It had three flat sides, like a pyramid stretched out to a point. He'd never been allowed to touch it while his father was alive, but he'd taught himself to use it because he had nowhere to run and nobody to look after him. He could throw it pretty well now. He practiced a lot. He could hit any target, moving or otherwise.

"What's it like being a soldier?" he asked.

Munin shrugged. "Often boring. Sometimes scary. You travel a lot. You make the best friends you could ever have. You really live. And sometimes—you die too early."

"Do I have to follow orders?"

"Orders keep you alive."

It wasn't quite dusk, but Falin could hardly keep his eyes open, and he sank into a delicious numb fatigue as the world receded. He tried to stay in that twilight state because sleep inevitably brought the dreams; but he was just too tired. At one point he was aware of being picked up and carried, but he didn't wake fully and the last thing he felt was settling into a pile of warm blankets in one of the shelters that smelled of machine oil, smoke, and dried fish.

It was then that the dream started again. He knew he was dreaming, but it didn't help. He walked through the front doors of the house on Surcaris, all the walls shattered and fallen with just the doors left intact, and he didn't recognize what he stepped on as his mother until he saw the blue fabric of her favorite tunic. He looked around for his father.

Papa was lying by the remains of the window, and Falin knew something wasn't right, but it took him a few moments to work out that most of his father's head was missing. He knelt down to take the knife from his father's belt and thought he saw him move.

It was always then that he woke up. It hadn't been like that in real life—he'd huddled next to the bodies for ages before he decided he had to run and hide, and took the knife to defend himself—but in the dream, it was all faster, different, more horrible. He jerked awake, heart pounding.

"Papa's head . . . ," he sobbed. "Papa's head's broken."

Munin Skirata hugged Falin to his chest. "It's okay," he said. "I'm here, son. I'm here. It's just a bad dream."

"I want it to stop. I want to stop seeing Papa's head."

Munin didn't yell at him for crying. He just held him until he stopped. Falin clung to him and sobbed until he couldn't get his breath anymore. He realized that the three-sided knife was on his belt now, in a new leather sheath, and he didn't know where that had come from.

"It'll stop, Kal," Munin said. "I promise. And nobody's ever going to hurt you while I'm around. You're going to grow up strong, and you're going to be happy."

Falin decided he didn't mind being called Kal if it made the nightmare go away. Somehow, the two things were now connected: if he stopped being Falin, he stopped seeing his parents' bodies. Munin Skirata sounded so certain and felt so strong and solid that Falin believed him. You could change if you wanted to. You could do *anything* if you wanted to.

"I'm not really a *nibral,* am I?"

" 'Course not, Kal," Munin said quietly. "I shouldn't have said it. There's no word for what you are in Mandalorian."

Falin—Kal—didn't understand. He looked up into Munin's face for an explanation.

"Hero," Munin said. "We don't have a word for hero. But you're a real little hero, Kal Skirata."

Kal Skirata. It was who he was going to be from this moment onward. He fell asleep again, and when he woke the next morning—no dreams, no nightmares—he saw that the world was a different place.

2

Ba'jur *bal* beskar'gam,
Ara'nov, aliit,
Mando'a bal Mand'alor—
An vencuyan mhi.

Education and armor,
Self-defense, our tribe,
Our language and our leader—
All help us survive.

—Rhyme taught to Mandalorian children to help them
learn the *Resol'nare*—the six tenets of *Mando* culture

Arca Barracks, Special Operations Brigade HQ, Coruscant,
736 days after the Battle of Geonosis—
second anniversary of the outbreak of war

Scorch raised his rifle and sighted up on the two sergeants
on the parade ground below the window.

The DC-17's upgraded optics were a definite improvement on the last version. The reticule settled on Kal Skirata
within a narrow imaginary band level with his eyes and the
indentation at the base of his skull; a perfect cranial vault
shot, the ideal for instant incapacitation. Scorch could see
the Mandalorian's mouth moving as he spoke to Walon Vau.

Yeah, it's getting like downtown Keldabe around here. It's
not as if I don't like the guy. But . . .

Sergeant Vau—and he would *always* be Sergeant Vau,
civilian or not—was the nearest Scorch had to a father. Vau

and Skirata seemed to be deep in conversation, both talking at once while they stared down at the ferrocrete surface of the parade ground, no eye contact at all. It was a weird thing to be doing at daybreak.

"I thought you said you could lip-read," Sev said, munching on a handful of spiced warra nuts.

"I can, but he's not making sense."

"Maybe they're talking *Mando'a*."

"I can lip-read *Mando'a* just fine, *mir'sheb* . . ."

"You'd think they'd have the sense to wear their buckets and use the internal comlink."

"Maybe it's nothing confidential." Scorch could smell the pungent spice on the nuts from across the room. "Look, you know what happens when you stuff your face with those things. You get indigestion and wind. And I'm not going to put you over my shoulder and burp you."

Sev belched. "You'll miss me when I'm gone."

"Make yourself useful and take a look, will you?"

Sev made a long, low rumbling noise at the back of his throat, finished the handful of nuts, and sighted up with his own Deece. He was a sniper. He spent even more time staring through optics than Scorch did.

"They're reciting something," he said at last, and leaned his Deece against the wall again to sit on his bunk and resume munching. "They're both saying the same words."

"Yeah? And?"

"Don't know. Can't make it out."

For as long as Scorch could remember, Skirata and Vau had been at loggerheads about everything from tactics and how to motivate troops to the color of the mess walls, sometimes to the point of fistfights. But the war seemed to have softened their outlook. There was no affection between them—not as far as Scorch could see—but something kept them together as brother warriors, tight and secret.

Neither of them needed to be here. Vau's bank raid—and they didn't talk about that, no sir—had probably netted millions. They were men with a mission, driven by something Scorch didn't quite understand.

He cranked up the magnification. But it didn't help. "Maybe they're having a really boring conversation."

"It's *names*," said Sev at last. "They're reciting names."

Scorch sighted up again, transfixed. "How old is Skirata?"

"Sixty, sixty-one, something like that."

"What's that in clone years?"

"Dead."

It was a sobering thought, and Scorch wondered why it hadn't struck him that way before. He'd never worried about getting old. He never thought he'd survive, for all Delta Squad's general bluster that the Separatist hadn't been born who could kill them.

"You think the crazy old barve is going to find his magic cure?" he asked.

Sev tossed a nut in the air and caught it in his mouth. "For what?"

"Our premature exit from this life. He is always talking about it."

Sev rumbled again. "I still reckon he killed Ko Sai. And I still reckon he got her research, and that's why he killed her, to shut her up. So yeah, I'd bet on him finding a way to stop us aging so fast."

Scorch suspected that Vau was as deeply involved in the death of Kamino's renegade cloner as Skirata; he was still fiercely loyal to Vau, because the man was the reason Delta were all still alive today, one of a handful of squads that had survived intact since the Kamino days. Vau raised *survivors*. "You're not going to mention that to Zey, are you, Sev?"

"Nah. I hate giving him sleepless nights."

"But if Sergeant Kal's got Ko Sai's research, why hasn't he started dishing out the cure? It's been nearly six months since he gave you her head."

"You make it sound like a birthday present," Sev said. "Maybe he can't make some of the formula work. Or he's just milking the Republic for all he can get before he bangs out with his stash."

"Kal wouldn't leave without his precious Nulls." Scorch turned to look at Sev and met a raised eyebrow. "Would he?"

"If they deserted, would you shoot them?" Sev asked.

Scorch shrugged, trying to look disinterested, but the idea of putting a round through a brother clone didn't sit well with him. The Nulls were Skirata's adopted sons, too, his precious little boys even if they were grown men—*big* men, dangerous men—and if any barve so much as looked at them the wrong way, Skirata would have his guts for garters.

Even us.

"We wouldn't have to," Scorch said. "You heard all about Palpatine's death squad standing by if we step out of line."

"Don't avoid the question. *Would you shoot them if ordered?*"

"Depends," Scorch said at last.

"Orders are orders."

"Depends who's giving them."

"The longer this war goes on, the less I feel the Nulls are on the same side as us."

Scorch knew what Scv meant, but he thought it was a harsh judgment all the same. He couldn't imagine the Nulls siding with the Seps. They were crazy, unpredictable, even Skirata's private army, but they weren't traitors.

"Come on," he said, grabbing his helmet and heading for the doors. "Let's see what the old guys are up to. I can't stand the suspense any longer."

The parade ground was a platform edged with a low retaining wall and a border of manicured bushes, all trimmed to regulation height—there *was* such a thing, Scorch was certain—and it didn't see many parades. More often than not these days, it stood empty except for the occasional impromptu game of bolo-ball. The two veteran sergeants stood in the center of it with heads slightly bowed, oblivious of the commandos approaching.

But Skirata was never really oblivious of anything. Nor was Vau. They had eyes in their backsides, those two. Scorch still hadn't worked out how they'd managed to keep such a close eye on their respective training companies back in Tipoca City. To a young clone, they'd seemed like omniscient gods who could not be deceived, evaded, or outsmarted, and they still came pretty close now.

Scorch could hear the mumbling rumble of low voices. It

had a sort of rhythm to it. Yes, they were reciting a list. Now that he could hear, he caught sounds he recognized.

Names.

They *were* reciting names.

Sev was the first to hesitate. He caught Scorch's elbow. "I don't think we should interrupt them, *ner vod.*"

Skirata turned slowly, lips still moving, and then Vau looked up.

"You want to join in, *ad'ike*?" Vau said kindly, and he was not a kindly man. "Just commemorating brothers gone to the *manda*. You forgotten what day it is?"

Scorch had, although it should have been etched in his memory. Seven hundred and thirty-six days ago, all ten thousand Republic commandos had been deployed to Geonosis with the rest of the Grand Army at zero notice, a scramble to board ships that left no time for farewells to their training sergeants. Of the ten thousand men who shipped out, only five thousand had come back.

Scorch felt like a fool. He knew what the two sergeants were doing now, and why: they were reciting the names of fallen clone commandos. It was a Mandalorian custom to honor dead loved ones and comrades by repeating their names daily. He wondered if they went through all those thousands every single day.

"You didn't memorize every name, did you, Sarge?" Sev asked.

"We remember every lad we trained, and we always will," Skirata said quietly, but Scorch saw that he kept glancing down at a datapad clutched in his hand. Five thousand names—plus those killed after the Battle of Geonosis—was an impossible feat of memory even for Skirata's devotion. "The rest . . . we only need a little prompting."

Scorch couldn't now name half the squads in his batch at the Tipoca training center, let alone the men in them. He felt ashamed, as if he'd betrayed them. Vau gave him a nod and gestured with his own datapad, indicating he was transmitting, and when Scorch checked the 'pad clipped to his belt the list was there, highlighted at the company currently being recited. He joined in the reading obediently. So did Sev.

There were many clones with identical nicknames based on their numbers—a lot called Fi, or Niner, or Forr—and it gave Scorch a shudder to say the name *Sev* more than once.

It probably didn't do much for Sev's morale, either. Scorch glanced at him, but he looked unmoved as usual, eyes fixed on his datapad.

"Baris, Red, Kef . . ."

". . . Vin, Taler, Jay . . ."

". . . Tam, Lio . . ."

The list went on. After a few minutes, their voices synchronized; there was a strange hypnotic feel to it, like an incantation, a rhythm and pitch that left Scorch almost in a trance. It was just the effect of simple repetition, but it still unsettled him. He wasn't the mystic sort.

Behind him, he heard the faint crunch of boots, but he didn't dare break the spell and turn to look. Other commandos were joining the ritual. There were never many men in the barracks at any one time, but it seemed like they were all turning out to pay their respects.

So many names.

Is mine going to be on that list this time next year?

Fi was on it; Fi, RC-8015, Omega Squad's sniper. Skirata didn't even blink when he said the name, and neither did Vau, even though word was getting around that Fi wasn't dead. It was a strange moment, repeating the mouthy little *di'kut*'s name as if he were gone. Scorch, feeling suddenly guilty at escaping so much personal bereavement, saw Sev take a slow look to his left as if he'd spotted someone. Scorch didn't want to break his concentration. He didn't look to see what had distracted Sev.

Reciting the list of the fallen took well over an hour. Eventually, when the last name was read, Skirata and Vau stood silent for a moment with their heads bowed. Scorch felt he'd been woken abruptly, suddenly aware of sound and harsh sunlight as if he'd stepped out of a dark room, and he was almost expecting some momentous end to the ceremony; but in typical Mandalorian style, it simply ended because all that needed to be said had been said.

Skirata looked up. A couple of hundred commandos had

assembled, some with helmets and some without, each man in individual painted armor that looked incongruously cheery for such a solemn event. But that was very *Mando,* too. Life went on and was there to be lived to the full, and constant remembrance of lost friends and family was an integral part of that. *Aay'han.* That was the word for it: a peculiarly Mandalorian emotion, a strange blend of contentment and sorrow when safely surrounded by loved ones and yet recalling the dead with bittersweet intensity. The dead were never shut out. Skirata's *DeepWater*-class submersible was called *Aay'han.* That said a lot about the man.

"What are you waiting for, *ad'ike*?" Skirata asked. He always called them that: little sons. Scorch wondered if he'd formally adopted all his squads. That was Skirata all over. "Just make sure I don't have to add any of your names next year, or I'll be very annoyed."

"You reckon there'll be a next year, Sarge?" The commando who asked wasn't a guy Scorch knew, but then Delta kept to themselves. His armor was decorated with navy-blue and gold chevrons. "I like to plan ahead. Who knows, I might have a social engagement . . ."

Skirata hesitated for a moment. "You know how the war's gone so far. Maybe we'll all be here in *ten* years."

"Your grandson will be big enough for full armor by then."

There was a ripple of laughter and Skirata smiled sadly. Scorch expected him to be happier at the mention of the baby boy that one of his kids—his *biological* kids—had dumped on him. He certainly seemed to dote on the child. But it looked as if something had taken the happy grandfatherly gloss off the situation.

"My dearest wish," Skirata said, "is that you all get to see him grow up."

Well, it wasn't a day for hilarity anyway. They'd just stood there on a big, empty parade ground and recited the names of thousands of dead brothers, so Scorch felt it was a suitably downbeat note to end on. Nobody was singing much about *darasuum kote*—eternal glory—these days, although Scorch thought a verse of *Vode An* might have been appropriate.

But the impromptu assembly broke up in silence, and Skirata walked off with his usual limp, Vau ambling beside him. Out of curiosity, Scorch kept an eye on the two sergeants all the way to the hangars on the far side of the barracks.

"Come on," said Sev. "Can't hang around all day. Got a mission briefing before lunch. I need to calibrate my HUD."

"What do you think they're up to?"

"Getting old and working out how to spend Vau's bank haul."

"No, they're up to something serious. I can tell."

"Mind-reader now, are we?"

Scorch couldn't understand why Sev never saw what he saw. They'd grown up with those two old *shabuire,* and when either of them had some scam running, they had this *look* about them, subtle but discernible to clones who relied on subliminal detail for recognition in a sea of near-identical brothers. Skirata had his scam face on, for sure.

"He definitely knows something we don't," Scorch said.

"Whatever it is, then, it won't hurt us."

Skirata and Vau paused at the entrance to the armory. Then Scorch saw something that vindicated his paranoia. Two familiar figures that he hadn't seen in a couple of years— figures in *beskar'gam,* traditional Mandalorian armor— emerged from a side door and greeted the two sergeants with that distinctive hand-to-elbow grip. Mandalorians shook hands by mutually clasping above the wrist. Vau said it was to prove you had a strong enough grip to haul a comrade to safety.

Maybe they'd arrived to mark the anniversary. Nobody outside the Grand Army seemed to bother about it.

"What are *they* doing here?" Sev muttered. "Why now?"

Wad'e Tay'haai and Mij Gilamar were two of the *Cuy'val Dar,* the training sergeants recruited personally by Jango Fett to train clone commandos in Kamino. Most were Mandalorians, and most had disappeared again once their contract was over, living up to their title: "those who no longer exist." But now they were reappearing in ones and twos. It just made Scorch feel that his general suspicions were justified.

"I don't know," he said. "Maybe Kal's decided he likes the company of intellectuals." He paused. Tay'haai still had that ancient bronzium spear slung across his back and a *beskar* flute hanging from his belt. They were both lethal weapons. "You think he ever uses those things?"

"Sure of it," Sev said. "I heard Zey was trying to recruit *Cuy'val Dar* again to cross-train ordinary troopers."

"Smacks of desperation."

"In case you hadn't noticed, we *are* desperate."

The four Mandalorians exchanged a few words and disappeared. Without his helmet systems, Scorch couldn't overhear anything at that distance. "Why *did* Fett recruit any non-*Mando* sergeants at all?"

Sev shrugged. "He said it was for the skills mix, but I reckon he just couldn't find a hundred Mandos to front up for him."

Scorch followed Sev back into the accommodation block. He often wondered how the commandos trained by *arueti-ise*—non-Mandalorians, a word that could mean anything from foreigner to traitor—felt about being surrounded by others who were so steeped in Mandalorian culture. There weren't that many left, though. Out of twenty-five hundred or so who completed training by *aruetiise,* fewer than a thousand remained. It said a lot for Mandalorian training.

"We could train the white jobs better ourselves," Scorch said. "We've got experience to pass on to them."

Sev picked up his helmet from the table and inverted it to begin calibration. "You fed up with fighting, then? Want a nice desk job?"

"No, just saying . . ."

Scorch tried to avoid thinking too much because life was now full of questions that were beyond his power to answer or even influence. They crept up on him at unguarded moments: in the 'freshers, or while he sat in the gunship en route to an insertion, and just before he fell asleep. Where was the Grand Army going to get more troops? If they started cross-training more meat-cans as commandos, who backfilled their positions? Things looked more stretched every day.

And where were all those zillions of *shabla* droids the Separatists were supposed to have? They had plenty, but if they had as many as Intel claimed, they must have been having a party somewhere and sitting out the war. One of the Null ARCs swore blind that there was only a fraction of that number deployed.

The Nulls knew a lot that they didn't share with the commando squads. When they *didn't* know something, Scorch got worried. He kept forgetting how many zeros there were in a quadrillion, but whatever it was, it was a lot more droids than he'd encountered.

"Maybe Palpatine will have to start recruiting citizens," he said hopefully.

Sev laughed. He didn't do that often. "I'd rather work shorthanded than have to serve with mongrels. You've seen what they're like as fleet officers. You want them as infantry?"

"At least the war would be over quicker. We'd win or lose horribly."

"True. Brutal, but true."

But what happens to us when it ends?

It was the kind of question that whiny bunch Omega kept asking. Scorch couldn't plan that far ahead. All he knew was that the Grand Army would run out of troops in a year or so, if casualty rates held constant, and he wasn't seeing anywhere near enough replacements coming in.

"Someone said that Palpatine's started producing clones on Coruscant because he doesn't trust the Kaminoans not to get their facilities trashed by the Seps again," Scorch said.

Sev huffed and got on with calibrating. "Yeah, like the rumor that we were getting some super-duper new ion cannon . . ."

He was right. It was another dumb rumor like so many they'd heard before. If the Chancellor was breeding more clone troops, he'd have told everyone, just to boost morale and scare the Seps. And if he had them, he'd deploy them.

Scorch had seen evidence of neither.

But if he *was* breeding them . . . they wouldn't be ready for a long time. Kamino clones took ten standard years to mature.

No, it was all *buzz,* the stream of tall tales, general half-heard gossip, and occasional nuggets of truth that circulated among the ranks. There were no extra reinforcements on the horizon.

Galactic City, Coruscant, 737 days ABG

Surveillance was an art, and so was evading it.

Republic Treasury agent Besany Wennen had tailed a good number of frauders and embezzlers in the last six years, but she'd never been the subject of a investigation herself. As she headed home from the office after a late finish—some work was best done while colleagues were absent, especially the kind of work that would get her arrested—she slid her hand into her pocket out of habit to check two things. One was the Merr-Sonn blaster that Mereel, Null ARC trooper N-7, had given her; the other was her datapad, full of heavily encrypted data that should never have left the Treasury mainframe.

I'm a spy. I'm working against my own government. I was always such a good girl, wasn't I, Dad? And now look what's become of me.

Her father would have understood, though, she was sure. He'd taught her to stand up for what she believed. The blaster was simply the kind of precaution you had to take when you were meddling in the Chancellor's secrets. At night, even under the garish lighting of a quarter thronged with beings from every part of the galaxy, Besany felt utterly alone and *hunted.*

Every day—sometimes in the morning, sometimes on her way home—she was convinced someone a few paces behind was watching her. She'd turn, seeing nothing but commuters with woes other than hers on their minds, but the uneasy feeling wouldn't go away. Sometimes it even happened in the office. She wondered if one of the shapeshifting Gurlanin spies was still shadowing her; but they'd left Coruscant now, and if they put their minds to it, not even a Jedi could detect them.

This time, though, the sensation of being stalked wasn't just her guilt talking.

Just as the Gurlanin had warned, someone *was* following her. A man had caught her attention at the speeder bus platform near the Treasury building. She was used to attracting stares—she was very tall, very blond—but this scrutiny was different, a kind of fixed, slightly-past-her glance that meant the man was keeping her carefully in his peripheral vision, trying to look as if he were taking no notice of her. Some might have said Besany was just paranoid, but she was a professional investigator, and she just *knew.* Her gut was rarely wrong.

The man was graying, middle-aged, and portly, an anonymous-looking human male in a well-worn, high-necked business suit just like millions of others. He seemed to change his mind about waiting for the speeder bus to the university and walked ten meters behind Besany.

She caught sight of him reflected in the transparisteel walls of Galos Mall. He *was* tailing her, no doubt about it.

And if you've not arrested me yet, chances are you can't . . . or you don't know what I'm up to.

It was hard to imagine what *can't* meant for a government that seemed to use emergency powers with such careless and unopposed ease. Besany had been waiting in silent dread for a knock on the door in the middle of the night ever since she'd first started bending the rules, and then twisting them out of all recognition on behalf of Sergeant Kal Skirata— *Kal'buir,* Papa Kal—whose extraordinary paternal charisma made her throw aside the caution of a lifetime.

It was for a moral cause. She never had any doubt about that. It was just a healthy fear of getting caught.

She glimpsed her stalker in the transparisteel shopfront again, and her stomach churned.

The more she dug into the accounts of the Grand Army, the more anomalies she found—bogus companies, credits being channeled into cloning facilities far from Kamino— and yet there were no extra troops appearing to bolster the beleaguered Grand Army, now stretched dangerously thin across the galaxy. Numbers were her life; but the numbers in Chancellor Palpatine's defense budget didn't even come close to adding up.

You're building another secret army, aren't you, Chancellor? And that's why the Kaminoans are worried. They know something's up.

Besany didn't break her pace. She kept on walking, still relatively safe among the crowds, and tried to decide whether to carry on to the air taxi platform, grab a cab, and escape her apparent pursuer, or to divert down the next walkway to nowhere in particular and flush him out.

And then what? Run away? Shoot him?

The man was still behind her as she stepped onto the moving slidewalk that linked the lower level of Galos Mall to the fashion floors. She leaned one-handed on the safety rail as the moving belt carried her past the holodisplays of garments, letting her gaze sweep over him before turning to look at the other side. When she reached the ready-to-wear section, she stepped off at the last moment and thought she'd lost him, but after a few minutes she caught sight of him again riffling through impossibly frilly underclothes on a rail as if shopping for his wife. His air of bemusement looked authentic.

Of course, I might just be paranoid after all . . .

Besany spun around and headed back to the slidewalk down to the walkway level again. If he followed her this time, she decided, she'd grab an air taxi, or maybe even confront him. Yes, she could do that: she'd walk right up to him, look him in the eye, smile charmingly, and ask him if he knew her.

Do I just want to shake him off, or find out who he is?

If Palpatine's agents wanted to kill her, they'd had plenty of opportunities. This man was probably just finding out who she associated with and where she went. The slidewalk dipped at a gentle gradient down to the walkway, and she stepped off at a race-walking pace to the air taxi rank. His only option then would be to follow her home, and then—*then* she would have an excuse to shoot him.

But even if you do . . . there'll be another one to take his place.

How much did they know? Treasury security was her

business. She was certain they didn't realize she was downloading data from the budget system.

Ahead of her, a tower of black transparisteel hung like a waterfall, a different-themed restaurant on every floor. She could see the diners and the sporadic burst of flame as chefs prepared cojayav wings at the tables; and she could still see the man in the suit reflected in the ambling crowd behind her. They were well inside the entertainment district now. The walkways were packed with well-heeled Coruscanti and offworld tourists out to sample the best cuisine in the galactic capital. Crowds were useful insurance, but they were also places where the worst could happen.

Besany slid her datapad into the inside pocket of her coat, pretending to fumble for her transit identichip, and gripped the blaster in her pocket.

It was purely for comfort. There was no way she could use a weapon here in this crowded, very public place. Her newfound friends in the Coruscant Security Force could make the problem go away if she opened fire, but they couldn't make thousands of people turn a blind eye. Attention was the last thing she needed right now.

The plaza was growing more packed as she neared the taxi platform. A line of diners waiting for tables at the Vesari fryhouse had formed a dam in the sea of visitors, slowing the flow of foot traffic so much that the crowd began to form eddies. Besany was losing ground to the man in the suit; she could see him as she turned to avoid the queue, so she darted sideways into the colonnade of small tapcafs to bypass the crowd.

She was banking on him not trying anything stupid—as in *fatally* stupid—in public. The colonnade led to a parking area for private speeders, so if she cut through there she could rejoin the main walkway by the taxi platform. But the permacrete square was a deserted maze of vessels crisscrossed with long black shadows, and she realized she'd made a dangerous mistake. She should have stuck with the crowds.

Hand on her blaster, she turned. There was no point running. She was almost face-to-face with the man now, a matter of paces away, and she met his eyes.

He seemed surprised when she drew the blaster from her pocket. But his wide-eyed expression wasn't directed at her. It was because someone else was suddenly right behind him, an arm clamped around his neck, and his sharp gasp was cut short. Besany heard a faint gurgling. The man's right leg flailed a couple of times, and then he seemed to be standing frozen on tiptoe, motionless.

"Just because you're following someone," said a familiar, much-missed voice, "doesn't mean *you're* not being followed." Clothing rustled. "Let's just check what you're carrying . . . oh, a nice DH-seventeen. That's not quite your style, is it?"

A battered gray delivery speeder dropped out of nowhere and Besany didn't have time to move past complete confusion into fear. Its side hatch opened: a huge hairy Wookiee arm shot out and hauled the man inboard. Captain Ordo— Null ARC-11 Ordo, *her* Ordo, her lover—shoved the taper-nosed DH-17 blaster inside his jacket and beckoned impatiently to her. He was supposed to be on deployment light-years away, not here. She hadn't even spotted him following them.

Neither had the man in the suit, it seemed.

"Ordo, you said you were in the Outer Rim," she whispered, looking around to see if there were witnesses, heart hammering. "How long have you been following me?"

The speeder dropped a little lower, and he put one boot on the hatch rail. Ordo looked very different out of his pristine white ARC trooper armor: in nondescript dark street clothes, he could have been anyone from a bodyguard to a thug from one of the local gangs that preyed on unwary tourists.

"I like to keep an eye on you," he said. "Get in."

"What are you going to *do* with him? If his control knows he was following me, then they'll know I'm involved."

Ordo seemed disturbingly relaxed. It was as if he'd never been taught that kidnapping people was wrong. But Skirata's special forces squads abducted, assassinated, and spied for the Republic, and there was an inevitability if you bred hyper-smart, ultra-hard fighting men: sooner or later, they understood their power, and used it for their own ends if those ends weren't met by the Republic.

"Can't stand around chatting," Ordo said. "Get in, *cyar'ika.*"

Ordo always exuded unshakable confidence in a crisis, and Besany now understood why troops would follow some officers anywhere. Before she could even think about it, she found herself scrambling into the speeder's open hatch, following orders without argument. A stench of cooking oil and stale mealbread—the speeder's previous cargo, probably—hit her. In the gloom, a Wookiee sat crammed awkwardly into one of the human-sized seats with a firm grip on the man in the suit. It was Enacca, one of Skirata's fixers. *Kal'buir*'s associates were an eclectic mix of species and professional backgrounds, from the respectable to the outright criminal, but mostly the marginal beings who needed to duck and dive to get by. Skirata was very good at getting a motley crew to work together for mutual advantage. He'd missed his vocation, Besany thought. Politics needed a man like that.

Enacca made a quiet rumbling trill deep in her throat. Ordo shrugged in response.

"No, I haven't a clue who this *chakaar* is," he said. "Get this crate airborne and we'll find out."

"What do you want?" the man asked. "My wallet? My speeder?"

He was trying to play ordinary, and failing. He wasn't scared enough—or even angry enough—at being plucked off the street. Any normal being would have been reduced to a quivering heap if they were kidnapped by a Wookiee and a man who looked the way Ordo did right then.

Ordo held out one hand, palm open. His other hand drew a short-barreled custom Verpine pistol. "Not that I think you'll be carrying your *real* identichip, but let's have a look."

Besany shrank back against the bulkhead. She was now perfectly safe but even with a Wookiee and a Null ARC trooper taking care of her problem, she felt uneasy sitting so close to someone who'd been tailing her. Her adrenaline was starting to ebb. This wasn't how she saw her sober career in the Republic's civil service panning out. Ordo had literally crashed into her life a year ago, and her galaxy had been changed out of all recognition. Today was just the new normality.

Enacca lifted the speeder clear of the parking area, banking over the artificial cliffs and canyons of Coruscant. Besany could see the nightscape through the small viewport at the rear. She wondered where they might be going; Enacca's specialty was procuring vessels and safe houses—safe for the clones and Skirata's associates, anyway. Wherever they were taking this man wouldn't be safe for him at all.

"My name's Chadus," the man said, eyes following Ordo's hands as he rifled through the contents of the wallet. "I work the late shift at the transit authority."

"Sounds like a load of *osik* to me. Why were you following this woman?"

"I wasn't."

"You always hang around attractive females in the lingerie section, do you? There's a word for men like you."

"I wasn't following her. I was looking for something for my wife—"

"I'm the jealous kind. I don't like perverts stalking my girlfriend."

"I told you—"

"Why were you carrying a serious piece like a DH-seventeen?"

"In case you hadn't noticed, Coruscant is getting pretty rough."

"A hold-out blaster's a wise precaution. So many riffraff about." Ordo, still holding the Verp on Chadus, reached into his jacket and drew out the DH-17 blaster. He admired it for a few moments before flicking the safety catch off and handing it to Besany. She took it reluctantly. "But that's an assassin's weapon. Why else would you need a flash suppressor and low-light optics?"

"I got it from a buddy."

"Your buddy must work in a rough business, then. Look, we can keep this game up as long as you like, but I missed dinner tonight, and that always makes me cranky."

"You're a kriffing clone, aren't you?"

"And you're Republic Intel."

Chadus snorted. "I'm just an office clerk."

"Okay." Ordo took out a hand scanner. "Besany, if he moves, blow his *gett'se* off. Let's see who he really is."

Besany wasn't sure how she'd aim at anything other than the man's chest, but she tried to hold the DH-17 convincingly. There wasn't much Chadus could do thousands of meters above the city anyway except submit to the scan. Ordo flashed it in front of his eyes to check his retinas, and then made him press his fingers onto the pad.

"What's that going to tell you?" Chadus asked. He was definitely looking nervous now. "I haven't got a criminal record."

"I'll bet." Ordo read the display with a little frown. "Well, Agent Lemmeloth, Arbian J., you've got remarkably high security clearance for a clerk. Two more promotions and you'll report directly to the Chancellor."

"How the stang did you access *that*?"

"Because I'm much, *much* smarter than you, mongrel."

Besany had never known Ordo to show the slightest embarrassment at being a clone. In fact, he seemed to take great pride in it: his genome having been selected and enhanced to create the raw material for the perfect soldier, and—however much the Kaminoan clonemasters believed the Null prototypes were a failed experiment—intensive training from infancy had produced a super-fit, hyper-intelligent, but unmanageably idiosyncratic black ops commando. As far as Ordo was concerned, he was the best, and therefore any randomly conceived being like Chadus was a poor second or worse. He had a point.

And now he also had the agent's biometric access to the Republic's most sensitive information. He could slice into some priceless files. But he had to do it now, before Republic Intel missed Chadus, or whatever his name was. The Nulls were very adept at data stripping—even better than Besany was, in fact. Yes, they really *were* the best, and that made them especially dangerous to cross.

Chadus—Lemmeloth—seemed to have reached the same conclusion.

"Try to use my access, and you'll be caught right away." He looked really agitated now, staring into Ordo's face as if he was more shocked than scared. "What are you doing, anyway? You're programmed to be *obedient*."

"You should have paid more attention in genetics class," Ordo said. "Genes only predispose. Environment's what counts. Programming . . . no, human beings don't work that way. *Trainable*. Not programmable."

"You're a soldier of the Republic. I order you to land this vessel and release me."

Ordo made a little snorting noise of distracted contempt. "You can kiss my *shebs*. And you still haven't told me why you were following Agent Wennen."

"Who are *you* working for, clone?"

"I like to be my own boss. The hours are better. Now answer me before I have to start breaking things."

Besany had questioned suspects in the course of her job, but accounts that didn't balance or unauthorized expenditure didn't usually involve abduction and persuasion with a blaster. Lemmeloth turned his head slowly to fix on Besany, as if he could get farther with her than with Ordo.

"It's not too late to turn yourself in, Agent Wennen," he said. "We understand. You talk to some malcontent like Senator Skeenah, he puts unhelpful ideas in your head about the direction of the war effort—"

"You're bluffing," Besany cut in, hoping he was. If Lemmeloth had opened the batting with that, then he probably didn't have the worst dirt on her—that she was ripping data on the clone production program for Skirata. "I'm just a simple auditor. Numbers. Balance sheets. Budget estimates."

"Are we done here?" Ordo asked quietly. "Last chance, Lemmeloth."

Some things dawned slowly on Besany, for all her mental acuity. There was only going to be one way out of this for Lemmeloth. Ordo couldn't just give him a black eye and tell him not to hang around her again. They'd snatched a spy; and spies didn't forget. Even if Jusik had been here, he might not have been able to memory-rub Lemmeloth enough to guarantee the man would have no recollection of following her.

"If I don't report in," Lemmeloth said, "you're the last contact I was tailing. None of this is going to go away for you, Agent Wennen."

"No, but *you* are." Ordo didn't look up from his datapad. He seemed engrossed, tapping away at the screen. "I'm into your secure comm system now. I've just sent a message saying Wennen went straight home, didn't make contact with anyone, and that you'll call in later tonight."

"So you're working for the Separatists. That's what we get for letting Mandalorian scum train our troops, I suppose."

"Usually," Ordo said, holding a gloved hand out to Besany for the DH-17, "folks beg me for leniency at this point."

Lemmeloth was ashen. His gaze tracked discreetly around the speeder's cramped cargo area, as if he thought he stood a chance at seven thousand meters if only he could get to the hatch. "It's not going to happen, is it?"

"No." Ordo adjusted the force settings on the blaster. Besany felt her gut tighten. "But I'm not a savage. Professional courtesy and all that."

Then—no speeches, no insults, no warning—Ordo simply raised the DH-17, held it to the agent's temple, and fired. It discharged with a loud *bdapp*. The man slumped off the seat and hit the deck with a thud. It was fast, dispassionate, and shocking. The smell of discharged blaster and seared skin overpowered the odors of food.

Besany found she couldn't speak or cry out. She froze. Enacca looked over her shoulder from the pilot's seat and made a low, rumbling growl.

"No, I *don't* expect you to do all the housework," Ordo said, still utterly matter-of-fact. "I'll do the disposal myself."

Enacca yowled.

"Okay, keep the blaster, but dump him in the lower levels, the derelict zone, so that a borrat can dispose of the body." Ordo began stripping the corpse of everything vaguely incriminating or useful, as if he did it regularly. Besany realized he probably did. "The rats are pretty thorough. And recycling's our civic duty."

Ordo glanced up as if suddenly aware that Besany was staring at him in horror. For all the terrible jobs he had to do, he still had an incongruous innocence about him, a kind of wide-eyed embarrassment whenever he thought he might have made a social gaffe. Besany had never seen anyone killed before, let alone shot an arm's length from her by her own lover. She knew Ordo's work was dirty and difficult, but there was knowing, and there was *seeing*.

"Sorry," he said, suddenly a guilty little boy caught throwing stones. "I should have told you to look away."

"It's—it's okay." Try as she might, though, Besany *couldn't* make it okay. Something had stalled in her. She felt as if her heart was waiting for a safe moment to beat again. "I realize you couldn't . . . just let him go."

Ordo pulled off the man's belt with some effort. The bantha-hide strap snapped like a whip. "If it had been the other way around, what do you think he'd have done to me? Or you, come to that? He'd have killed either of us without a second thought. It's not like I tortured him or anything. Clean death. That's the most any of us can hope for."

Besany had hoped to die of extreme old age in her sleep. Most beings did, she suspected, even Mandalorian warriors. "Does . . . did he know what I was really up to?"

"I skimmed your file details off the Intel mainframe." Ordo shook his head. "According to that, it was just your meeting with the Senator that made them jumpy. Best thing you can do now, *cyar'ika,* is to tell your boss that a pervert's stalking you and that you're scared. That'll cover your behavior and weapons, if anyone asks questions, and make you look like you've got nothing to hide."

Ordo had been trained to kill efficiently, and given no other choice of career. Besany tried to remember that when Enacca dropped them off at her apartment and the speeder vanished into the night. He switched from assassin mode to harmless domesticity the moment the doors opened, trotting into the kitchen to make a pot of caf. Besany watched, unable to stop the trembling in her legs. It wasn't that she felt sorry for Lemmeloth, but just a few hours ago he probably had no idea he was going to die. She wasn't sure what had disturbed her most: being present at an execution, or realizing how very tenuous the link to life was for some in this war, and that the people she loved and cared for were as close to oblivion at any moment as that agent.

Outside this room, Coruscant went on shopping and dining and watching the holovids. The war was reality for someone else.

"I'm starving," Ordo said, opening and closing cupboard doors. Clones were always hungry. Executions didn't seem to dent his appetite. "Shall I make supper? I've learned to cook spicy grassgrain. You like that."

"Just caf for me." Besany was sure she'd throw up if she tried to eat anything now. She opened the conservator and pointed to neat rows of containers, prepared meals for two weeks, all labeled and dated because she was a label-and-date kind of person. "Help yourself."

Ordo laid the table for two anyway. He had a very precise way of doing things, as if every eventuality in his life had a drill, and she knew that if she measured the spacing of the cutlery it would be exact. He pulled back a chair and gave her a nod to sit down.

"It's my job," he said quietly. So he understood what was troubling her, then, and maybe his snap-change to domestic trivia was displacement. "I don't kill for fun."

"I know."

"It's time you left Coruscant, *Bes'ika*. You'll be safe on Mandalore. You can't go on like this."

"You need me inside the Treasury."

"But I can slice into the system. Mereel can. We *all* can, since you turned over your codes to us."

Yes, she'd done that pretty well the first night they'd met. *Shot by a Jedi, abducted by a clone. And I* trusted *them? Yes, I did. They're as good as family now.*

"It's still easier for me to do it."

Ordo placed a cup of caf in front of her with the handle at precisely ninety degrees, as if it was a private ritual. "The nearest I've ever come to arguing with *Kal'buir* was over whether we were putting you at risk for our own ends."

"I went into this knowing the score, Ordo."

"But you think you have to face danger yourself to be able to look me in the eye, don't you?"

He knew her a lot better than she realized. "I'm not going to sit on my backside in Kyrimorut while you're on the front line," she said. "I still have my uses." Stang, she'd forgotten all about her datapad. She took it out of her pocket. "Here. I found another black hole in the procurement budget. New contracts for Rothana Heavy Engineering."

Ordo took the datapad and looked as if he was calculating, lips moving slightly. "I make that an order for five hundred larties."

"Exactly." The LAAT/i gunship was the workhorse of the Grand Army, and replacements were always needed; five hundred was a drop in the ocean for RHE, whose yards could churn them out like cheap family speeders. "Now look at the delivery date."

Ordo raised his eyebrows. "That's nearly a year away. Are they knitting them by hand or something?"

"It gets better. I tied up that order authorization with the delivery date and the corresponding budget estimate for the next financial year, and not only do they not match, but the expenditure's coded under domestic security. I thought the decimal point was an error, but no—it's off by—well, see for yourself. That much can buy a few thousand Acclamators."

Besany waited for Ordo to react. She'd brought him a prize at great risk: she realized that she was waiting for a pat on the head.

"Either Palpatine's ordered some gold-plated custom larties to show us clone boys how much he cares, or he's building a huge new fleet." Ordo scratched his chin thoughtfully. "Lots of *big* ships. *Shab,* I need a shave."

"He's got to have somewhere to put his new clone army," Besany said.

"But KDY and Rothana can lay a keel and launch a warship inside five months, and they can handle hundreds, thousands if they drop all other contracts. Where's the other hardware they're building in the meantime?"

"Unless they're replacing ships a rivet at a time, I couldn't find any other big orders due for completion before that time period."

"So Palpatine's stocking up with clones and ships, but not

for deployment anytime soon. What's so im...
year's time? Why that timing?"

Besany knew enough about the fighting—the ...
HNE rarely covered now—to realize that every day w...
all-out, final effort for units of the Grand Army somewhe...
But throwing much bigger resources at a war suggested finality. "You think the war might be coming to an end?"

"It's only just started. Maybe he's finally taking notice of our warnings that the Seps just don't have anything like the number of battle droids they claim to have. But I still don't understand the delay. Either way, *Kal'buir* will find this information useful."

Ordo sent the data by comlink to Skirata there and then. The numbers in this war didn't add up; it was a sore point with the Nulls, and especially with Skirata. They kept finding evidence that the Separatist droid armies weren't the much-vaunted quadrillions but hundreds of millions, yet it didn't seem to change the tactics dictated by Palpatine. Those were still bad enough odds for such a small clone army. But it explained why the Separatists hadn't overrun Coruscant.

Besany preferred to think of this as the beginning of the end. She was a data-rational woman, her world built on demonstrable evidence and irrefutable numbers, but there was always room for optimism. She also preferred to think of Ordo as a victim of a regime that damaged him, not a stone-cold killer. He rummaged through the conservator and sat down with a plate of cold roast roba and thin slices of sheet-bread, chewing happily as if he hadn't a care in the world. How could he possibly react like a normal man, anyway? He'd never had a childhood, and not even Skirata's doting paternal presence could change the fact that everything about Ordo and his brothers—from their genome to the intensive training to maximize that genetic potential—had been designed to make him a lethal human weapon.

"You're afraid of me," he said suddenly, with the outspoken perception of a child again. There was still a lot of the boy left in Ordo. "*Cyar'ika,* I'd never hurt you, I swear."

"I know, sweetheart." That slightly desperate, wounded

tone, so at odds with his powerful physical presence, always made Besany angry with the world. Ordo deserved better. "I'm just shaken, that's all. It's not every day I see someone shot like that."

For Ordo, of course, it was routine. A clone's life was cheap and disposable to both his Kaminoan creators and his political masters, and if men were indoctrinated to believe their sole purpose was to fight and die for the Republic, it was inevitable they would see others' lives as equally expendable. The war was very distant for most Coruscanti, a conflict without personal consequences fought by men they never met. The two worlds—soldier and citizen—were utterly separate, and Besany thought that could only turn out badly for society.

"This is much better roba than we ever get in the mess," Ordo said, distressingly innocent again. "It's really tasty."

"I like you to have the best," said Besany. "You deserve it."

Ordo looked blank for a moment and then fished in his belt pouch. What he placed on the table in front of her was nothing short of shocking. A gold pin with three enormous brilliant blue gems—one central stone flanked by two smaller ones—glittered in the harsh kitchen light, showing hints of deep forest-green fire.

"I meant to give this to you months ago," he said. "But the time never seemed right."

Besany was almost afraid to touch it. "Ordo, are those what I think they are?"

"Shoroni sapphires, yes."

Shoroni stones were rare and ludicrously valuable. Clones didn't even get paid, let alone have personal fortunes. Besany had to ask. "Where did you get them?"

"Sergeant Vau. He raided his family's safe-deposit box on Mygeeto. He's a disinherited Irmenu aristocrat. Anyway, he said you'd do the stones justice." Ordo spooned pickled majroot relish onto his plate. "They're worth ten million."

"Ordo!" Besany's stomach hit the floor and bounced hard. It felt like it, anyway; if she had one more shock tonight, she wasn't sure she could handle it. "The police are going to be *looking* for these."

"You don't have to take them . . . and if the cops haven't found them yet, chances are they never will."

It's stolen, a voice said in her head. *It's wrong.*

So was stripping confidential data from the Treasury mainframe. So was handing over her passwords to Kal Skirata. So was extracting a badly injured clone from the hospital at gunpoint and making him disappear from the Grand Army's system. So was sitting back in a seat and watching while a Republic agent doing his lawful job was dispatched with a single bolt to the head.

She'd done it all.

And I'm going to keep doing it.

Besany didn't know how to handle a gift of that magnitude, stolen or not. She steeled herself to picking up the pin, and turning it to make the light dance off its facets.

"Shoroni gems appear green in daylight," Ordo said, matter-of-factly. "It's the crystalline structure. Bi-refringent and bi-axial. It's—"

"Can't Kal sell it? Kyrimorut needs the creds."

"You could keep *one . . .*"

They were magnificent stones, but it was Ordo's anxious expression that forced her hand. She was as damned now as she would ever be; she'd thrown in her lot with Skirata, and his rules were now her rules. Did it matter if she added one more crime to the list? She'd placate Ordo now, and work out how to square it with her conscience later. "Thank you."

"If I got paid, I'd buy you something wonderful." Ordo sometimes had an anxious, apologetic tone when he felt he'd fallen short of perfection, a rare lapse in his apparently unassailable confidence. That was what happened, Besany thought, when a child was told it had to die for failing to meet standards. It ripped her apart every time; not even Skirata's influence—constantly telling them they were perfect, wonderful, brilliant—could totally erase that trauma. "This is the best I can do right now. Do you want to marry me?"

Ordo was a slave by any other name, an object manufactured for a task, minus rights and a vote. Besany understood now why Etain had also had a moment of apparent insanity and had Darman's baby. The clones had a right to be men.

Their future was all the more precious because it would be so brief.

"Well . . . yes."

"Oh, good." Ordo seemed to have very fixed ideas about what a man should be and what he should do, no doubt swallowed whole from Skirata's philosophy. He placed his elbow on the table as if he was challenging her to arm wrestle. "Take my hand, then."

She did, palm-to-palm, because Ordo had that way with him. She *trusted* him. She didn't know if he was going to squeeze her fingers fondly or slam her hand to the table and declare victory.

"Mhi solus tome, mhi solus dar'tome, mhi me'dinui an, mhi ba'juri verde," he said, eyes fixed on hers. "Now you say it."

"What's that?"

"A *Mando* marriage contract. If you agree, repeat it. It means we're one whether we're together or apart, that we share everything we have, and that we'll raise our children as warriors."

It wasn't exactly the way Besany had imagined her wedding. But then she had never imagined a day like this one at all, ever. Her normality barrier had been smashed down twice in an hour, and the hammer was coming down for a third time.

"Okay," she said. She couldn't refuse; she didn't want to, even if this was brutally pragmatic in that conflicting Mandalorian way, strictly business one moment and tearfully sentimental the next. It was as if he'd made up his mind, and so had she, and he didn't see any point in messing around any longer. *"Mhi solus tome, mhi solus dar'tome, mhi me'dinui an, mhi ba'juri verde."*

Ordo smiled. "I'm glad we've got that sorted," he said, letting go of her hand. "You look like you need some more caf."

I'm still in shock. That must be it. People do rash things like this in wartime.

Besany now lived a life at the extremes, *with* the extremes, with the most marginal in society, an existence few beings around her would ever know.

"Good idea," she said, voice shaking.

She tried to blot out all thoughts of Lemmeloth's wife, if he had one, being told he was never coming home again. She couldn't. It would always plague her in the quiet moments.

That, she reminded herself, was war.

3

If we were given just one word of information in our entire history, how we'd treasure it! How we'd pore over every syllable, divining its meaning, arguing its importance; how we'd examine it and wring every lesson we could from it. Yet today we have trillions of words, tidal waves of information, and the smallest detail of every action our government and businesses take is easily available to us at the touch of a button. And yet . . . we ignore it, and learn nothing from it. One day, we'll die of voluntary ignorance.
—Hirib Bassot, current affairs pundit, speaking on HNE's *Facing Facts*—a low-audience politics show, axed shortly after this broadcast for poor ratings

Enceri, Mandalore, market day, approximately six months later—937 days ABG

Mandalore was paradise.

It was desolate, backward, and lacked most of the limited comforts Fi had been used to even as a clone commando, but here he was no longer a soldier among civilians. Mandalorians understood military life. They were *all* soldiers, one way or another, and that made this an easy place to be. He stood in the unrelenting drizzle that had reduced Enceri's marketplace to a quagmire and tried to remember why he'd agreed to meet Parja here.

She'd told him. But these days, he forgot so much. The war was over for him now. He wondered if he would ever be fit to fight again.

I don't know how to do anything else, do I? What use am I now?

"You okay, *ner vod*?" A stranger—a man in full Mandalorian armor, like everyone else here—put his hand on Fi's shoulder as if to get his attention. Fi must have looked lost. It was a voice that Fi felt he should have recognized, but he couldn't. "Can I help?"

Fi could follow the map Parja had given him. Some days he knew he'd forgotten something important, and some days he didn't realize it until someone told him. But just *knowing* there was something he'd missed was progress. Just over a year ago, he'd been on life support and declared brain-dead. His recollection of his recovery was a patchwork of memories that could easily have been dreams.

"I'm waiting for my girl," Fi said, steadying himself on the *bevii'ragir* that Parja had given him. It was a hunting spear with a removable counterbalance weight on the other end, and although he was in no fit state to hunt, it looked more respectable than crutches or a walking stick. He had his pride. He still struggled to find the right words, and he knew he sounded confused, but . . . yes, he was making progress. Parja told him so. "She told me to meet her here. I forget things lately. I was blown up."

The man, in that mid-green armor so many Mandalorians wore, stared at the sigil on Fi's helmet that marked him as a wounded veteran, and paused for a few moments, but didn't ask for an explanation.

"You're younger than I thought," he said. Fi's voice must have surprised him; maybe he expected an older man inside the armor. "I'll wait with you until she shows up, then."

It was a kind thing to do, as if Fi needed protecting here. He'd been used to being the one who provided protection. It rankled to be needy.

You've got Parja and you're alive. Be grateful.

But Fi wasn't grateful. Since he'd arrived on Mandalore, he'd come to understand how free men lived. Now he resented every moment he'd spent serving a society in which he had fewer rights than a droid.

"Who were you fighting for?" the man asked after a long,

awkward pause. Mandalore had supplied the galaxy with mercenary troops for generations, and the topic of commercial soldiering counted as social small talk. "Did they pay well?"

"Grand Army of the Republic. What pay?"

Another pause. Mandalore wasn't Republic territory, not by a long chalk. And now the Mandalorian knew Fi was a clone, too, not even accorded the respect of being paid for his fighting prowess. But that didn't seem to be a stigma here.

"Deserter," the man said, no hint of disapproval.

"Discharged dead." Fi groped for the words. He knew what he wanted to say, but getting his mouth to obey him was another matter. He could feel sweat beading on his top lip. "Like a regular medical discharge, only a bit more serious."

"It's okay, *ner vod,* you're among friends here," said the man. "Fett was a disgrace for letting the Kaminoans make clones for the Jedi out of him. It's not your fault."

"Don't feel sorry for me," Fi said defensively. He didn't want pity. The Kaminoans didn't care any more than Fett did if the clone army was happy and well treated, just as long as it won wars, but he'd had Kal Skirata looking out for him. "Our sergeant took good care of us. He adopted me as his son. We did fine."

"So I heard."

"You've heard a lot."

"It's a small planet. A fair few *Cuy'val Dar* came back here when they'd finished training you."

So the guy *did* know. The Mandalorian training sergeants handpicked by Fett hadn't all been fond of him, but they respected his prowess. And they'd been griping about life in Tipoca City. Well, there were no more secrets left to keep. Everyone knew about the Grand Army of the Republic now.

It was dawning slowly on Fi that Fett, *Mand'alor* and bounty hunter, had been a good advert for Mandalorian grit, but his heroic status wasn't respected by some of his own people. The Alpha ARC clone troopers, hard men literally made in Fett's mold, were scared of him, utterly loyal to his orders even after his death. But Fi realized that some *Mando'ade* here thought he was a selfish *chakaar.*

Mandalore didn't have any leader at all now, and life still went on regardless. Fi could imagine the chaos on Coruscant if the Chancellor was killed and nobody was around to succeed him. Mandos just got on with life. It had happened before, they said, and it would happen again, but no nation worth its salt fell apart just because there was nobody on the throne.

"You got any kids?" asked the man.

Fi shrugged. "I'm working on it."

Sometimes Fi's old self surfaced unexpectedly. He'd been superbly fit, an elite commando, and—most painful of all—he'd had what Skirata called *paklalat,* the gift of gab. He'd had a way with words. But the explosion on Gaftikar had put an end to that, and now he was an invalid, dependent on the care of a nice woman called Parja Bralor who didn't seem to mind that he wasn't quite the prize he'd once been.

The man looked past Fi as if he'd recognized someone approaching in the bustle of armored figures lugging flexiwrap bags of preserved vegetables, machine parts, and an occasional five-liter container of *tihaar,* the local triple-distilled alcohol that could actually be used to degrease engine parts.

"Is that your missus?" he asked. "Heading this way, on your six."

Fi turned. Parja's dark chestnut braids swung beneath the chin level of her helmet, secured with red copper beads. With her deep scarlet armor, the overall effect in the gray drizzle was one of vivid autumn fruit. "Yeah. That's her."

"I'll leave you, then. You're in safe hands again."

Again. What did he mean?

By the time Fi turned around, the man had melted back into the market-day crowd. Parja shouldered her way through the press of armored bodies with the focus of a laser cannon and caught Fi's arm, pulling him to her to tap the forehead of her helmet against his. It was the only way to give someone a kiss in full armor. That was probably why some *aruetiise* believed Mandalorians head-butted one another as a greeting. *Aruetiise*—foreigners, enemies, traitors, or anything in between—would believe any old tosh, Fi thought.

"You made it," Parja said, all approval. "Well done, *cyar'ika*. Making new friends, are you?"

"Don't know." Fi couldn't see the man now. He'd vanished. "He was worried about me."

Parja reached up and patted his helmet. She'd painted it with the Mandalorian letters M and S for *mir'shupur*—brain injury—just like a battlefield medic might do for triage purposes. On Mandalore, the symbol functioned as a blend of a general warning to give the wearer a break, and a medal for combat service. "He saw the sigil on your *buy'ce*. It told him you were disabled and why. Saves a lot of daft questions, you see, and folks know how to treat you."

Fi had never thought of himself as disabled. Injured, maybe, but not *disabled*. He told himself it was still early days, and that Bardan Jusik was putting him back together a cell at a time with his Jedi healing techniques.

"What are we doing now?" he asked.

"You've got to find your way to the cantina," Parja showed no trace of impatience even though he realized she'd probably told him a dozen times. "I'm not going to prompt you, either. Use the map. And what else have you got to do? Come on, tell me."

"Notes. Make notes as I go."

"Good. Make notes. Then all you have to remember to do is to keep looking at your datapad."

Enceri was a small pimple on the map compared with just one of Coruscant's teeming termite-hill neighborhoods, and the nearest settlement to Kyrimorut, Skirata's refuge for clone deserters deep in the northern forests. It was more a trading post than a town. But from Fi's perspective, it was as complex and confusing as a labyrinth. He took the stylus from his forearm plate and checked his datapad. Events a couple of years ago—even his artificially brief childhood—were vivid, but he couldn't retain the day-to-day memories that everyone else took for granted. He oriented himself the way he'd once been trained, getting his bearings from landmarks like the grain silo on the edge of town and the basic magnetic compass on his forearm, and then trudged off.

Once he learned to cope with that, he'd learn to use his helmet's head-up display again.

One step at a time, Parja had said.

She trailed after him. "You're doing okay. Really, *cyar'ika,* you're getting better every day. I'm proud of you."

How could Parja love him in this state? He felt crushed. But they'd met when he was already injured, and she never knew the Fi he'd been. She loved him for what he was now. Things could only get better.

"I miss my brothers," he said. "I miss Ordo, too."

There were messages, occasional comlink conversations with Omega Squad and the Null ARCs who were his only family in any sense of the word, but Fi had lived his whole short life among other men like him. He'd never really been this *alone.* He felt suddenly guilty that Parja wasn't his entire world; she'd nursed him in those awful days after he was rescued from Coruscant, fed and cleaned him like an infant, and her constant encouragement had made him walk again every bit as much as Jusik's Force healing skills. Once, Fi could imagine nothing he wanted more than a nice girl who cared about him. He never thought that she might end up caring *for* him.

"Ordo's bound to drop by soon," Parja said. "You know the Nulls don't exactly run to a timetable. Anyway, *Bard'ika*'s due back in a few days for your next healing session."

Fi thought it was worth asking. "Can I go home?"

Parja blinked. "This *is* home, Fi. You don't mean Coruscant, do you?"

"Yeah."

"No, you're not going back *there.* They were going to kill you, remember? They wanted to switch off your life support because they didn't think you were worth keeping alive. They'll probably confiscate you at Customs as stolen Republic property. You don't need to go back to that stinking *dar'yaim.*"

Parja was angry about it, but it was a very distant brutality for Fi, something that he knew was terrible but hadn't *felt* because he'd been mercifully unaware in a coma. As he paced the route to the cantina with mechanical care, checking the

map at every alley and crossroad, he tried to imagine Besany
and Captain Obrim desperately trying to save him from a
callous system that put down permanently disabled clones
like animals. Ordo said Besany had pulled a weapon on the
medcenter staff and kidnapped him at blasterpoint. He
seemed fiercely proud of her. Sheer guts like that had the
same effect on a Mandalorian male that a pair of long legs
did on *aruetiise*; female courage was irresistible.

"I can get past Customs," Fi said. "I'm a *commando*."

"Besany went to a lot of trouble to get you *out*."

"I know." Fi couldn't square Besany's daunting blond
glamour with the rather lonely, methodical woman inside, let
alone one who could start an armed siege. "Never said
thanks."

"You want to thank her? Wait till she visits."

"But I could say hi to everyone," Fi persisted. He rounded
a corner, and the cantina was exactly where the map said it
was. It was a small triumph. He took off his helmet and let
the rain wash over his face, hating himself for talking like a
simple kid. "It's easier for me to go to them."

"Your brothers are deployed all over the galaxy."

"And I could see Etain's baby . . ."

"That's a dangerous secret, Fi."

"It's not fair that Dar doesn't know he's a dad."

"The galaxy's an unfair place. It's safer that he doesn't
know yet."

Fi finally blurted it out without thinking. "I don't belong
here, *Parj'ika*. I should be fighting. It's all I know how to do.
I thought I wanted out, but—I don't know what to do."

The cantina doors were beaded with rain as if they had just
been painted, the only part of the building that seemed to have
been maintained in years. Concentrating on their glossy black-
ness kept the frustration and anger at his own helplessness
from overwhelming him. But part of his mind never stopped
whispering that he was nothing now, that he had no purpose or
pride. It was his *indoctrination* surfacing. Sergeant Kal said
so. *Kal'buir* reminded Fi a couple of times a week by comm
that he was a free man and he didn't *have* to have any purpose
beyond living his life to the full.

It didn't feel that way right then. Fi couldn't shake the guilt that everyone was fighting the war except him, and that he was a burden on Parja. She slipped her helmet off and clipped it to her belt.

"You've had quite a battle to get where you are now," she said quietly, and nodded toward the doors. "And you can be a soldier again, if you want, but not yet. I know it's hard. Try to be patient."

"I don't have *time.*"

Parja seemed to flinch every time he reminded her that time was running out twice as fast for him as it was for a normal man. They didn't talk about *Kal'buir*'s plan to stop the accelerated aging now. The genetic engineering secrets needed to stop it seemed as far away as ever; he was still searching for the right geneticists to make sense of Ko Sai's research.

"You'll *get* time." Parja had a way of dropping her voice that got Fi's attention—and compliance—a lot better than yelling at him. *Quiet menace* summed her up. "Even the way things are now, time's still on your side."

"Yeah."

"Fi, *look* at me." She clamped her hands on either side of his face and made him meet her eyes. "You've got years ahead of you, either way. So *live* them. And I'm not putting you back together so that you can run off with some *aruetyc* hussy with a fancy Coruscant manicure when you're fit, so you better marry me. Okay? Mandos marry young. We're both past the age. It's not right."

Fi's first thought was that he needed permission from someone, probably *Kal'buir.* But he didn't; and that was scary. He could do whatever he wanted. All his life he'd had army rules and regs and procedures to follow, a structured existence, and now he was adrift on a sea of choices he never thought he'd have but without the capacity to make the most of them.

"I'm no use for anything," he said. "Why do you want to marry me?"

Parja's eyes narrowed. They were very blue. "I'll be the judge of what you're good for. You're Fi, for a start, and that's a good enough reason. Now get your *shebs* into that cantina and show me you remember how to order *ne'tra gal* and a meal."

Fi was sure it was all bluster. He was amazed by her patience: she never cared how many times he dropped things or couldn't recall the right word. Her aunt Rav Bralor, one of the *Cuy'val Dar* who'd trained them on Kamino, said the engineer in Parja hated leaving any broken machine unfixed. Fi was the kind of restoration project that she relished.

"Will you still want me when I'm better?" As he walked through the cantina doors, the bar seemed a more intimidating target than any beachhead. "I might be too . . ." The word eluded his lips, although his brain had selected *gorgeous*. ". . . good to look at."

"Then I'll just have to wear a welding visor to shield my delicate sensibilities," Parja said. Several people in the cantina paused to look up. It was a small town on a small planet where everyone knew their neighbor's business, so they recognized Fi as a stranger. "Or you can keep your helmet on at all times."

"Okay, I'll marry you, then."

"Don't let me twist your arm . . ."

"Maybe I can learn a trade."

"When your coordination improves, you can pull your weight in the workshop."

It was always *when* with Parja, never *if.* Failure never occurred to her. As Fi stepped up to the bar, heart pounding because he wasn't sure he'd be able to find the right words to order ale, he was aware of two men to his right taking extra interest in him. He could hear them muttering over their drinks. Their helmets were stacked on the floor beside their table. Whatever else was wrong with his brain, Fi could still filter a conversation out of a hubbub of noise if it was about *him.*

"That's not the guy, I tell you."

"You can't tell."

"But he *looks* like him, I give you that."

"*Too much* like him."

"Who's to say where Fett sowed his *bas neral,* eh?"

They looked up as if they were suddenly aware that Fi was staring at them—he was, and with irritation—and changed the subject. Mandalorians had the tact of a drunken Wee-quay, so they must have thought he would have been pretty offended by their comparison. Fi tried to keep his mind on the task at hand and fumbled for a credit chip.

"Two ales," he said. And all Mandalorian cantinas could rustle up a couple of bowls of soup. "And two soups."

The barkeep, an older woman with the kind of thin, gaunt face that made her look as if she got her kicks by sucking the juice from sourcane, gave him a long and cautious stare.

"You're not from around here," she said in Basic. Every-one from Enceri spoke *Mando'a,* but Fi had enough trouble with Basic these days. She tilted her head slightly to one side to look at the helmet under his arm, and her expression soft-ened. "Ah. Okay, *verd'ika,* is it *gi* dumpling soup, or red gourd?"

Verd'ika. It was an affectionate term for a soldier. That warning sigil worked just fine. "Gourd, please."

Gi soup was too much for him. Fi couldn't face fish now, not after what happened to Ko Sai. The Kaminoan scientist was always referred to as *gihaal*—fish-meal—and now that she was dead and dismembered, fish made Fi feel oddly queasy. He handed over his credits. Parja claimed a table in a dim corner and settled him in a seat.

"You're doing fine, *cyar'ika.*"

"Who do I look like?" Fi knew he looked like every single one of his clone brothers, and—as far as he knew—like Jango Fett had at the same age. He indicated the two men still huddled over their ale with as discreet a nod of his head as he could manage. "Fett's dead, and he was a lot older than me."

"Not Fett," Parja whispered, taking a vise-like grip on his hand as if to shut him up. "One of your brothers. Spar."

Spar—ARC trooper Alpha-02—had deserted even before the Grand Army was first unleashed at Geonosis. As Skirata always said, the man might have been an Alpha plank but he wasn't a fool. "He's not my brother."

"Well, they say Fenn Shysa wants him to pretend he's

Fett's heir, just to keep up appearances. In case you hadn't noticed, we don't have a *Mand'alor* at the moment."

"Did you notice when you had one?"

Parja paused and looked as if she was going to smile. "The point is that *not* having one gives the *aruetiise* the idea that we're in decline. Let's face it, we never really recovered from losing our best fighters at Galidraan. We haven't had to— yet."

Fi hadn't noticed the place falling apart. *Mando'ade* didn't need much leading, although they did like to have a figurehead, if only to gripe about. A vivid memory sprang into his head, and the language to express it. "Fett's already got a son. Boba. He must be about twelve now. Cocky little jerk. Ordo shoved his head down the 'fresher for bragging that his dad could wipe the floor with *Kal'buir*."

"We need more than a kid right now, Fi, even if anyone could find him. He's vanished."

"Takes after his father."

"Careful, or Shysa might ask *you* to play the fruit of Fett's loins . . ."

"Test tube, more like." Fi recalled seeing Fett in Tipoca City from time to time, a solitary, distracted figure who sel- dom mixed socially with the *Cuy'val Dar* he'd recruited. Fi wondered if the *Mand'alor* got a kick out of seeing millions of copies of himself all over the place, or if it disturbed him. "Why doesn't Shysa take over? Or one of the chieftains?"

"The Fett name still makes the *aruetiise* tremble."

Aliit ori'shya taldin. Mandalorians always hit the nail on the head with their sayings; family definitely *was* a lot more than blood. Technically, Fi was as much Jango Fett's flesh and blood as Boba was. Fi thought it was interesting how he didn't feel the man was anything like a father.

"I'm *Mando* A-list, then," he said. "Pure Fett. But with better luck with women."

Parja submitted to the grin she'd been trying in vain to suppress. She rubbed his forearm with vigorous enthusiasm. "*Kandosii!* Jaing said you had a way with words. I do believe it's coming back."

Fi felt a little brighter. Yes, maybe he'd be as good as new one day, or near enough. He ate his soup with the unsteady hand of a child learning to feed himself, facing the wall so that nobody would see if he spilled it down his chin. He did. Parja reached out a discreet hand and wiped it for him before he could fumble for a cloth.

"Six months ago," she said, "you couldn't even walk upright without help. You're doing good, *cyar'ika*."

She knew exactly when he needed reassurance. *I'm lucky. My friends saved me. They put me back together again.* He'd once thought the bond with his original squad, the brothers he was born and raised with, was the strongest he would ever experience, and their deaths had devastated him; he couldn't imagine being that close to another living being again. Then he found an equally deep bond with Omega Squad. Now his bonds extended to a wider family, a ragbag of clones and nonclones, and even something that had once seemed unattainable—a woman who loved him.

"Okay," Fi said. "When I don't look so broken, we'll get married."

He wanted to be his old self for her. She looked at him with a slight frown, and it occurred to him that she might have thought he was fobbing her off. Maybe she just didn't understand what he was trying to say. Words often didn't come out as he planned these days.

"Better get fit fast, then," she said.

Kal'buir had trained his boys to set goals, no matter how small. The next ridge, the next morning, even the next footstep if things were going badly—you had to keep your eyes fixed on that, and use it for strength and focus.

By this time next year, Fi decided, he would be the man he was before the explosion. He picked up his mug of *ne'tra gal* and tilted it slightly in Parja's direction, managing not to spill any, and forced a grin.

"I'll paint my armor specially," he said. Maybe it was time he stopped looking like the ghost of Ghez Hokan, whose red-and-gray armor he'd scavenged. "Any color you like."

But Parja was looking past him toward the doors of the cantina, and her expression had taken on that tight-lipped, narrow-eyed, I'm-going-to-punch-your-head-in look that he found oddly endearing. He turned carefully to see what she was scowling at.

A man in green armor swaggered up to them and looked down at Fi. Then he lifted off his helmet, releasing wavy blond hair in need of a good trim, and extended a gauntleted hand.

"Well, look at you," he said. "Chip off the old block, or at least what the old block might have been if he'd had your start in life. You doin' all right, *ner vod*?"

Fi didn't have a clue who he was. He seemed to be the only one who didn't, though. The cantina was silent, one communal held breath.

Parja stared the man in the face. "You weren't just passing," she said sourly, and put her hand on Fi's forearm in a grip that said *keep off*. "So before you even ask—my old man's not available. Can't you see he's injured?"

The blond man didn't seem remotely offended by the rebuff. He just smiled, all charm—not that it worked on Parja—and clasped Fi's other arm *Mando*-style.

"You look baffled, soldier," he said. "The name's Fenn Shysa. How'd you like to do your bit for Mandalore?"

Omega Squad observation point above the Hadde-Rishun road, Haurgab, Mid Rim

Darman had never been a gambling man. Now he knew why; he watched his creds disappearing as Atin's racing beetle powered to victory, unchallenged and unstoppable.

The bug wasn't exactly greased lightning. But at least it knew where it was going, a skill that seemed in short supply among the local insect life. As the rest of the squad's beetles scuttled around chaotically, Atin's trotted on a straight, determined course toward the finish line—a strip of detonite tape stretched across the upturned ammo crate that formed the makeshift racetrack.

The others rushed back and forth, buffeting the walls and bouncing off them time after time as if they might eventually batter an escape route through the side of the crate. They just didn't have that single-minded focus that made a *winner.* Darman gave them five points for sheer persistence.

"Kandosii!" Atin cheered. Sound carried for kilometers on the still air here, but inside a soundproofed helmet, a commando could yell to his heart's content. It had taken Omega Squad days to find the path up to this vantage point, and they wanted to lie low. "Go on, *ner vod,* show 'em what you're made of . . . that's my boy . . ."

Omega had time on their hands while they waited for Separatist rebel convoys passing through Haurgab's Maujas desert, and beetle racing was literally the only game in town. It was a blistering noon, one of those days when climate-conditioned Katarn armor was a cool haven from the killer heat outside. Maybe it was too hot today even for the local insect life.

Darman reached out to put his beetle back on course with a careful forefinger. Its iridescent scarlet wing cases reminded him of the daywings that he'd seen on Qiilura, flies that lived for one frantic, gloriously colored day and then died. Darman had once thought that going out at the top of your game was a noble exit for a commando, but after a couple of years exploring the wide world beyond Kamino, he'd worked out that it wasn't glorious at all. It was *unfair.*

Life was short—especially for a clone—and increasingly depressing.

Daywings just showed you in fast-forward what was going to happen to you all too soon. Darman sometimes felt just like the racing beetles, too: trapped, shunted from location to location without really knowing what the greater plan might be, and banging his head against the wall of a war that seemed neither winnable nor losable.

He was fed up finding things in common with insects. He was a man, and he missed his girl. He wanted to go home—and he had no idea where home was.

Fi said it was Kyrimorut. Darman decided it would be wherever Etain wanted it to be.

Sometimes she touched him in the Force to let him know she was thinking of him, a distant and almost disturbing sensation as if someone was creeping up behind him. Dating

your Jedi general was a very bad idea, and he knew it, but the
war had to end sometime; and then he would have what
Sergeant Kal called a normal life. What normality might turn
out to be for a fast-aging clone and a prematurely retired Jedi
he had no idea, but he was willing to give it a go.

He prodded his racing beetle back on course again. "Get a
move on, *di'kut.* It's *that* way."

"Hey, no cheating." Corr turned to Niner for adjudication
as course steward. "Disqualify the unsporting bounder,
Sarge. His beetle's doped."

"Okay, I know I've lost already." Darman tossed a credit
chip at Atin to pay the bet, then picked up his beetle and
turned it toward the finish line. Comic relief had been Fi's
job, but he was gone; Corr, his replacement, did his best to
fill the role of squad wise guy and general cheering-up oper-
ative. "I just hate to see the poor thing bumbling around like
that, all confused and pathetic."

"You'll never be a successful trainer if you get sentimental
about the bloodstock, Dar . . ."

Niner edged across the ground on his belly and peered
into the box, his shadow falling across one of the beetles. It
paused to wave its antennae and tested the suddenly cool air
before trotting over to Corr's chosen creature—brilliant
turquoise, very shiny—and making amorous advances to it.

"I don't think its mind's on the race, somehow, *ner vod,*"
said Niner, getting back on all fours. Atin's beetle pottered
on, as steady and single-minded as its temporary owner, and
crossed the finish line. "Yeah, Atin's done it again. Drinks in
the winner's enclosure . . ."

They were on self-recycled water now. Darman fantasized
about fresh cold water from a faucet, and however much the
procurement techies insisted that the filter system *guaranteed* that the recovered water—"personal" water, they called
it—was as pure as a Naboo spring, he still didn't like the idea
that he'd drunk it and excreted it several times before. It was
unsettlingly warm in his mouth as he sucked the tube from
the reservoir inside his armor.

Still, it beat drinking someone else's.

A big jug of iced water, a shower, and a nice soft bunk . . .

Atin made a discreet fist, victorious. "*Oya!* Pay up, losers." He held out his palm. "That's eight straight wins."

"We'll make you a little trophy, *At'ika*." Darman picked up a cup-like desiccated husk from some long-dead plant. "You can put the winner out to stud now. Breed thoroughbreds."

"Will I get striped ones or mauve ones if I mate it with Corr's?"

"It's not like mixing paint. You don't know much about genetics, do you?"

Niner scooped up the beetles in his hands and tossed them into the air. They scattered in a dazzling display of gem-like wings, vanishing into the heat haze.

They could fly just fine. Why did they never try to escape from the racetrack? Why did they keep buffeting their stupid little heads against the sides of the ammo crate when they could just look up and fly away?

Niner repositioned the blaster cannon on its tripod with its muzzle nestled discreetly in a cleft in the rock and fidgeted with the optics. He seemed increasingly restless and withdrawn these days, as if he had doubts about everything and couldn't discuss them with the squad. Maybe it was Fi; not just his absence, which was hard enough to take, but what had happened to him. If Fi had died, they might have handled that better than knowing he was brain-damaged. They hadn't seen him since Sergeant Kal whisked him away to Mandalore. Sometimes he sent comm messages, but apart from mentioning some Mandalorian woman called Parja, who seemed to be a permanent fixture in his new life, he told them little.

Jusik said he was improving, though. Darman recalled just how much Fi had wanted a girlfriend, and now that he had one, Darman had no need to feel guilty about Etain. Most human beings seemed happier when they had something that someone else didn't, but Darman—like most clones, he realized—was uncomfortable when he had some advantage over his brothers.

As far as General Zey was concerned—not that Zey believed a word of the cover story, of course—Fi was dead. He was so far away now in every sense that he might as well have been.

Jusik was gone, too. The whole team was drifting apart.

Darman settled down in prone position and sighted up on the dirt road below, the only open terrain for kilometers, to wait for their target. Atin made a faint slurping noise as he sipped from his water supply. A shadow cast from the remains of an ancient fortress, three crumbling walls of baked mud bricks, provided some cool spots in their laying-up position. A lot of battles had been fought at this pass.

"Speaking of genetics," Atin said, "what really *did* happen with Ko Sai?"

Darman shrugged. "When *Kal'buir* wants us to know, he'll tell us."

"I heard some weird stuff."

"How weird?"

"That Kal took her research and killed her."

"Who told you that?"

"Sev."

Atin had been one of Vau's trainees, like Delta Squad, and Darman knew they still gossiped despite old feuds. "Sev's talking through his *shebs* as usual," he said. "Ko Sai got what was coming to her, either way."

"I know, but what does *Kal'buir* want her data for?"

At least Atin wasn't feeling sorry for the aiwha-bait. Darman had built up a good solid hatred of Kaminoans since leaving his cloistered existence in Tipoca City, and sometimes wished he'd felt this way when he was close enough to settle a few scores. It was amazing how much human beings could accept as normal if they had nothing else to compare it with.

"I don't know," said Darman. "Maybe he's going to sell it to the highest bidder."

Niner locked a new power pack into his Deece. "Have you asked him?"

"No," said Atin. "Why don't you ask him, Dar? You're one of his favorites. Like Ordo and Fi. And maybe he wants a half-Jedi grandchild one day."

Corr laughed. "But he's got *Bard'ika,* so he's got a full-Jedi son, hasn't he?"

Darman felt uncomfortable. He didn't want to alienate his brothers, and he'd never thought of any one of them as being treated differently. "*Kal'buir* doesn't have favorites. He probably thinks I'm the idiot of the litter who needs looking after. You want me to ask him?" Darman didn't know how he'd broach it, but Skirata had infinite patience where his boys were concerned. "I'll *ask* him."

But now the question had started to bother him. It didn't make any difference how Skirata treated them, but the doubt had wormed its way into his head and it wasn't going to go away. He settled down into a more comfortable position, Deece resting in the crook of his arm and his visor's magnification set on maximum range, and waited.

"Which moron in Procurement ordered Deeces with the clip on the left?" Corr muttered. He'd never seemed to like the commando-issue DC-17 very much; the original brigades of commandos had been raised with the rifle since they were old enough to hold one, but cross-trained men like Corr came to it new, and they griped. "And on the sidearm, too. Can't holster it right."

"A moron who never had to fire it to save his life," said Niner. "Or thought that if you aimed right-handed, then your left was free to reach for a reload . . ."

"What a bunch of useless *bev'ikase.*"

"Did you make that word up?"

"That's the right word, isn't it? It means—"

"Well, yes, but I've never heard it used as a term of abuse before . . . just anatomical."

"He's right," said Atin. "I reckon that's the real reason we were trained to be ambidextrous. To allow for those *or'dinise* in Procurement."

Darman *liked* his Deece. Okay, the clip *was* a nuisance, but the thing never jammed in heat, cold, or dust, it was accurate, and even swapping out the attachments was no more trouble than reloading.

"I'd like a Verp," he said. "They're lovely. Remember when we went out tagging terrorists with them on Triple Zero?"

Atin rolled his head to ease his neck muscles. "That was you and Fi."

"So it was," Darman said, missing Fi badly but careful not to hurt Corr's feelings by saying so. Corr was a good comrade. After a few weeks, it had felt like he'd been part of Omega forever. But if Fi could have come back as well, it would have been great.

The heat haze broke the ocher desert into shimmering mirages, dark pools that came and went as Darman stared at them; the Fleet Met forecast said there was an 80 percent chance of sandstorms. Haurgab was yet another backworld whose strategic value Darman couldn't work out. Yes, there was ore mining here, and the Separatists needed plenty of ore if they were going to keep churning out droids, but why didn't Palpatine concentrate on hitting the major population centers of Sep worlds? Why was the clone army spread so thinly?

Darman answered himself aloud. "All he's doing is stretching our supply chains."

"Kal'buir?"

"Old Slimy. Palps. He should leave the military stuff to the generals. Typical *shabla* civvy. The strategic genius sitting on his backside in his nice safe office."

If there was anywhere that typified the thoroughly stupid strategy of this war, it was Haurgab. The GAR had too few resources to take the place, but too many to be so thoroughly defeated that the politicians took the hint and withdrew. It was a nicely sustainable operation. It could keep simmering at this level of grinding misery for years, and probably would.

Across a riverbed that hadn't seen flowing water in decades, about twenty klicks to the northeast, two companies of the 85th Infantry were shoring up the regional government at Hadde. A distant *boomp-boomp-boomp* like a slow heartbeat started up, answered by the higher-pitched and more rapid bark of cannon fire. Darman saw fresh palls of black smoke forming in the distance. He could almost set his chrono by the regularity of the bombardment; the local Mauja clans rolled out their collection of artillery pieces just after lunch, driving Hadde's population into shelters at the hottest time of the day, and made the city a miserable place to be until the wind picked up at nightfall and the Maujasi went home for the night. It was as if they were doing a day's work, using their contracted hours for a bit of bombardment, then heading home to watch the holovids.

Two companies: fewer than three hundred men. It was pitifully inadequate and there was little air support. The rest of the battalion was scattered across the region in platoons, taking ground one day and losing it again the next.

That was why the squad had been sent in. They had one target—a key Maujasi leader called Jolluc. Now they were waiting for him to show.

"You know," said Corr, "if we just committed a few more air assets to this and bombed the *osik* out of the settlements around this dump, nobody would have to boil their *shebs* off and we could all go somewhere with better nightlife. Look at the place. It's all mountains."

"Hills," said Atin.

"They're still in the way. *Air assault.*"

Corr had started life as a bomb disposal trooper, so he was still learning *Mando'a* as he went along. Predictably, he picked up profanities and slang first, just like Etain had. He was even creating his own.

"*Cor'ika,* we'd be sent somewhere equally pointless to do it all over again," Atin said. "And we've been told to win hearts and minds. No obliterating civilian villages."

"Civilians, my *shebs*. They're all armed. They don't need a uniform to be hostiles. Why does every species with a grievance against its neighbor end up being classed as a Sep and added to our list?"

"They're not even a different species here." Darman joined in the grumbling. "Not like Gaftikar, where you could see who was who. They're *all* humans. They all look the same, too."

A tiny dust storm on the horizon indicated ground vehicles moving in their direction. Niner clicked his teeth, mildly annoyed. It was a habit he seemed to have picked up from Skirata. "I hate it when he thinks. Thinking just makes you dissatisfied."

"Yeah, that's *my* job," said Atin.

"Heard from Laseema?"

"Not yet, Sarge."

"She'll send a message. Don't worry."

"I *know* she will," Atin said peevishly. "We're getting married."

"What?"

"You heard me."

The news didn't take their attention off the road, but it certainly diluted it. Darman's gut flipped over. This was a whole new world. This was—

"Impossible," Niner said. "You can't get married. You're in the army."

Atin meant stubborn in *Mando'a,* but it wasn't a negative word to Mandalorians. It implied tenacity and courage rather than bloody-mindedness. Atin was quiet and relentlessly methodical until something really riled him, and then he reverted to type as one of Vau's men—fighting mad and unwilling to back down until someone *knocked* him down. Vau had beaten an animal reaction into them, a savage will that he said would keep them alive long after more reasonable men had given up and died.

"Show me the regs," Atin said. Darman could see his chin jut out in defiance, even with his helmet in place. "Go on. Show me the regulation that says we can't marry."

"We were never intended to have families."

"But there are no specific regs *against* it, are there?"

"No. But it's still stupid."

"Why?"

No clone needed to see his brother's face to know what was going on in his head. Darman could tell from the faint clicks and breaths over the helmet comlink that Niner was jumpy, as if he was panicking about something. But Niner was definitely not one of life's panickers. He was *upset.* He was trying to make an uncomfortable reality go away.

"Because you don't get a salary," Niner said at last. "So you can't support a wife and kids. There are no married quarters, either. There's—"

Atin dug in for the full argument. He sounded as if he'd

clamped his teeth together. "Laseema's a Twi'lek. Twi'leks and humans can't interbreed. And she's got an apartment. *Kal'buir* paid for it. And she's got a *job*. So I don't need to support her. Bang goes your case, Sarge."

Corr muttered to himself. "Kept man, eh? Nice work."

"You're still crazy," Niner said. "And it's not *my* case. It just *is*."

Darman's plans for some kind of domestic happiness were now under threat. He pitched in to back up Atin. They were men, not droids; they had a right to expect more from life. Skirata told them so.

"You think we can't marry because we're *property,* Sarge?" Darman asked.

Niner's voice hardened a fraction. "I don't know. Go ask General Zey."

"Zey won't give a *shab*," Atin snapped. "And if he did, what's he going to do about it? How's he going to tell the difference between what we do now and what happens when I've exchanged vows with Laseema?"

"He's got a point," Darman said. "It's academic."

"And I want a *life*." Atin was getting really angry now. "If I survive, then I'm not going to be a soldier forever." He paused for a few moments as if gearing up for something difficult. "I want out. I want to leave."

It was the first time any of them had said that aloud. Maybe it was the first time any of them had wanted it. Fi's departure had somehow opened the door to dissent and real ambition beyond the GAR.

In the awkward silence, Corr seemed to be studiously avoiding the argument. Sometimes he still behaved in a temporary I'm-just-filling-in kind of way, even if it was clear that Fi was never coming back.

Niner had his sergeant's don't-argue-with-me voice on now. "Your mind should be on the operation, not on getting out of the army."

"It *is*," Atin said, moving up beside Corr and taking a firing position next to him. "I can do both at the same time. In fact, one helps me do the other . . ."

No, it wasn't Fi's escape. Darman decided it was the arrival of Skirata's grandson that had started it. The child had given all of them the feeling that real life was going on without them and leaving them behind. If they'd been like the white jobs, the regular clone troopers who had limited contact with normal civilian life, then they might have managed to kid themselves that things weren't so bad. But they'd all spent time doing things that nonclones took for granted. By giving them as much freedom as he could, Skirata had made them far less satisfied with their lot.

"What about you and Etain, Dar?" Atin asked.

"What, you mean are we going to settle down?"

"Yeah."

Etain would have to leave the Jedi Order. They didn't hold with relationships—*attachment,* they called it—but they didn't expect Jedi to be celibate, either. That seemed to be asking for trouble, Darman thought. One day they'd get some lovesick Jedi doing something crazy, whatever the training was supposed to knock out of them, and it wouldn't end well. You couldn't turn flesh and blood into unemotional droids, neither clone nor Jedi. It wasn't healthy. It wasn't *fair.*

"We haven't talked detail," Darman said. "But yeah, that's what I want."

"Kids?"

Darman thought of Skirata's grandson. Babies were all demand and hunger. Force-sensitive babies—well, Etain would have to sort that out. It was all a long way off, if ever, and he didn't have to think about it.

"One day," he said. "But not yet."

"Better get cracking on it," Corr said helpfully. "Before you get too old."

"Talking of cracking on," said Niner, "stand by . . ."

Darman's gut knotted as it always did before action. He scrambled into a better vantage point and spotted what had grabbed Niner's attention: a thin line of repulsortrucks carrying routine supplies from the port, kicking up dust like a smokescreen. Atin released a reconnaissance remote, tossing the tiny sphere into the air to make its way across the narrow pass and hover, relaying images from the ground beneath.

Corr scrolled through magnifications in his HUD; Darman could see his brother's changing field of view in the point-of-view icons in his own head-up display. It settled on the southern wall of crumbling cliffs that flanked the road, and when Darman switched to the same view he could see shapes suddenly emerging from the fissures like insects.

"I still reckon they've got tunnels into those positions," Corr said irritably. "Or we'd have seen them move in."

Niner had a good line of sight down the wadi. "Well, as long as they didn't see *us* move in . . . remember, we're only after Jolluc. Don't waste ammo on anyone else unless you need to."

Each week, a rebel platoon had come along the dirt road to intercept shipments moving to Hadde from the port city of Rishun, and Omega had let them, simply observing and collecting intel. It was Jolluc they needed to take out; smart, resourceful, and the main man for planning, Intel said. Now the rebels were getting *lairy,* to use Mereel's favorite word. They weren't taking as many precautions.

It still seemed pretty pointless to Darman, seeing as the Mauja tribes weren't actually a threat to the Republic. He doubted they could even spell *Separatist.* They just liked thieving and didn't like their government, which sounded an awful lot like Skirata. They wanted whatever they could grab. Hadde probably looked like a nice place to pillage.

But they'd fire back when Omega targeted them, so Darman's vague sympathy evaporated faster than spit on the hot rocks around him. He sighted up. The rebels had to assault the convoy at close quarters if they wanted to pillage, because an artillery bombardment would trash everything they wanted to take, and that made them vulnerable. Jolluc would be with them—if Intel was right—and fair game in open ground.

"They could have a *warren* of tunnels in there." Corr was persistent. "And we won't even dent that if we can't call in air strikes. When we're clear, I say we wander down and run a few scans. See what we can do to shut them down."

Some of the Maujasi spilled down onto the road carrying parts of dismantled repeating blasters, and sprinted across to scramble up the rocks and take up positions on the other side and assemble the weapons; there were now around thirty of them. There was no sign of Jolluc. Darman had various images of the man in his HUD, checking them against each rebel he could get a clear focus on through the DC-17's optics.

"A few more than usual," Atin said. "Maybe there's nothing worth watching on HNE today."

Niner shook his head. "Intel didn't say there was anything different about this supply run."

"Here we go again." Darman sighed. "Intel's as useful as a third nostril. Stop listening to them."

The convoy of repulsortrucks was a few minutes from the ambush point now, their security speeders riding ahead. They knew they'd have company. They always got hit one way or another. It was just a question of how hard, so why didn't the Republic just supply Hadde with air transport to freight supplies into town? They were as stupid as those *shabla* beetles. It would have stopped this ritual. It just proved to Darman that Palpatine was either running out of creds and resources, or he hadn't a clue how to run a war, or maybe both.

"Stand by," said Niner.

"We should warn the convoy we're here."

"I'm not risking it. One minute they're government sympathizers, the next they're rebels . . . you can't trust any of 'em."

Darman planned to put a grenade or three into the northern face of the slope if things got too hot, starting with the rebels' rotary blaster position. The thing looked ancient. Warfare was a lot less high-tech here, but underestimating it was a good way to end up dead.

There was still no sign of Jolluc.

"Two hundred meters," said Niner. Darman heard the repeater's magazine click into position. "Boy, there's definitely more of them than usual . . ."

"We could abort," Atin said.

Niner had his finger on the trigger. The rebels were now all between Omega's position and the convoy. "Not now."

"I make it thirty-one."

On top of a rock in the middle of nowhere. We're going to have to run for it . . . should have brought the speeder bikes . . .

"When you see Jolluc, take him," Niner said. "If you don't see him, hold fire, shut your eyes, and leave the convoy to look out for itself. No heroics."

It was brutal, but they weren't here to babysit supply chains for civvies. Darman motivated himself with the thought of the jug of iced water back at base and checked the range on the Deece. The reticule lined up on the antique rotary and the grenade's charge glowed red.

The first *bdapp* of rebel blasters split the heavy afternoon air. The convoy's escort returned fire while the convoy tried to scatter, but there was no open ground.

"No Jolluc," said Niner calmly.

"Give it time . . ." Atin turned away from the assault below. "*Shab,* I hate this."

"We're not here to police traffic."

It was still tough to stand back and let the convoy take it. Darman itched for an excuse to open fire. He'd gone charging to the rescue before on Qiilura, breaking cover to save civilians, but he'd been a kid then on his second deployment. The longer you spent fighting, the more cautious you became. Battle hardening meant that you knew how dead you could *really* get. Darman would leave the derring-do to the new boys now.

What new boys? We're going to run out of reinforcements.

Blasterfire spat and flared; smoke roiled, and Darman made an effort not to react to the screaming and yelling. Niner reached out and put his hand on his shoulder, saying nothing.

"Got him," said Corr. He paused and made a low rumbling noise in his throat for a split second, just like Sev. "By the lead vehicle. Look at that filthy *hut'uun.*"

For a moment Darman couldn't work out why Corr had suddenly taken Haurgab's civil war so personally, but when he magnified his HUD image he understood. Jolluc—yes, it was him—was sporting a few pieces of white plastoid armor, *trooper* armor. He swaggered through the smoke as if there wasn't a firefight in progress.

There was only one way he could have acquired it, and that made this battle suddenly very personal indeed.

"I wonder what happened to the poor white job he took *that* from," Corr whispered, taking aim. "Well, *shab*-face, here's where you find out that trooper armor isn't as hardened as Katarn kit . . ."

Niner swung back to the repeating blaster. They hadn't bargained on this many rebels showing up, so they'd have to leave it behind. One good shot, and the Maujasi wouldn't be able to pinpoint the location in all this confusion.

"Soon as we're sure he's down, bang out," Niner said. "Got it?"

Corr squeezed the trigger without another word. Darman saw the plume of hot vapor like a puff of smoke rise from Jolluc's head, and the rebel leader—nothing special, balding, maybe fifty—seemed to leap for a moment before falling backward against a burning truck.

"Still moving," Darman said.

Atin squeezed off a shot. "Not anymore . . ."

Niner scrambled to grab his Deece. "Okay, job done—let's go."

They could be down the slope and out into the rocky hills before the Maujasi had worked out what had happened. They *could* have.

"Sniper! *Sniper!*"

The shout rang out across the wadi, and the firing paused for a moment. Then something whooshed a meter or so above the crumbling wall of the fort, sending Darman and the others diving for cover. A mortar exploded some distance behind them.

The next one would probably get the range right.

"We're screwed," Corr said wearily, and snapped off his Deece's sniper attachment to replace it with the ion pulser. "They know we're here."

"By the time we get to the bottom they'll be waiting for us." Darman counted again; maybe twenty rebels still standing. "We can take twenty."

Niner knelt down and aimed the repeater. "I'll give them something to think about and you lot bang out."

Darman ignored him and loaded a few grenades. Atin and Corr didn't jump to obey orders, either.

"Don't start that, Sarge," Atin said. "You know we don't do that. Let's go."

Some repulsortrucks had now managed to pull back and were making a run for it back toward Rishun. Another mortar round shaved a meter over the squad's heads, way too close. The air was thick with pulverized rock and smoke from a burning vehicle. Darman switched filters on his visor with a couple of blinks and saw chaos in the haze, more debris than he expected and a lot of bodies.

"Okay, go. *Go.*"

Darman ran at a crouch for the exit point, thinking the others were following, but the faintest movement in Niner's HUD point-of-view icon caught his eye. Through the haze that hung in the narrow pass, there was a growing tide of movement. Shapes—ones and twos at first, then dozens—were pouring out of openings in the sides of the wadi.

"I make that about a hundred . . . ," Niner said quietly, stacking what ammo he still had next to the repeater.

Corr swallowed audibly. "Tunnel network," he said. "Told you so."

The rebels had a lot more troops than Intel—or Omega—had thought, and they were all coming out to play. And they knew exactly where Omega were now.

It was one thing to fight past twenty rebels when you had armor and they didn't. A hundred—that was a different matter.

"Oh . . . *shab,*" said Darman.

**Private booth in the Haunch of Nerf cantina,
Coruscant university quarter**

Mandalorians were lying savages, loyal to nobody and congenitally violent. They'd steal anything that wasn't nailed down; they'd kill for a bet.

That was what a lot of folks thought of *Mando'ade,* and Kal Skirata was now relying on that thuggish stereotype to cover his tracks. The last thing he wanted any *aruetii* to know was that he needed information for purely emotional reasons. It always made negotiations harder.

"So, can you help me out or not, Professor?" He fixed the biologist with his best I'm-not-just-some-ignorant-grunt expression and leaned back so that the shoulder holster under his best bantha-hide jacket was partially visible. Nobody took much notice of armored Mandalorians on Coruscant, but he preferred to work in plainclothes here. It just provided one connection too many if anyone bothered to join up the dots. "I don't know how much university biology professors make a year, but I'm betting it's not millions."

Gilamar was sitting in on the meeting to add a little medical expertise, and Mereel provided a credible impression of hired muscle. The professor was Dr. Reye Nenilin: he was a gerontologist, the best in his field, and that was the kind of expert Skirata badly needed.

"I have a comfortable lifestyle," Nenilin said. "I'd have to have a very good reason for putting that at risk."

"They say you know more about the aging process than any being alive."

"Do you mind my asking what your interest is?"

Mereel—Null ARC Lieutenant N-7—stood behind Skirata. "My father's not getting any younger."

"He's such a cute kid," said Skirata. "Takes after his mother. Okay, let's just say I have some parts of a puzzle, a puzzle that might make a lot of creds when complete, and I'm looking for someone who can help me work out what the missing parts are."

"Is your interest professional?" Nenilin asked.

"I'm a Mandalorian," said Skirata. It didn't do any harm for the guy to realize what he was dealing with. "Do I look like I might be motivated by a Republic Accolade for Scientific Advancement?"

"Pecuniary, then . . . and if the topic is the process of aging, then which parts of the puzzle do *you* have?"

"I bet I know what you're thinking," said Skirata.

"I'd be very surprised if you did."

The prof was remarkably lippy for an unarmed desk jockey alone in a room with three Mandalorians, even unarmored ones. Skirata thought it was a shame he couldn't slap some respect into him. "You're thinking this is about some rejuvenation scam."

"Most entrepreneurs are on the brink of discovery, if only I can give them a *little* help . . . you'd be surprised how many pharmaceutical opportunities I get offered, Master Fal."

Fal. It was an alias Skirata hadn't used before; he wondered why he'd chosen to use the name after so many years. *Skirata* had been his only reality since childhood.

"Actually, it's an industrial process," he said, forgetting about Falin Mattran. The only thing he could remember about Kuat now was a green transparisteel wall in his parents' apartment that made the whole room feel as if it was submerged in shallow tropical water. "If I can resolve one aspect of it, it'd be worth a great deal to the cloning industry."

Mereel was usually the one who skated on thin ice when it came to shaking down a target. Now Skirata heard the Null inhale slowly, carefully, as if he was getting ready to interrupt.

Hide stuff in plain sight, son. I taught you that, didn't I?

"I'm struggling here," said Nenilin. "I don't know much about commercial cloning."

"Well, that's an oversight for a clever boy like you." Skirata smiled, all acid. "Commercial cloning's banned now under wartime legislation. That's bad news if your business is based on clones. It means you can't replace them. They age fast, you see. It's partly the mechanism for maturing them fast, but it's also common sense—if you make clones, you want repeat business, so you build in obsolescence. Great for clonemasters, but right now plenty of businesses can't replace clone labor and they want to make the most of the workforce they still have. They'd like to stop them from aging so fast."

Nenilin looked at Skirata long and hard. Skirata decided he didn't like the man much. He wore an old-fashioned tunic, the kind that out-of-touch aristocrats still favored,

which probably explained why he hung out at the Haunch of
Nerf. The place was tricked out to look rough-hewn and ancient, its tables inaccurately imagined replicas of antique
rural feasting trestles, and instead of porceplast plates it
served its meals on pleek trenchers. The ale was specially
brewed to make sure it remained authentically cloudy and
full of unidentifiable lumps. Nenilin probably thought this
was how the working classes once lived, in some bucolic
idyll of coarse plenty that never actually existed, and that
somehow this was a desirable state to revert to.

You've got no idea, chum. You should try the real thing.

"I'm not sure I want to be complicit in the exploitation of
cloned sentient beings," said Nenilin. Mereel sat down next
to him and gave Skirata a weary look. "It's tantamount to
slavery."

What a great time to find an aruetii *with half a conscience.*
Skirata decided it was one he only wore in public, and looked
to Gilamar to pick up on the technical stuff. It wasn't his area
of expertise, but he'd been a proper doctor once, and he knew
how to phrase the science stuff.

"Do you know how Arkanian Micro grows human beings
to adulthood in a year or so?" Gilamar asked. "How *any*
cloners operate?"

"In theory, yes. Do you work for the Arkanians?"

Skirata didn't have to say yes or no. Nenilin's assumptions
did the lying for him. "If we worked for Arkanian Micro,
we'd be breaking the law by working on cloning projects
with a ban in force, wouldn't we?"

"I suspect that turning their production over to pedigree
nerf bloodstock wasn't an option."

"I couldn't say."

But Nenilin couldn't resist filling in the gaps. He enjoyed
being clever. He probably thought all Mandalorians were
semi-literate grunts. "If I were Arkanian Micro, I'd want a
stopgap solution—a way of extending the life of my product
during the ban, but one that I had the option to reverse."

"An aging switch," Skirata said.

"Something of an impossible dream, in normal beings.
But with organisms designed to mature and age faster, it

would be more a matter of restoring the status quo for the species in question."

"Exactly." Skirata kept Gilamar in his peripheral vision, waiting for the point in the conversation where he would have to step in and discuss technical stuff with the prof. "And we're talking about humans. Which is your specialist area."

"I'd need to see . . . a specimen genome."

Gilamar leaned forward slightly. "This is highly confidential data, and we'd like some reassurance that you understand how very *sensitive* this is."

Nenilin looked irritated. "Like Master Fal said, any cloning activity, direct or ancillary, is illegal within the Republic unless licensed."

"And of course, no researcher in your position would compromise their reputation with illegal work."

So they all understood each other. If Nenilin helped them, he'd lose more than his job if he revealed his source. And he seemed hooked now. Finding out exactly how clonemasters controlled maturation was heady temptation for a gerontologist. Most commercial cloning research took place in-house, each company with its own closely guarded industrial secrets. Cloning companies spied on one another, didn't share data, and weren't averse to enforcing nondisclosure agreements with staff the hard way—with a blaster, or worse.

Skirata could almost see Nenilin's thoughts forming like a hologram above his head; the glittering bronzium globe of a Republic Science Accolade, and rippling applause.

Gotcha.

Gilamar held out a datachip. "Here are some sequences for you to examine. The geneticist on this part of the project was silencing genes H-seventy-eight-b and H-eighty-eight, one by zinc and one by methylation."

"Interesting," said Nenilin, inserting the chip into his datapad and frowning at the screen. "I'd have expected some manipulation of telomere length via checkpoint genes. Not *those* two . . . yes, that's very interesting indeed." He paused as if framing a delicate question. "Are you *really* a Mandalorian?"

"You mean how come I can use big words and don't walk

on my knuckles? Well, some of us evolved." Gilamar
snapped his thumb and forefinger together in demonstration.
"See? Give us a few more weeks and we'll invent the wheel."

Nenilin had clearly riled the doc. Skirata willed Gilamar
not to take a swing at him.

"I meant that you sound as if you had a scientific education," Nenilin said carefully.

"Just a country doctor," Gilamar said. "I don't think Mandalore has produced a geneticist of note since Demagol."

Nenilin's expression said that he felt he ought to have
known who Demagol was, but he didn't, and so had no idea
if Gilamar was mocking him or not. When he found out—*if*
he found out—he'd discover the insult. But Skirata could see
that the biologist was now firmly hooked by insatiable curiosity, and a small matter like comparison with the most no-
torious and loathed scientist in Mandalorian history wasn't
going to divert him from his quest now.

There was always the chance that Nenilin would fail to
come up with anything useful. Ko Sai, filthy aiwha-bait
though she was, had been an exceptional genetic engineer,
perhaps the greatest ever. She'd be a tough act to follow.

"This isn't the entirety of your material, is it?"

"Of course not," said Skirata. "But we have associates
who'd be emphatically disappointed if we handed you the
whole file . . ."

Nenilin looked to Gilamar as if he was the *Mando* with the
brain cell. "What do you want me to do, then?"

"Look at the data I've given you and tell me if the silencing of those two H genes would affect any in the cluster at
chromosome Nine-A, or possibly Fourteen-B."

"You've pinned that much down, then."

"You tell me."

"It's more than just telomere activity you need to control if
you want to stop accelerated aging. But I suspect you know
that. Do you mind my asking the obvious, though?" Nenilin
had a smug little smile. Skirata thought he probably spent far
too much time with adoring students who thought he was a
god. Maybe he should have let Gilamar smack Nenilin after
all. "If your . . . associates managed to achieve controlled ac-

celeration of aging, then they'd know the route to roll back from that to an unaltered genome."

Gilamar managed a smile even more smug than Nenilin's. "They're not just manipulating *maturation* of humans," he said. "I can't reveal too much, obviously, but they might even be adding material from another individual's genome or . . . building wholly artificial genes. You know the havoc that would play with the expression of characteristics."

Nenilin's eyes seemed to light up at the mention of artificially created genes. Maybe that was a daring new adventure for these lab jockeys. "Or does this data come from a rival, and so you're lacking critical parts of it?"

Skirata cut in. "Let's just say the geneticist who could best help us is a little indisposed, because she's *dead.*"

That knocked the smirk off Nenilin's face. Skirata hoped that his cloudy mock-rustic ale choked him, but not before he did something useful. He hadn't even asked how much he'd get paid. Skirata didn't trust anyone who didn't have a price.

"I have a condition," Nenilin said.

Skirata nodded. *Nice normal greed. That's a relief.* "Of course."

"If I can solve your little puzzle, then I want to be able to use the research for my own study. No embarrassing revelations about the source, of course. I give you my word."

It wasn't as if the guy would forget it once he'd worked it out anyway; you didn't forget that kind of stuff, and so it was bound to influence whatever experiments he was running at the university. But Skirata didn't give a mott's backside what Nenilin did with the data as long as he got what he wanted, a way of stopping the relentless accelerated aging in clones, specifically *his* clones, *his* boys—his sons. The definition of Skirata's responsibility had expanded since he'd first decided to look for a solution, and now he was ready to offer the cure to any clone in the Grand Army who wanted it, but his immediate circle, his *family,* came first.

"*Shab,* we'll even *pay* you," Skirata said, and casually tossed him a high-denomination cash credit chip as if the scientist was a waiter. "That'll help you make a start. Buy some test tubes or whatever it is you use."

"It's refrigeration, hydraulic shearing machines, and cuvettes," Nenilin said. "But thank you."

"We'll be in touch every week, by comm." Skirata got up and headed for the exit. "Pleasure doing business, Dr. Nenilin."

Mereel and Gilamar followed Skirata out into the main salon of the cantina, through a noisy, braying crowd of well-spoken patrons with the same air of faded nobility that Nenilin had. *And they say clones are all the same, do they?* Skirata's ingrained mistrust of the social classes above him came from more than just his Kuati roots. It was the way they combined detached cluelessness with their certainty that they knew best. *That* was what got his adrenaline prompting him to take a swing every time. He inhaled the cool air in the alley outside; it felt as if he was surfacing from drowning. Even the alley was built in a mock-ancient style, trying to pass itself off as some baronial fort. It was a year old if it was a day.

Skirata pulled three strips of ruik root from his pocket, handed them around, and chewed thoughtfully. "What do you reckon, Mij?"

"Let's see what he comes up with."

"Is he talking through his *shebs*?"

"Well, if he is, then at least we'll know what his methodology is so we can rule it out," said Gilamar. "Knowing what doesn't work is as useful a clue as any in genetics."

"Promise me you won't kill him until you get something useful out of him."

"It'll be a challenge," Gilamar said. "I could have fun testing a large-gauge rusty syringe on that guy. Now, you want me to look in on *Kad'ika* before I pay my respects to Zey and tell him where to shove his offer?"

"See Zey first. And no insertion instructions . . ."

"Wad'e and I . . . well, we're not exactly persuaded that training more covert ops troopers is a productive use of a *Mando'ad*'s time."

Here we go again. Covert ops clones had been tasked to

assassinate renegade ARC troopers. Gilamar and Tay'haai had taken that news very badly, although maybe not as badly as Darman, who'd ended up killing two of them. The Republic was rotten at its core; more maggots tumbled out every time Skirata shook it. Clones forced to kill clones—yes, Skirata could see it was one insult too far.

"Mij," Skirata said, "the more of us back on the inside, the better."

"You can get any information you want. Jaing and Mereel can slice into any system in the Republic—including the Treasury. Why don't you just fleece Palpatine of his reserves and we can all thin out?"

Skirata concentrated on not blinking. Gilamar had no idea how accurate that comment was. Skirata hated deceiving him, but what he didn't know couldn't get him into more trouble. He knew what he needed to know, and no more.

"Yeah, but you can steer events . . . ," Skirata said. "You want to see Priest or Reau back in?"

"You *wouldn't*. Not them." Gilamar boiled. He loathed both of them to the point of violence. "They had the makings of the Death Watch in them, those two. Him and that perverted secret fight club, her and that let's-conquer-the-galaxy-again *osik* . . . that's not what either of us want Mandalore to be, is it?"

"I know how to get you going, don't I?"

Gilamar scratched the bridge of his nose thoughtfully. The conspicuous break in it from a particularly fierce game of *get'shuk* made him look more like a man who handed out injuries than one who healed them. That was also true, of course.

"Just keep me away from them. Him especially. Jango must have been mad to recruit him."

"Joking, Mij . . ."

"Okay, tell me what you're really looking for."

"Any clue about the timing of a shift in strategy," Skirata said. "Like I said before, there's a big sea change coming and I want plenty of notice so I can get our boys out."

Gilamar stood with hands on hips, staring down at Skirata's boots. "Okay, just for you. And get that leg fixed, will you? It's a simple op. What are you, a martyr or something?"

Maybe I am.

Skirata had lived with the aftermath of that ankle injury for nearly forty years. He rationalized it as a reminder of stupid risks, but perhaps it was a penance. He couldn't sleep in a bed now, either; on the night he'd rescued Ordo and his brothers from the Kaminoans, he'd slept in the chair to keep an eye on them, and from that point on he felt that rest in a comfortable bed was off limits to him until he fully secured their futures. Ritual—ritual to keep the fates appeased, to focus him, whatever—had eaten a big chunk of his life.

"You're right," Skirata said. "I'll get it fixed."

Gilamar went on his way. Mereel, unusually quiet, strolled in the other direction toward the speeder parking area.

"Well, our professor's bold moral stance on not exploiting poor downtrodden clones like me didn't last long, did it?" he said. "He's got the breaking strain of a warm butter-loaf."

"Son," said Skirata, "if all scientists had nice shiny consciences, we'd still be fighting with stone axes. Who do you think developed all those handy blasters, lasers, and ion cannons?"

"A lot of academics don't support the war, though."

"Yeah, but if you went back in there, told our overeducated friend what you were, and asked him to liberate you and your clone brothers, he'd be out the doors so fast you wouldn't see his *shebs* for dust. It's a theoretical principle for him. It's not *personal*. Worse than that—he's not even motivated by creds. I hate a man who's driven by a *vision.* You can't trust him."

"And you're busting a gut to free us just for the cred chips and the plunder, of course . . ."

"That's different. You're my boys."

"Anyway, it's not as if we're stuck with him. He's just one scientist working on a fragment of the data. And he's not going to be chatting about the approach over a caf in the university common room, is he? None of them will. They'll all potter away on their own section of the genome, thinking they're privileged with some secret, and never have the full picture."

"Sooner or later, we're going to have to try it out. The cure, I mean."

"Try it on me."

It had to be tested on a clone. Skirata didn't see any of them as expendable, even rank-and-file troopers he'd never met, but the thought of trying some unproven therapy on any of his own boys scared him. He couldn't try it out on himself. It was the one sacrifice he could never make for them, however much he wanted to.

"We'll make sure we know how to undo the effects of it before we get to that stage," Skirata said, ruffling Mereel's hair. "I won't take risks with your health."

Mereel laughed. "Lots of nice healthy firefights instead."

"You could go home to Mandalore now and never fight again." Skirata felt instantly guilty. It didn't take much where his kids were concerned. "Nobody's forcing you to fight now, son."

"I'm not sitting on my *shebs* while my brothers fight, either." Mereel seemed more interested in an illuminated sign a little farther ahead than avoiding premature old age. He quickened his pace. "Sooner or later, though, we might have to use *Kad'ika*'s tissue samples."

Skirata shook his head. Etain hadn't objected to letting Ko Sai take a look at her son's genome, but Ko Sai had been their prisoner, held in isolation. There was nothing the Kaminoan could have done with the knowledge. Once some other gene cruncher got wind of the fact that Darman and Etain had a son, though, the baby would be a valuable commodity. Half Jedi, half perfect soldier: that was a genome a lot of companies—and governments—would kill to get their hands on.

"It's too dangerous, *Mer'ika*," Skirata said. "They can detect the midi-chlorians. They'd know."

"Maybe only the Jedi Council has the kit to do that."

"Wouldn't they see there was material in the cells that didn't add up?"

"*Kad'ika*'s the only child of a clone that we have, and some of the aging genes aren't present—or at least what we *think* are those genes." Mereel didn't sound desperate, just patient, as if Skirata didn't realize things and needed a biology lesson repeated with helpful diagrams of squalls and jakrabs. "I thought the maturation genes the Kaminoans added to the basic Jango model were recessive, for their own business reasons, but it's never quite that simple in genetics. Add, take away, or change one gene—even move its position—and it can have a massive impact on the expression of all the others. They're all connected somehow. It's not a simple case of chopping bits out of gene sequences or adding them. If it was, cloning wouldn't be such a profitable or secretive business. It's very hard to get right."

Skirata didn't want to argue. The whole quest was his idea; he could hardly turn around now and say there was a limit to how far he would go to save his clone sons from an unfairly early death. Skirata wasn't sure now if his own reluctance was based on fear of exposing *Kad'ika* to discovery, or just a general unease about *using* the kid for genetic research in any way. That was all too . . . *Kaminoan.*

Kid? My grandson. He really is *my grandson now.*

"We can approach it from the embryology end, too," Mereel said. "Dr. Elliam Baniora. Everything I've read suggests he's the top man when it comes to development. Let's tell him we want to see if we can clone humans with extended active life spans for manual labor."

Cover stories needed to have just enough truth in them to look like the real thing. Skirata wondered whether to just tell them the truth: that he'd been one of life's losers until his unhappy life had been transformed by a bunch of clone kids who needed him simply to survive, and so now he would do anything, absolutely *anything,* to give them a normal life and the life span that went with it.

If the scientists wanted the biotechnology as the price of saving his boys, he'd pay it. He didn't care. He just wanted them to have lives like other men.

"You know what I find funny?" Skirata unlocked his speeder, the spoils of war commandeered from a Jabiimi terrorist who was too dead to need it now, and realized the sign that had caught Mereel's attention was outside a confectionery store. Clones, always peckish, tended to have a very sweet tooth. Maybe it was linked to their maturation, the metabolic need to fuel all that fast aging. "That the guy could look you in the eye and still not know what you are. Even now, most *aruetiise* here don't know what a clone trooper looks like."

Nor did they care, by and large. But some did, like Besany Wennen, and when they cared they could move mountains.

Mereel paused. "Can you wait a few minutes while I get something, *Kal'buir*?"

"Candied nuts . . . nut slice . . . ?"

"I hear that store does *very* good nut slice."

Skirata fished in his pockets automatically and crammed a stack of credit chips into Mereel's hand.

"Time we got some bank accounts sorted out for you all," he said.

Mereel shrugged. "We're not short of creds, any of us."

"I mean real bank accounts, not skimming off the Republic's budget. In case anything happens to me."

"*Buir,* we can slice into any banking system in the galaxy, like Mij said. We're big boys now. And nothing's going to happen to you."

Skirata walked a precarious line between wanting to protect his adopted sons from an unforgiving galaxy and giving them the space the Republic denied them to be independent. It was a parent's dilemma, magnified many times and complicated by their accelerated, compressed life spans. He didn't want to dole out pocket money to them like kids; these were fighting men, and they deserved the wherewithal to lead their own lives, all the simple routine choices that citizens had.

"I don't mean money laundering," Skirata said. "I'll get Jaing to set up personal accounts for you all. Private, to spend as you like. None of my business."

Mereel laughed and strode off toward the brightly lit sign. "I'll only blow it all on fast speeders, slow women, and overpriced candy . . ."

Skirata sat in the driver's seat and waited for Mereel to return with his booty, checking the messages on his comlink to pass the time. No, he didn't have to worry about Mereel. The lad was sociable, confident, and guaranteed to find a way of fitting in wherever he went. Of the six Nulls, he was the one best able to deal with the demons the Kaminoans had forced on him. But the others—A'den, Kom'rk, Jaing, and Prudii— kept Skirata awake at night to varying degrees. And Ordo . . .

I'm too protective. Ordo can cope. He's a grown man. And he's got Besany.

Skirata stared at the comlink's miniature screen without really seeing it. He tried not to have favorites, but from the moment two-year-old Ordo had aimed a blaster at a Kaminoan to try to save his brother Nulls from termination, the kid had been his heart and soul.

And now he'd sent Skirata the usual stack of sitrep text comms. There was a file of budget data, with more information on the big procurement projects due to deliver around the third anniversary of the war. That time slot appeared to be increasingly significant. Ordo had added a terse line: I THOUGHT ANOTHER REP INTEL AGENT MIGHT BE TRAILING BESANY. I SUGGEST WE PERSUADE HER TO LEAVE FOR MANDALORE BEFORE SOMETHING SERIOUS HAPPENS. REMEMBER THIS IS MY WIFE.

Skirata read the last terse line a couple of times. He'd raised his boys as good Mandos, and the pressure to marry young must have seeped in deep without Skirata noticing he'd even put it in their heads. The Nulls were late starters by *Mando* standards. Marrying at sixteen was common.

My boy's grown up and left home.

It was a private deal between a couple, nothing to do with anyone else, but Skirata had felt a little excluded by the suddenness of it, and scolded himself for feeling that way.

Ordo was still playing the big brother to everyone just as he had in Tipoca City, but Skirata shared his worries; trouble *was* coming. They could even guess at a possible date for it. All that mattered now was getting out in one piece with as much capital as possible and a method for reversing accelerated clone aging. Skirata's priority was his underground escape route for clone deserters—something that had started with his Nulls, then spread to include his commando com-

pany, and now extended to *any* white job—the ordinary
clone trooper—who wanted something else out of life.

It was Skirata's sacred mission. He was wedded to it.

*But how many of the white jobs want to leave the army?
How many of them can even conceive of the life they've been
denied?*

He couldn't save one million men, let alone three. He'd
save as many as he could. They had, after all, saved him in a
way that went far beyond stopping him from getting killed in
combat.

Come on, Mer'ika. *You buying the whole store or something?*

Skirata scrolled through the remaining messages. Most
were business; fencing all the valuables that Vau had stolen
from the Mygeeto bank vaults was taking time, as was laundering the bonds and credits. Then there were updates from
Rav Bralor on Mandalore, letting him know how the construction of the bastion in Kyrimorut was going.

He almost missed the last message. It was very short.

DAD, RUUSAAN'S MISSING. WE HAVEN'T HEARD FROM HER IN
MONTHS. WE NEED TO TALK. YOURS, IJAAT.

It was from one of his sons.

Not his clone sons, the kids he put everything on the line
for; it was his biological son, Ijaat, whom he hadn't spoken
to in many years and—with his other son, Tor—had declared
him *dar'buir,* no longer a father.

Aruetiise didn't understand *Mando* family law, but to be
divorced by your own kids was one of the worst disgraces for
any Mandalorian.

Ruusaan . . . Skirata hadn't seen his daughter in years,
either. But she hadn't signed the *dar'buir* declaration, and
that had always given him some hope that she didn't hate
him for the divorce.

My little girl. She's missing.

The hatch opened and Mereel slid into the passenger's
seat, pockets bulging, but the grin died on his face.

"Buir?" He stared into Skirata's eyes. *"Buir,* what's
wrong?"

Skirata hadn't realized his shock and fear were visible. He hadn't realized tears were running down his face, either.

"My daughter," he said. "My girl's missing."

Skirata had two families, both in need, and no Mandalorian could ever turn his back on his kids forever, even if they'd disowned him.

"We'll find her, then, *Buir*," Mereel said, matter-of-factly. "After all—she's family."

Skirata hoped she was. Family took a lot more than genes to hold it together.

4

No, I'm not going to play Mand'alor. *Okay, you can tell everyone I'm Fett's son if that makes them happy, but you can keep the politics. And I want payment. It'll crimp my mercenary earnings.*
—Spar, formerly ARC-02, to Fenn Shysa, unconvinced that Mandalorians need him to masquerade as Fett's legal heir

Kragget restaurant, lower levels, Coruscant, 938 days ABG

"**H**i, sweetie." The Twi'lek waitress greeted Etain with a big smile. "The usual?"

"That'd be great," said Etain. "Thanks."

Nobody wandered into the Kragget by chance. It was a place for regulars, a greasy-looking diner right on the edge of the lower levels, and so it was popular with those who spent a lot of time in the lawless neighborhoods nearby—the Coruscant Security Force. Jedi general Etain Tur-Mukan was now a regular here, too, but it wasn't the Kragget's lavishly greasy all-day breakfast that lured her. It was brief and secret visits to see her son.

She'd named him Venku, but now he was known as Kad—*Kad'ika,* Little Saber.

Kad was now nearly a year old and Etain's heart broke anew each morning at the prospect of being separated from him for another day. The fact that he had a small army of doting babysitters did nothing to dull the pain of having to keep her motherhood secret from everyone, including Kad's father.

The longer this went on, the harder it would be to tell Darman that he had a son.

Etain settled at a corner table and got a nod from CSF officers she knew by sight but not by name. Her brown Jedi robes gave her a kind of anonymity, much like the clones' armor; nobody asked why she was slumming it down here, because Jedi often did marginal jobs, and anyway—she was Kal Skirata's buddy. CSF, and Captain Jaller Obrim in particular, were very chummy with Skirata and his boys.

One of the officers paused in midchew as Etain sat down at a nearby table. "General, have you heard from Fi lately?"

"He's doing okay," she said. The CSF officers knew Fi wasn't dead. They'd helped Besany rescue him. Etain was comforted to know she wasn't the only sane woman who did crazy, dangerous things for the welfare of clone troopers. "He's even got a girlfriend now."

There was a ripple of approving comments from surrounding tables. The cops liked Fi. Everyone did, because he was a funny, friendly guy, but he had legendary status within CSF; he'd once thrown himself on a grenade to shield CSF officers, and that bought a man serious respect. Katarn armor had saved him that time. It hadn't saved him from brain trauma on Gaftikar. Even Fi ran out of luck sooner or later.

"If he ever comes back here," said the officer, "tell him to drop by the social club, won't you?"

"I'll do that."

Soronna, the Twi'lek waitress who managed the Kragget day shift, sidled over to Etain and put a cup of mild-brew caf in front of her.

"Laseema's running a little late," she said.

"Anything wrong?"

"No, she's been out buying baby clothes." Soronna gave her a knowing wink. She was *getting on a bit,* as Darman put it, but still magnetically glamorous, with the flowing walk of the dancer she'd once been. "*Kad'ika*'s outgrowing everything. That's a baby in a real hurry to grow up. Takes after his grandfather for sheer impatience."

My baby.

That's my *baby. I'm not the one choosing his clothes. I'm not the one who feeds him and puts him to bed each night.*

Did Soronna know he was really Etain's? She hadn't shown the slightest hint that she did. But Skirata tended to surround himself with people who knew the rules and kept their mouths shut. The stakes were high.

So what? So what if the Jedi Council kicks me out for fraternizing with Darman?

She was on the point of comming General Zey to confess, as she was at least once a day. But she'd lose her rank and command. She couldn't turn her back on the Grand Army now, not when they needed every Jedi officer they could get.

Bardan's not a Jedi anymore, though, and he's still making himself useful . . .

Her whole reason for keeping her child a secret had evaporated when Bardan Jusik turned his back on the Jedi Order. It hadn't changed a thing. He was as deeply involved in the war and helping clone troops survive as he'd ever been. Etain stared into her mug of caf and wondered if she'd just become too comfortable with her rank, or even if she was more worried about what the Masters of the Jedi Council thought of her.

They say that however old you are, you still want your parents' approval, deep down.

The doors opened. Laseema walked in carrying *Kad'ika* on one hip and a shopping bag in her free hand, looking the part of the busy young mother. Etain couldn't pretend it didn't hurt. She tried to look casually interested, as any woman might when admiring a friend's child, but it was hard; when he started crying it tore at every nerve in her body. She wanted to grab him. It was an urgent, primal instinct.

Several cops stopped Laseema to coo over *Kad'ika*. His crying was a halfhearted grizzle, more a long complaint than anything, and he squirmed in Laseema's grip.

"They all want to be uncles," she said, dragging herself away from the chorus of *oohs* and *aahs*. She held the baby out to Etain as if she had to persuade her to take him. "Here. Want to hold him?"

Etain scooped *Kad'ika* up in her arms. He became instantly quiet, and everything around her suddenly ceased to exist. He smelled clean and wonderful and *hers*. The cop at the next table put down his caf and leaned across to make faces in the way people did when in the presence of infants. Etain wiped dribble from the baby's chin as he stared mesmerized at the officer with huge dark eyes—Darman's eyes.

"Who's gorgeous? Who dat *gorgeous* baby?" The cop was a big, square man who looked as if he spent his days kicking down doors, but now he was reduced to sentimental mush. He glanced at Etain. "You look like that comes naturally," he said, with no idea how deep the comment cut. "You've definitely got the secret of calming babies."

"Jedi mind influence," Etain said, forcing a smile. It was time to move somewhere more private before the pretense crumbled. Jedi or not, her hormones seemed still to be in disarray, her emotions made more erratic by the strain of being separated from those she loved most. "I think he needs changing. Come on, Laseema. Let's do the necessary, or Kal will complain that we're neglecting his grandson."

Laseema's apartment—the one Skirata had bought to get her out of Qibbu the Hutt's clutches, and provide them all with a base away from the barracks—was part of the same grim permacrete complex that housed the Kragget. By slipping through the rear doors and into the kitchen, Etain could reach the apartment via the turbolift and a flight of stairs. The place had the feel of a fortress, and that was probably why Skirata chose it. It occupied a whole floor.

Laseema followed her. The apartment doors opened into a big living room that had probably once been a warehousing area, and that bore all the signs of three very different people trying to coexist there with a small baby. It smelled of cooking, laundry, and air freshener. On a subtler level, the Force told her that Jusik was scared but more content than he'd been in years, that Laseema spent sleepless nights fretting about Atin's safety, and that Skirata . . . Skirata wasn't the swirling darkness Etain had first sensed. The pit of violence and anger was still there alongside the selfless passions, but there was also a small deep pool of profound contentment, a softness she hadn't sensed before. On the table was a chaotic pile of electronic circuits and mechanical servos that had to be Jusik's latest project. Skirata tended to leave no physical traces, as befitted a man who lived up fully to the nomadic side of Mandalorian culture.

"How long can you stay?" Laseema asked.

Etain settled down on the nearest chair and let *Kad'ika* totter around the room by holding on to furniture. He landed on his backside with a bump, giggling. "Two days."

"Oh."

"I'm doing *Bard'ika*'s old job now. Two days is a long period of leave when you're looking after a commando group." Etain checked *Kad'ika* over and saw how much he'd grown. "I ought to sleep, but I don't want to waste a moment."

Controlling nearly five hundred commandos was an impossible task. They were almost entirely self-directing, and the most she could do was pass them their objectives, deal with their requests and problems, and visit them in the field. There were too few Jedi to go around.

So there's one more reason why you stay . . .

And the commandos were all so *different.* Apart from the men trained by Skirata, their cultures seemed to vary from squad to squad, even those trained by Walon Vau and Rav Bralor, whose style she knew, and who were now among her band of unlikely friends.

"I talk to *Kad'ika* about you," Laseema said suddenly. "Even if he can't understand. I always say *Mama's coming home soon,* and things like that. You never know how much they take in."

Etain looked up. Laseema was a typically pretty Twi'lek, a young woman with a wretched past who had been used just as callously as the clones she'd found kinship with. Now she looked anxious, as if she felt guilty for looking after *Kad'ika.*

"It's okay," Etain said. "I'm grateful to you. It's my fault we're all in this mess. Without you . . . well, I know he's loved and well cared for."

"I'm not trying to take your place."

"I never thought you were, but I could hardly complain if you did."

Laseema looked at her with a slightly baffled expression for a moment. She looked very different these days. She'd taken to wearing very sober, high-necked clothing, not the usual low-cut, tight-fitting cropped tops that most Twi'lek females wore. It was as if she was making it clear that she wasn't the unwilling entertainment at some sleazy Hutt cantina any longer. Etain decided she would remind herself of the average Twi'lek girl's lot whenever she felt tempted to complain about her own restricted life.

"Kal absolutely adores him," Laseema said, as if trying to make harmless small talk well away from the minefield of absentee parents. "He's very good with babies. You wouldn't believe it, would you? Mandalorians look so hard-bitten."

Skirata typified the *Mando* ideal of responsible fatherhood and devotion to his clan. He was a sucker for helpless kids. "And *Bard'ika*?"

"Loves being an uncle. He plays little Force games with *Kad'ika* so that he gets used to his abilities."

"Really?" Etain was instantly worried, but it made sense; the baby's Force powers were as much a part of his development as learning to walk, and he would have to learn not only to use them but also to conceal them. "I'd better talk to him about that . . ."

Laseema looked as if she wished she hadn't mentioned it, and changed tack. "He's such a gorgeous baby. Rarely cries, smiles at everyone. Kal says he's exactly like Darman was at the same age."

And I'm missing it all. I'm not seeing him grow up.

Etain was hardly the first mother to have duties that took her away from her child. It was just something that no Jedi was supposed to experience, and she understood the ban on attachment better now than she ever had. It was a harsh rule, and she worried that Jedi raised other Jedi in a constant soulless cycle of detached, cold indifference, but at times like these she understood how disruptive it was to have someone whose welfare mattered so much to you that it clouded your judgment.

But if we don't experience this . . . how can we possibly sit in judgment on non-Force-users? How can we understand why they do the things they do?

Etain wondered what suppressing natural emotions did to Jedi in the end. She rearranged *Kad'ika* on her lap, but he could sit pretty well on his own. She realized she just wasn't used to doing this, and that she *should* have been. *Kad'ika* turned his head to look into her face with intense curiosity, then grinned again and said what sounded like, "Ka! La!" They weren't quite words, but Etain squealed with delight and surprise. The baby stared back into her face with wide-eyed shock at the reaction.

"He's talking!" she said. "Clever *Kad'ika*! Who's Mama's clever boy? Say *Mama*. Can you say *Mama*?"

Kad gurgled as if he was going to break into laughter. It dawned slowly on Etain that her son was probably trying to say *Kal* and *Laseema*. It was logical, because those were the names he heard every day. But she couldn't deny that it hurt.

"Mama!" he said suddenly. "Mama-*mama-maaaa*!"

He laughed, obviously delighted with himself, eyes locked on hers. That was all Etain needed. It was a moment of perfect connection between them, and she would treasure it for the rest of her life. She nuzzled him and rocked him to make him laugh more.

"Clever Kad! Yes, it's Mama!"

Kad pointed at Laseema. "Lala! *Lala!*"

Laseema beamed at him and got a heartbreaking smile back. "He's growing so fast."

For any other parent it would have been a source of pride, but for Etain it simply rekindled the fear that her son might have inherited his father's accelerated aging. Mereel had re-assured her that the Kaminoans had made sure the trait wasn't passed on. She wondered why they didn't just make clones sterile, but it could have been anything from complications with gene expression to simply seeing what happened if clones reproduced. Kaminoans didn't think like humans, and they didn't see clones as anything more than

product, just organic droids. She hoped Mereel was right
about inheritance. She'd read far too much about epigenetics
during her pregnancy, and now worried that Kad's genes
were somehow undetectably tainted by whatever had happened to Darman.

Kad babbled incoherently and made a lunge for the hank
of hair draped over her shoulder. Etain caught him as he
rolled to one side like an amiable drunk and threw up.

Laseema rushed to mop up, but Etain was determined to
do the messy work herself. Babies were always getting sick,
the experts said. "I hope this is normal development."

"Every mother worries about everything," Laseema said.
"Not that I know, but they said my sister did."

There was a whole world of misery wrapped up in those
two sentences. Etain realized how very little she knew about
the Twi'lek. Maybe Laseema's family stayed in touch, but the
way she said it made Etain think that she was alone, sold into
the awful servitude that awaited most Twi'lek girls with more
looks than family connections, and as long as she intended to
stay with Atin she could never bear children of her own. And
here she was having to look after someone else's baby. That
must have rankled. Mandalorians might have been hard-
wired to take in any needy kids as their own at the drop of a
hat, but Etain didn't feel that way at all.

He's mine. Kad'ika'*s mine. I want to be with him.*

She was a second away from grabbing an air taxi, storm-
ing into Zey's office at Arca Barracks, and telling him she
was giving up her Jedi status. The thought was becoming
ever more frequent and feeling like a rehearsal. Kad looked
up as if searching her eyes for something. Then his face
crumpled; he let out a small wail that tailed off into a whimper, and flooded her with his unhappiness. He was reacting
to her anxiety.

*When I was a baby . . . did the Jedi who raised me sense
how I felt? What did I feel of their emotions?*

She had no recollection. She didn't recall the family she'd
left, either. All she knew was that it wasn't going to be that
way for *her* son. His Force powers would have to find some
other outlet. She made an effort to concentrate on happy

thoughts, visualizing Darman and herself in a peaceful garden with Kad on her lap, the best way she could communicate reassurance on a Force level. Force-sensitive babies needed more than cuddles and a lullaby.

"Look at us," Etain said. "Jedi, Twi'lek, clone trooper. We're all locked into a path in life because of our genes. But we don't have to take it, do we? None of us. We can all be what we want to be."

Laseema, looking more like a bank clerk in her sober dark tunic, took a feeding bottle of juice from the kitchen and handed it to Etain. Kad intercepted it, two-handed.

"I don't dance any longer," Laseema said. "And you don't dance to the Jedi Council's tune. I think we've all stopped dancing, thanks to Kal."

The future seemed a little brighter now and alive with possibility. The war was survivable; Etain didn't think in terms of winning any longer, or even what the Republic might turn into if it *did* win. It wasn't the democracy the Jedi seemed to think it was. She felt that she was struggling to the peak of an unforgiving mountain, that a little more effort and courage would get her to the summit alive, and then she could make her way to safety.

But climbers said the most deadly and dangerous part of mountaineering was the descent.

"Come on, sweetheart." Kad sucked at the bottle with ferocious determination. Normality; he was like any other baby of his age, pretty well running to the timetable of normal human development that she'd memorized. The last thing she wanted was a prodigy. He'd had enough of an unusual start in life already.

Etain imagined Zey's reaction if he could see this scene. Laseema unwrapped the baby clothes and held them up for Etain's approval.

"When are you going to tell him?" she asked.

She didn't mean General Zey. She meant Darman.

It was the question Etain now put to one side every time it came up. It was easier to deal with Zey first. Darman had as good as said he wasn't in any hurry to have children, but sooner or later she had to tell him that not only was Kad her son, he was also his. Hindsight was a poisonous thing. Etain wished now that she'd told Darman from the start, but Skirata had probably been right. It was one complication too many for Dar, who looked and behaved like a grown man but still had many of the emotional vulnerabilities of a kid.

"I think I'll do it sooner rather than later," she said at last. "And if he takes it badly, at least he knows."

Forty-eight hours' leave was trickling through her fingers like water. It was unfairly short. But it was a consequence of the path she'd chosen. She watched Kad gulping down the contents of the bottle and reached out in the Force to Darman to check that he was okay.

She knew exactly where he was now. She could comm him anytime, even redeploy him; she was a group commander in Special Operations, and he was one of her resources. And he wouldn't thank her for cosseting him. Kad sucked on a now empty bottle and looked up at her with a distinct it's-time-you-refilled-this expression.

"I'll tell Dar when he returns from Haurgab," she said. "But I doubt I shall ever tell Zey."

Kad was going to have a life as unlike hers as she could make it.

He would have *choices*.

Laseema's apartment, Coruscant

Jusik had never worried about what clothes to put on each morning until now. He stared at himself in the mirror, minus his beard for the first time in years, and wondered if he'd pass for a government health inspector.

As a Jedi, he'd owned next to nothing, just the brown robe he stood up in, a couple of changes of tunic, pants, and underclothes, his lightsaber, and a lot of gadgets—none of which actually belonged to him. It all fit in one scruffy bag. Now he had armor, although portability was still paramount, and he had *disguises*.

Today he was disguised as a regular human being; a suited bureaucrat, folio case in hand, clean-shaven. He had a prison

to visit. Dr. Ovolot Qail Uthan had been moved from one facility to another, and then apparently vanished in the system,
but it was impossible to hide much from the Nulls. They had
been trained to infiltrate any system, and the Republic's was
more vulnerable to them than any. The security codes for the
Treasury had opened a particularly rich seam for Jaing—
ARC N-10—and he was working his way via crawler programs through separate systems in government departments,
using the interfaces between them to jump across departmental barriers.

Joined-up government—more efficient cooperation among
the Republic's bureaucratic fiefdoms—was an idea whose
time had come. It also made slicing their data a lot easier.

"Say bye-bye, *Kad'ika*. Say bye-bye to Uncle Bardan."
Etain, cradling her son in one arm, took his hand and made a
little waving gesture with it. "Ba-da!" he said. He seemed
happy with words that ended in *a*. Jusik waved back. Kad
looked bemused by Jusik's sudden change in appearance and
frowned slightly at Etain as if looking for confirmation of his
identity. "Yes, it's *Bard'ika*. He'll be back soon."

"Just pinning down locations," said Jusik. "Won't be
long."

"You're wondering how I can do this, aren't you?"

Etain radiated regret. There wasn't much that one Jedi
could hide from another.

"I'd find it impossible," Jusik said carefully. He wondered
if the separation was good for either her or the baby. "But I
understand. All the time Darman has to fight, so do you."

"If anything happens to me—"

"Jedi casualties have been few and far between in this
war."

"Hear me out. If I don't come back, make sure the Jedi
Order doesn't find Kad."

Jusik fiddled with his high collar. Armor wasn't half as re-
stricting as a business suit. "Nothing's going to happen to
you," he said. "Like I said, we lost a lot of Jedi at Geonosis,
but very few since."

"Bardan . . ."

"They'll have to get past Kal's small army first. But yes, if you want my word—I'll give my life to protect him."

Etain made a little "uh" sound and when Jusik turned away from the mirror, she looked on the brink of tears.

"I don't expect you to—"

"I know, but *I* expect me to." By the time he returned from his mission, she'd be back on duty, and Laseema, Besany, or Skirata would be here holding the fort. "Now, no foolish heroics. May the Force be with you, Etain."

Jusik didn't look back. When he took his leave of someone, there was always a final moment when he had to break eye contact, a degree of pain to be faced, so he always got it over with fast. Moving through the city unnoticed was second nature to him now; all transactions by cash credits, multistage journeys by public transport, avoidance of areas with security cams. He could mind-rub and disable surveillance holocams with a thought, but he didn't want to leave a wake of renegade Force-using behind him.

And if there were any loose ends despite his care . . . Jaller Obrim could probably tie those up.

The Valorum Center looked like a midmarket spa from the outside, and only the impressive security—double gates, and a sequence of doors that could have doubled as an air lock on Mustafar—gave a hint that it was a judicial psychiatric unit. Not all its guests were criminals; many were a danger only to themselves, but they were all there because the courts had ruled that they needed locking up. It attracted surprisingly little attention, but then there were any number of government buildings with unwelcoming façades springing up on Coruscant these days, and it wasn't a residential area.

Jusik presented his identichip to a droid at the gates that looked more like an ion cannon emplacement. It scanned the details and swung back to let him pass.

It was very easy to fake a civil service ID if you had a civil service contact willing to give you his or her chip for electronic cloning and modification. Besany Wennen's original chip had now spawned bogus employee identities across the whole tangled spectrum of Republic administration. A bureaucracy that didn't actually know how many staff it employed on any given day was ripe for infiltration. The last time Jusik had sliced into the payroll system, the full-time workforce alone stood at eight million, more than twice the size of the Grand Army.

Denel Herris was just another pen pusher who might or might not have existed. Jusik wore him like a coat.

"I won't keep you long," he said, looking suitably harassed as the deputy chief administrator with PELBION, DR. S. on his ID badge led him through the soothing pale green corridors. "Just preparing a response for the health minister. Another hoo-hah about dangerous patients being released into the community too early."

"I'm still not sure how we managed to mislay your request. I'm very sorry."

"No matter." Jusik already had the ground plans for the facility—courtesy of the unsuspecting utilities administration—but it did no harm to record the layout, too. He clutched his comlink in his hand while he walked as if waiting for some important transmission, but the integral holocam was active, recording in detail to be examined later. "Will I be able to see the director at such short notice?"

Say no. I won't mind. I could bluff my way through it, but . . .

"He's out of the office today, I'm afraid."

"Well, I'm sure you can give me the figures." Jusik strode on, trying not to look as if he knew where he was going. "Just how much of a risk are the patients you have here? How many are actually a threat to other citizens? Aren't they mainly troubled souls more likely to throw themselves off buildings?"

"Mainly." Pelbion was a thin human male in his fifties who kept looking over his shoulder as they passed through each set of security doors, as if he was expecting an attack. "But we do accommodate some high-risk patients on a short-term basis. The truly dangerous ones are then transferred to the isolation facility on Jevelet. And I can assure you that our clinical assessments of risk are much, *much* more exacting than some other institutions. We do *not* put faith in pharmaceutical cures or convincing interviews with assessment panels."

The facility was remarkably quiet and empty. Jusik had somehow expected something more like a hospital, with at least droids moving around, but this wasn't a place where visitors or activity seemed to be encouraged, and the doors were all locked. The farther into the complex that Jusik walked, the more unsettled he felt. This was a miserable place for a Force-user; Jusik could sense emotions. Wave after wave of anxiety, fear, wild elation, and even occasional oddly misplaced *certainty* swept over him almost like whispers emerging from each locked room. He'd never been this close to so many people all in . . . all with . . . he wanted to say *torment,* delusion, insanity, but that wasn't it at all. Some were very unhappy, but some were very happy indeed, quite manic in fact. It took a lot to rattle Jusik, but this shook him. It was made worse by *seeing* nobody, just *sensing* them. He felt surrounded by ghosts.

"What proportion do you release into the community?" he asked Pelbion, trying to center himself again. Sometimes he envied ordinary beings. All they had to do was look. But he didn't dare try to shut out the clamor of emotions because he was seeking one mind, one person who he had reason to believe was being held here.

He was looking for Dr. Uthan. If she wasn't here, then he'd run out of secure facilities to search, and the trail had gone cold.

"Only three percent ever leave this institution," Pelbion said. "We take quite extreme cases, after all."

Jusik concentrated. It was like sifting through a thousand conversations going on simultaneously, looking for one word, but he couldn't walk every corridor without arousing Pelbion's suspicions. Ahead of them, a med droid and a female Mon Cal in a pale lemon lab coat wandered down the corridor deep in conversation before turning left into an office. Jusik was beginning to think there was nobody else walking free in the building, and he felt oddly comforted by seeing them. He could hear voices, too; muffled by distance and heavy doors, but snatches of senseless conversation he tried to follow despite himself.

He even thought he heard some words of *Mando'a*. The human brain had a wonderful ability to zero in on the apparently familiar. He strained to listen to the voice—a woman, alternately crying and cursing by the sound of it—and some of the words seemed to be Mandalorian, but some were totally alien. He could have sworn he heard *chakaar*. No . . . it was *shekker*. Whatever that was, it wasn't *Mando'a*. He had to move on.

Don't get distracted. You have a mission.

Anxious for some focus to his search, he tried to open up a line of questioning. There was no mind influence he could use yet because he had no idea how to frame the question; if Uthan was a patient here, then Pelbion wouldn't have her in a cell marked SECRET PRISONER.

"I would find this job very depressing," Jusik said, knowing that might flush out a fuller response that he could steer and pick apart. "Most medical staff have some expectation of curing their charges. The best you can do is to stop them being a danger."

"Or keep them in as content a state as we can manage," Pelbion said, defensive, opening yet another pair of doors under the scrutiny of a chunky droid armed with a stun stick. "That's a goal in itself."

Jusik felt the opening. "They must all be wretchedly unhappy."

Uthan would be, if she was here. The Nulls had already picked up intelligence that the geneticist was selectively breeding soka flies to keep herself busy, although there was no guarantee she would be allowed to keep insects in this pristine, sterile place. The building smelled of that particular cleaning fluid that Jusik associated with dentistry—a faint spicy scent that caught the back of his throat.

"No, some are very happy in their delusions," Pelbion said. He seemed content to chat aimlessly, perhaps because it seemed to appease Jusik. "So much so that I envy some of them."

There were a lot of angry people in here, too—anger that

seemed without focus for the most part. Whoever was behind one set of doors made Jusik step up his pace to pass
them faster, so strong was the urge for bloody destruction
that emanated from them. If any Jedi wanted to learn about
the dark power of rage, then this was the place to bring the
younglings.

"Any you feel sorry for?" Jusik asked. He needed a break
now; he scanned as best he could for beings that felt more
like himself, more *normal.* "Do you feel that any of us might
be in that state, but for providence?"

"Oh, we have a dozen physicians in here, at least," Pelbion
said. "It's quite sobering to look them in the eye. And beings
who *think* they're doctors, and some of them seem more
competent than the qualified ones . . ."

Jusik forced a smile. *You want to tell me more.*

Pelbion blinked at Jusik's careful manipulation of his
mind, unaware of it but reacting to a thought that wasn't his.
He didn't discuss individual patients. It jarred with him, but
there was something in there, something else not so much
troubling him as *bothering* him.

Jusik nudged him a little more.

*You want to tell me about the patients you're not sure
should be here. You want to take me to them.*

"Some of them . . . well, even I wonder if they should be
here," Pelbion said at last. He was walking with purpose
now, not just ambling along at Jusik's side, as if herding him
toward the most impressive aspects of the facility and away
from the worst. "They're so internally consistent about their
imagined lives that I have to remind myself why they're
here."

Show me.

You want to show me.

*You want to show me how tough your job can be, so I file
a favorable report on this facility.*

Jusik had to nudge Pelbion again. It was risky. The man
wouldn't realize he was being influenced by a Jedi technique, but he might decide he wasn't feeling too well and
call a halt.

A faint breath of familiarity brushed Jusik, and he found

himself staring at cell doors bearing the number 7885 in black letters. He'd never met Uthan. He couldn't feel her, but he could feel someone normal, someone sane, someone who *didn't belong*.

"Like this one?" Jusik said, gesturing to the cell.

"No, his family committed him after he had an . . . unfortunate incident at home." Pelbion seemed to be debating with himself. "Okay . . . follow me."

But the sane person's in there . . .

For some reason, that distracted Jusik for a moment, the sudden realization that there was someone nearby who wasn't disturbed or crazy at all, but locked up anyway. The sense of betrayal and hopelessness was now overwhelming, and he could hardly leave it alone. Something deep inside said, *Help him, help him, you can't just walk away.*

But he did; this mission was critical. He abandoned a being in need.

As cell blocks went, the Valorum Center's Hesperidium Wing was comfortable and—apart from the smell of cleaning fluid, and all those security doors—didn't look that institutional. Jusik followed Pelbion into what seemed to be an older part of the building with higher ceilings, and then through more doors. Jusik recorded it all. Had any of the Nulls been with him, gifted with eidetic memories because the Kaminoans thought it would make them better troops, they'd have memorized the route and every detail along the way instantly.

Pelbion stopped outside a set of doors and fumbled for a passkey. "Yes, this woman troubles me," he said, as if answering Jusik. Pelbion didn't respond the same way as most beings to mind influence, that was clear. "She's perplexing."

Jusik knew even before the doors opened that he'd find a sane but disoriented woman in there. He could feel her: not quite as he expected, dulled somewhat, but not in need of psychiatric care—yet. When the doors parted, revealing a second toughened transparisteel set within, it was all he could do not to cheer.

The cell—quite a pleasant suite, actually, but without any

natural light—was full of small transparent cases stacked on a counter. Black specks moved around inside them.

Soka flies.

Pelbion lowered his voice conspiratorially. "She thinks she's a Separatist scientist working on a doomsday virus. It's really very impressive, because she obviously has scientific training and a brilliant mind. She almost had me convinced at one point that she'd been kidnapped by Republic forces on the Outer Rim, shot in the back, and brought here to be forced to reveal her secret research."

"Quite *extraordinary*," Jusik said. Uthan recalled the Qiilura raid, all right. "What a *detailed* delusion."

"According to her file, she was committed by the Public Safety Department because they thought she might actually be qualified enough to create some plague for real. I must say she's doing some fascinating genetic research on those flies, even without proper lab facilities. We help her out occasionally, you know . . ."

"Good grief." *Oh joy.* "Should you be telling me this? Isn't it classified?"

"I don't think you can classify psychotic episodes, Master Herris . . . although scarring shows she really has been shot by a projectile at some time."

Jusik stepped into the room. A well-groomed middle-aged woman with red-streaked black hair glanced up from her makeshift desk and looked hard at him, datapad in hand.

"This gentleman is from the Coruscant Health Administration," Pelbion said, smiling nervously at her. "Just showing him around. How's the breeding program going?"

Uthan—it was definitely her—raised one contemptuous eyebrow. "You might be medicating my meals, you mediocre quack, but my brain is still functioning better than yours," she said wearily. Then she fixed on Jusik again. "So you're from the government, are you? Well, I'm a prisoner of war, and as such I have rights. I demand a lawyer—*again*. My name is Dr. Ovolot Qail Uthan and I'm being held incommunicado."

Jusik gave her a slightly pained but compassionate smile, his best. The Chancellor was a clever man; what better way to hide Uthan than this, in plain sight, letting her tell her story in an imprisoned community where *everyone* had a crazy story?

"Of course you are, madam," Jusik said. "I'll get right on it."

She'd be out of here, all right, only not the way she'd hoped.

"Absolutely consistent," Pelbion said on the way out. Jusik disrupted a few surveillance holocams as he went, fogging the images. "Every detail."

"Sad," said Jusik. *No, brilliant. Wonderful. Hope for my brothers.* "Now, about those figures . . ."

"Right away, Master Herris," said Pelbion.

It probably wasn't necessary to rub the man's memory, but Jusik erased enough of their conversation to reduce his visit to a minor annoyance that would be quickly forgotten the natural way.

All the way back to the apartment—four changes of speeder bus, a couple of long walks, and doubling back once or twice, just in case—Jusik felt his triumph being tarnished slowly by a small nagging, worrying voice.

It wasn't the welter of disturbed minds that left him most unsettled, or even coming face-to-face with a woman whose job was, effectively, genocide.

It was finding that she was not the only wholly sane person being imprisoned in Valorum. And there was nothing he could do about the other one. He couldn't pursue the man's case, because Herris now had to disappear. He'd made too much of a splash as it was.

There were always casualties in war. Not all of them occurred in combat.

Hadde-Rishun road, Haurgab, 1510 hours local time

"Dar! *Dar!* Get down!"

Hordes of heavily armed Maujasi had come out of nowhere, and now Omega were stuck in the remains of the ancient fort, under fire and running out of luck.

The convoy had vanished except for the vehicles still burning in the pass. Darman threw himself flat as another mortar whooshed overhead and detonated somewhere behind the crumbling wall, ripping more chunks out of it. Darman found himself looking at the world from a ninety-degree angle, noticing that the front wall providing cover didn't look so solid now, either. Voices filled his audio link.

"Where the *shab* did they come from?"

"Told you, kriffing *tunnels*."

"*At'ika,* can you move the remote? Come on, look for a route out. We can't sit up here all *shabla* day waiting to get picked off."

"On it, Sarge—can you see that?"

"Oh *shab* . . ."

Niner rarely swore. Things had to be worse than Darman thought. He scuttled on all fours across the ground, pushing the ammo crate out of the way. When he checked his HUD icons, the view from the remote wasn't encouraging. From a position nearly two hundred meters above them, it showed the terrain in all its depressing reality: a sheer drop on three sides, and a long rocky slope down to their rear, the only access to the old fort. It was also the only route out. The fort had been a great vantage point in its heyday and easy to defend, but even four Republic commandos couldn't hold out here forever against hundreds of Maujasi.

"I'm calling for extraction," Niner said.

Darman began calculating how far they'd get if they tried to storm their way out. "Who the *shab* is going to lift us out of this?"

"The Eighty-fifth have larties."

"Let's see if they have a window in their busy manicure schedule."

The view from the remote showed Maujasi moving around to the rear of the peak. It would take them maybe half an hour to pick their way up the long slope, longer if Darman made life more interesting for them by bringing down some rock on their heads.

He reloaded with grenades and began crawling toward the

path, which fell away sharply as if the peak had been sawn off by a giant hand to create a level base for the fort.

"I'll delay them while you call a cab," he said.

Niner had his right hand cupped to ear level. He always did that when comming in a tight spot, as if it made voice traffic easier to hear, despite the sophisticated audio in his helmet. "Roll a det down, for fierfek's sake, Dar. Don't expose yourself."

Corr, propped on one elbow as if he was sunning himself, listened with a cocked head. "They sound like they've got another repeating blaster or a cannon down there."

"They could just blow the top off this stump, then . . . ," said Atin. "But that would kill us, and that means they want us alive."

Darman had a good idea what *taken alive* meant around these parts. It wasn't how he planned to bow out of this life. "Let's hope they don't manage to conjure up their own air support."

"Hadde Base, this is Omega. Hadde Base, this is Omega. Request immediate extraction." Niner kept repeating the call, but it didn't sound as if he was getting a response. Darman could hear the fizz and crackle of the comlink. "Hadde Base, repeat, this is Omega. We're pinned down at the old Churt fort, twenty klicks southwest of your position. Low ammo, enemy strength estimated at . . . between one fifty and two hundred, with cannon and heavy repeaters. No anti-air that we can see. Hadde Base, this is Omega . . ."

Darman had reached this point in combat several times over the last couple of years. There was a very good chance that he was going to die. The more times that happened, the more confident he was that he could get out of it, but there was also the realization that this time might well be the last.

It was a long way down and there were an awful lot of Maujasi down there. In the way of knife-edge moments, he found himself thinking things unconnected with the prospect of an unpleasant death. He hadn't called Etain and he hadn't spoken to Fi in months. Apart from that, he'd made his peace with the world.

It was suddenly quiet. Niner, leaning back against the mud

bricks, checked his ammo. "Well, even if we get past that lot, we're on foot, and that's not exactly a fast getaway. And Fleet Met says sandstorms are on the way."

Darman checked his HUD. Nobody liked flying in a sandstorm even if they had the filters and other countermeasures to venture out in it. It was a lousy time to need extraction.

"How many thermal dets have we got?" Darman asked.

"I've got three."

"Two," said Atin.

Corr pulled three out of his belt and held them in a cluster like fruit. "Being a man who knows about things that go bang, I estimate we have enough baradium yield between us to reduce this peak to rubble, or make a hole big enough to swallow it."

Darman's mind raced. Lots of bad guys, one way down, not enough ammo, but a big explosive capacity. "Yeah, I was hoping that would be the result."

"Only problem is . . . we're sitting on it."

"I'm still thinking."

"Well, it beats being interrogated by the locals."

"Quitter," said Darman, but Corr had a point, and he wondered when he'd take off his armor so that he died outright and didn't linger injured like Fi. If he was going to go, he wanted to go *clean*. Suddenly he wasn't just bothered that he hadn't said good-bye to Etain; he was devastated that he might never see her again. "Look, if they're going to come and take us, then they've got to come up that slope. The path's two meters wide. Logjam."

"You thinking of playing skittles with them?" Atin asked.

"Well, the blast radius is five meters. I can throw a bit farther than that." Darman had started life as the squad's ordnance expert. He'd picked up so many new skills since Geonosis that—

Fierfek, I forgot the anniversary.

I forgot. But I remember them every day.

Sorry, Vin . . . Jay . . . Taler.

"And?" Niner reloaded the repeating blaster. "What if we don't kill that many?"

Darman shrugged. "Every little bit helps, as they say."

The odds were bad. Katarn armor technology meant that they could take a considerable pounding from blasterfire and even grenades, but close-quarters combat—hand-to-hand, probably—made them vulnerable. They could be brought down by sheer numbers. Then the armor wouldn't do a thing to save them.

Atin took a noisy pull of water. "I don't want to rush you, Dar, but if you take a look at the remote view, you'll see we have visitors."

Darman tested his vibroblade, ejecting it from his gauntlet plate with a satisfying *shunk.* If they wanted a fight, they'd get one. Corr continued to call for extraction while Darman pried the plates off the dets to wire them together. Another mortar found its target, now way too close for comfort. Atin edged forward to lay down fire.

"They don't know how many of us are up here."

"Well, they will if they reach the *shabla* top, *At'ika . . .*" Corr paused, listening for some response in the comlink interference. "If I live through this, first thing I'm going to do is shove my vibroblade in some Intel guy's—"

"I make that *two* mortar positions," said Niner. "And yeah, I'll join you."

Darman couldn't see what was happening behind him. Cross-wiring thermal dets was a fiddly job, and it didn't seem to occur to the others that the jury-rigged device could just as easily kill them all without any help from the rebels. All Darman could think at that moment was that Jusik would have been really handy to have around now. He was great with gadgets. And a spot of Force-created avalanche would have been just the job.

"Okay, I'm done," he said. "How far have those *chakaare* got?"

Atin steered the remote. It was too small for the rebels to notice at that altitude. "They're about fifteen meters up. Another ten and they'll be on scree. Bring that lot down, and you'll probably block the path. It'll take them hours to dig past it."

The wired dets formed a loose ball about the size of a human head, and as near to spherical as Darman could make

it. He wasn't so sure he could throw it accurately enough
now that he realized how ungainly a shape it was; he'd have
to roll it and detonate remotely. And that meant split-second
timing, or he'd miss and detonate the device behind them.

"Okay, *At'ika,* you talk me through it," he said, and ran for
the edge of the path. He had to get on the slope and line up
as best he could. "Ready?"

"Ready."

Behind him, Niner's repeater spat and boomed as another
mortar shook the fort. He skidded down the narrow path for
a few meters until he could hear the occasional shout from a
rebel to *go left* or some other order.

*If I roll it now, it'll reach the detonation point in eight sec-
onds.*

Who was he kidding? He couldn't be sure of that. He
waited for Atin to refocus the remote. Now he could see
clearly. What seemed like an endless stream of rebels were
scrambling up the slope with rifles slung across their backs.
It was probably only fifty, but it felt like hordes somehow,
and he knew there were more behind them.

"Stand by."

"In your own time, Dar."

"Dets away."

Darman let the ball tumble down the narrow path. It
bounced and skidded—*don't blow early, you* shabuir, *please
don't*—and he watched its progress via the remote view with
his forefinger resting on the control in his left palm.

Bounce, bounce . . .

Heads. He could see the tops of heads, and he pressed the
button.

For a silent moment he thought the device had failed. Then
a deafening explosion shook the ground under his boots, and
all he saw in his HUD was a blinding fireball and flying rubble. Fragments peppered his armor, bouncing around him; he
felt as if he was falling and reached out instinctively to grab
something solid. His hand caught an outcrop and he found
himself sitting solidly on his backside.

He couldn't feel anything under his boots, though. A panicky flash of a thought seized him: *No, I couldn't possibly have broken my spine.* He swung his legs just to be sure.

"Dar? *Dar!*" Atin's voice filled his helmet. The rest of the squad could all see the images from the remote, he knew. "Dar, you okay? *Dar!*"

Darman glanced down. He was sitting on a ledge of rock, staring down from a brand-new cliff. The dets had blown out a landslide. Rocks were still clicking and groaning, pebbles bouncing. His legs were fine; there was just nothing under his boots to *feel*.

"We didn't need Jusik after all," he said, appalled. "I don't think they're going to get up to the top anytime soon."

"Oh, *shab* . . ." Corr's voice sounded more stunned than angry. "And we're not going to get down, are we?"

Darman shuffled back from the precipice and scrambled to his feet to run back up the remains of the path.

At least we're on the highest peak. Nothing's overlooking us. We've got cover. And a few less enemy than we had a few minutes ago.

It still couldn't make up for the fact that they were marooned on a plug of rock 150 meters above ground level with no way down, no support, and dwindling supplies. As Darman dropped down behind the wall again, nobody said a word. The firing had stopped for a while.

"Go on, yell at me," he said.

Atin shrugged and directed the remote to a higher altitude. Darman could see chaos—temporary, he knew—while the rebels rushed around trying to rescue their comrades and regroup. He'd bought some time, but it would be no use to Omega now.

"Any luck, *Cor'ika*?" Niner asked. He could hear Corr's transmissions as well as the rest of them, but it was his way of chivvying everyone along. "Because if the Eighty-fifth don't respond, we've either got to kill every last rebel or learn to kriffing *fly.*"

"Or both," Atin said. "We can try a descent, but we'll be completely exposed to fire if we try to climb down."

Three seconds, five meters. That was about as long and as far as you could run before a sniper got a fix on you. Climb-

ing down a sheer rock face—Katarn armor or not—was asking for it. The rebels didn't have state-of-the-art blasters, but
they had mortars, and that would finish off anyone.

"Where's the rest of the convoy?" Darman asked. "Some
got away. They must have called it in by now."

"Except they don't know we're here, and we'd have looked
like some bunch of local trouble to them," Niner said. "If
they saw us at all."

Corr laid out his ammo in front of him in descending
order of stopping power. It wasn't a comforting sight. It
looked as if he'd prepared for a last stand before, but he'd
never talked about the action he'd seen. It clearly wasn't just
bomb disposal. The last item in the row was a small grenade.

He looked up and caught Darman staring at him. "For
me," he said. "I don't expect much of local hospitality."

"Good idea," said Niner, tossing a similar device in his
hand.

Darman looked at Atin, but neither of them set aside a
quick end for themselves. Maybe it was knowing they had
someone waiting back home.

"Keep trying the Eighty-fifth," said Niner.

Atin shook his head. "No, flash HQ. They should be able
to get through to them."

It normally took time they didn't have, but time wasn't an
issue now. The rebels who had regrouped and were making
their way back up the cliffs surrounding Omega—*they* were
the issue. Them, and their repeating blasters.

Etain would hear they were in trouble. Darman preferred
not to worry her. But now he didn't have a choice, and he
took some comfort in the fact that the fort was thirty or forty
meters higher than the rest of the terrain, and it still looked
as if the rebels wanted to take them alive.

The rebels could sit it out, of course. Even in climate-
controlled Katarn armor with fluid recycling, commandos
couldn't hold out indefinitely on a rock in a burning desert.

"Arca HQ, this is Omega," Corr repeated quietly, as if he
was ordering a carry-out meal. The squad kept their communal audio link open. "Arca HQ, this is Omega, request urgent
forwarding for immediate extraction. Arca HQ, this is . . ."

It would be dark in a few hours. Darman and Niner hauled and rolled whatever solid objects they could find to shore up the blast-pocked walls of the ruin that provided their only protection. A volley of blaster bolts smacked into the rock a meter below, seeming more like a ploy to torment them than a serious attempt to kill.

"Omega, this is Arca HQ," said a male voice. "Say again."

"Captain Maze . . . I see you're answering the comms today, then . . ."

The ARC trooper captain—Zey's aide—wasn't known for his cheery camaraderie. "Omega, your position's noted. Comm trouble?"

"Can't raise the Eighty-fifth. Request *immediate* extraction from these coordinates. We're surrounded and low on everything."

"I'm alerting Hadde FOB now. Stand by."

Corr switched to a private comlink channel that Maze couldn't hear. "How are you, Omega? Can we help? We're really concerned that you're stranded on a *shabla* rock surrounded by an infinite number of armed locals who'll cut your *gett'se* off when they haul you screaming from the summit." He switched back to the open circuit again. "Thank you, Captain. Standing by."

It was relief, Darman knew. Corr vented his tensions through acid sarcasm. *I know what Fi would have said. Fi would have said, Captain, you never call, you never send flowers . . .* Darman hoped Fi was happy on Mandalore. He really did.

"I make it about seventy *chakaare,*" Atin said. "Not *infinite.*"

"They've got buddies back home who could show up any time," Corr said. "And stop being pedantic. It'll make you go blind."

"He didn't say they were sending a larty. He didn't say *when.*"

"He said *stand by.*"

Corr snapped a fresh clip into his Deece. His POV icon showed that he was scanning the cliffs at high magnification, so he'd noted the open-ended nature of Maze's response, too.

Darman moved across to the north wall and set his HUD on maximum magnification; Hadde was wreathed in black smoke and now that his mind wasn't so firmly fixed on his own predicament, he could hear the *whoomp-whoomp-whoomp* of artillery fire. The 85th probably had their hands full. That was probably a detail that Maze didn't want to depress them with.

"So what's the problem with the comms?" Niner asked.

Maze's gravelly tones interrupted him. "Omega, air evac's coming from Neska instead. One standard hour subject to the storms. Hadde FOB's lost a comm relay in the shelling. You do pick your moments."

Maze didn't ask if they could hold out that long. If they couldn't, it was too bad. Neska was the closest base after Hadde, and nobody was riding to the rescue any faster.

"Thanks, HQ," Corr said. "Tell General Zey we have a confirmed kill on Jolluc, by the way."

"Not a wasted journey, then, Omega."

"You have a nice day, too, Captain . . ." The link went dead and Maze was gone. "Maybe get your hair done. A bit of shopping."

"ARCs get cranky when they're cooped up on desk jobs," Darman said, feeling he had to make excuses for Maze. "They'd all rather be at the front."

"You really think any sane man wants to get his *shebs* shot off? It's not like he's got some need to be with his brothers like the Nulls."

"The Alphas have buddies, too," Darman said, recalling Sull and his anger at the fate of a brother ARC executed for going AWOL. "They're no different from us."

Corr puffed contemptuously and didn't answer. Three brilliant bolts of hot white energy shaved the top of the wall and sent brick dust flying. Niner opened up with the repeater and blew a chunk out of the facing cliff, taking what looked like a couple of bodies with it, but all across the rock slopes Darman could detect movement—lots of it. The rebels were reinforcing. Yes, those tunnels needed some serious attention from a ton or two of five-hundred-grade thermal plastoid.

"Fifty-five standard minutes," said Atin, aiming through a

gap in the wall. At least there was nothing to the rear now—just on all the other flanks. You had to look on the bright side. And a LAAT/i was on its way. "Counting down."

"Remember, eke it out, *vode*," Niner muttered. "Don't expend more than you absolutely have to, in case our ride's delayed."

Atin steered the remote. "Or if the *chakaare* turn into mountain nerfs . . ."

The remote view showed that one party of Maujasi were preparing for a climb. They had grapples, lines, and what could have been launchers.

"How far down?" Darman asked. "Exactly?"

Atin's POV icon showed he had superimposed telemetry on the remote's view. "One hundred and fifty-eight meters forty centimeters." Atin paused. "To the datum line."

The rappel line built into commando armor was a hundred meters, tops. Darman visualized a last, last, *last*-resort escape that might not break his neck if he hit the right angle and rolled the last fifty-odd meters, but once he was on the ground with *shab* knows how many rebels converging on him, he'd be fresh out of ideas. And luck. But there was always the sandstorm. They could use it for cover.

It could also end up being the death of them.

"Jetpacks," he said wistfully. "Really should get jetpacks as standard. Mandos aren't daft."

The Maujasi climbing team fired a grapple and line. It bit into the cliff face with a chattering noise, and when the first climber was twenty meters up the slope, Corr put a blaster bolt through the top of his head.

"Maybe I should have waited for him to get higher . . ."

Darman kept an eye on the remote view and tested his gauntlet vibroblade a few more times. Yes, he was getting scared, larty inbound or no larty inbound; standing your ground was one thing, but being trapped like a staked feshu waiting to be eaten was another thing entirely. He began to wonder how many he could take with him if the worst came to the worst. "They've got some *gett'se*, seeing as they don't know what we can do to *them* once they reach us."

"Well, they definitely want us alive," Niner said. "Or else they haven't got enough heavy ordnance to cream us totally."

An hour was a surprisingly long time. Between monitoring the remote—which the rebels obviously hadn't detected, or else they'd have tried to disable it—and resisting the ingrained reflex to hose the source of incoming fire, Darman had time to watch the horizon to the north.

Hadde's canopy of black smoke was now invisible, swallowed up by a mass of rolling yellow cloud that looked as solid and implacable as a tidal wave. The wind was picking up strength; debris whipped and whirled around the fort. Darman did a rough calculation and worked out that the storm front would be upon them in minutes.

"Heads down, *vode*," he said. "Here it comes."

The sand couldn't penetrate their vacuum-resistant armor, and the Deeces had filters. Their HUDs enabled them to detect their surroundings in the thickest smoke; the screaming wind could be silenced by their helmets. But being caught in a storm like this was nerve-racking. Darman heard the first sprays of windborne sand rattle against his Katarn plates and huddled in a ball in the lee of a wall with the others.

"Oh, *shab* . . . ," Corr whispered.

The whirling grains engulfed them, utterly silent as Darman cut his external audio so he could hear the rest of the squad on the helmet link. All they could do was sit it out. The rebels wouldn't be climbing now, that was for sure. He thought of Etain and hoped Maze had passed on the sitrep.

"Fierfek, this must be a big one . . . ," Niner said. The storm didn't seem to be abating; the sand cloud must have covered hundreds of square kilometers. "We won't get extracted until this passes. You wouldn't even get a TIV pilot out in this."

Sicko would have tried, Darman knew. But he was long gone, and for a brother they'd known only briefly, his death still cut way too deep.

Visibility was now zero. Darman opened his external audio cautiously so that the roaring storm was a whisper. He thought he heard another sound, but that was impossible. It had to be the buffeting of the storm.

Chakka-da-chakka-da-chakka . . .

No, he wasn't imagining it. It was getting louder.

Chakka-da-chakka-da-chakka-da-chakka . . .

It was a regular mechanical noise with another constant rising and falling note underneath, almost like a faint siren. No, not a siren; a drive struggling to cope.

Whatever it was, it wasn't a LAAT/i. That was a sound he'd know anywhere, sweetly familiar and comforting enough to make his chest feel hollow and heavy with emotion.

"Shab," he said. Darman measured the crisis level of any given day by the number of times they used the *S* word. Today was a hundred-*shab* day, getting close to *shab* saturation point. No other word offered such relief when you were tired, in pain, incredulous, or just facing imminent oblivion. *"Shab,* it's not one of ours—"

They looked up, even though they didn't need to. The remote could have shown them the worst if they'd switched it to infrared.

No, it wasn't a LAAT/i. The drives struggling against the abrasive, sand-laden wind sounded alien because they *were*. The vessel's undercarriage was visible through the swirling amber haze, brilliant turquoise with angular black designs half scoured down to bare metal by past sandstorms. It was old. Darman caught a glimpse of jutting hydraulic lines and piston-shaped servos.

"Shabuir," said Corr, groping for the anti-armor attachment and slapping it on his Deece. "Okay, if *we* don't go home, *nobody* goes home."

Darman aimed at what he hoped was the hydraulics reservoir. The wind nearly took him off his feet. Atin collided with him; Niner, repeater held in both hands by some astonishing feat of raw muscle, was yelling at them to get clear.

He fired. Darman fired. Maybe they all fired; but all Darman knew right then was that a fireball blinded him and laid him flat on his back as red-hot metal debris, rock, and oily fluid spattered his visor.

Fi was adamant—or at least Parja was adamant, and therefore he obeyed. He would *not* help Fenn Shysa by playing a
Fett.

"We're only here so you can see Keldabe, okay?" Parja
had hold of his elbow as if she was a possessive wife rather
than someone supporting a man with mobility problems. "A
trip to the big city, that's all. You don't owe him *anything*."

Keldabe wasn't exactly big. Fi still found it overwhelming, but he remembered to consult his datapad to navigate.
The Mandalorian capital was a cluster of stone, wood, durasteel, and plastoid buildings clinging like determined fungi
to a granite outcrop. Beneath the granite cliff, the Kelita River
was busy cutting a ravine. The place was somehow scruffy,
majestic, defiant, and inviting at the same time. It was what
the lower levels of Coruscant would have been if they'd been
given some attitude, bundled into a city-shaped lump, and
dumped in unspoiled countryside. Fi loved it immediately.
The sun glinted off the tower of MandalMotors' engineering
works, a landmark that pilots used for their approach to the
landing strip.

And the air smelled of resin trees, a delicious woody
sweetness that lingered at the back of his palate.

"Lovely," Fi said. *"Lovely."*

"It's a slum," Parja steered him. "The *shebs* of the galaxy.
But it's ours."

They walked across one of the bridges and into the heart
of the city. Alleys threaded between buildings so unalike and
eccentric that it was clear the phrase *Mandalorian town
planning* didn't exist. It was everything that Coruscant
wasn't.

"Does he have a palace?" Fi asked.

"Shysa's just a minor chieftain, if that. Not even Mandalores have a palace these days. I'm not sure if they ever
did."

"Where are we going, then?"

"The tapcaf."

"Why a tapcaf?"

"Convenient." Parja paused to stare at a shopfront. It was full of tools and machine parts, and she gazed at it the way Fi had seen Coruscanti females stare at fashion shops. "Everyone knows the *Oyu'baat*. It's been here since Canderous Ordo was a glint in his mama's eye, and it never closes, ever. They say the pot of stew over the fire's been simmering for a thousand years, and that all the cooks do is throw in more meat and veg every day."

"Yuck," said Fi. "I hope they wash their hands."

Mandalorian informality fascinated Fi. He'd been raised on military precision, a place and a regulation for everything. Somehow, in this please-yourself, hierarchy-free chaos there was still a powerful sense of social purpose that could come together into a formidable army at a moment's notice. He took off his helmet to feel the breeze on his face, and a passerby paused to look at him.

"I'm gorgeous," he said. "See?"

Parja giggled. "Bardan's going to be pleased with your progress. Listen to yourself."

Yeah, but I used to be able to rappel off the Erelan HQ building, do two hundred press-ups before breakfast, and drop a moving target at a thousand meters. I was special. I was the best.

"He's meeting us here?"

"Why not? It'll take two minutes to tell Shysa where to ram his dumb idea, then we pick up some supplies and head back home so Bardan can do the healing thing."

Fi counted the days between Jusik's visits. Not only was he pleased to see a dear friend, a precious connection to his previous life, but the healing sessions held out the prospect of more improvement. He felt the strength seeping back into him like a bellyful of hot food at the end of a freezing patrol. Jusik always seemed tired afterward, though. It was as if he was draining himself. Fi wished he could understand how Jedi could harness the activity of cells like that.

"Found it!" Fi said triumphantly.

The *Oyu'baat* was a sprawling cantina with a motley collection of windows that didn't look as if the builder knew what a perpendicular line or level was. It seemed to be a collection of buildings that had grown together over the centuries. Fi drew himself up to his full height and walked through the doors into a scent of a wood fire, yeast, and rich food perfumes that was irresistible. Sitting near the crackling fire was Shysa, boots up on a chair, hands clasped behind his head, holding court with two men who had their backs to Fi, both in mid-green armor. When he spotted Fi, Shysa sat up straight and looked earnest.

"Ah, the prodigal son and his good lady," he said. "What are you drinking?"

"We're not staying," Parja said. "We're here to meet a friend."

The two men with Shysa turned around just as Fi got to the table, and he wondered why he hadn't recognized them the moment he walked through the doors. Even the backs of their heads—identical, the same close-trimmed black hair—should have clued him in.

They were clones, just like him. No, *not* exactly like him: they were ARCs. One was Sull, formerly A-30, the deserter Omega had tracked down on Gaftikar before Sergeant A'den had booted him off the planet. The other—Fi took a guess at Spar.

"I suppose I ought to thank you," Sull said. "Seeing as your brother whacked those two covert ops clones sent to kill me."

We buried them, showed them respect. They were just doing what they were ordered to do. It really upset Dar.

"Moz and Olun," Fi said. He was proud that he could remember their names. It was the kind of detail he thought he'd forgotten. "Like you care."

"What happened to you? You never stopped yapping on Gaftikar."

Parja very nearly snarled. She was magnificently scary. "He took an explosion full in the face, that's what happened, *chakaar.*"

"Hey, sorry."

Shysa shoved Sull in the shoulder. "Come on, leave the man be. Spar, pull up some seats for my guests."

So it *was* Spar. He'd deserted long before the Grand Army

even left Tipoca City. Fi wasn't sure what to make of him. He didn't look happy.

"We'll pass, thanks," Parja said.

"If you won't drink with me, then I'll put this to Fi straight," Shysa said. "Mandalore needs someone to stand up and say they're Fett's heir. You said no, Sull's said no, and Spar's said no. And you're the only three lads who I can ask right now. It's an easy job. All you have to do is play figurehead."

"Is there a pension plan?" Fi asked.

"It's just keeping up appearances for the *aruetiise*. We live in nervous times, and the job's been vacant for too long."

"I don't get why the clans don't just fill it the usual way," Spar muttered. "Either Mandalore needs a real leader or it doesn't. If you're going to put up a sham one, you might as well go the whole way and select a proper one."

"The Fett name puts the very fear of *haran* up the *aruetiise*." Shysa had an earnest manner that Fi found hard to dislike. The glib charm fell away fast, leaving a man who seemed genuinely worried for his world. "Whatever happened to Jango in the end, he killed Jedi with his bare hands. Folks don't forget that. And if you leave the clans without a focus for too many years . . . well, we don't want another Death Watch starting up. Right now, we don't have an obvious candidate for the job."

Fi didn't yet understand Mandalorian politics, but Parja seemed to. She didn't sit down; she leaned on the back of Fi's chair, one hand on his shoulder.

"Why don't *you* step in, Fenn?" she asked.

"Ah, me, I'm just an odd-job man," he said, spreading his hands. It didn't look like false modesty. "A bit of this, a bit of that. A foot soldier. We need more than a pair of fists leading us these days."

"We need someone to keep the clans together, and I think you'd be pretty good at that."

Fi simply didn't understand a society where nobody made a grab for power when they got the chance. Perhaps there was nothing to be grabbed, only whatever burden landed in the *Mand'alor*'s lap. He concentrated hard on declining the offer himself rather than let Parja speak for him. She was right. It was crazy, even if he could see Shysa's point.

"So, Fi, will you do it?" Shysa asked.

Fi felt sweat beading on his top lip again. He could hear Skirata in his head, warning him to look after number one first. "I can't walk straight, I can't talk properly, and anyway, Fett has a real son somewhere. Sorry. Can't do it."

Shysa smiled sadly. "Okay. You can't blame a fella for tryin'. Concentrate on getting yourself fit, *ner vod*."

"Count me out, too," Sull said. "I'll fight if you want, if I get paid, but I'll stay in the background. My . . . previous employers weren't exactly thrilled by my sudden resignation."

They all looked at Spar, and he shrugged. "You can use me as public relations, Shysa, but it's going to wear thin pretty fast. And I don't owe Fett any kriffing thing."

"How about Mandalore? You don't think you owe your own?"

"How *about* it? I never bought Fett's tosh about serving the Republic, so I'm not the patriotic kind." He turned to Fi. "Like I told you, *ner vod*—Fett didn't give a mott's backside about anything other than himself. He got paid for helping churn out cannon fodder like you and me. And that's what Mandalore wants as a symbol of its power? Terrific."

So it was Spar who'd talked to Fi in the Enceri marketplace. Fi wondered if the ARC trooper felt guilty about deserting even before the war started. He didn't seem the guilt-ridden kind, but there was something about him that smacked of regret.

"So it's okay," said Shysa slowly, "for me to put about the story that you're one of Fett's sons, and that Mandalore is *considering* having you take his place."

Spar had that typical ARC expression of disdain now: one eyebrow raised, lips pressed together. They must have picked it up from Jango. "Okay, as long as you don't advertise that I'm a deserter, or I'll have a death squad after me, too."

"Thanks, pal." Shysa raised his mug, and they seemed to have reached some agreement. "That could well be all we need for the time being."

Fi still couldn't work out why Shysa didn't just step in and take the *Mand'alor*'s role, seeing as he was doing most of it anyway. Parja seized the opportunity to haul Fi away to a quiet corner of the cantina.

"I'm glad that's over and done with. And you did well, *cyar'ika.*" She kept glancing at the door, looking out for Jusik. "You've more than done your duty. Now's your time to be selfish."

Fi had never been good at saying no and meaning it. Skirata had raised his squads to believe they could do *anything,* because they were the best; and deeply ingrained confidence like that was only a short step away from feeling *obliged* to tackle every task simply because he could. Fi now struggled with a vague guilt that chewed quietly at him, telling him that all he had to do was sit around looking Fett-like and making *Mand'alor* noises.

"Wouldn't have been a good advert anyway," he said, arguing aloud with himself. "Mandalore the Drooler."

Parja squeezed his hand hard. "Don't . . ."

"Joke."

"As long as it *is* a joke."

The *Oyu'baat* was very quiet for the hub of Keldabe life. He'd expected it to be full of clan chieftains brokering deals and playing that awful board game that involved stabbing the squares, but maybe it was the wrong time of day to watch the loose and chaotic business of Mandalorian governance taking place. Eventually the doors parted and a slight figure in green armor appeared.

Jusik really looked the part now, as if he'd never been a Jedi, but his lightsaber still hung from his belt. Fi knew what most Mandalorians assumed when they saw the weapon, and why they gave the man a wary glance. They didn't think they were looking at a Jedi. They thought Jusik wore it as a *trophy.* It gave him an instant reputation.

He clasped Fi's arm and then Parja's like any *Mando'ad* and pulled off his helmet, revealing short hair and a complete absence of beard. Fi expected it to make him look younger. It had the opposite effect.

"How are you feeling, *ner vod*?" Jusik gave him a big grin. "You're looking more like your old self."

"Tired," Fi said. "It'll be nice to get home."

"I can stay a few days this time. Ready when you are. And I have some interesting news for you about . . . well, an old friend, shall we say."

Parja stood up and retrieved her helmet. "Got some parts to collect from MandalMotors, and then we can be on our way."

Fi decided to explain the whole Shysa deal to Jusik later, but he noticed Jusik looking discreetly around the cantina as if he was admiring the décor, and there was an expression on his face that Fi had come to know from operations. Jusik could *feel* something. His gaze swiveled in the direction of Shysa and the two renegade ARCs.

"Ah," said Jusik. *"Vode."*

"Spar and Sull," Parja whispered.

Jusik nodded gravely. "Let's go."

Fi was so used to thinking of Jusik as being on his side— Jedi or *Mando'ad,* it didn't matter—that he hadn't considered how folks here would react if they found out he was a Force-user. Your past didn't matter, they said; once you put on the *beskar'gam,* you were family, *aliit.* Fi wondered if that clean slate extended to all newcomers to the *Mando* way.

But Sull turned slowly. He might have been checking on Fi, or it might have been the general wariness that Jango had instilled in all the ARCs he trained. Whatever made him look, he looked. And he stood up.

"Do I know you?" he said.

There was only a handful of people in the *Oyu'baat* at that moment, which was just as well. Jusik stared back calmly at Sull. Shysa and Spar watched as if it didn't concern them.

"You tell me," said Jusik.

Sull walked slowly over to Jusik. Fi found himself instinctively moving between his friend and the ARC, and Parja stepped in, too. There was no telling which way this would go. The ARC looked him up and down, and nodded knowingly at the lightsaber.

"Never met you face-to-face," Sull said quietly, "but I know that voice from a few comm messages, don't I?"

"I've got no argument with you," Jusik said.

"We're not on Coruscant now, and we're not under GAR rules. Who authorized the covert ops guys to kill our own men, General?"

Now they had an audience, however small. Fi could see two men in the corner straining to listen. He could have stopped this by now if he'd been his old self. Come to that, so could Jusik; Fi had seen him smash heavy doors apart with a single gesture. He could defend himself in ways they couldn't imagine.

"I'm not a general now, either, Sull." Jusik was very still, weight evenly on both feet. "And do you seriously think I'd harm a clone?"

"I think," said Sull, "that you hypocritical mystics would waste every last one of us if it served your purposes."

"Watch your mouth," Fi said. "That's my *vod* you're talking to."

Now Spar decided to get involved, wandering over with apparent casual ease to stand by his brother ARC. "Problem?"

"Jedi." Sull spat out the word, hand straying way too close to his blaster. "A kriffing *Jedi,* all gussied up like one of *us.*"

It was the hand that triggered Fi. Part of his brain must have been working just fine, a part that connected his fists to his animal instincts, because he brought his gauntlet up hard under Sull's jaw and sent him staggering backward into Spar.

"Get away from him!" Fi snarled. "You touch him and I'll gut you—"

It took Parja and Jusik to hold him back. He wanted to rip Sull apart, and he had no idea where the rage came from, but all he knew was that it was eating him alive and he wasn't nice, funny Fi any longer. Shysa was on his feet in an instant, grabbing Sull by the collar and parting the three clones. Fi had no idea how he'd landed that punch in his condition— but he had, and it hurt like *haran.* Sull was bleeding from the lip.

"It's your boyish high spirits, and I know you lads enjoy a scrap," Shysa said, arm locked tight around Sull's neck. "But sort this out over a nice friendly drink or two, whatever your problem is. Okay?"

"Come on, Fi." Parja bundled him toward the doors. "Not worth it. Walk away."

The barkeep watched, chin resting on one hand as he leaned on the counter, as if he saw fisticuffs like this all the time. Fi pulled away from Parja. "You stay away from *Bard'ika*," he warned, jabbing a finger in Sull's direction. "You hear me? You so much as *look* at him, and you're dead."

The moment he got outside in the cool air, Fi felt instantly ashamed and confused. He *never* lost it like that before he was injured. It wasn't him at all; his heart hammered so hard it almost hurt, and he felt he had no control whatsoever over the animal part of him. Jusik took his arm and helped Parja steer him across the square to sit down by the bridge.

"Well," Jusik said, balancing his helmet on his knee. "I see you've got some higher motor skills back, and a good degree of verbal fluency . . ."

"Sorry. I just saw his hand . . . the blaster."

"No problem. Thanks."

Parja kept looking back toward the *Oyu'baat* as if she expected the two ARCs to come after them. She patted her sidearm. "Sull's just mouthing off. Rav says ARCs are all mouth and *kamas*."

"I can't blame him," Jusik said. "He knows ARCs won't get a happy retirement, and it must be hard to trust a Jedi when you've been used like they have."

"Is everyone going to treat you like that?" Fi asked. It did more than anger him: it upset him. Jusik was his buddy, his brother, as close to him as Ordo or his squad brothers. They'd had near misses and narrow scrapes, and when Fi had needed him most, he'd been there, no questions asked. "Is everyone going to spit on you for being a Jedi? Because I can't stand that. It's not fair."

"Ah, they'll get used to me." Jusik gave Fi a playful headlock and forced a grin, but he was acting, Fi knew it. "And it's only Sull, after all. ARCs are all nuts. A'den said he nearly had to head-butt him last time. And didn't he bite Dar?"

Fi thought back to Gaftikar. Darman and Atin had captured Sull when he deserted, and he'd sunk his teeth into

Dar's hand. It was a mess. "Yeah, he's got Cyborrean rabies now . . ."

"Now *there's* a word you couldn't say a month ago." Jusik got up and began walking. "We're going to have you back to full spec in no time, *ner vod.* Come on. Home."

Jusik whistled tunelessly to himself, helmet in one hand while he twirled the hilt of his lightsaber in the other, looking for all the world like another swaggering *Mando* without a care in the world. But Fi knew it was going to be hard for him here. He wasn't a Corellian, or a Togorian, or any one of a thousand species that Mandalorians would accept without murmur; he'd been a Jedi, and *Mando'ade* didn't have a good history with them. Now there were small but growing numbers of disgruntled clones who felt the Jedi were to blame for a lot of their woes.

It was going to be the ultimate test of traditional Mandalorian tolerance, *cin vhetin,* the virgin field of snow that everyone who put their past behind them to become a Mandalorian had a right to walk upon.

Fi had been taught caution. You didn't take chances; you had to know who was watching your back. He knew he'd have to watch Jusik's back for the rest of his life.

Jusik had put him back together again. It was the least Fi could do for him.

5

So . . . we're building more ships for the Republic, far more ships than they have crews to run, in fact—and how much more armor? Have I missed a decimal point here or something? I mean, this is an even bigger order than Kamino placed twelve years ago. Doesn't that sound weird to anyone? And how many kriffing years are we going to have to store it this time?
—Production line supervisor at Rothana Heavy Engineering, checking the confidential advance workflow schedule

Omega observation point, Haurgab, 938 days ABG

Getting your gunship shot out from under you would normally sober anyone. But it didn't even slow down the Maujasi rebels.

Darman scrambled to his feet, visor smeared with hydraulic fluid, expecting to see a downed vessel and body parts everywhere. The gunship was a mess, all right, all buckled metal and in flames, but the Maujasi—they just poured out of the crew compartment into the sandstorm *fighting*.

Darman ducked back behind the cover of the wall and began laying down fire. He couldn't see a thing. All he could do was rely on the HUD sensors to pick up temperature variations and metallic composites in the rebels' weapons.

"Dar! *At'ika!*" It was Niner. Darman could hear but not see him. "Get down!"

Blue blasterfire cut through the whirling yellow haze; red and white bolts spat back. The rebels had dropped down behind the ancient rubble of a collapsed wall. "Where the *shab* are you, Sarge?"

"I can see you, Dar. You're left of me, eight meters."

The HUD view shimmered. It was like watching a scrambled HoloNet channel on which the vague shapes of what could have been bodies never resolved into anything instantly recognizable. "Got you, Sarge."

Corr let out a shout. Darman couldn't tell if he'd been hit, even though the upgraded biomonitors in their suits relayed their physical status. The stupid readout was set at the most awkward place on the HUD when you were busy being shot at. He hated Republic Procurement more each day.

"*Cor'ika,* you okay?"

"Yeah."

"*Shabuir*—" Corr grunted as if he'd punched someone. "*At'ika,* watch your left, I can see one going wide—"

Darman raised his shoulders to launch an anti-armor round, but a blaster bolt hit him like a fist in the chest and winded him for a moment. Recovering, he aimed two grenades in the vague direction of fire. The ancient wall rained down on him. He ducked: Atin swore. Something had hit him, hard, and Darman shook off the debris. There was a moment of relative silence—screaming wind, but no shots, no shouts—and he was sure he'd finished off the rebels until something hit his back plate so hard that he thought more rubble had fallen on him. Firing started again.

As Darman rolled over, eyes streaming with the pain, a Maujasi loomed over him, his face suddenly very clear and close. His blaster was point-blank in Darman's face. No thought, no coherent words: Darman ejected his vibroblade and lunged, ramming the blade so hard into the man's thigh that when he fell back again he couldn't pull his hand free for a few moments. The guy didn't so much scream as yelp in surprise. Adrenaline was a great anesthetic. But it didn't stop the arterial spurt, and suddenly there was blood everywhere.

It's not mine, it's not mine, it's not mine . . .

That was all that mattered. Darman got up and bolted the

few meters to where he thought Niner and the others were clustered. The wind was still scouring his armor like shot-blasting, but the sand seemed to be thinning out and he could see more shapes and flashes of light.

How many Maujasi rebels could you pack in an assault ship?

A lot more than Darman thought. A *lot* more.

"*Shab,* why don't they just *die*?" Atin said.

Judging by the hail of red and white energy bolts that greeted him, there were twenty or twenty-five of the *chakaare* still functioning, and that wasn't good odds now. Darman was on autopilot. He was just returning fire in a continuous stream, part of his brain telling him that the moment he stopped he'd be dead, and part warning him he was running out of ammo even faster. Omega were now almost on top of the Maujasi. It was like trench warfare. They couldn't have been more than ten meters apart, with only the piles of rubble and stumps of the walls for cover.

"When this storm drops, we're stuffed," Corr said.

How long would it take to get killed? How many blaster rounds would finally destroy their Katarn plates' energy-diffusing properties? The better protected you were, the more complex and frightening the death that awaited you, Darman decided. Without it, a clean shot would end it all. With it—well, you couldn't design for immortality. Just delaying the inevitable, that was all it was.

One way or another, he didn't plan to be captured. *Sorry, Et'ika. Didn't even leave a last message, did I?* Darman loaded his last ion pulse clip and aimed at the incoming fire.

He could see the far wall now. The storm was dropping. Hand to hand, in the end. Yeah, he'd do whatever it took. Between bursts of fire, he reached down to his belt to check the last det was still there.

"I hope I'm not hallucinating," Niner said. "Listen."

Darman held his breath. Nothing: he couldn't hear a thing beyond the battle.

Corr exhaled. "Can't hear anything, Sarge."

Then a loud voice right in his ear made Darman gasp. Someone interrupted his audio circuit.

"Omega, keep your heads down. We see you. Hold on. It's going to get busy."

Now Darman could *hear* it, because it was right overhead; a rapid metallic stuttering noise with top frequencies that went right off the scale, the sweetest sound in the world—a LAAT/i gunship.

"Shab," Niner whispered. " 'Bout time."

The pilot wasn't joking. The instant they dropped flat in the lee of the last remaining pile of rubble, the larty's forward laser cannon opened up and the ground under them shook. Darman half expected the rock to split and slide just as it had when he blew out the side of the slope. He thought the deafening noise was never going to stop until the firing ended in a ringing silence and the gunship dropped like a stone onto the smoking chaos in front of them. The crew bay hatch opened. The first thing Darman saw was a white-plated arm reach out as if to haul them inboard.

"Omega, shift your backsides, will you?" It was a sergeant, a regular trooper. The hand gesture became impatient. "We don't want a missile up the chuff. Come on, chop-chop . . ."

They piled in, numb and shaking with adrenaline. The LAAT/i lifted even before the hatch closed. As the gunship banked over the desert, Darman caught a glimpse of laserfire through the gap, and the larty shivered as if something had hit it. Its cannon opened up again. The airframe shook as if the thing was coughing, and Darman found himself clinging to the grab rail, realizing that his left shoulder hurt and his knee didn't feel too clever, either.

"Thanks," said Niner.

The sergeant tapped two fingers to his helmet in mock salute. "No sweat. Which genius blew up the mountain?"

"That'd be Dar."

The sergeant cocked his head. "I bet he paints himself into corners, too."

When Darman went to remove his helmet, his finger snagged in the fabric trim around his neck. It took him a few moments to work out that a blaster bolt had seared a hole in it.

"Lucky your head's still on," Corr said casually.

"This fabric's supposed to be blaster-resistant."

"At point-blank range? Nah."

It was pointless chatter fueled by relief. Nobody would get emotional about the rescue, not yet, when actually all Darman wanted to do was to fling his arms around the sergeant and the pilot and the crazy guys manning the cannon and tell them they were all his best buddies forever.

Fierfek, we made it out alive again.

No, Darman *was* going to say it.

"*Ner vod,* you have *no* idea how glad we were to see you." Darman cradled his helmet and inhaled the cool conditioned air inside the crew bay. "I thought those *chakaare* were going to be wearing my *gett'se* for earrings."

The sergeant was probably staring at him. His head was in a position that looked as if he was, but he said nothing, as if he hadn't heard right.

"What?" he said at last.

"Things were getting *shabla* hairy down there." Maybe he didn't understand what the Maujasi rebels did to their enemies for revenge. "Thanks."

"Is that the local language?"

"What is?"

"Nair vowd," the sergeant said carefully, as if it was the only phrase he'd caught.

Darman didn't expect white jobs to understand *Mando'a.* It was only the Republic commandos trained by Mandalorians like Sergeant Kal who spoke the language. But every trooper flash-learned the words to the marching song *Vode An,* and some phrases—like *ner vod* and the best profanities— had percolated through the ranks fast.

Not to this guy, though. *Odd.*

"You Eighty-fifth?" Darman asked.

"Fourteenth Infantry," said the sergeant.

"Okay, maybe we'll get you a crash course in *Mando'a* so you can exchange chitchat with Shiny Boys like us."

"Sorry," said the trooper. His accent was different from the rest of the white jobs Darman had come across. "Never heard of it. I'm new."

He was new, all right. As the man moved forward to the cockpit, hand over hand on the grab rail, Darman replaced his helmet to talk privately with the squad.

"Does that look like reinforcements to you? New clone intake?"

Niner clicked his teeth. "If it is, they've changed the training program on Kamino. The meat-cans all learn *Vode An.*"

Atin secured his restraints, leaned back on the seat with arms folded across his chest, and stretched out his legs, indicating that he planned to sleep. "Maybe the Kaminoans think the *Mando* thing is getting out of hand and making the lads too uppity."

"Maybe they're cutting corners in production," said Niner.

"Maybe they told some aiwha-bait to *kovid lo'shebs' ul narit* once too often," Corr said, and laughed.

It was a small thing, but life and death in this business hung on the apparently inconsequential detail. Darman made a mental note to tell Skirata. Then he switched out of the squad link with a couple of blinks, and opened a private comlink to Etain's code.

She needed to know he was okay, wherever she was.

**Republic Fleet Auxiliary support vessel *Redeemer*,
off Thyferra, 940 days ABG**

"What's your name, Commander?"

The Jedi looked up at Etain as she leaned over the hangar deck gantry. She was a human female, brown-haired, maybe Etain's age, but she didn't look like any Jedi that Ordo had seen before; no traditional brown robes, just clean but well-worn overalls as if she'd stepped straight out of a factory. Only the lightsaber she was checking over gave any indication of what she was, and even that was different from those Ordo was used to seeing. The blade was yellow, and the handle was carved with sea creatures. She wasn't one of Zey's regulation-issue Jedi.

Ordo was dismayed to realize he found her rather attractive. Guilt consumed him for a moment. He felt disloyal to

Besany for even *noticing* another female, and made a mental
note to ask *Kal'buir* if this was a terrible failing. There was
no point asking Mereel. He seemed to think it was compul-
sory.

"Callista, General," said the Jedi. "Callista Masana." She
nodded politely at Ordo. "Captain."

"Delta Squad are on their way." Etain seemed at a loss for
the right words, as if there was something about Callista that
bothered her. "Thank you for responding. Every pair of
hands counts."

Callista gave her an equally odd look back. "You'll get
used to our funny little ways, General."

The woman walked away toward the LAAT/i on the
hangar deck, where a few other equally un-Jedi-like Jedi had
gathered. Ordo was fascinated, as much by Etain's reaction
to these unusual officers as by their behavior. Callista put her
arm around one of the young male Jedi and gave him a kiss
on the cheek that was definitely *not* comradely. They were, as
Mereel would have put it, clearly an *item*.

"Master Altis has some unconventional views on how Jedi
should conduct themselves," Etain said quietly, giving Ordo
a gentle shove toward the hatch. "He and his followers hark
back to a less rigid and ascetic age."

*Jedi kissing in public. And Etain has to hide her relation-
ship with Darman? These people need to work out what they
stand for.*

"This Master Altis," Ordo said, following Etain to the
briefing room. "How does he feel about marriage and children? Is this what Callista means by *funny little ways*?"

Etain took a breath as if she was preparing to give him a
rehearsed speech. "In the early Jedi Order, there was no ban
on attachment, and Masters could take as many Padawans to
train as they liked—even if they were adult. It was all *much*
more informal. Altis is a back-to-basics kind of Jedi."

"Maybe you should join him."

"They've joined us." ·

"You know what I mean, General . . ."

"What do you think Bardan would say?"

Jusik had rapidly become a kind of moral compass for the

younger Jedi as speculation about his resignation spread. He had a reputation even before he walked out; he'd already berated the Jedi Council about its stance on the war. To some he was an example they wished they could follow, but Ordo had the feeling he shamed others, and they seemed hostile in their polite Jedi way.

"I think he'd tell you that everyone has to make their own decision," Ordo said.

"And I'd say that joining a more liberal group of Jedi would be trying to have the best of both worlds, and ignoring the issues that made Bardan leave."

"You plan to leave the Order."

"I certainly do."

And that was the least of Etain's challenges. Every day that she didn't tell Darman that Kad was their son made the revelation harder. Ordo had racked his brain trying to think of a gentler way to break the news, but there was no good way to do it.

When they reached the briefing room, Delta Squad were listening intently to the air group commander with two other commando squads—Orar and Naast—that were made up mostly of Rav Bralor's former trainees. None of them paid any attention to Ordo and Etain slipping in at the back. The rest of the seats were taken up by infantry troopers and pilots, but there was no sign yet of Ordo's five brother Nulls.

There was rarely an operational need to meet face-to-face, but they missed one another, and Kom'rk had been out in the field for a long time on his own.

"What are you doing here, anyway?" Etain whispered. "Kal sent you to keep an eye on me?"

"No, I'm here to keep an eye on *Kal'buir.*"

"Anything wrong?"

"Maybe."

Etain turned her head slightly to stare at him. "You'd better finish the sentence."

"One of his sons contacted him to say his daughter was missing."

Etain closed her eyes for a moment. "Poor Kal. He never said. Missing *how,* exactly?"

"I don't know. I'm waiting for *Kal'buir* to tell me."

She let out a long breath. It wasn't so much a sigh as the sound of sheer fatigue and disillusion escaping from her. "I would so like a simple life for us all, however hard the work."

"We shall have it. Make no mistake, we *shall* have it."

Ordo rarely felt pity, but when he did—and if it wasn't for his small circle of brothers—he felt it for Etain. He felt it all the more now that he knew that there were Jedi who did things differently, and that if Etain had been born in a different place, or a different time, that she might have been old enough to choose whether she wanted to be a Jedi, not simply taken as a helpless baby and indoctrinated. And she could have chosen to love without fear of censure.

If the galaxy had been that different, there might not even have been this war to worry about.

"We won't wait until the end of the war, will we?" she whispered, lips barely moving. "But when will we know when the time is right?"

She was referring to desertion—getting out, leaving the war behind. It was an odd question for a Jedi to ask. Ordo had always thought that their senses would tell them when momentous events would happen. He realized he had a far better chance now of predicting that from intelligence than Etain had from listening to the Force.

"*I'll* know," he said. "And so will *Kal'buir*."

There was no point finding a way of stopping accelerated aging if nobody survived to have the therapy. And that meant leaving millions of brother clones to fight on while the small and fortunate circle of *Kal'buir* fled.

Yes, Ordo understood now why Etain couldn't bring herself to follow Jusik out of the Republic's service.

"Do you think Callista and her freethinking friends are up to the task?" he asked. On the dais at the front of the briefing room, the air group commander was still demonstrating with the aid of a holochart how they would insert troops to secure the spaceport. "They've never led troops, and we know what happened last time that role was dumped in Jedi laps without training."

"I have no idea," Etain said. "But I've told the squads to

ignore them if they give suicidally stupid orders. They know that."

Etain was a smart woman. She knew what she didn't know, and she trusted her troops. Ordo took his leave of her with a nod and slipped out into the passage to look for his brothers.

The RV point was one of the engineering spaces where the only interruption was likely to be by a maintenance droid. It wasn't ideal, but *Redeemer* was more or less in a convenient place at the right time, and thanks to Etain, Ordo had numerous excuses for being there. There was no sign of the other Nulls when he stepped through the hatch, but Skirata was already there. He didn't seem to hear Ordo enter and carried on talking on his comlink in fond tones, his back to the hatch. "I know, son," he said. "But other than that, do you need anything? Is everything okay?"

He seemed to listen for a while, laughed ruefully, and said *"Ret' "* to end the conversation. Then he tapped in another code and waited. *" 'Cuy, Gar'ika. Me'vaar ti gar?"*

Ordo had thought he was talking to one of his real sons, Tor. But he was doing a regular call-around of his commando squads, just chatting and seeing how they were. It was important, he said. Men needed to know that someone cared if they lived or died. Etain had taken that to heart, because she was visiting every single squad in her commando group, all 125 of them.

Ordo waited until Skirata came to a natural pause and coughed politely. Skirata jumped as if someone had discharged a blaster behind him.

"Sorry, *Kal'buir*."

"Son, you know I'm a bit deaf." Skirata turned to swing his leg over a metal bench and sit astride it. "Just catching up with the *ad'ike*."

It was a compartment of Skirata's life that Ordo and the other Nulls weren't quite part of, like the family the veteran sergeant had before he came to Kamino. Skirata somehow kept all three separate; the Nulls had barely known the commandos under *Kal'buir*'s care until after Geonosis. Ordo rationalized it as Skirata's way of avoiding any comparison between the amount of time he devoted to the Nulls and how thinly his attention was spread among a hundred or so young commandos.

"I've called the *vode* together," Ordo said. "We need to get a few things straight."

"All of you?" Skirata looked embarrassed. "That sounds ominous. Going to give me a talking-to?"

"Yes."

"Look, I'll book an appointment to get the leg fixed. I swear. Next week."

Ordo opened his datapad and checked the calendar, thumbing through the medcenter codes. Mereel had fixed a slot for the surgery. "No need, *Buir'ika.* Done."

Skirata wasn't himself. The news from his estranged family had hit him hard. Ordo thought it was unjust that his sons could disown him and yet expect him to come running when something went wrong; they were grown men, old enough to have grandchildren of their own. But this was his *daughter* in trouble. She hadn't declared him *dar'buir.* Ordo was prepared to give her some benefit of the doubt for Skirata's sake, with one hand on his blaster in case she turned out to be trouble that his beloved father didn't need.

Am I jealous? Am I worried because he's our father, our buir, *and we don't want any interlopers?* It wasn't a very *Mando* thought. Ordo suppressed it. It was another guilty moment that made him wonder what he really was.

"You don't need to be a Jedi to feel something's shifting," Skirata said. "And I've had word from Omega."

"They're okay. I checked."

"Yes, I know, but Dar said they've come across troopers who don't seem to know *Vode An.*"

In the context of a galactic war, it was less than nothing. In the context of what the Nulls had discovered on Kamino—the looming end of its clone production, facilities set up on Coruscant itself—and the evidence Besany had turned up about a clone program on Centax 2, it was significant; it meant that there was a new basic training schedule. The aiwha-bait were nothing if not mind-numbingly consistent. The song was part of the flash-learning module that taught young clones the purpose and nobility of the Republic's cause.

"Is this the first of our Centax batch?" Ordo asked. "Because I've not noticed any real increase in troop numbers. Believe me, *Kal'buir,* I've been monitoring that very closely."

"They'd have to test a few in combat, wouldn't they? Or maybe give the new clones a chance to assimilate. But if they weren't trained on Tipoca, and Kamino didn't provide embryos for Centax, the dates Besany found for cloning materials being sent to Centax means we have fully grown troops being produced in a year or less."

There was only one way of doing that as far as Ordo knew. "Spaarti cloning."

"Arkanian Micro?"

"I don't think even they can beat the year barrier yet. They'd have to come from Spaarti Creations on Cartao. Or else Palpatine's brought in some ex-Spaarti clonemasters, which is more likely."

"He's got Kaminoans somewhere on Coruscant, too," Skirata said. "The man's quite the recruiter."

Ordo didn't even need to consult his datapad. His eidetic memory summoned up an entire report from nearly two years before of the Separatist destruction of the Spaarti facility on Cartao. "I think he picked up a few scientists after the attack on Cartao, *Kal'buir.*"

"Spaarti clones, then. How much use do you think they'll be if they churn them out in a year?"

Ordo felt uncomfortable to hear these men—men exactly like him in most ways—referred to like that, even benignly, and even by Skirata. "It's not just the process," he said. "It's the genetic material they're grown from. The Kaminoans weren't happy with results from second-generation tissue, which is why they kept Fett around."

"We need to do some *serious* digging."

"Why? All we need to keep an eye on is when the Chancellor plans to deploy them. That's our cue to leave."

"I wasn't thinking of asking Besany to take more risks, son."

"I know."

The comment hung between them for a moment or two. Then the hatch opened and Kom'rk stuck his head into the compartment.

"So, nobody missed me," he said. "I'm gone a year, and nobody baked a cake."

"Kom'ika . . ." Skirata got up and embraced him with a crunch of armor plates. Ordo waited his turn. "Come on, get that bucket off and let's take a look at you . . . *shab,* son, you're looking thin."

Kom'rk shrugged, clipping his helmet to his belt. His face did look drawn. Ordo took advantage of the moment and moved in to hug his brother. Then the rest of the Nulls showed up and the engineering space was suddenly very crowded. It was just like old times, the seven of them together, ready to take on anyone.

"I've been babysitting him, *Kal'buir,*" Jaing said. "Someone has to keep him away from Mereel and his wild debauchery, after all."

Prudii gave Ordo a friendly shove in the back. "It's *Ord'ika*'s turn to explore the Outer Rim now."

It was. Ordo didn't want to leave Skirata's side if he could help it, but he was always conscious that he spent more time at base than any of the Nulls. *Kal'buir doesn't have favorites.* "I'll swap drafts with you, then."

Mereel took off his helmet and grinned. "Yes, and I can look after Agent Wennen while you're gone."

The others laughed. Ordo bristled. "We're here to read *Kal'buir* the riot act, *vod'ikase.* Remember?"

"I thought that maybe we could grab a meal in the wardroom and celebrate still being alive," Skirata said. "After you've had your say."

"We'll make it quick, then," Prudii said. "One, you show up for surgery and get that ankle fixed, and no crying off like all the other times. Two, *we'll* find your daughter, and that way if your no-good offspring is trying to bleed you because he thinks you're rich now, we'll cut off his—"

All Skirata had done to stop Prudii in midsentence was look faintly pained.

"You don't owe him anything, *Kal'buir.*"

"*D'ika,* he's my son."

"He disowned you. Your wife wouldn't let you bring up your kids as Mandos, but they accepted your creds happily enough, didn't they? Funny how they declared you *dar'buir.* It was the only Mandalorian custom they ever observed."

Ordo watched the color drain from Skirata's face. It was a question he'd never dared raise, because there was only one reason why sons who'd turned their backs on their Mandalorian heritage would use the ancient law to disown their father; they knew it would *hurt* him. They knew how much it mattered.

"Whatever they do to me," Skirata said quietly, "they'll never stop being my kids. Now, why don't we get a meal, and you can all tell me what you're up to. Jaing, how's the fundraising going?"

Jaing followed Skirata out through the hatch. "On target, and the investment income is starting to roll in."

"Nice job, son. And you, Kom'rk?"

"Grievous still comes and goes on Utapau, *Kal'buir,* and he gets visits from interesting allies we didn't know he had. The Regent of Garis, in fact."

"And there was I thinking he was in the Republic camp."

Kom'rk handed Skirata a datachip. "A crumb to toss to Zey—here's the voice traffic between the two of them, minus the locations, of course. We don't want Windu or Kenobi charging in there and blowing it before we've milked the situation." He lowered his voice. "And Grievous keeps asking Dooku what's happened to all these gazillions of droids he was promised, poor old dear. I think he's been set up."

"Told you so," Skirata said. "All propaganda. All *osik.*"

"Can I have a change of scene, then? It's boring out there."

Mereel raised an eyebrow. "You need to learn to find your own entertainment, *ner vod . . .*"

The Nulls laughed all the way to the wardroom. They breezed in, took a table, and Skirata ordered nerf steaks all around from the steward droid. The wardroom was usually the preserve of nonclone officers, but those who were there sensibly made no comment about an influx of ARC troopers, and nothing about the presence of two sergeants—if they even recognized Skirata and A'den as such. They knew what ARCs did, and that it was a good idea to avoid them.

The meal was as much a rare celebration as a meeting, and the Nulls even had a few glasses of Chandrilan wine. "I should have done this many years ago, *adi'ke*." Skirata raised his glass. "*Ni kyr'tayl gai sa'ad*—Mereel, Jaing, Kom'rk, A'den, Prudii. There. It's formal, legal. You're my sons and heirs."

"And *we* won't bankrupt you," Jaing muttered.

"Not with the amount you're skimming, *ner vod*," Mereel said, raising his glass in return. "Thank you, *Buir'ika*. An honor."

At least one cause for guilt had been lifted from Ordo's shoulders. He was no longer the only Null formally adopted by Skirata. It was a legal detail, nothing more, but Ordo didn't want to be singled out as the favorite. He already felt he had a far easier time than his brothers. They carried on chatting—nothing confidential, not until they were back on the secure helmet link—until Ordo noticed a couple of the mongrel lieutenants, the nonclones in their drab gray fabric uniforms, looking past him toward the entrance with mild amusement.

Ordo turned. Behind him, a young ensign stood glowering at the Nulls, and caught his eye.

"Clone!" snapped the ensign. "What's the meaning of this?"

Clone.

It was never a good opening line. Mereel stifled a smile. "Remember, no entrails, *Ord'ika*. Folks are still eating."

But Ordo couldn't laugh it off. Not only was it a gross insult, it was also a test; if he allowed this upstart to disrespect him, he encouraged him to treat all clones badly. A lesson was needed.

"Ensign," he said slowly. "I'm not *clone*. I'm *Captain*." He tapped his red pauldron meaningfully. "*Captain* Ordo, ARC en-one-one, Special Operations Brigade, Grand Army of the Republic. And you'll address me *properly*."

The wardroom fell silent. The ensign had taken on an

ARC trooper, and he was going to get his *shebs* handed to him. Ordo could sense their anticipation without any need for telepathy.

"You can't talk to me like that," the ensign said. "You're a *clone.*"

Ordo stood and ambled slowly toward him, both thumbs hooked in his belt, coming to a halt almost nose-to-nose. It was hard not to hit the brat and be done with it. He wanted to very badly, and noted the COMPOR pin next to the ensign's flash. *Political ideologue, eh?* It was the Commission for the Protection of the Republic, strutting little twerps who wanted firm government as long as it was imposed on lesser beings and not them.

"And proud to be one," Ordo said, feeling his throat tightening and his pulse accelerating. "Designed to be superior. And looking at you, I can see why the Republic had to buy in a *real* navy. What's your problem?"

"You can't bring noncommissioned ranks into the wardroom." The ensign hadn't backed down, so he was doing better than most. "Officers only—"

"Quote him the regs, *Ord'ika.*" Prudii laughed. "Chapter and subsection. That'll teach him."

But the ensign was on his suicide run now. He pointed at Skirata. "And as for bringing the hired help in here, that *mercenary*—"

Up to that point, Ordo had balanced on that fine edge between finding things almost funny and being irritable. He was aware of his moods and occasionally explosive temper. They said the Nulls were all psychos, screwed up by too much genetic tinkering, and Ordo knew his reactions weren't those of a normally socialized human being. But he had bigger issues on his list than satisfying this ensign's desire for a sergeant-free wardroom, and he let his instincts take over. His instincts were very, very angry.

"GAR regulation five-six-one-one, subsection A—an officer may invite guests into the wardroom," Ordo said. "And you'll apologize to Sergeant Skirata *right now.*"

"I will do no such thing. I'll have you court-martialed."

Ordo answered to nobody but Skirata. This little gut-worm *had* to apologize. It was a matter of honor, and not just his. "Really? Court-martial *this*." He brought his head down sharply in a well-practiced head-butt and the crack of bone—not his—split the wardroom air. The ensign fell backward with a shocked *oof* sound, hands cupped to his nose. There was plenty of blood.

"I'm sticking you on a charge," Ordo said calmly, picking up a pristine white napkin to wipe his forehead. Without a helmet, it always hurt more than he expected. "Insubordination. What's your name?"

The ensign was stunned, in more ways than one. "Lu . . . Luszgoti."

"And now, Ensign Luszgoti, you'll say the magic words." He grabbed the kid's collar, hauled him upright, and stood him in front of *Kal'buir.* "Apologize to Sergeant Skirata."

The ensign glanced around, maybe calculating his chances of dropping Ordo, maybe looking to more senior officers to back him up. Nobody else moved. Ordo tightened his grip.

"I apologize," the ensign said at last. *"Sergeant."*

Skirata raised his glass. "Apology accepted, son. Now *usen'ye* before my boys really lose their tempers."

Ensign Luszgoti left to a polite ripple of applause from one corner of the wardroom. He obviously wasn't popular. A steward droid trundled up to the table with a jug of ale that Skirata hadn't ordered.

"Most entertaining, Captain." A commander sitting at a nearby table nodded, indicating the drinks were on him. "How I've longed to do that."

The ensign would think twice about treating another clone like dirt. But so would the more polite officers here. Violence had its place in education.

"K'oyacyi," said Skirata. "Cheers."

It was a telling phrase, *k'oyacyi;* it was a command that meant "stay alive." And so it was a toast, or an exhortation to hang in there, or even to come home safely. Staying alive and making the most of each day's living underpinned much of the Mandalorian language.

"K'oyacyi," A'den said. *"Oya manda."*

Ordo, never fond of alcohol, stared into his glass and wondered what the Republic's armed forces would be like if they had to recruit wholly from nonclones. Whoever had ordered the clone army had excellent foresight.

But, as Fi had once said, they might have set up the whole war anyway, not that a carefully planned war looking for an excuse to start was anything remotely new in the galaxy.

It was still important to find out exactly who could plan so far ahead, and so well.

Hangar deck, *Redeemer*, two hours later

Skirata found a quiet corner of the hangar deck as he waited for the transport, staring at the comlink in his hand for a long time before keying in Tor's code.

It had taken him three days to work out what to say. He thought he'd comm his estranged son straight back and demand to know what had happened to his daughter, buoyed up on a wave of anxiety, but there was too much water under the bridge, and the boy was a stranger.

Boy.

Tor was thirty-nine now. Maybe he even had grandchildren. That was possible, if he'd been Mandalorian and married very young as *Mando'ade* did; but his mother wouldn't have allowed that. Ilippi thought the *beskar'gam* was dashing when she married Skirata, but his long absences on deployment started to wear on her with three small kids to care for, and then she hit the big cultural wall—Tor was coming up on eight years old, and Skirata wanted to do as all *Mando* fathers did, to take his son to train and fight alongside him for five years.

Skirata could picture Ilippi now, five-year-old Ruusaan and six-year-old Ijaat clinging to her legs, crying, while she yelled that no baby boy of hers was going to war. From that argument—and she shouldn't have yelled like that, not in front of the kids—their marriage went rapidly downhill. The next time he came home on leave, the kids were with her parents on Corellia, and she told him she wanted a divorce.

It took thirty seconds, *Mando*-style—a short oath to wed,

and a shorter one to part. Skirata handed her all his earnings and left for another war.

Every credit. Every credit I didn't absolutely need to survive, until the day I left for Kamino. Then I was dead and gone.

He waited for Tor to answer with comlink set on audio-only. He had no idea what to call him. Son? He called most younger men "son" by default. This time it wasn't a reflex.

"Skirata here," said a voice. For some reason he expected Tor to have rejected his name, and it shocked him into brief silence to hear it. "Hello?"

"It's me . . . Kal Skirata."

"I . . . I didn't think you'd call back."

Skirata plunged in as he would with Zey, and bit back the urge to ask every detail of their lives. They'd decided not to be his sons, and begging for crumbs would only make things worse. Cool distance was the only way to deal with it. "You used the word *missing*. Is Ijaat okay?"

"He's fine."

"Tell me about Ruusaan."

"We lost contact with her some months ago."

"And *now* you start looking?"

"We . . . drifted apart."

The adult Tor was a stranger; the Tor that Skirata was reaching out to had grown up and changed years ago. There was nothing familiar even about his voice. Skirata's finger hovered over the hologram key, wanting to activate it to see what his boy had grown into, and finally he gave in to thirty-two years of wondering.

The hologram shimmered into life, blue and unreal. Tor was dark-haired, thickset, smartly dressed, and that was all Skirata could tell. Low-res holograms were lousy on detail.

And Tor could see him and what was immediately behind him.

"Where are you?" he asked. "Who's—oh, wow, that's the Republic *army.*"

"They're clone troops," Skirata said. *My boys, too.* "I'm on the front line."

"You always were."

Tor was on neutral Corellia if his comm signal was real—
it would be, of course—and his only contact with the war
was probably via HNE bulletins. How could he ever understand his father? "Tor, tell me what happened to Ruusaan. I
need all the data you can give me."

"Yes, we thought you'd be best placed to find her."

"When, where, how?" *How can I talk to a kid I raised as
if he's a client?* "I need detail."

"She was living on Drall, last we knew. We didn't see her
more than once a year, but when her comm code didn't func-
tion, we got worried. Her apartment was cleared out and
there was no sign of her."

"Did you check her bank account?"

"Why?"

"Activity. Withdrawals, or a complete lack of them."

"No. I don't have any access. We weren't that close."

I would have raised you smarter, son. And we'd *have been
close.* "What does she do for a living?"

"She drifts. Security . . . bartending . . . a bit of *courier*
work now, she says."

*Please don't let her be a mercenary. I wasn't there to teach
her how to stay alive.* "Did you report her missing to the
Corellian cops?"

"They said she was an adult free to go where she liked,
and we'd have to come back with evidence of a crime before
they could get involved."

"Okay. I need her state ID number and a recent holoimage." *I've got her date of birth. She's my girl. She's still my
daughter.* "I'll do the rest."

"I know it'll cost you, but we can pay."

"No. Thanks."

"You look . . . like you've had a tough time . . . Dad."

So now Skirata was *Dad* again.

That hurt. In his peripheral vision, he could see Mereel
and Ordo chatting, thinking they were keeping a discreet eye
on him when he knew perfectly well that they were standing
by to pick up the pieces. Would he take Tor and Ijaat back?
Would he swap any of his clone sons for those he had some
genetic investment in?

*Never. Is that bad? Understandable? Noble? I still don't
know. It just . . . is.*

"I'm doing fine," Skirata said, struggling with the mix of
remembered heartbreak and resentment that he couldn't link
to the person he was looking at now. *I didn't want to leave. I
wouldn't have left. I sent you every cred I earned.* "Comm
me the data and I'll find her. It's what I do."

Tor seemed to be hovering on the brink of saying something. His fidgeting was visible. "I just want you to know
we're sorry. It was about Mama, that's all. We just wanted
you to be there when she was dying."

Skirata gave up trying to handle the welter of emotions.
He could see a red-and-white blur striding toward him, but
he didn't look up. "There's no point going over it now. We
did what we did, son, and for reasons that made sense to both
of us at the time."

Son. It slipped out. Ordo, helmet under one arm, moved
purposefully into the range of the holovideo pickup and put
his hand on Skirata's arm. It was a real hands-off-my-father
gesture.

"*Buir,* General Tur-Mukan needs to speak to you." Ordo's
tone was pointed, and maybe Skirata was imagining it, but
there was some emphasis on the *buir.* "She's about to leave."

It broke the spell. "Got to go, Tor," Skirata said. "Get that
data to me as soon as you can."

"*Buir?*" Tor asked. "He called you *father.*"

So how did you introduce your estranged biological son to
his adopted stepbrother? Skirata decided he wouldn't even
try. "Tor, this is one of my sons. Captain Ordo Skirata. Look,
tell Ijaat—tell him not to worry and that it's all going to be
okay."

Skirata closed the link abruptly and looked up at Ordo.
The Null managed to look both faintly disapproving and
guilty at the same time.

"Sorry, *Kal'buir.*"

"I wouldn't have known how to end the conversation anyway, son," Skirata said. "It's bothering you, isn't it?"

"Not exactly a joyous reunion."

"I'm not even sure Ruu's missing. They just don't know

where she is." Skirata decided to keep an open mind until he could hack into Ruusaan's bank account and see if it was still active. "She sounds like a restless spirit."

"I meant," Ordo said grimly, "that you're distressed by your sons."

"Are *you*?"

"If you want to be reconciled with them, we'll do whatever you want to ensure it's . . . trouble-free."

Ordo had never shown the slightest sign of jealousy as a kid. Each of the Nulls was—in that curious clone way—anxious not to have more privileges than his brothers; it was a way of avoiding conflict in a closed, stifling, wholly artificial clone society in Tipoca City. But the Nulls had also been genetically altered to maximize the potential for fierce loyalty in Fett's typical Concord Dawn genome. Their brutal infancy before Skirata rescued them had made that potential manifest itself fully, and if a Null liked you, he'd die for you. If he didn't, it was a good idea to run for it. They had no middle path.

"They're *never* going to take your place, son." Skirata gripped his arm. "And I wanted to tell him to *usen'ye,* but I have to be bigger than that, because a father's responsibility doesn't have an expiry date. I could have tried to stay in touch better than just transferring creds."

Ordo—very upright, thumbs hooked in his belt—tilted his head slightly. "They bled you dry and finally rejected you, and you still love them. Don't you?"

"I don't know, *Ord'ika.*" Skirata saw Etain making full speed on a collision course with them, two lightsabers swinging on her belt, and dwarfed by the huge concussion rifle slung across her back. "But if they hadn't, I'd never have had to take Jango's offer to train clones, and then I'd never have met you."

Ordo's head dropped a little. "And we'd have been euthanized, because nobody else would have thought our lives worth saving. If the tidy nature of fate is the point, I accept the argument, but that doesn't change what happened to you."

"Well . . . if you want something to shine bright, it has to

be polished hard." Skirata wondered exactly what Jango
would have done if he hadn't been there to stop Orun Wa
from having the Null kids put down. Jango talked tough—
was tough—but his callous attitude didn't extend to children,
however brutal it looked from the outside. "Jango might have
been a self-centered *chakaar,* but don't believe all that bluster about Boba being nothing more than his apprentice. He
wanted a *son,* no doubt about it. He knew what it was to be a
kid waiting to die, so I reckon he'd have given the aiwha-bait
a good hard *kov'nyn* and sent him on his way."

*Shame you didn't do a bit more for the other boys cloned
from you,* Jang'ika, *but I suppose you didn't have much pity
left after all that happened to you.*

Etain strode up and looked into Skirata's face. "What's
wrong?" she asked. "And what's a *kov'nyn*?"

"A head-butt," said Ordo. "A Keldabe kiss."

Etain wore a little frown of concentration. Skirata suspected she was memorizing every *Mando'a* phrase she
could, the better to be a good *Mando* wife in due course.
"Kal, the two of you are radiating trouble like a beacon. Can
I help?"

"Family strife," he said. "Your Jedi radar is pretty impressive."

"So is the strife," Ordo said cryptically, then squeezed
Skirata's bicep in parting. *"Ret', Kal'buir."*

Supply droids and repulsor trolleys began filling the deck,
transferring pallets of food, spare parts, and fuel cells from
stores to a replenishment shuttle. *Redeemer* was a heavily
armed warehouse. Etain and Skirata were about to go their
separate ways again.

"Any message for Veshok Squad?" she asked. "I'm paying
a field visit."

Skirata pulled out a packet of candied bofa fruit and
handed it to her. "Tell them to remember to brush their teeth
afterward."   •

"You miss them."

"Yeah." Skirata wondered what Etain was going through
being separated from her son so often. "In case you're still

wondering, I just spoke to one of my biological sons for the first time since he disowned me. It's never easy."

"It's your daughter, yes?"

"She's probably gone off on some adventure, but I'll find her anyway, just in case."

"I can't work out if Ordo's jealous or scared, but he's very upset."

"He's got nothing to worry about. That boy's my heart, and he knows it."

"Just let me get this straight, Kal. I did the sums. You were still supporting your kids financially when they were pushing thirty. None of my business, but I think you more than did your duty by them." Etain had an earnest little face dusted with freckles. Skirata sometimes found it hard to reconcile her durasteel will with that apparently fragile exterior. "The way you first described how they disowned you made me think they were still *children,* not grown men. And you didn't walk out. You were dumped."

"It was my rough *Mando* charm. Irresistible."

"I'm saying that you've got nothing to feel guilty about. I'm with Ordo on this. It's not healthy to be at their beck and call."

There was a small place in Skirata's mind where he knew that was true, but the rest of him felt he'd failed. Etain meant well. Like Ordo, she seemed only to want to protect him. "Now how about you?"

"I'm going to tell Darman about Kad when he comes back from Haurgab."

"Okay."

"And I'm going to leave the Jedi Order."

Skirata kept his reaction to himself. She'd sense it anyway. "Now?"

"No, but I'll know the right time. My work's not finished yet."

Someone called to her. A young lieutenant—not a clone, but a random human being—stood with one boot on the rail of a small armored shuttle. "General? Flight checks complete, ma'am. Ready when you are."

Etain gave Skirata a wink. "I'll make sure Veshok brush their teeth. Force be with you, *Kal'buir.*"

She walked away, still looking like an attachment to the conc rifle. He knew very few Jedi with a taste for the weapons of the ordinary soldier. So far, they'd all ended up in his motley gang.

Kal'buir. *She calls me* Kal'buir.

Skirata checked his comlink data display for files from Tor, and wondered what Ruusaan would call him when he found her.

6

As a Jedi, I was taught to preserve life. I led these clones—
no, these men—to their deaths. These were living, sentient
beings. What I have been asked to do is the opposite of
everything I was trained to do as a Jedi.
—Master K'Kruhk, in self-imposed exile on Ruul,
explaining to Mace Windu why he chose not to continue as
a general, shortly before returning to the
Order to fight again

Hadde forward operating base, Haurgab,
one and a half months later

"**W**hat happened, General—did we finally find something
worth pillaging from this planet?"

Etain just sighed to herself, but it wasn't directed at
Scorch. He knew that Etain was the most relaxed of generals
and didn't mind her commandos mouthing off. He shook his
head at the size of the Haurgab base, which had grown to
something approaching a small city itself, and wondered
why the GAR presence here was getting bigger rather than
smaller. This ball of rock wasn't worth the effort. If the locals
wanted to kill each other, Scorch could see no reason to get
in their way. The whole planet could turn Separatist and nobody would ever notice the difference.

"Ours is not to reason why, *ner vod,*" Sev said. "Bred to be
happy with our fate, and all that sewage."

"*Shabla osik,*" Scorch said. "Remind me to punch the next
dumb civvy that says that."

Scorch doubted he would ever get within punching distance of a civilian who knew enough about them to even say it, but it was a nice fantasy for a few seconds. Boss and Sev went off in the direction of the mess, and Fixer hung around like a little black cloud of disapproval. He examined the new ordnance.

"Yes, we should have put the civilian government back in the pilot's seat and withdrawn troops from here by now," Etain said. "But it doesn't seem to work like that. Grab yourself something to eat while things are quiet."

She strode off in the direction of the base commander's office. Inside a minute, there was a distant but deafening *whumppp* and the whole building shook. Scorch ducked instinctively as dust rained gently from the joists overhead.

"Incoming . . . ," a clone's voice called, feigning boredom, and everyone around laughed.

"Yeah, quiet." Fixer pried open an ammo crate with his gauntlet vibroblade and rummaged through the contents. "Regular spa retreat." He tutted loudly. "De-skilling, that's what this is."

"What is?" Scorch asked, thinking about his next meal. In this game, you grabbed whatever you could whenever you could, and as much of it as possible—food, sleep, water, laughs. There were a lot of clone troopers milling around, and he didn't recognize the unit flashes on a couple of them. Scorch didn't like not knowing things. He filed it mentally as something to catch up on later. "Going to lodge a complaint with the Galactic Union of Amalgamated Building Wreckers?"

Fixer examined the new Merr-Sonn entry grenade with sighing disdain. "Even a Weequay could use this."

"That's the whole idea, genius. You ought to suggest that to Merr-Sonn as an advertising slogan." Scorch took the grenade from him and attached the stand-off rod, then slid the grenade's housing over the muzzle of his Deece. A couple of troopers watched warily. It wasn't a smart thing to do inside a building. The device was designed to blow out doors from a safe distance—safe for the operator, anyway—to effect a rapid entry. "Personally, I don't mind trading professional exclusivity for an absence of pain."

Fixer held out his hand for the grenade. Scorch returned it, and the troopers appeared to relax again. "I thought you were a craftsman."

"I am. I just don't like being met with a hail of blaster bolts when I knock on doors, that's all."

Fixer slipped a couple of the grenades into his belt pouch. The two of them wandered off toward the scent of frying oil and hot sauce, removing their helmets to get a good deep lungful of the seductive aromas without air filters getting in the way. In the mess hall, white armor in various states of cleanliness, from snow-field to rolling-in-the-dirt, formed an unbroken sea except for a little craggy island of matte-black, burly Katarn Mark III rig. Etain was huddled at a table in conversation with Omega Squad.

"Thought she was heading to see the CO," Fixer said.

Scorch looked around for a splash of red and orange to spot Sev and Boss. They were in line, getting their plates loaded by a droid that seemed a little too obsessive about portion control for Sev's taste. Sev's voice carried across the burble and hum of mess-hall chat: "I need extra protein. Otherwise my aim wanders, and then I shoot tinnies. By accident, on account of being *starved*."

"She must have diverted." Scorch wanted to stay on the subject. "Well, she could hardly walk past Darman, could she?"

"It'll end in tears," Fixer said.

"Spoilsport."

"Seriously. It's not right. Clones shouldn't mix with officers. Let alone *Jedi* officers."

"What, in case we get ideas above our station? Don't know our place, to die nice and quietly so we don't upset the civvies?"

"You spend too long talking to Fi and those Null dingbats, Scorch."

"You've seen the average galactic citizen now. We didn't know any better on Kamino. If anyone's superior, it's *us*, not them."

Fixer just stared at him. It was the most dangerous thought Scorch had ever expressed. But he wasn't going to be made to feel he was less than fully human because he'd been hatched rather than born, because he'd seen plenty of natural humans now, and they weren't much to write home about.

He was the best of the best. He deserved the same respect as the next man, and maybe a little more.

"You're jealous of Darman," Fixer said at last.

"She's not my type." Scorch felt unaccountably angry. "But if you're saying I envy him for having the guts to live his life, not the life he's been told to get on with, then yes. I am."

"Di'kut," Fixer muttered.

Sometimes—too often, in fact—Scorch had nothing to do but wait, and thinking filled the time even when it was the last thing he wanted to do. He often thought about Skirata's new grandson. Clones, like all beings in the galaxy, speculated and gossiped.

"You reckon that baby is a clone's?" Scorch said at last.

"What baby?" Fixer targeted the menu suspended above the servery; they actually had a choice. Troopers parted to let him pass. "What's up with you today?"

"The baby Skirata brought into the barracks when Zey was away. His grandson."

"Snack-sized. Yeah. Why do you think that?"

"It's just weird to hand your kid over to a *Mando* who's fighting in a war. I mean, how bad must things be at home if the kid's safer with Skirata?"

"So why does it have to be a clone's baby? And maybe Skirata's family lives in the *shebs* end of the galaxy, so it's an improvement to have the old *shabuir* hauling Junior around minefields."

"Coruscant. Not exactly minefields."

Scorch thought of the baby's curly black hair and dark eyes. There was something . . . something very *familiar* about him. The kid could easily have been one of the younger clones back on Kamino, those baffled and serious youngsters who once stared at older clones like Scorch in the refectory. *That was me, not so long ago.* Scorch saw himself in their eyes: desperate to succeed, aware of yearning for something but not able to articulate it, feeling safe only among his immediate brothers.

Scared. Scared of everything.

"I think I'll have the minced nerf stew," Fixer said, like he was some kind of restaurant critic. Scorch couldn't recall if Fixer had ever had that wide-eyed look when they were kids. "You, Scorch?"

"Uh . . . whatever's the biggest portion. Chaka noodles."

Looking after a clone's kid was just the kind of thing Skirata would do. He'd been an assassin, a debt enforcer, any number of brutal and unpitying things, but he loved his boys to blind distraction. If any of them had found time to get a girl pregnant, he would take in that kid as his own kin.

"What if it's one of Omega's kids?" Scorch said.

Fixer turned his head slowly. He had to twist from the waist because his backpack frame was too high to glance over his shoulder.

"What are you yammering on about? Drop it."

"I said, what if the baby was fathered by one of Omega Squad?" Scorch tried to keep his voice down. "They're his favorites."

"Have you been drinking contaminated drive coolant again?"

"Okay, forget it."

Fixer was far more interested in his meal. Scorch turned very slowly to watch Etain and Omega chatting. It had been no secret when the two squads did joint ops on Coruscant that the general and Darman were lovers. Scorch had found that such a difficult concept to handle that he simply shut it out and reminded himself he didn't have time for anything but staying alive. He worried that he was getting like Fi. The smart-mouthed little *di'kut* had become a watchword within Delta Squad for doing everything a clone commando was supposed to avoid—he craved the outside world too much, he voiced his dissatisfaction, and he encouraged the same kind of dissent among his brothers. He was *subversive.* He should have known the only way out was in a body bag. What was it they were all told back in training? They had certainty, they had a purpose, and that was more than most beings ever got in their miserable lives.

Okay, so why isn't it enough?

"Might be Darman's love child with the General," Fixer said, seeming to tune back in to the topic. The droid slopped a brown liquid mass onto a mound of mashed vegetables. It would have needed a forensic test to confirm it was minced nerf in gravy, but this was still a long way from the bland nutrition cubes they'd been fed as kids and still carried as part of their dry rations. Hot, savory food was a luxury that Scorch never took for granted. "She disappeared to Qiilura for ages. Or maybe it's Captain Maze's, because he's such a smooth-talking rogue that no female could resist him."

Maze was an iceberg on legs, and a grumpy one at that. "Now *you're* the one drinking coolant . . ."

"I can have crazy theories, too. Can't get any crazier than that. I win. Now *eat.*"

They grabbed their trays and made their way to the table occupied—in the full military sense of the word—by Boss and Sev. Omega might have mixed with other brigades and ranks, but Delta still liked their own company, and whatever mood they conveyed to other clones usually made them want to sit somewhere else. Scorch wanted to wander over to the white jobs with the unit badge he didn't recognize and ask a few questions. But it could wait. He wedged his Deece and helmet between his feet and tucked into a mountain of noodles.

"So what's the General here for, then?" Boss worked his way through a pile of oozing red-fruited pie. "Other than visiting her favorite squad?"

"She hands out *candy,*" Sev said. "Every time she visits a squad in the field, she takes *treats* for them. Just like Skirata."

"Maybe he'll teach her to garrote folks as well as he does, too."

"She's been bleating about the number of men they've committed to this dump," Sev said. "I overheard General Mlaske say she's nagging Zey and Camas to withdraw the garrison and leave the locals to sort themselves out, because they'll be as much trouble for the Separatists as they are for us. Might tie them up here for free."

Fixer chewed. The table was silent except for the faint wet sounds of eating for a few moments.

"There's a sort of logic to—"

That was as far as Boss got. One moment the mess hall was lit by sunlight slanting through blast shutters set high in the walls, and the next Scorch was blown backward by an instant whirlwind of shattered duraplast into darkness and sheets of flame. Something smashed him full in the chest and winded him. It was the table. He groped for his rifle, but his helmet had gone flying, and he lay on his back trying to suck in breaths, succeeding only in swallowing dust that choked him. He couldn't breathe—

But he could hear. That was something.

The yelling began right away; no screams, just shouts to do this, check that, get medics. Scorch made a few attempts to sit up before he realized the table was still on top of him. Then the weight suddenly lifted. He was looking up at Sev through a haze of settling permacrete dust, so unsure of how long he'd been on his back that he checked the chrono display on his forearm plate and then realized he couldn't work it out from that anyway.

"Direct hit on the front entrance." Sev wiped his mouth on the back of his hand. His face was peppered with tiny beads of blood as if he'd had a bad time shaving. "You okay?"

"What happened to the perimeter defense systems? We're supposed to be secure here."

Sev hauled him to his feet but there was nowhere clear to stand. The mess hall was a mass of upended tables and chairs. It hadn't taken the full force of the missile, but the shock wave and debris had punched out the hall doors and flung anything that wasn't secured across the room.

It had flung metal trays like Kaski throwing-blades, turning them into lethal weapons. Scorch had that moment of trying to make sense of what he was looking at but not wanting to, because his brain was saying *Horrible, look away— no look, you have to, even if it makes you sick.* The trays had hit two men standing near the racks where they'd been stored, and one of them was in just his fatigues; a tray had taken off his leg at the knee. His buddies were kneeling beside him, giving him first aid. The other—they'd given up on him. The impact had sliced off the top of his head.

Some things in battle you shut out, and some you couldn't and would never stop seeing. Scorch felt this scene slot into his memory as if it would never fade. It was the incongruity of it, a scene of carnage with food and cups spread among the blood.

Then rage took him. He felt himself go from stunned slow motion to off the scale in a blink. *Nobody* expected to have to die while they were off duty trying to grab a meal. Out of all the death he'd seen so far, this was different, *he* was different, and he felt he'd tipped over an edge that he would never be able to draw back from again. He started sorting through the debris, flinging aside the plastoid tables, oblivious to everything around him except finding his Deece, locating the scum who did this, and blowing their brains out.

He was nearly at the shattered doors when he felt someone grab his right shoulder plate from behind.

"Scorch!" It was Boss, with Sev right behind him. Scorch was aware of frantic activity all around him and an alarm klaxon screaming close by, but he couldn't pay attention to it. It felt like it was all happening behind a transparisteel barrier. "Whoa there. You don't know where you're heading yet." Boss spun Scorch around and handed him his helmet. "And you'll probably need this."

Just being stopped in his tracks was enough to jerk him out of the blind rush to exact revenge. He found himself panting. The hall came back into focus; the sound was making sense now. The rest of his squad looked a mess, covered in fine dust, and then Omega came scrambling over to them, kicking chairs aside. Etain appeared from the other side, hair in a tangle but very alert.

"Everyone okay?" she asked. "Scorch, did you get hit by anything? Did you lose consciousness?"

"I'm not *concussed*," he said firmly. His voice sounded odd to him. Maybe he looked crazy to her. "I just want to kill the *shabuir* who did this. How did they get past the missile defenses?"

"I just raised the base security team," she said. "The security scanners show the trajectory of the missile, and it came from inside the city. Not from the rebel positions."

"Have they calculated a location yet?"

"To within one block," Niner said.

"Good." Scorch felt that they were staring at him, but even though he was back in control again, he still knew that only one thing would let him sleep tonight. "Time for house calls."

Treasury offices, Coruscant

"Ooh," said Jilka. She took Besany's wrist as if arresting her and yanked her hand up to inspect it. "That's *nice.*"

Besany should have known she could get nothing past Jilka Zan Zentis. The woman was a tax investigator. She could assess a defaulting taxpayer's net worth to the last cred just by sniffing him—blindfolded. She zeroed in on the ring that Besany had thought was discreet and understated.

"It's nothing."

"Doesn't look like *nothing* to me," Jilka said. Besany made an effort to herd her into a quieter corner of the archive area. "Looks like top-grade sapphire. Looks like you ditched soldier boy for a more upmarket model."

"Soldier boy," Besany said, feeling her throat tighten with temper, "has *not* been ditched. And I'm going to get Ordo out of the army." She swallowed hard, knowing it was unwise to say it, but she would *not* cover him up like some guilty secret simply because he was a clone. "We got married."

Jilka looked as if Besany had told her she was joining a Jabiimi terrorist group for a lark. "Can you even *do* that?"

"No law against it." At least it had distracted Jilka from a full assay of the stone. Besany willed her not to say that she couldn't marry a clone, because then she wouldn't be able to bite back a retort. "And I know what I'm getting into, before you ask."

Record droids whirred past in the corridor. "I haven't a clue what you're *getting into,* so I wouldn't ask," Jilka said. "And you don't talk about him much, so there's not much for me to warn you about anyway. Boy, are you *edgy* lately." She shrugged. "Well, congratulations. No nuptial cake to share?"

Besany was edgy all right. It wasn't just the small matter of slicing data from the Republic computer network on a regular basis. She'd almost grown used to the constant anxiety about that. It was the kriffing shoroni sapphires that were uppermost in her mind, possibly because they were so *visible,* and her data theft wasn't. She thought she'd put the problem to rest when Vau had the three gems recut into smaller stones for her by one of his dodgy Hutt contacts. That had shaved a lot off the value. But they were still worth millions, and they were almost impossible to trace. She'd weakened and had one made into a ring, to stop Ordo from feeling he'd been rejected. Once he was reassured that she'd have been as happy with a plastoid band, she'd sell it to raise hard credits.

It's wrong. I shouldn't benefit from this.

She kept the rest of the stones in her jacket, wrapped tightly in a small flimsiplast bag, because she wasn't sure what to do with them. One idea nagged at her like a begging child.

It's crazy. But someone I know has a very good use for those creds, for clones even Skirata won't be able to help.

"It's the war," Besany said, which was true.

"At least it'll be over." Jilka's eyes still strayed to the sapphire, but it was the cold appraisal of a professional calculating unpaid tax, not a woman admiring a bauble. "And it won't reach Coruscant."

"What makes you say that?"

"It just won't."

"I meant why you think it'll be over."

Jilka shrugged. She seemed to be picking her words, but Besany knew her well enough to know she was trying to avoid saying the obvious: that the Republic might have to give in to Separatist demands, because the war was stretching it thin. She would stop short of saying that clone casualties would be too high to carry on. That was too crass an observation, true or not.

At least she kept up to speed with the progress of the war. That was more than most.

"Costs too much," Jilka said at last. "Senator Skeenah's raised a question in the Senate about the large numbers of gunships being ordered that are taking too long to get to the front line. I think they've got a budget crunch, but the accounts are such a mess it's hard to know where to start."

Ah. Skeenah was a decent, moral human being who cared about the treatment of clone troopers. He was a few months behind Besany on this one; she wished he was less diligent. She didn't want attention drawn to the very area she was investigating. Maybe giving him the proceeds from selling the sapphires was too risky.

Start. Start?

"What do you mean, *start*?" Besany asked.

"Well, if he gets the Senate to back his call for a full audit, some unlucky person's going to have to do it."

Besany had always been good at covering her tracks.

For the past fifteen months or so, she'd mined the Republic's financial network for apparently routine data on exports and defense procurement, patiently piecing together a complex picture of ships being ordered from KDY and laboratory supplies heading for Centax 2.

"It'll be me," she said, wishing Skeenah had either shut up or started his finance crusade a lot earlier, when it would have given her better cover for her own activity. "And I could do without an extra project right now." Besany looked at the chrono on the archive wall and edged toward the doors with her box of datachips. "Got a lot to catch up with. See you later."

"Did you ever find that medical supplies company you were trying to track down?"

"No, I had to admit defeat on that one," Besany said, far too quickly.

Jilka would know that wasn't like Besany at all. Besany hoped she'd put it down to worrying about Ordo. When she was safely in her own office, she went through her daily routine of running a search for all new transactions on the Treasury ledger—sometimes as many as a million line items a day—and set it to look for defense and medical product codes. Anyone hiding those items probably wouldn't use them, but she had to start somewhere each day. She could refine them farther by delivery target dates; any expenditure was sorted by the quarter in which it was due to be drawn down from the budget.

What was she really looking for now, anyway? *Timetables.* She knew what was happening. She just needed as many clues as she could get for Skirata to decide when the time would be right to pull his boys out.

And me.

She'd never been to Mandalore, and she hadn't the first clue what a frontier existence on a backward rural planet might be like. As she glanced at her office-worker hands, soft and manicured, she decided it was too late to worry about that now, and concentrated on the scrolling lines of data in slight defocus, letting her eyes scan rather than trying to read.

The medical items weren't showing any pattern, but the defense procurement codes were clustering around the same period, about a month or two away. On its own, that was nothing; added to what she already knew, it just reinforced the time period that was becoming more apparent as the likely time for the big push. She made a copy of the defense budget data—perfectly legitimate in her current role—but transferred it onto her private datapad rather than her Treasury one for transmission to Skirata.

How much does he tell Etain?

Besany hardly saw her. It was just as well, because she wasn't sure what she could safely discuss with her. The two women could hardly sit down over a cup of caf and chat about the various scams she'd pulled. It was one deception layered on top of another, even within their own circle.

Besany stuck to her routine, going out at lunchtime to stretch her legs and transmit the data clear of the building. As soon as her encrypted system indicated that the data had been received, she deleted the files; the less time she had them on her 'pad, the better. A brisk walk around the plaza and a little window-shopping created the illusion that life went on as it always had for her, instead of the minutes ticking down toward the time when she would have to leave everything she knew.

As she walked, she felt the hairs on her nape prickle, as if someone was behind her again. She really had to shake this off. If she didn't, she'd be completely nuts soon. A casual glance over her shoulder confirmed, as it did almost every time, that there was nobody around but office workers on their meal break and shoppers, just like her.

These days, she saw clone patrols on the streets. It had started with a few outside main government buildings, and now she was seeing them daily, the same white armor she was used to, but some with blue sigils and plate detail, some with red. She made a note to ask Ordo who they were, and carried on shopping.

What matters more? An easy life, or doing what's right? You can *make a difference. So it's your moral duty to do it. That's what Dad would have done.*

She'd cope, because Etain would, and so would Laseema. They were all in this together. Back in the office, she leaned back in her chair and unlocked her terminal to begin today's task—real work, the stuff she was paid to do—checking a tip-off that catering contracts were being awarded to nonexistent companies, the credits pocketed by someone in the procurement service. It was a common scam in a big, complex budget.

"Just can't get the staff these days," she muttered to herself. "Okay . . . let's see . . ."

She accessed the Treasury database of registered companies, which was simple enough, but when she tried to crosscheck an entry with a CHA food hygiene inspection she hit a problem. Instead of lines of names, addresses, and registration numbers, she got only a portal screen; access was denied.

The system was usually more reliable than that.

"Jay-Nine," she called. "Jay?"

The support droid was usually wandering up and down the

corridor on this floor of the building, ready to be summoned to fix computer problems. He rarely had to be called. Normally, the sound of distant swearing was enough to summon him. She heard the faint hum of his repulsors as he glided down the corridor, the top of his dome just visible above the rail in the transparisteel wall.

"Agent Wennen," said the droid, hovering in front of her desk. "Problem?"

"I can't get into the CHA network, Jay. It's locked me out."

As soon as she said it, her gut knotted. *They've caught me.* In the weeks after Ordo had killed the Republic spy trailing her, she'd waited for that knock at the door or a hand on the shoulder to tell her the game was up, but nothing had happened.

"Central Tech took down the network during the meal break," the droid said. "They found what appears to be a virus in the system, so they activated the departmental firewalls. Nothing to worry about. All requests for data will have to be via comlink for a few days, that's all. Did you not receive notice of the shutdown?"

"Obviously not," she said. Relief of a kind flooded her, but it didn't stop that churning sensation that spread from her stomach and became a feeling of cold tension in her thigh muscles. "And why does neutralizing a virus take *days*?"

"We've never seen this before. It's very sophisticated. We're not even certain what it's *doing,* because it causes no disruption, but there's definitely something running across the network that wasn't installed by the Treasury and shouldn't be there."

I'll bet. Jaing and Mereel were gifted slicers. And she'd watched Ordo hack into the Republic Intel system with the ease of someone checking his stock prices. There was no magic or mystery in it, just the right inside information; almost every breach of security she'd ever investigated came down not to brilliant computer skills—although the Nulls *were* brilliant—but to someone being careless with passwords and verifications.

I opened the door.

I let the Nulls into the system within hours of meeting them.

She didn't regret it, but it didn't stop her from being scared.

And now she had a problem. Her access was severely limited, and the Treasury computer team had spotted that something was wrong. There'd be an investigation. Things would get too close for comfort. She was qualified in computer auditing, but the stuff Jaing could do—that was well outside her league, and she had no idea what he might have introduced into the system.

"Well, I'll just have to work around it, Jay," Besany said. "Have other departments been infected?"

"Still looking, Agent Wennen," said the droid.

It was all Besany could do to stop herself from making an excuse to leave the building to warn Skirata. She waited an hour so that if she was being watched, she didn't look as if she'd rushed to call someone as soon as she found her network access was down. Walking across the plaza in front of the Treasury building, she bought a mealbread stick from a vendor; then, casually as she could, she munched on it while she commmed Skirata.

"Kal?" she said. "I've got another one of my problems . . ."

Hadde, capital of Haurgab, half an hour after
the missile attack

Hadde was now enemy territory.

After months of regarding the capital as a safe haven, the GAR could no longer be relaxed about watching its back here. Darman provided top cover on Omega's patrol vehicle as it sped down the main road behind Delta's, both of them flanked by new Nek Pup armored gun platforms of the 85th Infantry as fire support.

"More of those guys from the Fourteenth," Corr said quietly. On either side of them, life seemed to be carrying on as normal, with shop awnings pulled down against the blistering afternoon sun and few citizens on the streets. The launch coordinates for the missile were in this neighborhood. "Look. Manning the right-hand gun."

The man looked like any other clone trooper, except for the discreet brigade markings. Darman tried to get a closer look. But his attention was needed on the street, to keep an eye out for trouble at ground level while the others scanned rooftops. The remote that Atin had sent out in front of them checked the route ahead for ambushes, trip wires, and disturbed ground, relaying images to their HUDs. The Hadde militia and civilian police had swept through a few minutes ahead of them.

"Are they some kind of special unit?" Niner asked. "Because I've only seen them in ones and twos. And that's odd. And we didn't know about them. That's even odder."

Etain, crammed into the seat behind Atin on the open-bay speeder, made a noncommittal grunt. "The Nulls weren't told about them, either."

"Is that a problem?" Corr asked.

"Well, it bothers *me,*" Darman said. "Seeing as they seem to know every time the Chancellor changes channels on HNE . . ."

"That's just talk to scare you, *ner vod.*"

"It's true."

"If the Nulls were Force-sensitive, too," Etain said carefully, "they'd be terrifying."

"Like they're not already?" Darman turned as far as he dared to look at her. *Fierfek, that's my girl. I've got a girl. I matter to someone in the outside world.* The heady sweetness of it distracted him for a moment. "I mean, they're our brothers, and we love 'em now that we know them better, but when they get that red mist—well, they scare me."

Corr sighted up fast on an apartment building, making Darman think he'd spotted something through the cloud of dust kicked up by the speeders. "They're only a danger to *aruetiise.*"

"Yeah, I'm more scared of Scorch at the moment," Atin said, but he didn't sound as if he was joking. Delta's speeder was fifty meters ahead in a wake of dust. "I think he's feeling it."

The road narrowed and they were in another neighborhood, all side streets and winding alleyways. They passed local Hadde patrols that waved them through intersections. *Feeling it* had become a shorthand throughout the Grand Army for the increasing agitation and hair-trigger anger that troopers experienced as the war progressed. Darman had his moments. Some nights—not many, but enough—he had nightmares; being engulfed in flames in the warehouse raid on Coruscant had come back to haunt him for reasons he couldn't fathom. It wasn't the shattered bodies on the battlefield or the faces of his first squad that disturbed him. It was the fire.

Poor old Scorch. Darman understood.

"I'll talk to him later," Etain said, adjusting her comlink earpiece. Her tone indicated that *talk* was going to be something a little more intensive. "Here we go. Cordon ahead."

Niner brought the speeder to a halt beside Delta's. Dozens of local militia milled around, heavily armed and watching every angle, but Darman still kept the repeating blaster on full charge. One of their officers jogged from the inner cordon toward Delta's vehicle. Boss redirected him to Etain with a jerk of his thumb.

"We sealed off the area within ten minutes, General," said the officer. "We might have lost them by now, but we've pinpointed one house as a launch site." He turned to indicate the road at his back and gestured left. "The street is shut off at both ends, as you requested. The houses are still occupied as far as we know."

"Haven't you checked?"

"No, ma'am. We left it for you. We didn't encounter any fire."

Etain didn't say anything, but her tight-lipped expression said she was underwhelmed by their commitment. Darman wondered why they didn't just arrest their own problem citizens and be done with it, but they were clear that they wanted the GAR to go in and kick down doors. And it couldn't have been because they felt Scorch needed the therapy. Darman bet that the show of GAR strength was a bracing reminder for any citizens thinking of going over to the rebels.

"Maybe the locals don't want to be seen dragging other locals away for questioning," Atin said, almost a whisper on the helmet comm circuit. The two squads could hear each other. "But it's okay for us to play the bad guys."

"He might just want to reassure people that we're here and we're cracking down," said Niner.

Corr had fallen into a new and totally un-Fi-like role: squad cynic. "Of course, it might also be that they're militia one day and rebels the next . . ."

"Can't trust 'em." It was Scorch. "Any of 'em. They'd all put a round in us given the chance."

Scorch wasn't joking. Darman could hear it in his voice. He could never predict what was going to be the final straw for anyone, and he wasn't sure why the attack on the base was any more traumatic for Scorch than previous missions. But it obviously was. Perhaps it was because Scorch associated the mess with sanctuary, and now even that haven was a battleground.

He'd ask him later.

"Okay, prepare to dismount," Etain said.

The eight commandos walked into the deserted streets under the cover of the two Nek Pups, split into two rifle teams. Darman checked the remote aerial view; there was nothing on the roofs, and nothing in the walled courtyards. Outside a door, a small dark brown animal of a species that Darman didn't recognize sat cleaning itself. He checked again and magnified the image.

In the rear courtyard of the largest house, a big patch of charred vegetation was clearly visible. It was easily big enough to be the downdraft burn from an Arakyd Huntmaster missile. You could haul those things anywhere and move them in minutes, and that was what had hit Hadde Base.

"Of course, the guy *could* have just had a barbecue," Darman said.

Sev cut in. "Well, let's go and check out his sausages, then . . ."

"I don't like this." Etain was still carrying the conc rifle, but this time she drew both lightsabers from her belt. One was hers, and the other was her dead Master's. *Shab,* had she changed a lot since Darman had first met her. But even then, back on Qiilura when she had been under cover for so long that she didn't even know there was a clone army, she knew that she didn't know it all, and she trusted her troops to put her straight. She activated one lightsaber and stared at the target building as if she was willing the doors to open.

"I can sense a lot of beings in these buildings . . . plenty of armaments . . . hostility. Let's hope they've got the sense to stay inside." She simply walked up to the doors—a bold move even for a Jedi—and hammered on them, lightsaber still clenched in her fist. "Grand Army—open up!"

"Wow," said Sev. "Bold. And *dumb*."

"Open up, or stand away from the door," Etain yelled. She had no concept of cover, but she was a Jedi, and she had her own early-warning system. Darman was watching her back anyway. He'd smack Sev later for the wisecracks. "Your call. Lay down your weapons and come out."

There was still no answer. Rapid entry with a Jedi wasn't quite the same as with a regular team, because she could sense things nobody else could, and when Etain cocked her head and then backed away from the door, Darman knew she'd detected something specific.

"Six or seven individuals in there, cannoned up," she said. "I'd hoped for a surrender. Never mind. Open the box, Dar. Let's see what we shake out."

"Ma'am," said Scorch, "permission to join the assault team?"

Scorch needed to do it, and Etain seemed to understand that. "Granted."

Darman was struck by how much more soldier she was than Jedi now. He liked that. She *understood*. It made him feel safe, certain that they were all going home in one piece. One Nek Pup moved up, its forward repeating blaster elevating to line up for a possible wall breach.

"Omega, *go*," Etain said. "Dar, stand by."

Darman had never used the Merr-Sonn breaching grenade before. The stand-off rod made his Deece feel oddly unwieldy, but at twenty meters he didn't think he'd miss the entrance. Atin, Corr, Scorch, and Niner stacked either side of the front doors, but much farther back than usual. Delta stood by as security, ready to deal with fire from other locations.

As Darman sighted up he held his breath for a moment, it was suddenly so quiet even with the steady burble of the Nek Pups' drives that he could hear a baby crying somewhere. Etain jerked her head around.

"The kid's streets away," Darman whispered. He could see it had distracted her. "We're fine. On your mark."

Etain gave him a grim, close-lipped smile as if she was going to burst into tears. It was just a second, no more. Then she was her old self again.

"Take it out," she said. *"Fire."*

Darman squeezed the trigger.

It definitely beat shooting out the doors from point-blank range. The rod struck the metal plating, and the sheets blew apart with such neat precision that there was just a loud explosion and a flare of dust before the doors simply fell in through the opening like an entry ramp. Scorch threw a grenade hard through the opening, the squad rushed the doorway, and the firing started.

Blue-white blasterfire lit the doorway and windows like a chain of pyrocrackers. Darman switched to blaster mode again and got ready to pick off any troublemakers, but overwatch wasn't a role he felt comfortable with when his squad were clearing a house.

I got separated from my squad at Geonosis.

Why he was thinking about that now, he had no idea. The flashing and cracking of blasters stopped suddenly. Then there was a massive *whoomp* and the roof of the two-story building erupted, sending tiles raining onto the street in a ball of dust and splinters. Etain ducked; debris diverted from her in midair, a neat trick if you could do it. Darman felt it rattle on his armor.

"*Shab,* Scorch . . ." It sounded like Corr. "Happy now?"

"Omega, we're clear." Niner's voice filled Darman's helmet. "Four live prisoners, three dead."

One Nek Pup moved in close to the house to provide cover while the other stayed focused on the silent homes around them. The neighbors weren't exactly craning their heads out the windows to watch. Three men and a woman came out with their hands on their heads, stumbling and unsteady, with Corr, Atin, and Niner at their backs, DC-17s aimed.

"Missile launcher in the rear lean-to," Niner said, "and plenty of rifles, mortars, and anti-armor rounds. Hey, someone get the militia to take these jokers, okay?"

And then Scorch came out.

He was dragging a body—a burly male, from the looks of what was left—by one leg. That was no mean feat even for a fit commando. He dumped it in the center of the street between the Nek Pups, making no attempt to maintain cover, and went back into the shattered building.

They could have left the bodies for the militia to sort out, like the damage to the houses on either side. Darman went to help him, but Etain stopped him with a touch on his arm.

"Just cover him," she said. "I wouldn't step in now if I were you."

She felt something nobody else could. But you didn't have to be a Jedi to know that Scorch was in trouble. Darman heard Sev mutter something, and Boss responded, "Negative, Sev. Don't."

It took him several minutes, but Scorch hauled out all three bodies and arranged them neatly in a row. Darman thought that was the end of it, an act of closure that the locals would note, and remember that helping out the rebels—if it meant attacking GAR personnel—was a dumb idea that would end in tears. As hearts and minds went, it was definitely negative. But Darman could see why Scorch wasn't in the mood to hand out candy to local kids.

Was it only two years ago that I wanted to save the locals from the wicked Seps on Qiilura? Wow, talk about being naïve . . .

Scorch, Deece held one-handed, cocked his head as if he was studying the haul of dead belligerents. Darman thought he was going to walk away, at least satisfied if not purged, but instead he took aim and sprayed the bodies with blasterfire. Darman heard the same intake of breath from at least three other helmet links. Then, as soon as he'd started, Scorch

stopped, pulled off his bucket one-handed, and spat elo-
quently on each smoking pile of remains; Darman didn't realize Scorch had that much spit in him. When he was
finished, he put his helmet back on and walked over to the
nearest Nek Pup to sit down on the running board.

"Just as well we got the right house . . . ," Corr muttered.

Folks around here would probably see Scorch's display as
contempt, a message—as if it needed underlining—that you
didn't mess with the Republic. But Darman saw a brother
who had been tipped over the edge and couldn't articulate his
anger any other way, maybe just temporarily, maybe for
good. Darman had seen it once or twice with clone troopers,
and how their brothers had swept up the pieces and kept
them together, but he didn't know what happened to the ones
who couldn't snap back to rights after a break. He thought of
what nearly happened to Fi, and realized he could guess.

Etain gestured to the militia waiting on the barricade to
move in. "Okay, the local force can clean up and search the
rest of the houses, just in case. Probably better if we stand
down now." She seemed to take Scorch's reaction calmly.
"I'll go see Scorch."

She sat down on the running board next to Scorch and
took his gloved hand in hers, which made Darman feel a little odd. He caught some of what she was saying. She was
telling Scorch that she understood, and she could make him
feel better for a while, as long as he didn't object to her influ-
encing his mind to get him through the rest of the day. A faint
click in Darman's ear interrupted his eavesdropping, indicating someone had switched to the squad-only comm frequency.

"Everyone okay?" said Niner. Darman knew what he
meant. He wanted to know if anyone else was going to lose
it like Scorch. " 'Cos let's talk about it if you're not."

No, you never knew what was going to get to you, and
sometimes it was the least expected things.

There was a sudden *pee-yong-pee-yong* sound and Atin
snarled.

"*Shab,* some *chakaar* taking potshots."

They all wheeled around to locate the position. There was

someone on a roof on the other side of the street. The guy from the 14th opened up the Nek Pup's repeater, and his first burst took the rain recycler off a nearby roof before he managed to concentrate his fire on the same place as everyone else. They'd already sighted up, returned fire, and withdrawn behind the barricade by the time Atin worked out that the round—a projectile—had been stopped by his armor.

"I'm okay," he said, sounding embarrassed and trying to twist his neck far enough to get a look at the gouge in the paint on his shoulder plate. "Mark Three armor, my best buddy . . . *shab,* that would have ruined my day."

"Nice shooting, *mir'osik,*" Darman called to the gunner from the 14th. Even a Weequay could have hit the target at that range. "Who the *shab* trained you?"

"Flash-trained," the trooper said, deadpan.

"Well, tell Flash he's *osik* at training . . . look, you want some marksmanship remedial class? Just ask."

"Leave the poor white job alone, Dar." Corr, relatively fresh from the meat-can ranks himself, sprang to the defense. "First deployment."

We were great on our first mission. What's his excuse?

Actually, it hadn't been great at all. The Jedi generals, utterly untrained, hadn't a clue. Half the commando strength at Geonosis had been killed, deployed as basic infantry, in the wrong place with no air support. Darman shut up. Corr had a point.

"Sorry, *ner vod,*" Darman said. "When did you leave Kamino?"

The trooper hesitated for a moment, as if he'd forgotten. He took off his helmet to wipe his forehead, and the expression on his face was one of very brief disorientation, not an attempt to be evasive.

"We arrived at HQ a few weeks ago," he said.

"I bet it's still slashing down with rain in Tipoca. It never stopped. Never a clear day. *Ever.*"

The trooper's frown deepened. He flipped his helmet over between his palms as if he was about to put it on again. "Bone-dry when I embarked," he said. "Don't recall it raining at all."

"Let me check your calibration," Atin said helpfully, and climbed up on the Nek's turret.

Darman was so thrown by the answer that he didn't even snap back with a smart one-liner about the trooper needing more time on the practice range. No rain on Kamino? Maybe the man's powers of observation were as bad as his aim.

Etain appeared from behind him. "Problem?"

"Yeah, that guy from the Fourteenth said it never rained on Kamino."

Etain scratched her cheek, looking preoccupied. "Is he being ironic?"

"Didn't strike me as the witty type." Darman's senses were still finely tuned to anything out of the ordinary among his brother clones, and if the 14th Infantry didn't know even the most basic *Mando'a*—if they came from a Kamino where it never rained—then there was something *wrong*.

And he was a poor shot. Darman had never seen any clone that inaccurate, not even the young kids.

"Do you think he's a spy?" Darman said, thinking of the two covert ops troopers he'd killed. They were just like him, and yet they'd been sent after their own brothers. "I'm just paranoid after Gaftikar, that's all."

"If he is," Etain said, "then he didn't graduate top of his class."

"It's still *odd*." Darman put his helmet back on and switched to a secure comm channel. Skirata needed to know about this. Small detail was the fabric of the bigger picture. "Better report it."

"Dar, there's something I need to discuss with you."

Skirata's channel was busy. Darman found his patience wasn't quite what it had been two years ago. "What, *Et'ika*?"

"Not here."

"Are you really telling Zey that we should pull out of this cesspit?"

"I am, yes, but—"

"Good. This is a waste of time when we could be taking on high-value targets."

"Okay." She looked suddenly weary. "I agree."

"What was it you wanted to talk about, then?"

Etain, hands on hips, stared down at her boots. "It'll keep," she said.

As soon as the militia confirmed they had the house searches under control, the small convoy headed back to Hadde Base. Darman waited for Etain to pick up where she'd left off, but he had the feeling he'd interrupted her train of thought yet again, and she'd forgotten what she had to tell him.

It couldn't have been important.

7

*We've invented a Separatist threat that's bigger than the
reality. The claim of quadrillions, quintillions, and even
septillions of Separatist battle droids is so ludicrous that
we'd rush to debunk it if someone didn't have a vested
interest in making us believe it. Nothing adds up—literally.
Do you know how big a quadrillion is? Let's use the
Galactic Standard notation—a thousand million* million.
*A quintillion? A million quadrillions. A septillion? A billion
quadrillions. Any coalition capable of producing even
quadrillions of* any *machine could roll over the Republic in
a few days. And the amount of materials and energy needed
to produce and move even a quadrillion droids is
immense—it would drain star systems. Either our
government is composed of innumerate idiots, or it's
inflating the threat way beyond the average citizen's math
skills so that it can justify the war and where it's heading.*
—Hirib Bassot, current affairs pundit, speaking on HNE
shortly before being found dead at home from alleged
abuse of contaminated glitterstim

Kyrimorut, Mandalore, 995 days ABG

Jusik pointed to the wall at the far end of the compound,
along the length of a strip of tape stretched in a straight line
across the dirt.

Fi, wearing just a pair of shorts and looking deeply uncomfortable, stood with his arms folded across his chest in
his I'm-not-playing mode.

"Walk that line, Fi. Off you go."

Fi took a breath as if he was going to object, but turned and started walking. Jusik and Gilamar stood behind him and watched his progress, recording his movements with a handheld holoscanner. Jusik couldn't help noticing that the device had a stenciled mark on it: PROPERTY OF REPUBLIC CENTRAL MEDSUPPLY.

"Nice piece of kit," Jusik said. "Free gift from a grateful Republic?"

Gilamar chuckled to himself but didn't look away from the small screen. The monitor was capturing reference points on Fi's body—spine, joints, skull—and analyzing his movement and posture. "Well, they left it loafing around," he said, "and I had a patient in need." He put one hand in his belt pouch, eyes still fixed on the monitor, and drew out a couple of small but expensive-looking instruments. "Stylus scanners. Encephaloscan and neurochemical assay. Best in the galaxy. State of the *shabla* art."

Fi reached the end of the compound, did a pretty good about-turn, and then began walking back again.

"You stole it all," Jusik said.

"I *liberated* it," Gilamar corrected. "The taxpayers can afford it, seeing as they're not paying for clone rehab centers. I've just got to locate a few more portable diagnostic tools and assorted toys, and we can have a pretty good field medical facility here. You never know what state those boys are going to show up in when the time comes. And brain trauma's common."

"I wasn't criticizing," Jusik said. "I was *admiring*."

Jedi weren't above appropriating goods and cheating their owners in the cause of justice, of course; Jusik had heard many accounts of Jedi Masters commandeering vessels and pulling other dubious tricks without the slightest thought of recompense for the owner. He couldn't see any difference between that and Gilamar's pillage of the Republic's medcenters for a socially purposeful cause.

"You'd be amazed what you stroll off with if you can talk like a medic, wear the right outfit, and know how to misuse medcenter security," said Gilamar. "I nicked a complete operating table once."

Fi finished his test walk and stood with his chin lowered, waiting for the verdict. "How did I do? Can I get dressed now?"

Gilamar turned the small holoscreen so that he could see it. "That's you, compared with one of your brothers at his peak fitness. See?" The screen, as far as Jusik could tell, showed percentages. "That measures how much your gait wobbles, how far you stride, how much bend there is in your spine, all that kind of biometric stuff. Look."

Fi frowned slightly as if calculating. "Eighty-nine percent, just over."

"Eighty-nine point two percent correlation with the benchmark," said Gilamar.

Fi let out a long sigh. "Oh well . . ."

"What do you mean, *Oh well*?"

"I'm never going to be a hundred percent."

"Never's a long time, *ad'ika,* and eighty-nine percent of a clone commando is probably about a hundred and fifty percent of a randomly conceived human. You're the luxury model of humankind. You can afford to lose a few points."

Fi didn't look convinced. "So I'm better than a mongrel. Great."

"Get dressed and we'll do your cognitive tests."

Fi trudged off into the bastion, and they followed. Jusik felt he'd failed him despite the huge progress he'd made. He was prepared to spend the rest of his life healing him, if that's what it took. But he was a Jedi, with a reasonable expectation of a longer life than a regular human, and Fi had drawn the short straw on life expectancy.

Healing took it out of Jusik. It was increasingly exhausting. The improvement in Fi's condition had been dramatic at first. But now it was marginal, the kind of changes that had to be measured with sophisticated equipment.

When Fi's happy—well, that's the only benchmark I can trust.

"It can take years to see any kind of improvement, and plenty of folks never recover," Gilamar said as they stepped into the main accommodations from the utility area, wiping their boots out of reflex because Rav Bralor had told them she'd skewer them if they messed up the new floors. "But it's no good telling him he's made an incredible recovery, because he won't see it like that. I've seen the sequence of brain scans. He had damage to at least two separate areas. How he ever survived at all—well, clone lads are built from Jango, and he had a tremendously robust physiology. Fi's still got damaged areas in the forebrain, though, and that's what's causing the memory blips and the temper."

Jusik considered how much effort had gone into getting Fi this far—saving just one man—and despaired at the numbers he would never know or be able to help. "He wants to come back to Coruscant with me and see the squad."

"Maybe that's what he needs." Gilamar consulted his looted medical sensors again. "I'd still love to know how you did it."

"I don't really know." Jusik healed by visualizing. He saw the fabric of the body at its most basic level, the ruptured cell walls and tangled proteins, and imagined them whole and straight again. It felt the same to him in the Force as the way he harnessed energy to Force-rip a door off its runners. "I have theories. I always do. I like to think of it as a mix of micro-telekinesis and stimulating the body's natural healing mechanisms."

"How precise is it?"

As a Jedi, Jusik had been taught to trust his feelings, and not to think. He never completely learned that lesson; he refused to, because he knew he could think very well indeed, and the Force wouldn't have manifested itself in him if it hadn't had some use for that intellect. And if the Force had no purpose—deliberate or accidental—then he wasn't inclined to let it rule him.

He grabbed a slice of fruitbread from the conservator, chewed slowly, and realized he had never been a very Jedi-like Jedi.

"As precise as I can imagine, *Mij'ika*."

"Well, when I *acquire* the right kit to do brain scans at neuron resolution, I'd better give you a crash course in brain anatomy. Then you can be very, *very* precise." Gilamar held out his hand for a share of the fruitbread. His armor was almost the same shade of dull gold as Skirata's, gold for vengeance, but he wasn't from the same clan. It was a personal statement. "You're even smarter than you think, *Bard'ika.*"

"The Masters at the academy told me that I thought too much and asked too many questions."

"Well, that's what any secret cabal that doesn't like its authority to be questioned *would* say."

Jusik couldn't resist the urge to ask. "Why the gold armor?"

"There you go again with the questions."

"Sorry. Didn't mean to pry."

"It's a fair question. I fell in love with a Mandalorian girl, married into the clans, and a *hut'uun* killed her. I know his name. I'll find him. And then I'll show him what it means to make a bad enemy of a Mandalorian with anatomical expertise and a scalpel."

The dark side could be very dark indeed in Mandalore. Jusik didn't shy from it. "May she find rest in the *manda.*"

"Do you believe in that possibility?"

Jusik saw nothing incongruous about the *manda,* the Mandalorian collective consciousness, the oversoul for want of a better word, even if he knew most Mandos didn't take it literally. "I use the Force, Mij. I'm prepared to give a lot of things the benefit of the doubt."

"Do your old buddies think you're lost to the dark side now?"

"Probably. I just wish they'd stop worrying about light and dark, and learn the difference between right and wrong instead."

Gilamar laughed loudly. Jusik was glad he could get a laugh out of him after making him remember grief, but he suspected that the man never forgot it for a minute.

"What's the joke?" Fi asked, appearing in the doorway. He was wearing his gray undersuit, no plates. "Is it the one about the Hutt and the trash compactor?"

"Just conjuring tricks." Gilamar took out his datapad. "Now see how far we get with this today." It was a program that flashed up images of objects, from the everyday to the obscure, and Fi had to name them. He still had a problem with that, and it seemed to be the source of much of his frustration. "And don't say *thingie,* because *thingie* will not do, soldier."

"I'm not a soldier anymore," Fi said quietly. His eyes flickered as the images scrolled. "Table . . . anti-armor round . . . bantha . . ."

No wonder he felt like a child again. He was doing better, but it was all about what Fi regarded as normal for Fi, not the average human male. Jusik tried to imagine waking up with no Force powers. He'd still be smart and capable, but with his extra edge missing he'd feel blind and deaf, he knew.

"That's an improvement," Gilamar said, showing Fi the collated results. Jusik didn't know if they made any sense to him. It was all numbers. "You're one of nature's miracles, even if you do need a haircut. Now let me check your blood."

Fi submitted to the probe pressed into his fingertip, watching Jusik with one eyebrow raised until Jusik got the hint and gave him some of the fruitbread.

"Sergeant Kal used to tell us every day that we would do the best because we *were* the best," Fi said, chomping enthusiastically. "Good enough isn't good enough."

"He didn't mean it that way, Fi." Jusik ruffled his hair. He'd spent so many hours with his hands on Fi's skull, healing him, that he knew the contours of it better than his own. "He was instilling self-esteem."

"Only way from *best* is down."

"Oh, you *are* a little ray of sunshine today, aren't you?" Gilamar said, tapping Fi gently on the nose like a naughty akk pup. Gilamar was a mercenary, and he'd trained some fearsomely hard men, but sometimes Jusik could see the physician he'd once been. He doubted that Gilamar had ever been the simple country doctor that he claimed, though. "Now, look at your progesterone levels. Still higher than normal. Are you pregnant? Have you been throwing up?"

"No. But I get cravings." Fi frowned. "Will I get stretch marks?"

Jusik always paused now to work out if Fi was being funny or if it was some odd disconnection in his brain. It had become a weather gauge of his recovery. But this was the old Fi, back for a while.

Gilamar kept a straight face. "Yeah, say good-bye to your figure. Everything sags from now on in."

Jusik rejoiced silently at Fi's improved mood. "Is the progesterone a problem, *Mij'ika*?"

"No," said Gilamar. "Every human's got progesterone. Males can't make testosterone without it. But it might explain how you've been able to get Fi's brain to repair itself—it's been shown to aid healing in brain trauma. Your Force shenanigans might be stimulating secretion."

"You'll have to bill me later, *Bard'ika*," Fi said. "I'm a bit *boracyk* until payday."

Jusik took out a cash credit and shoved it in Fi's hand. Creds—largely untraceable—were no problem in the alternate morality of Skirata's renegade gang. Jusik was only occasionally surprised at how quickly he'd come to see it as acceptable. "*Ba'gedet'ye.* Here's something to tide you over."

Fi studied it. "Did you rob a bank?"

"No, Vau did."

"Where am I going to spend it? Nearest shop is Enceri, and I can't drive a speeder . . . yet."

There was a heartfelt plea in the statement. Fi was imprisoned here without transport. "Parja can drive you in the meantime."

"She's had to powder my *shebs* like a baby too often. It's time I grew up again."

Fi got up and rummaged in the conservator, head down. While his back was turned, Gilamar mouthed a silent warning: *He needs a break.* Jusik nodded.

"Well, I must be going—I've got an embryologist to threaten." Gilamar pulled on his gauntlets and helmet. "The barve said he'd have the research ready for me today." He winked at Jusik. "We're getting there. Nothing definitive yet, but we'll have a *very* good data library for Uthan to work from."

Fi watched Gilamar go and stared at the doors for a long

time afterward. "Talking of pregnant," he said, "Dar still doesn't know about Kad, does he?"

"No," said Jusik.

"It's wrong. It's not fair to him." Fi stood up. "Can we go to Keldabe? I can't keep hanging around Parja's workshop. She's got a business to run."

Jusik knew that Parja would have thrown the business out the window and lived on water and dead borrats if she had to choose between the workshop and Fi. But Fi wanted to be out and about. Keldabe seemed to do him good, even if it sometimes seemed overwhelmingly complex to him.

"If you're good," Jusik said, "I'll let you take the speeder controls. And you can visit the barber. But no brawling if we run into Sull."

Fi grinned "It's just like old times."

Yes, it was. They were just two young men having a day on the town. It didn't matter at all that one had been a Jedi and the other had been a clone bred to serve him.

Mandalore was like that. It was a great leveler, and a fresh start.

Special Operations Brigade HQ, Coruscant

"How have you been keeping, Kal?" Zey asked.

Skirata sat down without being invited. Zey knew him well enough by now not to take offense at his lack of respect for rank. He'd even laid out caf. Outside the window, a platoon of clone troopers selected for commando cross-training were being put through unarmed combat drills by Tay'haai and Vau. Vau kept saying he wasn't GAR personnel any longer, but it was awfully hard to tell. Where would any of them have ended up without the army?

"Not bad, General," said Kal.

"You had your leg fixed, I see."

"It was slowing me down."

"I'd ask how the family was, but that would put you on the spot, wouldn't it?"

"Not really." Skirata took a gulp of the caf. Zey was probably still angling to find out what had really happened to Fi. Why did it bother the man so much? He didn't care what happened to clones, except in that theoretical Jedi way. Skirata decided to lob in a verbal grenade, just to show Zey that mundane beings could beat Jedi omniscience. "My daughter's still missing."

Zey did a freeze-and-turn that told Skirata he hadn't been expecting that, and didn't feel the need to hide his reaction. "I didn't know you had a daughter," he said. "I'm very sorry. Can we help?"

"When I say *missing*," Skirata went on, satisfied at having scored a point, "I mean that she appears to not want to be found. Ruusaan's over thirty, so she can look after herself."

"How do you know she's all right?"

"She was still using her identichip up to a month ago."

"How do you *know*?"

"I'm her father, and fathers know that kind of stuff." Skirata wondered if it had been a good idea to remind Zey that his skills ran to slicing into secure records. *Shab,* Zey knew the kind of stuff the Republic asked the Nulls to do. Zey was the one who did the asking, obliquely enough to be deniable, of course. "Just keeping a watchful eye and all that."

"I meant your grandson. When I asked about family, that is."

Skirata had never taken Kad anywhere near Zey for fear of the Jedi sensing the baby's latent Force abilities. Skirata didn't trust Jedi not to abduct and indoctrinate him, and he was never sure if gossip about Etain and Darman ever reached Zey's ears. The man heard a lot more than he let on.

"Kad's terrific," Skirata said carefully. "He's into everything. A real handful. Look, I can see this social chitchat is a trial for you, General. What do you want?"

"The Treasury needs some special Null expertise."

Skirata felt his gut somersault. If he hadn't already had warning from Besany that Jaing's spyware had been detected, it would have done a lot worse. Zey must have felt his reaction in the Force. It was too strong to miss.

"Yes, I know they're not where they should be, Kal," Zey said, guessing wrong. "My professional blind eye is still turned to their extracurricular activities, whatever they might be."

The nice thing about the Force was that it was so *vague*. Etain had told him that. All Zey knew was that either the mention of the Nulls or the Treasury had made Skirata jumpy, and he opted for Nulls. *Ha. So much for omniscience, Jedi.*

"I have such wayward kids," said Skirata. "What do they need to do?"

"Jaing and Mereel are the information technology specialists, aren't they? They've certainly cracked a few Separatist systems."

And yours. "Correct."

"Then I need them to investigate a very clever program that was installed on the Treasury mainframe. It erased itself as soon as the technicians started trying to isolate the code, and they have no idea what it was doing, but it shouldn't have been there, and Intel fears a Separatist sleeper in the camp."

"Okay, I'll call them in and you can brief them. Who's vetting the Treasury staff? Do they have any idea where it was introduced into the system?" Skirata actually needed to know. If Zey could sense his panic and urgency, he wouldn't be far wrong. "It might be a long shot, even for my boys, but they'll do their best."

It could be worse.

Zey nodded. "The Treasury wants its own senior auditor on the job, too. Some woman called Wennen."

Then again, maybe it couldn't.

Skirata's immediate reaction was that Zey was shaking him down. He *knew;* or at least he looked as if he knew. "So you want us to look for spy programs and dodgy staff."

"Yes. I'm recalling Omega and Delta from Haurgab, and not just to stop General Tur-Mukan from nagging me to death about the fruitlessness of the operation. They've both done urban ops here and they know how to hunt operational terror cells. Apparently Intel were involved in something at the Treasury that didn't pan out, and to which I'm not privy, so word's come down from the Chancellor's office that they want the job done right."

"Nice to see they have faith in Special Operations."

So now Skirata knew something that Zey didn't: that Intel had sent some hapless spook after Besany, a spook who never made it home again. Skirata, proud of his well-honed paranoia, juggled a range of scenarios in his brain that began to feel like the hall of mirrors at the Republic Day carnival. Was Zey shoving him into this position to force a confession, knowing about Besany's and Jaing's involvement? Or was he an unknowing instrument of Intel, and they knew now what was happening? It had the whiff of a technique that Jaller Obrim favored—breaking down family murder suspects by getting them to do a news conference begging for their loved one's safe return.

And Jaller says he's amazed how often they can sail through it . . .

There was always the possibility that it was an honest and logical coincidence. Jaing and Mereel were the best at slicing. Besany was the senior agent for defense budget investigation, and if the Seps wanted to glean any information, it wouldn't be data about street cleaning in the lower levels. And yes, Omega and Delta had operated undercover on Coruscant, the only Republic commandos who had, and they were way better at it than Intel's bantha-brained operatives.

It made sense, but Skirata's gut said that setups always did. How could he refuse?

He couldn't. But he could shake Zey a little and see what fell out. Pretending that Besany knew nothing of the Nulls would be too big a cover story to maintain. The operation at the GAR procurement center was too easy to check out.

"I know Wennen," Skirata said. "She was on an undercover op and my boys crashed into it. Bit of an awkward moment, but it all ended friendly enough. Not a face any man would forget, either."

"Oh, she won't mind the Nulls trampling all over her turf, then." Zey betrayed no reaction. He really did sound as if it was just an annoying concession to keep the Treasury quiet. "Some civilians can be very *judgmental* about clones."

And Jedi can't, of course. "Yeah, I hear Master Vos is *judgmental* about our lads, too." Skirata seethed; come the glorious day, arrogant *shabuire* like that would be the first up against the wall. "I'll get right on it."

"Do you really think of them as your boys?"

It was one of those out-of-the-blue questions that Zey was increasingly prone to. Skirata couldn't work out if he used it as a tactic, or if his job had become so stressful that he had a million things buzzing around his head the whole time.

"They're my sons," Skirata said. So what if the man knew he'd adopted the Nulls? It was *Mando* business, outside the petty rules of *aruetiise,* and nothing Zey or even Palpatine did or said could change the fact. "And I'd die for them."

Zey refilled his caf and didn't look up. "That's very moving. I realize how much you care for them."

"No, I mean they *are* my sons. Legal heirs. I adopted them under Mandalorian law and custom."

Now *that* caught Zey with his *kute* around his ankles. He blinked a couple of times, seeming lost for words. Skirata noticed how gray he was looking now, and not just his hair.

"Well, I can't think of a regulation that prohibits it," Zey said at last, and winked. "And if I could, you'd just ignore it."

"I'm glad we understand each other, sir," Skirata said, and left.

Covering his tracks by randomizing his route back to the apartment had become routine for Skirata now, which was a bizarre irony in itself. He changed speeders, took different skylanes, and even walked. As he set the speeder of the day to pick up the skylane's automated control, he commed each Null and summoned Besany. Maybe Jusik would make it back from Mandalore in time, too. This wasn't quite a crisis meeting, but it was definitely more than keeping up to speed. He had to implement the standby for *ba'slan shev'la* now— the Mandalorian tactic of strategic disappearance, vanishing to regroup and pop up again when least expected.

No, this is making a run for it.

I'm going to need to break it to Omega now.

Who else? Who else can I safely tell now *that there's a safe haven for them if they want to desert?*

Skirata's mind raced. Omega had a vague idea that there would be a future for them, but they didn't know the full story of the hunt for gene therapy, and Skirata had never actually spelled out that he wanted them to desert, to do a runner. He had no idea how they'd take it.

And Zey . . . he wanted to hate the man as easily as he'd hated other Jedi, but it was impossible not to see Zey as a man stuck in a system that stank, trying to influence it from the inside, and who'd never chosen his path in life any more than the clones had.

Don't go soft on them. A Jedi can walk out. A Jedi can say no. Bard'ika *did.*

After a fuel-wasting detour or two, noting the extra clone troopers on duty outside public buildings, Skirata landed close to the Kragget and walked the rest of the way. It was like going home. *Home* was something he hadn't defined for many years, not even narrowing down a planet, but the Kragget and the apartment now felt almost as safe a haven as Kyrimorut, maybe more so; the bastion on Mandalore wasn't full of armor noises, cooking smells, and boisterous conversation—yet.

He cut through the restaurant, scanning quickly to see who he didn't recognize, a *Mando* habit that had stood him in good stead. He knew all but three of the diners, and two of them were in CSF uniform, cops on their meal break.

Captain Jaller Obrim sat at his usual table, working through a pile of nerf strips. The two men exchanged casual pats on the back.

"What's up?" Obrim asked.

"That obvious, eh?"

"Yes, Kal. It is."

"Things are getting a bit *warm.*" If Skirata couldn't confide in Obrim—a man who'd bent every single police regulation to help Skirata, not to mention the law itself—then he could trust nobody. "You know my *vacation* plan?"

"Winter sports, you mean?" Obrim knew about Kyrimorut, even if he didn't have the exact location. "Got a firm date in mind yet?"

"Might be earlier than expected. Before the big melt."

"Ah."

"Yeah."

"Why don't we have a chat somewhere quieter, Kal? Maybe I can give you some skiing tips—"

A conversation interrupted them, and they both turned at the same time. Laseema had appeared with a tray of meals, working her shift even though she didn't need to. The Twi'lek insisted on earning her keep. At a table near the kitchen doors, a man—one of those Skirata hadn't recognized, the one in civvies—said something to her. She put the tray on a vacant table.

Skirata only caught scraps of the sentence.

". . . hey, I was just being friendly. You Twi'lek girls . . . well, it's kind of nice for us patrons to see your—"

The man had his arm resting on the table. He didn't finish the sentence. Laseema drew a blade from nowhere and slammed it into the tabletop, pinning his sleeve with a loud thud. She reached forward with her free hand and grabbed his collar, almost pulling him out of his seat.

"Listen, *shabuir*," she hissed. "Us *Twi'lek girls* . . . I'm not your entertainment, I'm not your sport, and I'm not for sale, understand? This *Twi'lek girl* can cut your *gett'se* off."

In the second's absolute frozen silence that followed, Skirata heard two things: the distance tuneless whistling of someone working in the kitchen, and the rasp and whir of a dozen blasters being drawn from holsters—CSF regulation-issue—and charged to fire. Every cop in the restaurant had drawn his weapon and aimed. Skirata had drawn, too, without even thinking.

"Is that the time?" said Skirata. "My, son, I think you need to get back to the office. *Now.*"

Laseema pulled the blade out of the table and stepped back. The man got up and left, which was probably his only option under the circumstances.

"No tip?" Laseema called as the doors parted to let him escape intact. "Tightwad."

She picked up the tray as if nothing had happened and went on serving meals. Everyone resumed eating. This was no longer a restaurant for casual visitors. It was a CSF and GAR canteen by default, and it was a bad place to hit on the waitresses.

"Kal, you have some awe-inspiring daughters-in-law," Obrim said, sliding his blaster back in its holster. He mopped up the sweet melted fat on his plate with a chunk of meal-bread. "To think that girl was too scared to speak when you first found her."

"I have an uncanny knack for helping folks realize their full potential," Skirata said. "I'll catch you later. CSF Social Club?"

"Eighteen hundred hours. See you then."

Skirata headed to the rear exit, the least observable route to the apartment. As he passed Laseema, she gave him a smile, and he paused.

"Besany's with Kad," she said, anticipating a question. "He keeps saying *Da-da*. It's his word today. Etain sent a holomessage, and he was completely mesmerized by it."

"I was going to ask how *you* were."

"Never better, *Kal'buir*."

"You sure? That *chakaar* . . ."

"I've never had the choice of saying *no* to a man before." Laseema had the most beatific smile, as if she'd had some wonderful vision. Skirata knew all too well what happened to Twi'lek girls from poor families. They were for sale, and nobody lifted a finger to stop the trade. "It feels good."

Skirata was going to train her how to defend herself, but it looked as if Atin had beaten him to it. It wasn't the first time that he'd wondered why he was still fighting for the Republic, given how thoroughly corrupt it was to its core. If Zey and his Jedi pals thought that Grievous was evil, then they hadn't looked too closely under the Republic table at which they sat.

"Not long now," he whispered. "Before the year's out, we'll be gone. Chin up, *ad'ika*."

Tonight they'd finalize plans. When the time came to run, they'd have minutes—not days, maybe not even hours—to get out.

In the end, it didn't matter if the Republic won or lost the war. The people Kal Skirata cared about most would be crushed between the warring factions either way.

GAR Station Nerrif, Mid Rim, 996 days ABG

"I vote," Corr said, "that the minute we get back to Coruscant, we get the chiefs of staff, the defense committee, and that oily *mirshebs* Palpatine, line 'em up against a wall, and show them the business end of a Deece."

The transport waited to dock at Nerrif, maintaining a three-hundred-meter separation from the other transports waiting to land at the space station. Niner, arms folded across his chest and apparently asleep, creaked a little as he moved. Etain watched her squads with a concerned eye. Scorch's recent fall from the grace of his usual relaxed detachment had worried her.

"That's mutinous talk, Private," said Niner. "And you haven't got a vote."

Atin patted Corr's shoulder. "I'll hold your coat, *Cor'ika*."

"Well, it's dumb. It's just *dumb*."

Corr always had an opinion. Etain had learned fast that the commandos were freethinkers and pretty vocal, but the speed with which the rank-and-file troopers adapted to a less circumscribed life took her aback. She expected them to be like cage-farmed nuna, not entirely sure what to do when someone opened the cage and tried to shoo them out. White jobs, as the commandos called them, didn't take long to work out that they could fly when given the chance.

"Why's it dumb?" Etain asked. "Not that I don't agree with you."

"About giving the government a nice bracing volley of blasterfire?" Corr asked.

"Well, it was disapproval of the conduct of the war, actually, but . . ."

"It's not mutinous, anyway." Corr directed his ire at Niner. "Contingency rules. If they're not fit to retain command, we can boot them out. Even slot them."

Etain was mildly interested, but she wanted to hear Corr's views on Haurgab. "Really?"

"*Cor'ika*, we've got a hundred and fifty *shabla* contingency rules, everything from arresting the Chancellor if he goes gaga to reducing key allied worlds to slag if they switch sides," Atin said. "Including shooting the whole Jedi command if they go over to the enemy. It doesn't mean you have to go out and do it now."

"Come on, Corr," Etain said. Contingency orders were long, tedious lists of worst-case scenarios, and she didn't want to hear all 150 again. "Spit it out."

"Well, if you want to make Haurgab people love us, then you can't just send in special forces to blow the *osik* out of the place, especially as the government there is as bad as the other side. They need AgriCorps Jedi and engineers. Give 'em a reliable water supply and some crops, and they'll all calm down."

"He's got a point," said Atin. "When did we ever try anything other than head-on confrontation? With anyone? All that happens is we end up fighting on more fronts and spread all over the chart. You don't believe me? Go look at the deployment schedule. Map it on a holochart, like the one they've got at HQ. Look."

Atin activated his holoprojector, and their small corner of the crew cabin filled with complex threads of light dotted with planets in three colors: red allies, blue enemies, and yellow neutrals. Then he changed the sort criteria, and the schematic of the galaxy became a totally different picture. The red dots showed deployed Jedi commanders, with purple dots indicating non-Jedi nonclone commanders— *mongrels,* as the squads called them—and green dots their forces. The pattern was very spread out, with a lot of dots in the Outer and Mid Rims.

"*That's* what's killing us," Atin said. "I know we've been banging on about it for a year or more, and so have the Nulls, but this is just keeping the war ticking over. If we concentrated on one strategic target at a time and really brought one theater under control before we moved on to the next, the war could have been over by now."

"Could have lost it, too." Etain suddenly felt them all staring at her, even though she couldn't see their eyes behind the helmet visors. "Just saying. Could have gone either way."

Corr snorted. "Yeah, and *we* might even be better off under the Seps."

"I agree that it looks *flawed*," she said.

"It's so *flawed* that it looks as if all they're trying to do is to maroon as many generals in as many stupid places with inadequate support as they can."

It didn't look good. It never had. All Etain could care about now was making sure that her boys—there she was, falling into Skirata's terms, Skirata's thinking—made it out alive. She thought about Commander Levet, and Bek, and Ven; she never forgot their names, and she reminded herself to check if Ven survived, and how Levet was doing. Levet said he liked the idea of having a farm, having seen them at close quarters on Qiilura.

Clones could think outside the confines of their military world, all right. Once they did, they weren't dumb and happy with their lot. She thought the only reason General Kenobi talked about them like a proud akk owner was that he couldn't admit even to himself that the Jedi Order was complicit in a thoroughly evil thing. But at least he didn't refuse to use their names, like General Vos seemed to. Etain found it increasingly hard to find common ground with some of her fellow Jedi. She could see the Order foundering, unchanging over the centuries, hidebound by esoteric arguments about the unseen mysteries, and yet blind to its own moral decline in the real world.

Master Altis must think that way, too.

She thought of the very *un*-Jedi Jedi who had shown up to help the war effort, the ones like Callista, who had families and lived a life without a Temple or the rules of the Council. Mainstream Jedi regarded Altis's splinter group as dangerous. But for all their heresy, they didn't look remotely tainted by the dark side.

That was why she'd asked Callista to meet her here. There was a third way.

"Prep for docking," said the pilot's voice over the intercom. "You're off watch, and I'm not, you barves . . ."

"Shower, food, sleep," said Darman, prioritizing.

Atin shook his head. "Food, shower, sleep."

"Sleep," said Niner. "Then more sleep."

They looked at Corr. "Glorious revolution, then installing a military junta," he said. Etain stared, not at all sure about his hidden depths, but he laughed. "Or a nice big plate of minced roba patties. I'm easy."

The transport docked, sending a little shudder through the crew bay as it settled on its dampers on the hangar deck. Etain jumped down from the hatch and stood back to count out the squads—Omega, Delta, and Vevut. Vevut had been trained by Rav Bralor; it showed. They behaved like sons eager to please their mother.

"Come on, General, let's get you fed and watered." Dec, their sergeant, began steering her in the direction of the mess. "You won't be fit for much without some decent *skraan* inside you."

"I'll join you later," she said, checking her chrono. "Two standard hours, relief crew area, for briefing. I'll even stand you an ale in the mess."

Darman hung back. "When exactly are we shipping out again?"

"Tomorrow."

"Good."

"I told Zey that Triple Zero could do without you for another day, because I wanted you all to get a clear eight hours' sleep for once."

Darman just grinned. "I'll do my best."

"I'll bet." It was as good a time as any. "And anyway, I need to talk to you without the squad around."

"I don't mind. I don't have any secrets."

"It's private. *Really* private."

Darman's grin crumpled for a moment and what returned was an anxious smile. "Okay. Am I going to need a few ales to sustain me?"

"No." *Oh, fierfek. Yes, you will.* "You don't like ale anyway."

Etain turned and walked away before she ended up blurting it out there and then in a busy transit area. The last thing she needed was half the galaxy knowing she had a child. The urge for confession burned her up. Every moment she didn't come clean with Darman made it worse.

It shouldn't have been this way. It was all her fault, all her doing, but there had to be something wrong with a system that put two people in the positions that Etain and Darman were in.

She found Callista pacing around in a quiet corner of the med deck, one level below.

"Sorry if I kept you, General," she said. "I was just seeing if I could help. Quite a few wounded troops passing through."

It took Etain a few moments to realize she meant medical help. "Doing a bit of healing?"

"I'm not a good healer, but I try. A little bit of mind influence to lift their spirits seems to be what I do best."

"Do you ask their permission?"

Callista looked faintly offended. "Of course."

"Yes, you would." Etain's question had already been answered, but she went on anyway, because she needed to talk to another Jedi who wouldn't make pious noises about helping her get back on the right path. "I've come to see you about your funny little ways, as you put it."

"Something tells me you're not here to lecture me on our deviance."

The two women looked at each other in silence for a moment or two, tasting the subtle ebb and flow of the Force around them. "Not exactly," Etain said. "I'm not the kind of Jedi the Council wants as its arbiter of adherence to the tenets." *Go on, say it.* "I have a child they don't know about, and a lover I shouldn't have. I'm still serving in the Grand Army, but I can't carry on like this. Before I give up being a Jedi completely, I want to know if I can salvage any of my calling."

Callista put her hand on Etain's shoulder. "You want to join us? You know what'll happen if you do. We're effectively the lunatic relative that they don't talk about."

"Would I be accepted? What do you expect of your adherents?"

"Well, your family's welcome. You never need live a lie, for a start."

"You have a lover?"

"Of course. What's life if you shun the most powerful influence for good that any being knows?"

Etain wondered how Darman would fit in as the non-Force-using other half in a community of Jedi. Then she realized she was making yet another decision for him, assuming control, assuming that she knew best—just as she had when she decided to conceive.

"If I were to come to you, would we be obliged to live in your community?" Etain asked. Callista leaned her head as if she was struggling to hear her. The idea was already beginning to look like a bad one, and Etain's voice dipped accordingly. It was ludicrous to think that she could think of being a part-time Jedi, occasionally popping in to do a bit of Jedi work with Master Altis and his sect. "The father of my child might have to be based elsewhere."

Callista looked bemused. "I can't speak for Master Altis, but I can't imagine him turning you away if you wanted to spend any time at all with us."

Etain found it almost shaming that Altis and his people would throw their lot in with the Jedi Order to fight alongside them when they were effectively shunned by it the rest of the time. She was also shamed that the Order was happy to have them back on board when it suited them. She was starting to think like Jusik.

"I think I shall spend some time with you one day," she said. A few weeks was all she had in mind, just to be certain that she wanted no more to do with the Jedi path. "If you'll have me."

"This is very sad, you know."

"What is?"

"That you have to be so miserable simply for being a normal human being, Force-user or not. Master Altis says the Jedi Order has become more like a corporation than a spiritual body, all rules and infrastructure and committees. To continue the analogy, he says that the Order has lost sight of its core business, which is simply doing the right thing for others."

Etain thought of the Jedi Temple and its vast Archives,

technical facilities, and apparently limitless budget. Yes, it was hard to see where it had all started.

"I wish I could say we're stagnant," Etain said, preparing to leave before she poured out all her frustration and resentment on this woman. "But I feel we're decaying."

Callista gave her a polite nod. "One day, come visit us and bring that baby of yours. We'd love to see him."

As Etain walked back to the main mess deck, she couldn't recall mentioning that she had a son. It might have had no significance, just a better pronoun to use than *it*, but perhaps Callista was sufficiently Force-sensitive to tell.

She suddenly craved Darman's company. Nerrif was a huge station, a docking platform and resupply base for a quarter of the Mid Rim, and when she finally reached the mess, Omega weren't around. The deck was a sea of strangers, mostly clone troopers, with a scattering of gray-uniformed nonclone officers and a couple of Jedi Padawans. When she reached out in the Force, Darman felt peaceful and distant. He almost always did; sometimes it was hard to tell if he was awake or not from his impression in the Force. She commed him. It took him a few moments to respond.

"Dar, where are you?"

" 'Freshers, K-deck."

"The steward droid booked me into the officers' quarters, not that I asked for that. Private cabin, not a mess deck, so find cabin seventeen sixty-one, N-deck. I'll meet you there."

Darman's voice sounded suddenly husky and self-conscious. "I've missed you, too."

Etain could be slow on the uptake, she knew. Poor Dar; he was expecting a little diversion by way of romance, not the biggest shock of his short life. She'd have to play this carefully. "Talk first," she said. "Catch up on lost time afterward. Deal?"

"Okay."

She got to her cabin before him and waited, trying to meditate. Being a Jedi required maintenance. It was a set of skills, she realized, and once she stopped using them, they went off tune. She spent so long now in the mundane world that she rarely meditated, and even her kinetic skills needed sharpening up. Her duties were much less combat-oriented now. She had to get up to speed again, if only for basic survival purposes.

She could still sense Darman's presence long before he rapped on the doors, though. She kept that skill very sharp indeed. He still felt remarkably innocent in the Force, not exactly the child she'd first mistaken his presence for on Qiilura, and the bright optimism had definitely tarnished, but it wasn't shot through with dark vortices of anger and passion like Skirata's yet.

Scorch, though . . . she thought of Scorch, quiet despite the raw blazing fear and anger that she'd calmed at Hadde, and hoped the Force would spare Darman that. The war was grinding down even these soldiers, despite a genome selected for its potentially abnormal resistance to stress.

"Et'ika?"

"Good navigation. Come in, quick." She could sense nobody nearby, but the last thing she needed was to be spotted inviting one of her men into her cabin. "Did you get something to eat?"

"I lost the GAR record for bolting down ten roba sausages washed down with half a liter of caf," he said, setting his helmet and rifle down on the upper bunk. The cabins were cramped, the kind with washing facilities that folded up into the bulkhead. "Corr trounced me. The man's a sarlacc on legs. I hung on to the SO Brigade All-Comers' Pie-With-Unidentified-Fruit-Mush-Filling record, though. You can still be proud of me, *Et'ika*."

Darman had an utterly disarming smile. It made Etain feel worse, because the trust just shone out of him. She would be contrite. She would beg forgiveness. And he had to be told, but she worked up to it gently.

"I really like Corr," she said. "I'm astonished how political he is, how much he *thinks*. He's really rather *subversive*."

Dar began detaching his pack and armor, stacking the plates beside his helmet. There was no such thing as a quick change for a commando kitted out the way the RCs were. "Yes, us simple clones can even count, and we is *happy* to be dumb, yes *sir,* just churn us out and line us up in the shooting gallery, because we don't feel a thing . . ."

Etain was mortified. She hadn't meant it like that. It was simply admiration of Corr's ability to shake off the indoctrination that told him the only purpose of his life was to lay it down for the Republic. "Dar, you know I'd never even *think* anything so disgusting." She grabbed his hand. "You believe me, don't you? I'm not a bigot. I meant that—"

"I know. It's okay. Sorry. Just a bit fed up."

Darman was the most laid-back of men, so some mongrel must have said something out place to the squad. If she found out—well, if she found out it was a Jedi officer, she'd go and give them a very un-Jedi bawling-out they'd never forget.

And now she had to tell him.

"Dar, I love you. You know that, too, don't you?"

"Are you working up to telling me something bad?"

"Not exactly *bad.*"

"Because that's how Sergeant Kal used to start when he had to scold us as kids. *You know I love you, son, but you mustn't do that again.* But he *does* love us, so it's okay."

Etain knew now why Jedi—her brand of Jedi, anyway—feared attachment. She was now totally out of control of the situation, unable to be serene. Love messed you up something rotten. But she still wouldn't trade it for anything, including her next breath. It was the peak of her existence.

"Dar, I need you to listen to me." Etain took his arm. She wanted to grab him by both shoulders to keep him facing her, but he was too tall. "Dar, I'm going to tell you something I should have told you a long time ago. Please don't be angry with me, even though I deserve it."

That got his attention. "Is it Mereel?"

"What?"

"When I'm away."

Etain was shocked silent for a moment. "Fierfek, Dar, never! No, nothing of the kind. I'd never betray you like that." She'd been at this point so many, many times, and she hovered on the brink again. It was agony. *Do it. Tell him. Do it.* Stang, did he really think she'd cheat on him? "Dar, the reason I was away on Qiilura for five months was . . . I was pregnant. I had a baby."

As soon as the words escaped her lips, she could almost see them hanging in the air. They had a life of their own, form and meaning, reality and potency. However many times she'd picked up Kad and held him, he had never been more real than at this moment, even light-years away in someone else's care.

Darman just looked at her. She *felt* him: he was suddenly as blank as his expression. It was a bombshell. It had stripped all thought from him.

"What?"

"I had a baby."

They were the wrong words, but that was how they came out. Darman was struggling, blinking as if he was trying to process an alien language, looking her straight in the eye but not connecting with her. A vast chasm had opened up between them.

"It *died*?" The words escaped in a breath. "Oh, *Et'ika* . . ."

She wasn't expecting *that*. He'd totally misunderstood. She'd used the past tense, and it had thrown him. He didn't even ask if it was his. It was as if he didn't connect their relationship with the possibility of a child.

What did I expect him to say, after what I've done?

"No, Dar, he's fine. He's beautiful. He's yours. He's *ours*."

Darman's eyes never left hers. He stopped blinking and drew in a breath with his lips parted, like someone about to sneeze or cough. Etain couldn't even feel which way he was going to jump. She was now terrified. She knew it would shock him, but it had completely winded him.

"You never *told* me?" he said at last. "You never thought to *tell* me?"

It was far worse than that, of course. Did he even need to know she had planned it? Yes, he did, because she couldn't live with any more lies. He and Kad were her whole life now. There could be no secrets.

"I realized that if I told you I was pregnant, you'd fret, and you don't need any more worries when you're at the front." There was no purpose to be served by telling him Skirata had stopped her. She'd deceived Darman from the start, planning to conceive, making him think there was no risk of pregnancy. It was her fault: she would face the consequences alone. "And then I didn't know when to tell you. And I was scared of the Jedi Council finding out, for all kinds of reasons—they'd kick me out, they might take Kad away from me—"

"Is . . . is that his name?"

"Yes. Kad. I named him Venku when he was born, but then you said you liked Kad as a name for a son, remember? When . . ." Etain trailed off. She remembered when that conversation had taken place, and wished she hadn't reminded him. The eruption was coming. "We were talking about names."

Darman had superb recall. Not perfectly eidetic, like the Nulls' enhanced memories, but he could remember just fine. *When.* When Skirata had introduced Kad to the squad as his grandson. Now *Kal'buir* was in it up to his neck, too.

"That was *my son*," he said. Etain could hardly hear him. He was almost saying it to himself. *"My son."*

"It's okay, Dar." She reached out again and tried to take his hand, but he didn't grip hers in return. She was too scared to try to hug him now, although she wasn't sure what she was scared of. He now looked like a spring about to uncoil. "We'll make it work now, Dar. I'm *sorry*. I'm so sorry. I shouldn't have done any of this, I know it, but I so wanted you to have a son, to have some kind of future. That's what Mandalorian men want, isn't it? Heirs."

Darman didn't seem to pick up that it was deliberate and Force-shaped on her part, but that was like failing to notice the snowstorm when the avalanche had brought down half the mountainside. He simply took a step back from her, and cupped both hands slowly over his mouth and nose, as if he was trying to avoid inhaling something.

"Dar?"

He straightened up with his arms at his side. "Am I the last to know that was *my son*?" He looked as if he was replaying all the conversations from that day when they stood around in Besany's apartment admiring the new addition to Skirata's family. Skirata had even formally adopted Darman, in that on-the-spot, one-line, instant Mandalorian way. And Darman had told her he wasn't ready to be a father. If he was recalling all that, he must have been in turmoil now. But she could sense almost nothing from him. "Etain, did *everyone know except me*?"

"No. Just those who needed to know for Kad's safety."

Darman paused, staring at the bunk in defocus, and then began reattaching his armor plates. "Everyone except me and the squad, then."

Etain had no reason to think he would ever hurt her, but in that way of all very strong, very muscular men, he had a presence that could either be reassuring or menacing, and right now he scared her inexplicably. It was the silence—both kinds, the lack of sound and the lack of emotion in the Force. He fumbled with his helmet, and then seemed to give up on sealing it, tucking it under one arm.

"Dar, when you're ready to talk about this . . . ," she said.

He turned to the doors. "I just need to walk for a while," he said, voice hoarse. "Clear my brain a bit."

She listened, holding her breath until she couldn't hear his boots in the corridor any longer. Then she opened her comlink, and called Skirata to let him know what she had done.

8

Of course clones suffer. What makes you think they don't?
They've been at war continuously for more than two years
without a break, and it's been a hard war. Battle stress isn't
an if, *it's a* when; *if the GAR were made up of average*
humans, you would simply not have a functioning army
now. Clone troopers are optimized humans, and only two
percent of the population could ever be as tough, resilient,
and aggressive as these men are. But grind them daily like
this, give them no respite, deprive them of sleep,
give them no outlet or support—and even they *will*
break down eventually.
—Dr. Mij Gilamar, *Cuy'val Dar* and medical adviser to
Special Operations Brigade, assessing the Republic
Department of Defense claim that clone troops would not
suffer battle stress like other humans because they knew no
other kind of life, and were bred for it

Transit mess deck N, GAR Station Nerrif,
1910 hours GST, 996 days ABG

The benefits of a fully enclosed helmet had never been more apparent to Darman than now. He could sit and rage in full sight of any passing trooper, and as long as he didn't move, nobody would be the wiser.

There was little privacy in these temporary barracks. Omega Squad huddled in an open four-berth cabin area, icons of relaxed calm to anyone watching, but inside their *buy'cese* was a private arena for a painful conversation. The only drawback was that body language had to be suppressed;

but that was a skill all clones learned the moment they realized they could retreat inside their armor and create a private space that the Kaminoans couldn't enter. Darman wondered how many Jedi generals knew that the familiar *Copy that* . . . was nothing like the comments shared between brothers on private circuits out of officers' earshot.

"*Shab,* Dar, what are you going to do?" Atin asked.

"I don't know." Darman hadn't managed much more than that in the past hour. He didn't even know yet if he was angry. The closest comparison he had to this feeling was when Jay, Vin, and Taler got killed, once the immediate blind struggle to survive had passed—disbelief, numbness, a physical ache in his chest, and a complete inability to think straight. "I just don't know."

"He doesn't have to *do* anything." Niner fell into sergeant mode, trying to be the voice of reassurance in a crisis. "There's nothing he *can* do. The baby's a fact. It's being looked after. There are no regs that say he can't father a child. And Etain isn't going to sue him for child support credits, is she? So all he has to do is come to terms with the fact that she kriffing well had his kid and *didn't bother to tell him.*"

"Nothing major, then," Atin said, arms folded tight across his chest. It was a good way to avoid making gestures that would give outsiders any clue to what was going on. "He can just feel betrayed. He can manage that."

Corr had kept his mouth shut throughout the argument. He might have been annoyingly gabby on less personal topics, but he knew when to butt out. Dar felt he glimpsed the real man at those moments. He liked him all the more for it.

Darman ventured into territory he was reluctant to even think about. "*Kal'buir* knew."

"Yeah, but you said Etain would be in serious *osik* if the Jedi Thought Police caught her." Niner seemed to be going for mitigating circumstances. "And don't they take Jedi babies? She had her reasons."

But she *had* told him, and Kad wasn't any less at risk. The assumption was that the baby was Force-sensitive, or whatever they called it. That didn't make him a Jedi. Darman longed for a few sensible words from Jusik. He'd have the answers, and if he didn't, he'd still have some wise words on the situation that might make Darman see the positive side and a way of picking up again from here. It struck him that his first thought wasn't to pour his heart out to Skirata.

"Dar," Corr said carefully, "don't you *want* the kid?"

"Yes, I *do*." It just slipped out. "I didn't think I'd be interested, but he's *mine*. It means there's more to me than just what's sitting here. I can't explain it very well. All I know is that it matters. It makes me someone different."

Regular humans grew up knowing what families were, what parents did, even if they didn't have one. In Darman's wholly artificial world on Kamino, during the years that mostly shaped him, Darman had worked out something vital; that there was such a thing as a father, and Kal Skirata filled that gap in his life. He'd seen Jango Fett from time to time—and his son—and known that he was grown from the man's cells, but he never felt the connection with him that he felt with Skirata. Humans were just like any other creature in the galaxy. Their instinct was to breed and look after their young, and cloning humans and growing them in vats didn't change that one bit.

"I bet Ko Sai would have been shocked that her predictable clone units had such messy lives," Corr said. "She wouldn't have liked that at all."

"Shame she's dead, then. Would have been great to see her reaction."

Niner clicked his teeth in annoyance. "Well, you can forget the practical problems, and we can get you through the bad feelings. We always have. *Vode An,* right?"

Actually, Niner was wrong. He was *very* wrong. Darman was in a place he'd never been before, and it was about more than suddenly finding he had a child out there somewhere. It was about trust. The galaxy was all lies, and even his job was built partly on deception, but as long as there was one area that he knew was real and that wouldn't crumble under him, he felt safe.

That part wasn't Etain. It was *Kal'buir.*

"He knew," Darman said, "and he never told me."

"Kal?" Corr asked.

"Why *wouldn't* he tell me?"

"Because he knew you'd go off the deep end like this."

"Don't I have a right to know? I mean, he always told me I was a man with the right to control my own life, but now he decides what's good for me and what isn't."

Niner cut in. "Give him a break. *Kal'buir* wasn't the one who got pregnant and kept quiet about it."

"Well, if he had a reason for not telling me, it's either because he thought I was too stupid to handle it, or that Etain's problems were more important. I mean, it's not like I'd tell anyone else, is it?"

"Or," said Niner, "maybe he decided that because you and Etain *are* two adults, he was staying out of your private business."

It made sense. Niner always did. But it didn't placate Darman one bit. He was starting to find definite thoughts solidifying in the fog of painful emotions, and three of them loomed like rocks: that he wasn't trusted by people *he* loved and trusted, that he wasn't sure now if he could trust *them,* and that he had a nameless, formless, desperate animal need to see his kid, even if he wasn't sure what a father in his position was supposed to do.

Well, he could hang on to that. And he knew what a father's job was. He'd had what he thought was the best role model in Skirata, although doubts about that now gnawed at him.

He checked the incoming transmissions on his HUD. If he chose not to answer on the voice channel—or couldn't—the data could be stored as text to be read later. Skirata had been trying to raise him on the secure link. Etain had just left a reminder that they were embarking for Triple Zero—Coruscant, Corrie, Trip Zip, whatever she wanted to call it, because he didn't care right now—at 0600 GST.

He wasn't snubbing either of them. He just hadn't worked out what he wanted to say, let alone how he was going to react to the answers.

"It'll be all right, Dar," Atin said quietly. "Ups and downs of being with females. We'd have learned all this by stages if we'd been born the regular way on Corrie."

Darman was inclined to listen to Atin. Niner was just Master Theory about women, and Corr's romances lasted as long as he was in town, thanks to Mereel's influence. Atin had Laseema, and he knew the score even if he never had to worry that there was a kid out there he didn't know existed.

"Things used to be simple," Niner said, but it sounded as if he was talking to himself.

Things did. But life wasn't simple now, and Darman understood the occasional bliss of being ignorant.

Growing up at twice the speed that nature intended hurt in more ways than he first thought. It hadn't given him time to toughen up his heart.

Arca Barracks gymnasium, Coruscant, 0630 hours,
997 days ABG

Vau seemed to be in his element again. Scorch hesitated to use a word like *radiant* for a hard old *chakaar* like his sergeant, but the man looked like he had some blood in his cheeks for the first time in ages.

"You think *that* hurts?" Vau grunted. He had an unlucky trooper in an eye-wateringly painful grip on the floor. The *di'kut* should have known better than to volunteer for the demonstration, but he obviously didn't know Vau, and thought he was dealing with an old guy. He was. But Vau was an old guy who kept fit and knew plenty about pain. "No, *this* hurts."

The trooper squealed. It took a lot to get a reaction out of a man like that. They might have been meat-cans, but they were as hard as any ARC or commando. Scorch couldn't watch any longer. He called to Vau, more for his own peace of mind than the urgency of Zey's summons or to end the trooper's agony. Vau's technique was known as a Keldabe handshake, but hands didn't have a lot to do with it.

"Sarge!" he yelled. "Sarge, General Zey sends his compliments and wants to see you right *now.*"

Vau let go of a delicate part of the trooper's anatomy and the guy rolled over onto his side, out of action for a few moments. Well, at least he knew how to stop a human adversary with one grip now. Mird watched from the sidelines, yawning occasionally, with the air of having seen it all before.

"Get yourself off to medbay and have that looked at, *ad'ika,*" Vau said, tidying his rumpled fatigues. He didn't look half as scary out of armor. His looks lied. "Mird, watch them and make sure they don't slack off. You lot—by the time I come back, I want you to be able to make each other's eyes water. Got it?"

It was a weary chorus. "Yes, Sarge."

"Great Darakaer of Irmenu, I've been struck deaf for my sins. I said, *got it?*"

"Yes, Sergeant!" they barked.

Vau seemed temporarily satisfied. He accompanied Scorch through the corridors to Zey's office, smelling faintly of fresh sweat and bacta ointment.

"Are you on brigade strength again, Sarge?" Scorch asked.

"No. Still civilian status." Vau wore a slightly preoccupied frown that didn't seem to have anything to do with the business at hand. "That way I can tell Zey where to stick his orders without feeling I've lost my military self-respect. An army that refuses orders is a rabble."

Scorch had heard it all before. It was like a litany, and he knew his lines. "An army that refuses orders is a danger to its citizens."

"An army that refuses orders is dead."

"You ever disobeyed an order, Sarge?"

"Only when it was unlawful. And that's not always an easy call, not when the bolts are shaving your nose hair. I'll leave that wisdom to the lawyers sitting on their padded *shebse* years after the event." Vau had never been a chatty man at the best of times; maybe this was the private Vau, the one his squads rarely saw. "How are things with you?"

"Sorry, Sarge, say again?"

"I hear and see all. There's no shame in losing it from time to time, not in a fools' war like this."

Nobody could keep their trap shut, it seemed. But it was probably Etain who blabbed, not the squad. None of them would have told Vau they thought Scorch needed a bit of help. The old Vau would have given him a thrashing for what he'd done at Hadde—stupid risks, emotional outbursts, generally not being ice when it mattered. Today's Vau seemed a little more tolerant, and that was unsettling in itself. Scorch wondered if his own grip on reality was in a worse state than he thought.

"Bit tired," Scorch said. "That's all. Shipping out to Kashyyyk some time soon. We'll be there awhile . . ."

"I know, but I want to see you in my quarters at eighteen hundred, okay?"

Scorch's gut churned. "Right you are, Sarge."

There was always a chance this wasn't really Vau but a shapeshifting Gurlanin. Sometimes, Scorch heard, they didn't quite manage to get in character. Scorch felt fine now. He couldn't see what the fuss was about. He was just reacting to being surrounded by *chakaare* who enraged him. He had bad dreams, too, but everyone did. He'd tell Vau as much.

Boss, Fixer, and Sev were already waiting in Zey's office when Scorch opened the doors. There was no sign of Captain Maze. Zey had both elbows on his fancy blue lapiz desk, arms crossed, a sure sign that he was crawling the walls instead of just being extra-agitated.

"Gentlemen, this is a confidential briefing," he said. The doors snapped shut from the control on his desk. "What's discussed here goes no farther."

Scorch was offended. Every *shabla* job they did was top secret. He noted Vau's jaw take on a more set angle; definitely not a Gurlanin, then. The old martinet Vau was still in there.

"I think you can trust us to be professionals," Vau said. He adjusted the collar of his fatigues, probably ill at ease out of armor or formal clothing. "Whatever it is, how *bad* is it?"

"It's about the compromised computer networks."

"I know. You've already briefed us on that. We need some leads from the Nulls and the Treasury techs before we can get on with it. Shouldn't Omega be in on this, too?"

"That's the nub of the problem, Walon." Zey had the air of

a man edging his way across a rickety bridge. "I need someone to keep an eye on Skirata and his Nulls. And I don't
mean checking they've got enough caf and cookies to keep
them happy."

"What are you asking me to do, General?" Vau's expression was set in granite now. "You'll have to be explicit for
once."

It wasn't the first time that Zey had kept Skirata out of the
loop on an operation. He hadn't wanted him to know about
the mission to locate Ko Sai. But it was the first time Zey had
asked anyone—anyone in this room, anyway—to treat him
as potentially hostile rather than just prone to slicing up
Kaminoans that the Republic wanted alive.

"Much as I respect the man as a soldier, I want to be sure
that he's not misusing his position," Zey said. "I want you to
observe what he and his little private army are up to."

"You want me to spy on a comrade. Yes?"

"I want to be sure he isn't harming the Republic, Walon.
That's all. I know how much he cares about his troops, and I
know he bends the rules past breaking point, but I don't be-
grudge him whatever he creams off the budget—I know it'll
be for the clones' benefit. And I can't argue with the Nulls'
record on black ops. I just need to know Skirata isn't sabo-
taging the war effort, deliberately or otherwise."

Vau looked as if he was chewing it over before spitting it
against the wall. Delta Squad just sat there and said nothing;
the conversation was being conducted over their heads, as it
often was, and Scorch wondered if Zey just had them sit in
on these sessions so he could try to sense from their reactions in the Force if they knew anything. Scorch felt increasingly uncomfortable with that idea. It was like the constant
monitoring by the Kaminoans to check for deviance, reminding him of all the subtle ways that clones presented a
nice, tidy, unremarkable façade to avoid *reconditioning*.
Some never returned from that. You had to try to be as *un*-
individual as you possibly could, in case the aiwha-bait spotted you and carted you off.

"You must have some evidence of dodgy behavior to try to
enlist me," Vau said at last. "I don't like flying blind. Level

with me. Tell me where you think I should be looking, or he'll completely bamboozle me—or cut my throat for betraying him when I'm least expecting it."

"So that's a *yes,* then."

"No, it's a *tell me what I'm getting myself into before I say anything.* I'm too old to play guessing games."

Zey leaned back in his seat. "I have no doubt he's stealing."

"Well, they say that's what Mandalorians are like, after all . . . all the same . . ."

Zey ignored the barb. "But even Skirata couldn't purloin enough to put a dent in the conduct of the war. I'm looking for active sabotage of missions, withholding of information, unhealthy contact with Separatists, that kind of thing."

Scorch knew Skirata got up to all kinds of mischief, and he'd even taken part in some of it. So did Vau, come to that; but that was why the Special Operations Brigade had them on the payroll. It wasn't Junior Scout-Ranger work. They had to mix it with the lowest forms of life in the galaxy.

Vau was now a statue of self-control. Etain said he always seemed utterly calm in the Force, even when he was shoving a vibroblade down someone's gullet. Zey looked none the wiser.

"I've known Skirata for some years," Vau said. "He's a criminal by Coruscant standards. So am I. But an outright traitor—no. He's a professional."

"So Mandalorians never do double-agent work, Walon?"

"Not for the rates you pay, General."

Zey met Vau's unflinching gaze and looked away before reaching for a datapad, tapping to select something, and pushing it across the polished desk. Vau picked it up to read.

"That's a list of Separatist combatants taken prisoner during the last month," Zey said. "Recognize any names?"

Vau was still totally unmoved. "Yes."

"When Skirata mentioned his daughter was missing, I felt sorry for him, so I ran some name checks on government databases just in case she showed up at a medcenter or registered for work somewhere."

"And you found her in a Republic prison."

"I assume it's the right woman. He didn't spell her name."

"R-U-U-S-A-A-N," Vau said. "Ruu, for short. And you think that having a daughter fighting on the other side would make Skirata put his beloved clones at greater risk than they already are."

"She's his flesh and blood."

"You still don't understand *Mando'ade* at all." Vau let out a long and weary sigh that sounded real. "*Aliit ori'shya tal'din.* Family is more than bloodline. And if you looked at any *Mando* working for you—and doing a solid job, might I add—you'd find some of their kin fighting for one of the Republic's enemies at any given time. We've worked as mercenaries for millennia. When you hire a *Mando,* you get professional loyalty as part of the deal. Funny how you see us as private contractors fighting for the cause of freedom when it's *your* credits, but as amoral scum when we get paid by someone else. Maybe we're like all your fine Jedi who come from non-Republic worlds, perhaps . . ."

"I didn't call you in for a debate on the ethics of private military contractors, Walon."

"Yes, I realize this is one of those philosophical gray areas that you struggle with. But if you want me to slide a blade into a man I'd have to trust with my life in battle one day, I require grounds. Because clients come and go, but your professional community is with you forever."

"Very well," said Zey. "Intel says someone has been poking around in files and places that concern them greatly. They won't tell me exactly where, because apparently as Director of Special Forces I have no need to know. But I can watch the unseen by the shadows it casts, and I know this is Treasury, and I know this is Defense, and if there's anyone who has the wherewithal to get this far into Republic systems leaving no direct trace, it's Skirata and his very clever boys."

Vau still didn't move a muscle. Despite the office security soundproofing to thwart eavesdroppers and bugs, a sudden noise interrupted the hold-your-breath tension. It was the sound of claws scraping the doors. Mird had shown up.

"I can't argue with your logic," said Vau.

"In?" Zey didn't even ask Boss for Delta's position. It was irrelevant. "Or not in?"

Vau waited five beats. Scorch had seen him do that many times, and the longer he waited, the more scared Scorch always got. Five beats was a warning of serious displeasure.

"You're paying me," Vau said at last. "If I find him doing anything to help the enemy, I shall give you full details. But only because he'll be in breach of his contract with you. Our word is our bond. It has to be, or we're just savages."

Wisely, Zey didn't come back on that last line, but Scorch was never sure if Zey shared the common view of Mandalorians. He might have been ignorant of the culture, but he was a pretty tolerant guy for a mystic.

"Remember, I expect discretion." Then Zey almost said *dismissed.* Scorch saw his teeth come together and the shape his lips were beginning to form. He stopped short. "Thank you."

The doors parted as Vau walked toward them, followed by Delta. Mird sat patiently at the threshold and made no attempt to bound into the office. The strill trotted ahead of them down the corridor, nose almost welded to the pleek-wood floor in pursuit of fascinating scents. Scorch switched to his helmet circuit so that Vau couldn't hear.

"Skirata's going to cut off his kriffing *gett'se* and ram 'em down his throat if he finds out."

Sev snorted. "I told you it was getting a bit too much like Keldabe around here."

"Kal wouldn't scupper the Republic," Boss said.

"You sure about that?" Fixer sounded unconvinced. "More to the point, is Kal sure?"

Vau said nothing until they reached the doors leading to the training wing of the HQ building. He turned slowly, and stared at them as if their helmets weren't in place and he could see not only into their eyes but into their minds.

"In case you're wondering why, if, and when," Vau said, "this is *Cuy'val Dar* business, and I will *not* involve you in it. Stand from under—stay away from it. *Tayli'bac?*"

It was the most aggressive way a Mandalorian could ask someone if they understood, and if the question ever required an answer, yes was the best one. It was an order to back off. But Delta was tasked by Etain, and she was very much on Skirata's team. It put them in an awkward spot.

"Sarge," Boss said, "where does this leave General Tur-Mukan?"

Vau dropped his chin and gave Scorch that benign but I'm-not-joking warning look. "Like you stay out of *Cuy'val Dar* affairs, I keep clear of internal Jedi politics. Until you receive an explicit order to disregard her in the chain of command, she's still your CO."

Scorch liked to be clear. They all did. Sometimes he envied the white jobs for the clean lack of politics in their working lives.

"Well, *shab*," Sev said, watching Vau walk back into the gym again. "I'm going to start a sweepstakes. Place your bets, *vode*—who's going to be left still standing in Kal's happy little gang this time next year?"

Galactic City Utilities Department standby underground reservoir, Coruscant, late evening

"So when was he going to tell me that my girl's a prisoner of war?"

Skirata sat on *Aay'han*'s casing, so besieged by his torrent of problems that he'd overloaded and reached the relatively comfortable stage of simply picking them off as they floated to the surface. *Do what you can. It's all you can ever do.* Vau paced the edge of the permacrete quay as if he was measuring it for a carpet, head down, hands clasped behind his back.

"Try to look surprised when he finally does, Kal."

Skirata opened his palm and stared at the data crystal from Vau's concealed audio recorder. No *Mando* with two brain cells ever went into a contentious meeting without an electronic witness hidden somewhere. Vau always had one on him, in his collar or belt, even in his underclothes, *ret'lini*—just in case. It was a *Mando* mind-set. You never knew what was coming around the corner to ruin your entire day.

"Don't worry, I'll win an award for dramatic presentation," Skirata said. "Thanks, Walon. So—is he going to use Ruu to shake me down, or has he told you just to see if you'd come running to warn me?"

"Well, we know it's true—she's on the POW list. I checked. Better assume every malign motive until proven benevolent, though. But Zey's not a holo-chess player. He's just drowning in the war like everyone else, grabbing what flotsam he can to stay afloat."

"You're in full Imperial Irmenu Navy mode today, I see."

"It's the water. Brings out my inner sailor."

The underground lake, stored as an emergency supply for homes across Coruscant, cast rippling reflections onto a vaulted permacrete roof that stretched far out of sight into darkness. *Aay'han* was moored down here, courtesy of yet more folks who owed Jaller Obrim a favor and so turned blind eyes when asked. She could have been laid up on the surface easily enough, ready to bang out at a moment's notice; but this was a forgotten place, perfect for hiding a submersible starship. The exit, when the day finally came, was via the sluice bulkheads at the far end of the reservoir.

Ordo said the distance was enough to reach takeoff speed before the ship slipped through the narrow opening into the daylight and clear air. *Aay'han* was going to give someone a massive surprise when she punched out of the side of a utilities plant. No rehearsal was possible. Ordo had to get it right the first time, but he was Ordo, and so he would.

"My alarm bells went off when Zey said he wanted Mereel, Jaing, *and* Besany to investigate the virus," Skirata said. "It's the *get all the suspects in one room* approach. Like a Corellian holodrama."

"If I were laying bets, I'd say that's unhappy coincidence, but we plan for the worst. What's the state of play with Etain?"

"Well, the news gutted Dar and he's not talking to her at the moment." Skirata checked the chrono on his forearm plate. He preferred to work in full armor; it was as much tool kit as protective clothing. "They're due back at barracks from Nerrif in a couple of hours. With any luck, *Bard'ika* will make it by then, too. I think we have to treat this as the last big planning meeting."

"You're going to come *completely* clean with Omega?"

"Despite what happened with Dar . . . oh, I think I need to keep them away from any fallout from my mess until we're literally ready to move. So, not yet."

For a moment, Skirata's natural suspicion tugged at his sleeve and said: *Yeah, good idea, get all the gang in one place, and warn Vau so he can tip off Zey.* Not knowing now who he could and could not trust got to Skirata in a way few things ever could. But that was their *aruetyc* game—divide and rule, sow distrust, set *Mando* against *Mando* by adding a little poisonous doubt to the mix.

If Vau's set me up, and this is some clever double-double game, then I'm going to take my time killing him.

The trouble with war-gaming double-cross scenarios like this was that there was no logical point at which to stop. It was layer upon layer. It could drive you crazy. Skirata knew Vau all too well after being cooped up on a Force-forsaken stilt city on Kamino for years; if he was the double-crossing kind, it would be a first time for him. But . . . Skirata shook it off as best he could.

Mandalorians needed to learn to stick together, to look after one another and let the rest of the galaxy find its own fall guys to do the fighting and dying in their place.

"If you don't feel comfortable having me at this meeting, Kal, just say so." Vau squatted down to pet Mird, who had finished inspecting the makeshift dock and trotted back to report with a series of grumbles and whines. "Just because I'm good at this slippery two-faced stuff doesn't mean I enjoy it, and if there's another unfortunate coincidence, I wouldn't want to be seen as the leak."

Skirata wasn't sure if he felt ashamed or amused at hearing his very thoughts laid bare, but the comment made his gut flip for an irrational moment either way. "How long have you been the only telepathic *Mando,* then?"

"Long practice, overfamiliarity, convergent thoughts . . ."

"We've both known each other long enough to realize what the stakes are."

Mird seemed to approve of the subterranean berthing arrangements. It walked up to a handwheel set low in the wall and sprayed its territorial scent with abandon.

"Mird, when we bang out, you can do that all over Zey's office," Skirata said, trying to find something to laugh about. "It'll take irradiation to clean it off."

Aay'han was almost ready. She'd had a full refit, one discreet piece at a time, her supply lockers and tanks were full and cryosealed, and she looked a lot tidier down below than she had when he'd haggled her out from under that Rodian. She wasn't just a multitask submersible. She was a lifeboat for everything he loved and cared about.

Tied up alongside her in the water was *Gi'ka,* the tiny shark-shaped sports submarine they'd used to infiltrate Ko Sai's hideaway on Dorumaa. Mereel loved that thing. He came down here to pilot it occasionally when he was back at base, just letting off steam like a normal lad of his age. *He'll love thrashing that up and down the lake at Kyrimorut.* In the throes of plans crumbling to dust, there were still good things to look forward to.

No, Zey. I've not come this far to lose my nerve now. We're nearly there. You want to stop me? Then you're going to have to kill me.

Mird sprayed copiously into the water. Vau managed a rueful smile. "With Mird's contribution and *Aay'han*'s antifouling coating . . . remind me not to drink Coruscant water again, will you?"

"Good reason for leaving. Come on. Back to base."

Waiting for everyone to assemble at Laseema's apartment was taking longer than Skirata liked. Even with Kad on his lap, precious time he usually cherished, he still had that feeling of needing to get everything sorted and stowed, to be ready to run. Kad and Mird seemed to have developed an understanding; Kad babbled happily at the strill, which rumbled and even squeaked for a few moments, then disappeared for a while. It returned dragging the covers from Jusik's bed and it proceeded to build a nest from them on the floor. It was a ruthless predator, but it was also a devoted parent. Strills were almost the archetypal Mandalorian spirit.

Jaing arrived with Ordo and Besany just after midnight. Laseema put Kad to bed again, and within the hour all six Nulls—some in uniform armor, some in *beskar'gam*—and Gilamar had arrived. There was no sign of Jusik or Etain. Skirata waited a little longer, then decided they could catch up. He played the recording of Vau's conversation with Zey and waited for comments.

"How do you lie to a Jedi Master?" Laseema asked. "Without him sensing it, that is?"

"I didn't," said Vau. "I said I'd tell him if I found Kal doing anything *to help the enemy*. The minute that this little *shabuir* opens a comlink to any former Death Watch personnel, I shall gladly turn him in."

Skirata paused for a moment, then managed to laugh. "Do I know any?"

"No, but they're the only group I'd really call my enemy. So I didn't lie, and I was genuinely emotional enough for him to believe what his Force senses told him he wanted to believe."

Laseema applauded politely. "That's a *very* clever technique."

"Thank you, my dear. *Mando'ade* are trained to acquire certain states of mind for battle, so it's an easy switch."

"I'm sorry." Besany, perched on a chair next to Kom'rk, looked exhausted. "This is all my fault. The Gurlanin told me I was *crashing around* when I was doing my digging."

"*Shab,* no," Skirata said. "Ordo saw the file on you, remember? They haven't traced it back to you. You got good intel, *ad'ika*. You made the difference. We know about the second stream of clones, we know about the extra fleets, and we have a rough idea of when it's all rolling out. We might not know all the details, but we've got enough to save our *shebse* when the time comes. That's all down to you."

"Maybe *I* was too cocky," Jaing said quietly. "I'm the one who took the risk of introducing a program into the Treasury network to crawl through every linked Republic computer system to mine data. I should have stuck to short-lived programs that self-erased. Grabbed snapshots."

"Is that what it actually did?" Vau asked.

"You should see the quantity of data it transmitted back. Most of it useless, but . . . snapshots rely on you looking in the right place at the right time, so I thought it was worth the risk."

"You really *are* a clever lad."

"Well, they still don't seem to know what it did, only that it's been in the system and vanished," Besany said. "Unless, of course, they really *do* know I'm involved, and even the tech droid is instructed to lie to me."

Jaing shook his head. "They can't trace the entry point to your terminal, Besany. I sent the program via the main com-link, so if they can even find the route it entered by, it's not traceable to any individual user."

Skirata realized how much faith they all put in one another. He was no fool, but he really had no idea of the sophisticated technical skills that Jaing used as easily as Skirata drew his blade. He took it on faith—ironically, faith in the enhancements that the Kaminoans engineered into the Nulls—that they all knew what they were doing. Even Besany—no, he had no idea of the fine detail of her expertise, either. He was proud of his kids. He included Besany in that now; she was his daughter, because Mandos didn't draw the distinction of in-laws.

"I think we've got two issues," she said, with the earnest air of someone used to conducting meetings and commanding attention. "One, what happens when we start this investigation? Do we treat it as real, that they think we have nothing to do with the problem, or do we assume it's a shakedown? Zey's chat with Walon makes me think the latter. Either way, we have to find another way of monitoring activity in our areas of interest, and that's issue two. Follow the supply chain, not purchasing, from now on in. All we need is to keep tabs on the firms we know will supply the kit. KDY, Rothana specifically. Then there's Aurodiseal, *big* supplier to Spaarti Creations before the Cartao plant was trashed, and the data I pulled off the CSX and ISE company information service shows no fall-off in production or profits since cloning was banned. They say they're making water purification equipment now. Seeing as they lost their biggest customer overnight, I find it hard to believe they've found enough new business to fill that gap so fast . . . so we just need some way of getting an overview of their outputs and shipping activity. Check what they're shipping, when they're shipping it, and where it goes."

"Anyone got a contact in KDY?" Mereel asked, looking around his brothers. "If not, we'll have to get in there."

My father worked for KDY.

Skirata tried to honor the memory of his birth parents, but it had been more than fifty years, and it was getting harder than ever to summon up the scraps of the past. The apartment on Kuat was reduced to one view of a wall; but memory was also kind, because he could no longer recall the full detail of the scene he came back to after his home on Surcaris was bombed.

"I know a very reliable freight pilot," A'den said. "She helped our ARC deserter vanish, so she'll be good for a few trips to KDY."

"How do we get into Aurodiseal?" Skirata asked.

"Leave that to me," said Vau.

Skirata started to feel that things were coming back under control again. All it took was a task list and common sense. "Okay, now on to wet assets. We've got Uthan still in the secure mental unit, and my daughter Ruu in a POW camp. Ideally, we snatch them both within the same time window to minimize holding time here, and get them offplanet fast. *Bard'ika*'s keeping tabs on the secure unit, and I'll look after Ruu."

He said it as naturally as if he'd seen her last week. He didn't even know what she looked like as an adult until he got hold of her ID hologram. He searched her features for Ilippi's face, but found mainly his own; Ruu was brown-haired and pugnacious looking. Now he was practicing *not* seeing her as a stranger. None of the Nulls had said a word about it, but he could sense that they were standing by to intervene if things didn't go as planned.

He'd spring her from prison. Then it was her choice what she did next.

"Okay, what have we got left?" Skirata asked.

"Medical update and finances," Prudii said. *"Mij'ika?"*

"Nenilin came up with some interesting insights but no solutions, and I paid him off, with the reminder that if he opens his mouth, tenure won't save him from the weight of my disappointment." Gilamar didn't go into detail. Skirata could guess. "But there's excellent data from the embryologist, who's confirmed there are *no* manufactured genes in the sample, just manipulated naturally occurring ones. The aiwha-bait stuck to the basic blueprint. That's narrowed the range to what Mereel first suspected—that they just concentrated on rapid maturation, and on making sure the genes that influenced bonding and social compliance were fully expressed—to make clones as loyal and disciplined as possible."

"They learned their lesson with us," Mereel said. "Maturation is the bit we're interested in, which is, unfortunately, the most complex."

"Databases?" Skirata asked.

Mereel tapped his 'pad meaningfully. "We've ripped most of the data on cloning and genetics now, public sector and commercial. Uthan's going to have everything she needs. *Shab,* Arkanian Micro would *kill* to grab what we've extracted."

Rarely—very rarely—Skirata stepped outside himself for a second and saw what he did, plain and unvarnished. Extortion; blackmail; industrial espionage; theft; fraud; kidnapping; violence; even good old-fashioned spying on the state. He—they—did the lot. This was a crime syndicate.

My syndicate.

He never saw himself like some Hutt *chakaar* or other gangster. He didn't see himself as a paragon, either. But he could sleep at night for the most part, and he worked out that he could live with himself because—other than in war, which was another matter—everyone he'd hurt had been asking for it. There *was* collateral damage; the families of scumbags he shot, and they might well not have been scum, but they were unseen strangers. Thieving—he faced up to the fact that it was never victimless. And still he slept. The same or worse had been done to him and those he loved.

But he squirmed now. What had stabbed suddenly at his conscience was the awareness that he wasn't all that different from Zey. The Jedi seemed like a nice enough man. He treated Maze with courtesy. But when push came to shove, he did immoral things, and sent clones to die, because he could justify it. *Collateral damage.* They both had their rules of engagement.

Why am I not Zey? Why don't I think I'm as bad as a Jedi? Because I don't drone on about compassion and respect for life. Because I don't exploit slaves while polishing my principles. Because . . . it's personal. When I kill, I mean it. Even when it's just killing them before they kill me.

Skirata found that he was watching Ordo watching Besany, a strange act of observation that summed it all up. This was his son, not a throwaway organic droid made to order, but a man with powerful feelings, a man who was loved and who could love in return, and this random civilian, whose most remarkable quality wasn't her pretty face or her razor-sharp mind, was a woman who looked at Ordo purely as a man like any other, and loved him.

Jedi weren't allowed to love.

If you were forbidden to love a person you could see and touch, how could you ever learn enough compassion to treat strangers right? Jedi never truly learned to love anything beyond an idea, and that was the gulf that Skirata saw between himself and Zey.

He wasn't even trying to work out if he was standing on higher moral ground than Zey and his kind. He just needed to work out if he was, on balance, doing more harm than good if he carried on like this.

"*Kal'buir,* are you feeling okay?" Prudii put his hand on Skirata's cheek. "Talk to me, *Buir.* What's wrong?"

Skirata was jerked out of his thoughts so hard that the touch startled him and his heart hammered out of control. "Sorry, son." Embarrassed, he looked around at worried expressions and tried to joke his way out. "Trying to process too many thoughts with one brain cell. You smart lads don't know how hard it is."

"You need to get some sleep," A'den said. "We thought

you'd had a stroke for a moment. You're no use to us dead, *Buir.*"

It was an old *Mando* joke, the kind of thing that *beroyase* said to the bounties they'd hunted down and cornered, a hint to surrender quietly.

"Finance," Jaing said. "Want to hear the update? Might help you sleep."

Jusik was late. So was Etain. Skirata would get a few hours' sleep and then go find them. "Okay. Last item on the agenda."

Jaing had an oddly satisfied look on his face. Skirata waited for the punch line.

"Our current assets stand at one point three six trillion credits, rounded down."

There was a pause of such profound silence that Skirata heard Mird's stomach gurgle. He took a breath. His hearing was shot to *haran* from too many loud detonations too close, and he lived with that, but he hadn't thought he was *that* deaf.

"Say again, son?"

Gilamar seemed to think he'd misheard, too. *"Meh'shab?"*

"Just over a *trillion* creds, *Kal'buir.* You want me to count out the zeros?"

"Wayii!" Mereel started applauding. Ordo joined in, then Laseema and the others. *"Oya manda! Ori'kandosii, vod'ika!* You actually pulled it off!"

"I thought I was wasted being just a gorgeous hunk," Jaing said, grinning. He smoothed the fine gray leather gloves tucked into his belt. Skirata hoped Etain never asked too many questions about those. "I felt like being *creative* for a change."

The Nulls were extreme risk takers. Skirata now feared Jaing had gone too far; his spy program had been detected, and now he'd ripped off enough creds from the Republic to get attention. Oh, *shab* . . .

Skirata got up and walked over to him. "Just tell me how, son."

"You look worried, *Kal'buir.*"

"It's a *big* hole to leave."

"Not from several trillion bank accounts . . ."

The Nulls laughed like Skirata had never seen them laugh before. They really did think it was hilarious. They were giggling like kids.

"Spell it out for an old *chakaar*," he said.

Vau nodded. "And me."

"You know roughly what my programs do." Mird wandered over to Jaing and put its head in his lap as if to join in the adulation. Jaing didn't seemed bothered by the drool, but he moved his gloves to higher ground, to the clip on his shoulder plate. "They wander through computer networks, copying data and sending it back to me. So I created a version that wanders around bank networks skimming a credit or half a credit off each account it finds, and depositing it in another account. Well, this program did a *lot* more exploring than I counted on, thanks to the central clearing system Republic banks use. That let it into every bank on the grid. *Trillions* of accounts . . . and who misses half a cred on their balance statement? Who'd argue with their bank about it? Which bank would spend time investigating such a small dispute anyway? Next thing we know . . . thank you for choosing the Clone Savings Bank, citizen, you've invested wisely."

Skirata nearly wept. He was tired, so his guard was down, and he was prone to emotion anyway, but this was shock and joy. Besany just put her head in her hands, maybe amused, but probably hyperventilating in horror. The poor kid was an auditor. She was supposed to hunt men like Jaing.

"Look, it's not like I left any widows destitute," Jaing said defensively. He must have misunderstood Skirata's expression. "*Shab,* I didn't even leave any rich Hutt starving. And I only hit Republic banks. It's social taxation."

"You're . . . you're . . . a *genius,*" Skirata managed at last.

"Thank you for noticing, *Kal'buir.*" Jaing looked up as Vau leaned over and shook his hand. "The really clever stuff is making it stealthy enough to defeat security programs."

"And it's been laundered?" Vau asked.

"Laundered, pressed, starched, new fastenings sewn on,

and now it's being reinvested. You want to know how much interest it's earning per day, *Kal'buir*?"

"I'll live with my current level of shock, thanks."

"We now have a war chest."

"I think I'll join you in that suspected transient ischemia, Kal," Gilamar said. He looked as ashen as Skirata felt. "Those numbers cut off the blood supply to my brain."

They could now buy anyone or anything, and buy a lot of clones a new life if they wanted one. If those sorts of resources couldn't also buy a solution to the genetic aging puzzle, nothing could.

Skirata would have slept well in what remained of the night, if only Darman and Etain had walked through those doors having made up and forgiven. He slept in a chair anyway, as he always did, and waited, dozing fitfully and watching.

The doors stayed closed.

9

*Someone knows. I feel it. And I know someone single-
minded is looking for information about the new
clone army.*
*It's not a secret I could have hidden, not an operation that
big, but I didn't need to. Beings believe what you tell them.
They never check, they never ask, they never think. Tell
them the state is menaced by quadrillions of battle droids,
and they will not count. Tell them you can save them, and they
will never ask—from what, from whom? Just say tyranny,
oppression, vague bogeymen that require no analysis.
Never specify. Then they look the other way when reality is
right in front of them. It's a conjuring trick. The key is
distraction, getting them to watch your other hand. Only
single-minded beings don't join in the shared illusion, and
keep watching you too closely.*
*Single-minded beings are dangerous. And they either work
for me, or they don't work at all.*
—Chancellor Palpatine, talking to his personal Republic
Intel agents—known as his Hands

**Main computer control room, Treasury offices,
Coruscant, 0845 hours, 998 days ABG**

"Everything ready?" Besany asked.

"Yes, Agent Wennen," said Jay, the tech droid. "We've
maintained strict security. None of the staff knows it's an
audit investigation. As far as everyone is concerned, the shutdown is due to the virus infecting the network."

"Let's go," she said, and nodded to Mereel and Jaing.

Monitoring them from a few paces away was a Central Republic Audit Office employee with a name tag that read ELLIK, but Besany was sure the woman was an Intel agent. It didn't matter. She wouldn't find a thing. "Lockdown."

This was how it was done, by the book. No warning was given. Staff throughout the building suddenly found that their input devices wouldn't work, their computer screens were frozen, and they couldn't make comm calls. And then a small army of droids began searching their workstations, because it wasn't a job that anyone wanted a flesh-and-blood colleague to do. Droids were impersonal, impartial, and nobody had to look at them resentfully afterward. It made for more peaceful workplace relations.

Security droids also stood guard at the exits; actually locking staff in breached fire regulations. Besany found that almost funny under the circumstances.

"What would you like us to do, Agent Wennen?" Mereel asked, deadpan. "Lieutenant Jaing is ready to start."

The two Nulls stood to attention by the control console. All data storage and processing for the Treasury was done from this huge room; the staff—mainly human, but also Nimbanese and Sullustans—watched the two ARC troopers warily. Besany wondered whether to ask them to remove their helmets, so that the staff could see that there were real human beings under the white plastoid, seeing as the rest of the security rummage was being done by droids. She wanted them to know the difference. But now she also knew how much clone troopers relied on the helmet systems for comms. Jaing and Mereel would want to conduct unheard conversations.

We're here to get this done without digging ourselves in any deeper. The public relations will have to wait.

"You can run your forensic program now, Lieutenant."

She stood back to give Jaing control of the terminal. The CRAO officer glided up behind his seat like a ghost, watching in silence while he inserted the datachip, keyed in commands, and then sat back.

"What program are you running, exactly, clone?"

Besany braced for impact. It was a very emotive issue,

using the term *clone* when the woman knew both his rank and name. It said he was *nothing*.

"Routing analysis, to detect via which terminal the virus entered the network, and then purge it from the system, overweight female human," Jaing said.

The shock on her face gave way to outrage. "I *beg* your pardon?"

Jaing's tone remained even. "I thought we were using generic phenotype descriptions as a term of address, as you appear to have dispensed with name and title."

It really wasn't the best time to make a stand on courtesy, but that was a measure of how angry it made the Nulls. At any other time, it would have been funny. Officer Ellik looked as if she was trying to translate what Jaing had said into some language she understood. Besany silently willed Jaing to quit while he was ahead.

"How will this program detect that when our security scan couldn't . . . *Lieutenant*?"

"Because I wrote this program, *Officer Ellik,* and I'm a great deal more intelligent than those who produce monitoring systems for Republic Procurement."

It was impossible to take offense at Jaing. He was simply stating facts. Ellik didn't answer, but watched him carefully while Besany made an effort to look as if she was curious about what he might find.

"There," he said at last. "That's your point of entry. A comlink data portal."

"I thought we had adequate filtering for comlink-borne attacks," Besany said. "Jay, schedule me an interview with the head of system security, please. Let's get that plugged." Jaing didn't need that access now, anyway. "Lieutenant, can you suggest a solution for that?"

"Certainly, ma'am."

"Can you identify the incoming comlink?" Ellik asked.

Jaing pushed his seat back to let her look at the screen. "No, I'm afraid not. This code here shows—"

"Oh yes. The range of numbers is within the public node allocation."

"You're very well informed," Jaing said, keying in more

commands. "Yes, it's the public comlink node in the Fobosi district. The university."

Ellik shut her eyes for a moment. "If this is some student prank, they have some *very* sophisticated programming skills."

"Kids today," he said, shaking his head.

Ellik had switched from addressing Jaing like a droid to apparently thinking he had more to contribute than Besany. "You don't think it's a student slicing into our system for thrills, do you?"

"If I were a gambling man, Officer Ellik, I would place my credits on industrial espionage."

"Why not *real* espionage?"

"Because company secrets and the profits associated with them are bigger than planetary interests. Spying is small stuff by comparison."

"I don't know which should worry us more," she said.

"I could, of course, run similar checks for all the Republic contractors whose details are held on the Treasury system, starting with Defense. This spy program—and that's all it was, I think, because there are no corrupt data—has probably taken a look at commercially sensitive information."

"You're very definite about that."

"If it was military espionage, Officer Ellik, they'd be looking for totally different data—specifications, operating parameters, jamming frequencies. None of that data is held here. Anyone rummaging through the accounts wants financial information."

"Good thinking," she said. "Very well, I'll authorize your access to defense contractors to carry out whatever checks you need. I doubt they'll refuse our help under the circumstances."

Besany was left breathless by Jaing's sheer nerve. Had he planned this? Was he just *busking it,* as Skirata called it— making it up as he went along? He'd just talked his way into rifling through KDY's systems with the Republic's blessing. It was so casual, so effortless, that Besany wondered if Ordo was also really all he seemed.

"I *could* do what we call hardening a target," said Jaing.

"Try to breach their system security to see if it's robust enough. I'm sure they have paid professionals to do that, but so does the Treasury, and they didn't spot this spy program on entry."

Ellik nodded. "Start with KDY. I'll square it with the chief of staff and the Chancellor's office. Wait for my confirmation. Lieutenant, have your program sent over to our information technology division." She turned to Besany. "And I still want to see the results of staff monitoring, just in case. These people may have contacts on the inside."

"That's being done now, Officer Ellik." Besany turned to the control room staff. "As soon as you get the all-clear from the droid security teams, release the system lockdown."

Ellik left without shaking hands, which was no surprise. Besany, almost faint with relief, followed Jaing and Mereel outside into the service turbolift. Mereel ran his gauntlet around the interior as if he was feeling for a draft of air, then checked the display on his forearm plate.

"No bugs," he said, and took off his helmet. "Spook."

Jaing took off his helmet, too. "Definitely, spook. Nobody else would memorize public comlink node outgoing codes. Nobody sane, anyway."

"You pushed your luck there, Jaing," Besany said. She could feel her face burning now as the adrenaline dissipated. "Did I read that right? You're going to slice KDY's system on Republic time?"

"Please, miss, can I do some spying? I won't make a mess . . . ," Mereel mocked Jaing. "You little crawler."

"You're just jealous of my sheer animal magnetism, vod'ika."

"I *wondered* what that smell was."

Jaing affected a breathless, sultry tone. "Women can't resist me. Not even Ellik."

"Get over yourself." Mereel laughed. "But that did take some *gett'se,* I admit."

Besany watched the indicator charting their progress to the four hundreth floor of the complex. "I don't want to do that ever again, Jaing."

"With any luck, you won't."

They replaced their helmets. Besany tidied her hair to make sure that when she stepped out of the turbolift, she didn't look red-faced and guilty at having lied to cover up an even bigger mountain of lies.

The doors parted and they walked to her office past open areas where droids were still searching desks and cupboards, watched in grim silence by the clerks. Besany checked that her terminal was working again, then turned to Jaing.

"Are you really handing over your program to her?"

"I'm handing over *a* program to her. There's nobody working for her who'll know the difference. That's my intellectual property, and if she wants it for Republic use, she can pay me for it."

"And, of course, the Republic will never spot another Jaing virus with it," Mereel said. "Everything will look nice and clean."

Besany had to do a double take. "You mean you pulled *another* scam under her nose?"

Jaing shrugged. "Well, she *thinks* she's got a program that'll find all spy applications now, but she hasn't, so she might well have more viruses she'll never know about. So . . . yeah, I think I did."

"Remind me never to play sabacc with you."

It was the all-clear; this crisis, at least, had passed, and Besany was back to her normal daily level of fear of discovery. Somehow it seemed a lot lower.

"Agent Wennen?"

She looked past Jaing and Mereel. It was Jay, the tech droid. "All sorted, Jay? Back to normal?"

"Droid security team Eight-Seven Beta report finding evidence of improper access and use by an employee, ma'am."

Besany's shoulder's sagged a little. They were back to the routine of internal disciplinary trivia. Remote gambling, no doubt; some staff were hooked. *You'd think Treasury staff would know better . . .*

"Who is it this time, Jay? I hope the winnings made it worthwhile."

"Ma'am, it's Agent Jilka Zan Zentis. We've detained her for accessing suspicious files unconnected to her duties, and

transferring confidential data files to flimsi copy for removal
from the system."

The office perspective shifted violently like zooming the
focus on a holocam. Besany's relief had been cruelly short-
lived. The Nulls said nothing, acting as if they didn't know
the name.

"These—these are just procedural slips on her part,
right?" Some files never left the building, either on datachips
or hard copy. "She's just been careless. But what's this got to
do with me? She's Tax Enforcement. She's not in my department."

"But you're in charge of the defense data security breach,
Agent Wennen." Jay was patient, if a droid could be. Besany
always assumed they could. "And she appears to have been
accessing defense budget data."

"Oh, that can't be right." *I know it can't be true, don't I?*
"I'm sure this is just some mistake, and it wouldn't be the
first time. Let her go back to her desk. I'll talk to her."

"Apologies, ma'am, but you can't do that."

"Why?"

"Standing procedure says we're obliged to refer the matter
to law enforcement."

Ah, good old CSF. Captain Obrim would sort out this little
mess without a fuss. He'd made Besany's armed siege at the
medcenter vanish without a trace, after all. "I'll call CSF,
then. Just to square the books."

"No, ma'am, it's Republic Domestic Security for any
breach like this involving civil servants. The head of staff security has alerted them."

Besany found her stomach knotting again. RDS was new,
not part of CSF or any civilian law enforcement structure at
all, and reported direct to the Chancellor's office. The cozy
word *domestic* belied the true nature of the beast.

"Well . . . they'll find they have the wrong person, then,"
she said.

Besany *knew* they had the wrong woman, because she was
the perpetrator.

But there was nothing she could say to clear her friend that would not end in disaster for Skirata, Ordo, and everyone she now held dear.

Now she fully understood the term *collateral damage.*

Arca Barracks, Coruscant, later that day

There was something going wrong; Darman knew it.

"Shouldn't we be out hunting bad guys by now?" Niner leaned against the transparisteel wall that ran the length of the recreation area overlooking the parade ground. He rested his forehead against the clear sheet, hands in the pockets of his red fatigues. "No briefing? What's happening, d'you think?"

Darman, boots up on the low table opposite his chair, was psyching himself up to finally face Skirata, and he couldn't put it off any longer. But when he returned the comm call, Skirata didn't respond. Darman shoved the comlink back in his pants and rehearsed a long monologue to Etain in his head for the umpteenth time.

I can't sulk about this forever. I have to see Kad. He's mine.

"Dar?"

"Don't ask, *At'ika.*"

"I thought we were meant to be deployed with Delta. Where are they?"

"Look, we can't do anything until they get some leads for us to follow. You want to kick down every door on Coruscant?"

"Okay, Dar. Just asking."

"Why would *I* know? I'm just the coolie labor. I don't get told anything."

Corr didn't join in. He was examining one of his prosthetic hands, the synthflesh covering peeled back while he tinkered with the miniature servos. He'd lost both arms just above the elbow, and seemed to need to confront the loss head-on. Sometimes he dispensed with the synthflesh and went with the bare-metal look, even sharpening his vibroblade on the durasteel fingers the way some females filed their nails for diversion when bored. Darman took it as bravado;

losing one hand seldom bothered anyone in a society that had good medical care, but losing both somehow stripped you of a touchstone of humanity. Besany had been very distressed by it. Corr was the first trooper she'd got to know personally.

"Dar," Corr said at last, "do you want me to come with you?"

"Where?" Darman knew exactly where he meant. Clone brothers knew each other so well that they could think like one another, which was usually a comfort, but Dar felt more like he was under siege. "Why?"

"Because you shouldn't face this on your own. Let's go see your kid."

"I don't know where he is. I walked out before Etain explained any of that."

"Well, *ask* her."

Darman wasn't sure what he'd do when he saw his son. He'd been trying hard to recall his face from when Skirata had laid the baby in his arms—oh, *now* he understood, *now* he knew why *Kal'buir* looked so tearful—but the kid wasn't going to look like that now. They grew fast, babies. Clones were surrounded by their brothers at every stage of development in Tipoca City, because the Kaminoans didn't bother to hide the transparisteel gestation tanks. Darman felt he knew enough about baby boys to handle seeing his own.

"Okay," he said. He commed Skirata again.

Niner didn't need to be told what Darman was doing. He walked over to his brother and stood watching.

"Son." Skirata's voice sounded a bit breathless, as if he'd been pulled away from some crisis. Yes, he was really *was* Darman's dad now: it was official, legal, at least on Mandalore. "Son, I was worried about you. Are you okay?"

"Yeah . . . *Kal'buir,* where's my son?"

"He's with Laseema at the moment. You want to see him, don't you? He's a lovely kid."

"Yes."

"Etain's been trying to talk to you."

"I know."

"Don't shut her out, son. This is my fault. I'll put it right."

Darman heard Ordo say something to Skirata in the background, but he didn't quite catch it. "I can't bring him to the barracks while Zey's there. Jedi take Force-sensitive babies. But not on my watch. Look, we've got a few problems at the moment, but I'll be at the barracks in twenty minutes or so, and we'll work something out."

Darman had a long list of questions to ask Skirata, and had been able to ask none of them. He put the comlink away and couldn't marshal his thoughts. He knew what he wanted to do now; he was calmer, still shocked at the enormity of the news, but if there had been no constraints, no duties, he would have gone to Etain, picked up Kad, and walked out of the GAR to . . . well, wherever. Mandalore, probably. He didn't know where Kyrimorut was, and Fi said the location was secret because a haven for deserters and renegades had to show some discretion.

Darman missed Fi. His dream, which was a fancy word for the ideal he'd come to measure his current existence against, was having all his brothers around, and Etain, and Jusik, and all the other people he could trust, and now he added Kad to that—seeing Kad grow up with all these friends and *family* around him. It had to be *all* of them. He didn't want to be on the run, cut off from most of them forever.

"Better armor up," he said. "Can't loaf around in my reds all day."

Arca Barracks was eerily empty much of the time, with most of the commando squads deployed and only a handful there between missions to debrief, recuperate a little, and pick up any necessary retraining and new kit. Omega had the whole floor to themselves. Darman took a shower and washed his fatigues, then armored up and sat in the locker room, helmet on his lap, waiting. The other three ventured in. They seemed to be expecting him to explode if they said the wrong thing. It was a long twenty minutes.

"Here he comes," said Atin.

Two sets of boots clattered along the corridor, not GAR issue: Mandalorian *cetare,* definitely, from the sound. Skirata's gait had changed since his ankle was fixed. Now his walk sounded like any other soldier's except for the occasional scuff because he was still getting used to not limping. He wore full *beskar'gam* in the barracks, as if he was weaning himself off the *aruetyc* ways of Coruscant and its civilian fashions.

But Skirata walked through the 'fresher doors in his civilian rig—brown bantha-hide jacket and brown pants—which was slightly at odds with his heavy *Mando* boots. Vau stood behind him in his black *beskar'gam* with his helmet under one arm, Mird at his side.

"Dar'ika," Skirata said. "Come here, son."

And Darman did, despite himself. He stood up and let Skirata throw his arms around him. *Kal'buir* thought a manly hug sorted a lot of problems, and generally he was right. This time, though, it was going to take more than affection to fix things.

"I'm sorry," Skirata said. "I know you're upset."

Atin, Corr, and Niner leaned against the lockers, moral support for their brother. "Why didn't anyone tell me, *Buir*?" Darman asked. "Why did Etain lie to me? What did she think I'd do? Is she ashamed of me?"

"Shab, no, son." Skirata's face was anguished and exhausted. "She adores you. It was me—I stopped her telling you. She wanted to, right from when she knew she was pregnant, but I threatened I'd take the kid away from her if she didn't do as I said."

Darman didn't believe him. Skirata might have been a pitilessly hard man, no stranger to violence, but he was the kindest of fathers. He'd never have threatened Etain.

"Don't cover for her, *Kal'buir*."

"I'm not. It's true. Ask Ordo—he walked in on the row, and I'm not going to dress it up. I stopped her telling you, and that was wrong, whatever the circumstances."

Darman didn't like the feeling growing in his gut right then. Skirata had been the sole anchor in his childhood, the only adult he trusted, his shield against the Kaminoans and everything that scared him. He wanted this not to be true. Etain—Etain was a Jedi, and as much as he loved her, she wasn't a foundation in his life like Skirata had been.

"You put my son in my arms," Darman said, "and *didn't tell me who he was.*"

"I swear to you, son, *ori'haat,* we were going to tell you then. But you said that you weren't ready for babies. So we decided against it."

"We."

"All right, *me.* Leave Etain out of it. She's a kid like you, never had the chance of a normal life, and she did her best—because she needed something to love when she wasn't allowed to, ever. She loves you, and she loves Kad. *I'm* the one who should have known better."

Darman knew what was happening inside him now. He recognized it. So did Niner; he moved a little closer, as if he was going to take Darman's arm and tell him it was okay, and things would be better now.

Darman was angry and hurt. He knew he had to let that steam vent out carefully. "Why did you stop her the first time?"

"I thought it would distract you when you were fighting, and you'd get yourself killed," said Skirata. Vau was still silent. In a room full of soldiers, there was now really only Skirata and Darman. "And I didn't know if you could take it emotionally. A lot of men with more life experience than you run away when they find out they're going to be a dad."

"So am I a man, like anyone else, or am I always going to be a kid who needs everything done for him?"

"Look, I was *wrong.*" Skirata looked rough now; his eyes glazed with unshed tears, and his voice was shaky. "You *should* have been told. You *should* have been there when Kad was born. I took that from you, and I'll never forgive myself."

Yeah, this wasn't about Etain. Somehow, for all the knowledge he lacked of normal family life, Darman knew—*felt*—that she was in as big a mess as him, but Skirata was the grown-up, the seasoned warrior, the father, the veteran sergeant, the one who should have taken the situation in hand.

"I want to see Kad," Darman said. "When we go off duty tonight, I want to see my son."

"And Etain?"

Darman thought. Yes, he could face her now. He nodded. But he wasn't satisfied. The floodgates had opened, and he couldn't close them. He had to know *everything*. "What's happening, *Kal'buir*? I mean—the rest of it? We know we don't get told everything, but you're always up to something, and you don't tell us. You said *problem* when I commed you."

Skirata looked at Vau, who shrugged and went to stand guard at the doors with Mird. Skirata held out his hand. "Come on. Buckets—show me all your helmets are offline."

"Don't you trust *us*?" Corr asked.

"Of course I trust you. I just don't want any potentially live links while we talk. I'm getting paranoid about security breaches and the tech the *aruetiise* can get hold of. Things are *not* going great."

"Terrific," said Atin sourly, flipping his helmet upside down between his palms and showing a totally unlit interior, all systems down. "We're not amateurs."

"Neither is Jaing," said Skirata, "but some Republic jobs-worth knows someone's been in their network."

"What network?" Niner asked.

"Treasury."

Darman knew that Besany had slipped codes to Skirata from the start. He could guess what was coming, or at least he thought he could. "Jaing's been caught slicing? Or was it Besany?"

"Neither. Her friend Jilka's been picked up by the RDS bully-boys instead, and even Jaller Obrim can't make *that* problem go away. Jilka knows one thing too many. It might put Besany in the frame."

"But what's she *done*?"

"First things first," Skirata said. "I need to go in and shut Jilka up before she tells Palpatine's heavies too much."

"Shut Jilka up." Niner did his conscience-of-the-GAR act, that resigned expression that said he'd follow orders but he didn't have to like it—and he'd argue. "As in *slot her.*"

"If need be, yes."

Atin looked at Darman. "She's Besany's buddy."

"And it's Besany she'll implicate."

"In *what*?" Niner asked.

Skirata was talking about something to thwart the Chancellor. It was the first explicit proof Darman had that he was running his own operation—not in parallel with the Republic's interests, or outside them, but *against* them. Darman loved and respected *Kal'buir,* but he was under no illusions about his methods. He'd been up to something dodgy for a long time; Fi's extraction, the base on Mandalore, Ko Sai, the bank job on Mygeeto with Vau that Delta didn't talk about—something major was happening. Skirata was well off the chart.

And so were the Nulls.

"Just *tell* us," Darman said. "We're big boys now. Put your credits where your mouth is, if you meant what you said to me a minute ago."

Skirata paced slowly around the 'fresher with his head lowered, staring at the gray tiled floor as if he was working up to saying something awful. Vau was getting impatient at the doors, doing that sigh and head shake that meant he was going to cut in and tell them if Skirata didn't. But Darman wanted to hear it from *Kal'buir.*

"For *shab*'s sake tell them, Kal," Vau said.

Skirata let out a long breath. "*Ad'ike,* what I'm going to tell you must not, absolutely *not,* go beyond us. Do you understand? Not even if the Chancellor orders you to answer. *Especially* not then." He looked at Niner. "That means you, too. You're as straight as a die, son, but this isn't the time or the place for being Master Ethical."

So A'den had told Skirata about Niner's row with him over letting Sull desert and walk free. Niner drew his head back slightly as if he was hurt by the suggestion. "We're not going to like this, are we, *Kal'buir*?"

Skirata was all business again, eyes dry, as if they hadn't had the conversation about babies and lies at all. "This is a need-to-know job, not because I don't trust you, but because what you don't know usually can't drop you in it. *Usually.*"

"We get it," Atin said. "Just tell us."

"It's not Jilka who's been mining the Treasury's data. It's Besany. And I got her to do it. We don't live in a world now where you get a lawyer and a trial—you end up committing suicide whether you want to or not, like that HNE hack."

It was a tough line to follow. But Niner, being Niner, tried. "So you slot Jilka to save Besany."

"If you knew what Besany had found, *Ner'ika,* you'd understand. And it's not just about Besany."

"What the *shab* is it?" Darman snapped. "Come on, *Kal'buir,* spit it out."

Skirata dropped his voice almost to a whisper. "Palpatine's developing a new clone army. A *big* one."

It shouldn't have felt like a slap in the face, but it did. It was *reinforcements,* but it didn't feel like it. "What, you mean more of us? Well, that's—"

"More Fett clones, yes, but not from Kamino. He's fallen out with Lama Su. Got his own production plants, and building lots more ships. I think the clones from the Fourteenth are the vanguard. And the guys we're seeing around the city."

It was all getting too messy for Darman. There was something wrong. It was the kind of strategic information that special forces needed to know. If reinforcements were coming, they should have been told, just like he should have been told he had a son.

"About time," said Niner. "We're stretched thin enough to read a holozine through us. Okay, *Kal'buir,* that's all we need to know. But that still doesn't fully explain why Jilka's a problem."

"Niner, *ner vod*—shut up, will you?" said Corr.

"No, you need to know this, *all* of it, because it's going to blow up soon," Skirata said. "I want you to be ready to save yourselves."

It was so quiet in the 'freshers that Darman could hear a faint, distant, distracting drip from a faucet.

"Okay, full story," said Niner.

"The extra troops aren't going to be deployed for some months." Skirata held his hand up in front of his chest as if to quell argument that hadn't even started. "Palpatine's holding them back, but they're fully developed. Fast-grown Spaarti clones, we think, mature enough to fight within a year or so, not grown Kamino-style like you—millions and millions of them. He's got a big push planned, and the fact that nobody, but *nobody,* has been told about it scares the living *osik* out of me. So . . . okay, I'll blurt it out. When the big red button gets pushed, *we get out.* And I mean *we.*"

Darman heard Niner fidgeting. His armor rustled against the fabric of his bodysuit. They'd all talked around the subject, about what would happen after the war ended, and now—they knew.

Was the war going to end, though?

"Shouldn't *we* be there for the final big push?" Corr asked. "Do our bit? Seems a shame to leave the party early."

"Son, I don't know the full details, and it's not for want of trying." Skirata fastened his jacket, looking as if the snatched discussion was coming to an abrupt end. "But the more I find out, the less I think this is going to end well for the likes of you and me. I— The Nulls, Vau, and me, we've been getting an escape route together, and a refuge for any man who wants to leave the GAR without a body bag. And we're getting close to finding out how to stop your accelerated aging. It's a whole new life, *ad'ike,* a long one like any other human's. Are you in? Will you come with me when I say it's time to run?"

There was another communal silence.

Drip . . . drip . . . drip. Another leaky faucet joined the first in a quietly insistent chorus.

"So it's true about Ko Sai," Niner said at last.

"We didn't kill her, son, but we've got her research."

Every being needed some certainty in their life. Darman knew that some needed more than others, and he didn't need as much as Atin seemed to, but one thing he *did* need was to know that Kal Skirata was the honest foundation stone of the clones' sense of identity. Right now, there was nothing solid left under Darman. He was adrift. He couldn't rely on *Kal'buir* to level with him. The unknown and invisible was worse than incoming fire you could see.

"You never told us," Darman said quietly. "Again, *you* decide what we get to know."

"Dar, leave it," said Corr. "Soldier's lot in life, that is."

"*Kal'buir,* you kept us in the dark. Like you kept me in the dark about Kad." Darman found himself looking down into

Skirata's eyes, oblivious of everyone else. The pressure in his head, right behind his eyes, felt almost like a bad dose of flu that had hit him in just a few moments. He couldn't hold it much longer. "What else don't you tell us? How can I *trust* you?"

"Dar, I'm sorry." Skirata put his hands on Darman's arms as if to soothe him, but Darman pulled away. "That's why I'm telling you everything now."

"I said, what *else*?"

"I'm not holding anything back. At least I don't think I am—"

"You wouldn't even *know* if you were lying. It's all just one big lie."

Skirata's eyes changed. Something went out of them; light, life, whatever, but Darman had wounded him. "Son, I'm not exactly an Asrat holy man, I admit that. But whatever I did, however stupid it was, I did because I love you boys more than you'll ever know."

"Liar," said Darman. *"Liar."*

And he punched *Kal'buir* in the face.

The shock of the impact traveled up Darman's arm into his shoulder in slow motion. He heard the yells to stop, felt someone grab his arm, but shook them off. Skirata fell against the tiled wall. He started yelling, too; "Leave him, *leave him,* get out and *leave us*—" But the feeling didn't stop for Darman, not even when the punch exploded in pain, the feeling that his lungs were going to burst if he didn't get rid of this hammering pulse in his throat. Darman hauled Skirata upright and hit him again. He heard the *oof* and felt the spit on his face, but Skirata didn't hit back.

"It's okay, son," Skirata gasped, scrambling to his feet, arms held away from his sides. All Darman could see was blood, nothing else. "It's okay. Let it out. I asked for it."

Darman wasn't aware of much else for the next few seconds—maybe minutes, he had no idea—except hitting and hitting and *hitting* Skirata anywhere he could reach. No focus, no aim; there wasn't even Skirata, not really. There was just this weird rage, half terror, and Darman wanted it out of him because he couldn't draw another breath with it still inside him. Vau was shouting at the others to get out and *leave them to it.*

Then all Darman could hear was rasping breath. It was his own. Skirata was panting, too. When Darman looked down at his hands, they were raw and bleeding, and his first thought was that he hadn't put his armored gauntlets on, and he was glad. He landed back in reality, shocked.

"*Kal'buir,* I'm sorry, I'm sorry . . ."

Skirata leaned back against the wall, legs out in front of him. Darman could still only see the blood—not the face, just blood from the old sergeant's nose and mouth. Skirata wiped it with the back of his hand and smeared it everywhere. Darman was almost paralyzed with horror and regret; the smell of the blood made him feel unsteady. But he edged forward and lifted Skirata to his feet.

"Do you want to talk, son?" Skirata paused, put one hand on the wall to steady himself, and spat into the nearest basin. He could hardly get the words out. "Or do you . . . want to be alone for a while?"

"I'm sorry. *Shab,* I'm sorry, *Buir*—"

"I'm sorry, too. It's okay. Come here."

Skirata embraced him. He actually *hugged* him, although it felt as if he was also hanging on to him to stay upright. Darman felt he was now in a stranger's body, because he didn't know how he could ever have done such a thing to *Kal'buir.* He didn't know what had erupted from him. But it had gone away. And Skirata just held him as if he hadn't hurt him at all.

"Now, what do you need, son?"

"I don't want to talk," Darman said. "But I don't want to be alone, either."

"It's going to be fine, don't you worry." Skirata spat more bloody saliva. Something hard pinged in the basin. "Everything's going to turn out okay."

10

So what's wrong with being a mercenary? Is your war worth fighting? If it is, then why does it matter who fights it for you? Aren't we imbued with the righteousness of your cause when we take up arms for you? Would you rather your own men and women died to make the point? And if your war is so noble, so necessary—why aren't you fighting it yourself? Think of all that before you spit on us, aruetii.
—Jaster Mereel, *Mand'alor, Al'Ori'Ramikade,* speaking to the regent of Mek va Uil, ten years before dying at the hands of a comrade he trusted

Arca Barracks, three hours later, 998 days ABG

General Zey filled the corridor, robes flapping as he bore down like a bantha stampede.

At least it looked that way to Scorch. Zey was on the warpath. These quiet days when everyone seemed to be on the brink of screaming anger and nothing was getting shot, vibrobladed, or blown up—Scorch knew there was far worse lurking under the surface. He was fed up waiting for op orders when he could taste the tension in the air.

Vau and Mird walked head-on toward the Jedi as if he was a minor inconvenience.

"Sergeant Vau!" he barked. No *Walon,* then. "What in the name of the Force happened to Skirata? I've just passed him."

Vau was the only being Scorch had ever seen who could come to a halt *grudgingly.* "He's fine."

"He is *not* fine. He's badly injured. He can't even stand up straight."

Vau inhaled slowly. "We were having a philosophical discussion, as Mandalorians often do, and I asserted that the only demonstrable reality was individual consciousness, but he insisted on the existence of a priori moral values that transcended free will. So I hit him."

Zey didn't even blink. "You think you're so witty."

"No, I think you should stay out of *Mando* clan business. It's for your own good. Now, do you want a report, or not?"

Zey gestured Vau into a side lobby. So the old *chakaar* really *had* been spying on Skirata. Scorch was actually surprised, and even a little disappointed, but Zey had a point; and it was an inarguable order. Scorch stood to one side, trying to look—and feel—as if he wasn't listening intently.

"I see that arrests have been swift," Zey said.

"Some stupid clerk, General," said Vau. "So Skirata is *not* your traitor, even though he *is* a light-fingered little scumbag who'd steal your teeth if you smiled at him. But I don't think you'll see a continuation of his dishonest habits, because he now understands the error of his ways."

Scorch translated into plain language. So Vau had given Skirata a good hiding for causing trouble, and made him swear not to rip off Republic funds and kit again. That was . . . unexpected. Scorch had always had Skirata down as the alpha *Mando,* even if he had to stand on a box to head-butt Vau.

"I'm relieved." Zey nodded, shoulders relaxing visibly. "I didn't want to think I was that far misguided about his motives."

"We still have a job to do, General. The suspect—this tax clerk the RDS is holding. The Chancellor can set up as many internal enforcement agencies as he wishes, but I have no faith in anyone's interrogation ability but my own. I'd like to talk to her."

"Good luck," Zey said. "I'm just the Director of Special Forces. My wishes count for nothing."

"Exactly. So RDS won't share information with us any more freely than Intel does, so I'm planning to stroll over there and extract her if need be."

Zey spread his hands in mock helplessness. "My authorization will get you no farther than the front doors."

"No, I mean authorize me for the retrieval."

"That's extreme."

"So are the rumors I hear about a big enemy assault coming soon. I'll grab every source I can get."

Zey clasped his hands in front of him in that Jedi way, looking slightly sideways at Vau.

"Trying to sense any dark side in me, General?" Vau asked.

"You don't feel remotely dark. Quite serene, actually."

"I've been told that before, and that should set off your warning bells, *jetii*. Your senses need recalibrating. None of you can feel darkness right under your noses."

"Okay, agreed. Do it. If it goes wrong—you're on your own."

"I wouldn't have it any other way."

It was another nonconversation that had not taken place about a subject that wasn't for discussion; deniable. Zey strode off at high speed, boots thudding, cloak flapping like wings, a giant hawk-bat of a man.

"What do you want us to do, Sarge?"

Vau summoned Mird back to his side with a silent gesture. "Nothing."

"Sarge, we can—"

"No. You *can't*. Sorry. This crosses the line from soldier to . . . well, I don't want you involved with this. I needed Zey to know what I was doing, but it's better you don't ask why, either."

"Okay, Sarge." Scorch activated his helmet comlink, wondering if Vau didn't think they were good enough to take on RDS. "I'll get the schematics of the security cells, and we'll have you an operational plan inside half an hour."

"Scrap the plan, Scorch, but the schematics would be very welcome. Get some rest. Kashyyyk is going to wring you dry."

"Okay, Sarge." They had time to give him a bit of help. "We wouldn't foul up, honest."

"I know. But this is too dirty and political even for special ops. Concentrate on Kashyyyk. Real soldiering to be done there."

Vau gave him a thumbs-up gesture and walked away toward the accommodation wing. So what did he know about a big assault? There was always one coming, and Vau was good at leaving everyone wondering just how much he knew, just enough revealed to make folks take notice of him.

He knew an awful lot about Jedi, that was for sure.

Scorch slapped down his own curiosity and told it to behave. He didn't care how Vau knew. He was just glad that he did, and he trusted him, because Vau's words always came back to him from those first days on Kamino.

Everything I do from this moment on is to make sure you *survive to fight. Even if I don't.*

"Yes, Sarge," Scorch said. "We know."

Kyrimorut, Mandalore

"I want to come with you," Fi said. "I can go, can't I, Parja? Please?"

All Fi knew was that things were going badly wrong back on Coruscant. Jusik was packing up to go back, a day sooner than he'd said. He never broke his word; if he said he'd stay four days, then four days it was.

But he looked preoccupied as he stowed his bag in the burn-streaked Aggressor starfighter he used as a runabout. Jusik's metamorphosis from modest Jedi Knight to Mandalorian bad boy—not just in appearance—had been dizzyingly fast, as if he'd swapped one set of passionate beliefs for another without pausing to think. Maybe that was what being raised in a cult did to a man. He only knew how to surrender himself to an ideal. Fi knew how that felt, and how adrift you could feel when that certainty was snatched away.

Jusik's taste for fast, dangerous transport hadn't changed one bit, though. The Aggressor was the bounty-hunter special, with a decent hyperdrive and even holding cells.

"Your call, *F'ika,*" said Parja. "Just remember that you're a deserter, or you're dead, or you're stolen Republic property, whichever way they look at you. So you better not get caught if you *do* go."

Jusik fastened his bag, seeming not to hear. "One good thing about being a Jedi was that I never owned enough stuff to worry about packing. Now I'm working out what I need to get rid of to travel light."

"Me?" Fi said. *I know, I'll slow you down.*

"Now, I never said that . . ."

"I swear I won't be a burden."

"I've just commed *Kal'buir*. We've got a few problems to sort out. At least Dar knows about Kad now, and . . . well, that's resolved."

"So why are you rushing back?"

"We're in the final phase now, Fi. We've got a lot to do before we can pull everyone out, and Skirata needs all hands on deck."

"You said I was as fit as an average human." Fi made his mind up; he was going to go, even if he had to make his own way to the Core. "I'm probably as fit as *Kal'buir*, and you're not stopping him."

Jusik looked at Parja as if he was appealing to her to back him up. She didn't.

"*Bard'ika*, I'd rather he stayed here with me," she said. "But he can make his own decisions, and I'll still be here when he comes home. No *Mando* woman ever stopped her man going to war."

"You could come, too," Fi said. "And it's not exactly a war."

"You don't need me holding your hand any longer, Fi. Besides, someone's got to keep this place going, and I've got the workshop to worry about, too."

"It'll be a few weeks. That's all."

Jusik looked over his shoulder for a moment, as if he'd heard something, then shrugged and slammed the cargo hatch shut. "You're not going to give up, are you?"

"No."

"Take him, *Bard'ika*," Parja said. "I'll worry myself sick about him every minute he's away, but forcing him to sit it out won't help him get better."

Jusik didn't answer. He walked around the blunt tail section of the fighter and looked as if he was checking the airframe, but Fi knew him well enough to see that it was just marking time while something else—not the ongoing argument—was taking his attention.

"What's wrong?" Parja asked, drawing her blaster from her belt.

She did it casually, as if she was going to clean it. But when she flicked the charge button, Fi caught on. They had company. Nobody should have been able to find them here, but Jusik had sensed something.

"Maybe nothing," Jusik said, but he had his hand on his belt, too, and that meant he was feeling for his lightsaber. It was weird to see a *Mando* in traditional *beskar'gam* even handling that weapon. Jusik rarely activated it now, but like any soldier he defaulted to what he'd been trained to do. The body remembered; it didn't need the conscious mind. Jedi started lightsaber training when they were four years old.

Fi hadn't drawn a blaster in earnest for a long time, and the short custom WESTAR-20 still didn't feel right in his grip. Jusik turned to face out toward the field, scanning the landscape with slow care.

"Get down," he said. "Fi, Parja, find some cover."

Parja grabbed Fi's sleeve and forced him behind the protection of one of the Aggressor's twin manipulator arms.

"I thought we were hidden here," Fi whispered. "Nobody's supposed to be able to find us."

Jusik took a few steps forward. Fi heard his boots crunching on the gravel.

"There's two of you," he called out. "You're not sure if you're really bitter enough to kill me, or if you're desperate for help. I can even pinpoint your position."

The fields didn't answer. There were no engine or drive sounds, not even in the distance, just the sound of wind hushing the trees, and the distant rhythmic bark of a shatual buck announcing he was in town and looking for does.

It was a shame Jusik wasn't wearing his *buy'ce*. He could have sent Fi some coordinates to aim at. Come to that, Fi wasn't wearing his, either.

"Come on, I know what a clone feels like in the Force," Jusik called. "You're all different, *vode,* but I can still sense the things you have in common."

The seed heads on the grass fifty meters ahead rustled and shivered. Parja squinted down the optics of her blaster.

"I think I got 'em," she said. "Stang, that Jedi of yours is a human rangefinder. I reckon it's that *shabuir* Sull and his crazy buddy."

"Can you *see* them?"

"No, just the movement."

"Hold fire, then, *cyar'ika.*" Fi tried to follow her aim. He'd been a top-grade sniper. He felt the reduction to ordinary skill levels keenly. "They're ARC troopers. They're not that incompetent."

Jusik had always had an odd reckless streak. For the most part he was a methodical man, good at engineering and fixing things. But then he'd go and do something crazy, almost as if he wanted to test himself. Fi recalled a terrifying high-speed speeder bike ride through Coruscant on Jusik's pillion. Now Jusik walked slowly across the open ground and out into the knee-high grasses, making himself a target. Parja shifted her weight slightly, down on one knee with her elbow supported on a strut of the Aggressor's airframe.

"All right, get it over with," Jusik called. He held his arms away from his sides. "Parja, Fi? You will *not* open fire. Hear? Not unless Sull or Spar starts it."

A few moments later, the grass parted, and two figures in green *beskar'gam* got to their feet.

"*Osik,*" Parja said, adjusting her aim, "they were two meters to the right of where I thought they were."

"They're good at throwing you off." Fi had promised Sull he'd kill him if he messed with Jusik, and he was going to make good on that if the *shabuir* so much as twitched. "And they're too good at tracking us. We're getting sloppy."

Fi broke cover and went to back up Jusik, blaster still aimed. Parja covered him. Disappointingly, neither ARC had laid down his own weapon.

"If you've come to put a round through me, go ahead," Jusik said. Fi thought he was pulling some clever ruse, but then it dawned on him that he was *serious*; *Bard'ika* was standing there like a target, asking for some weird martyrdom. "If it gives you closure, do it."

Fi stepped into his path. "*Bard'ika!* Enough."

"Fi . . . either I believe in what I'm doing, or I don't."

Spar pulled off his helmet. "You're really full of it, Jedi."

"I'm not a Jedi now, but I was, and so I have to bear some of the guilt."

Spar holstered his blaster, and Sull followed suit. Fi didn't move. Parja walked up and pulled him aside.

"What's your problem?" she demanded, scowling at the two deserters. "Go spray your testosterone elsewhere. You don't even know how to be *Mando'ade*. But if you want a lesson, I'll give you one. It's more than putting on the *beskar'gam*."

"How did you find us?" Jusik asked.

"You fly a fighter like that, you get attention," Sull said. "Try parking it under cover next time."

Jusik put out his hand to shut Fi up even before Fi had formed the words, which was just as well. "You make a good point, *ner vod*. I was careless. What do you want from us?"

"We hear that Skirata might be onto something."

"ARC gossip, eh?"

"Is it true? Can he stop us aging so fast?"

"Not yet."

"So it's true that he's trying."

"If your gossip is that reliable, then you know the answer, and you know he'd help any deserter."

Sull looked at Spar. "Did he help *you* get off Kamino?"

Spar just raised an eyebrow. "He's okay, the old barve."

"We want in," Sull said. "How do we get to see him? Is he recruiting?"

"Room for eight in an Aggressor." Jusik gestured over his shoulder at the starfighter. "We're heading back to Coruscant. If you're up for some work, we've got plenty of jobs to keep a bored ARC trooper busy."

Jusik was insanely trusting. Fi wanted to grab his shoulders and shake him, and explain that he couldn't just dump two renegade Alpha planks on *Kal'buir* like that—or on

Ordo—but whatever Jusik picked up from the Force usually seemed to work out.

Except for forgetting that we need to camouflage all vessels, right away. Even here, even on Mandalore.

"Okay," said Sull. "Let's go."

Jusik popped the hatches and ushered them into the small cargo area. Parja nudged Fi with her elbow, hands on hips, chin down. Now that Fi was on the brink of leaving, the reality of being parted from her hit him hard. He missed his brothers, he felt useless, and he needed to get something back in his life—but he'd craved a girlfriend for so long.

I'm ungrateful. I get what I want, and then I forget what it was like to be that lonely.

"Well, I said you were worth fixing up, and Jusik and me, we fixed you up, so . . ." She looked resigned. "Want me to pack some food for you?"

"Just . . . well, my backpack."

"You be careful."

Fi was a little disappointed that she didn't beg him to stay. Maybe that really *was* how Mandalorian women did things: they gritted their teeth and got on with it while the men were away, if they weren't off fighting themselves. They didn't fuss and make parting even harder.

"You know I love you," he said. *Shab,* he couldn't remember the words of the contract. He had to open his datapad. "Now marry me."

Parja was still wearing her workshop overalls, spattered with lubricant, pockets ratting with tools. She wiped her hands on her pants and held out her hand to him to grip it in the Mandalorian way, hand to wrist. Fi took it.

"You know the words, *F'ika?*"

"I can read them out."

"Okay," Parja said. "We read them together."

She looked into his face. He found that he could repeat her words with just a fraction's delay, and do a pretty good job of making the pledge together, without the need to look at the words on his 'pad.

"Mhi solus tome," she said, and he joined in. *"Mhi solus dar'tome, mhi me'dinui an, mhi ba'juri verde."*

It was a very simple pledge, a contract, a business deal in its way: *We are one when together, we are one when parted, we share all, we will raise warriors.* There wasn't anything more that needed saying.

"Is that it?" Fi asked.

"Yeah, you're stuck with me now."

"Okay. That's good."

"Yeah, you'll do, too."

Jusik stuck his head out the hatch. "Fi, did I miss something?"

"We're married," Fi said. Did he feel different? Yes, he really *did.* "You can see Parja blew our savings on her wedding gown."

"You *mir'sheb.*" She gave Fi a big, noisy kiss. "You're lucky you've got a missus who knows how to replace a manifold gasket. Now, *Bard'ika,* you bring him back in the same or better condition, or this galaxy won't be big enough to hide from me."

It was always best to leave fast once you decided to go. Long drawn-out good-byes were painful; Fi discovered that for the first time in his life, and although it hurt, it was nothing like the pain of thinking he'd live and die lonely. It was a pain he could savor, to remind himself what he now had and what was worth living and fighting for.

The Aggressor lifted clear. Parja was still visible for a few seconds, a tiny figure in brown, then a dot. The camouflaged bastion just looked like uneven ground from the air.

"Aren't you supposed to celebrate?" Jusik asked, engaging the autopilot. Sull and Spar were aft in the hold. "I think it's really sad to marry and then part."

"It's not forever. And we had the honeymoon already, I suppose."

"Even so . . . okay, we can do the drinking and carousing later."

That was a nice thought. Everyone could attend then. There was an end in sight—of sorts—to the war, and even if Skirata never found a way of slowing the aging process, Fi would live the years he had left to the fullest.

Coruscant stood between him and that happier time. But

he was back in action again, and that made him feel whole. He gazed out the viewport at the starscape before the Aggressor jumped to hyperspace, and thought of Sicko, the TIV pilot killed helping Omega board a Separatist ship. Space was a big, lonely place to die.

"*Bard'ika,* I think *Kal'buir* is going to go nuts when you turn up with these two," he said, diverting himself from thoughts of Sicko. "They found us. The bastion's supposed to be off the chart. And how do they know about the aging cure? Why trust them enough to bring them along?"

Jusik gave Fi that look, as if he was wearing a sun visor and letting it slide down his nose so that he could look over the rim. "If they're secure in the hold, they're not wandering around blabbing about how they found us, are they? And Spar's almost certainly still got contacts in the ARC ranks. I'd put my bets on Maze talking to his ARC chums about Ko Sai's head showing up in a box . . ."

"That's disgusting."

"Yeah."

"Don't think that I feel sorry for her. She never saw us as anything that could feel pain. But when I look back at the things *I've* done that seemed normal at the time . . ."

"That's war, Fi. You don't have to feel bad about it. You *really* didn't have a choice. She did."

"You can tell what I'm thinking, can't you?"

"Sometimes."

"You're a good brother, *Bard'ika.*"

Fi calculated the time to Triple Zero; they'd be landing by nightfall in Galactic City. Now he was starting to get that tingle in his gut, like pre-battle anxiety, because Parja was right. He wasn't just returning to base. He was sneaking back as a man who didn't exist, and he couldn't afford to be caught.

It was like operating behind enemy lines. He'd had plenty of experience at that.

Coruscant, Triple Zero, was now enemy territory.

Laseema's apartment, Coruscant

Etain watched the doors, mouth dry and stomach knotted. She could feel Darman coming closer, and Skirata, too.

She knew their impressions in the Force so well that she could pin them down pretty accurately. There were variations from day to day, but they always had the same cores: Skirata, a whirlpool of intense loves and hatreds, and Darman, generally at peace with the world. Today, though, she could feel the change in both of them, from Darman's anguish and uncertainty, and from Skirata's raw pain.

But she still wasn't ready for what she saw when the doors parted.

"Kal, what *happened* to you?"

Skirata looked terrible. He was slightly bent over, as if his chest or stomach hurt him, and his face was a mass of cuts and fresh bruises. Someone had given him a thrashing. *Vau.* She'd thought the two sergeants had settled their long-running feud, but it seemed to have erupted again.

"I got what was coming to me," he said, his voice distorted by swollen lips. "Not the first time, either, and it won't be the last." He pushed Darman ahead of him with a careful hand. "Go on, son. You've got someone to meet."

"Kal—"

"*Et'ika,* just grab this time with Dar and Kad, and I'll sort myself out. You don't know when you'll next get a chance. I'll be back in the morning, and Laseema's staying with Jaller's family for the night."

Kal's injuries had rescued her from an awkward moment. Darman hadn't spoken to her since he walked out of her cabin on Nerrif Station a few days ago, and she'd had no idea how to break that ice again. But that was suddenly forgotten now. Darman's embrace was desperate. He buried his head in her shoulder, hugging her so hard that it almost hurt. Etain looked past him to see what Skirata was doing, but he was already gone. She heard his footsteps fade outside.

"Kad's asleep," she said. "I'll wake him."

"Is that bad for him?"

Darman was already the anxious father. "Of course not,"

she said. "He sleeps when he's tired. But it's hard to get him into a routine because we don't have one."

"Laseema looks after him?"

"Yes, she's wonderful. And Besany helps out, and Bardan and Kal. But . . . it's time he knew his dad."

"Okay." Darman swallowed. "I'm ready now. I really am."

"I don't know what else to say, Dar."

"Nothing you need to say. We can't change what happened, so it makes sense to forget it and start again."

That was Darman all over; he never bore grudges, and was the most easygoing of men. If anyone thought clones were identical, all they had to do was look at Darman and his brothers to see that they were as diverse as any random group of human beings.

"Am I forgiven?" she asked.

"Yes." He stepped back and pinched his top lip, a little nervous gesture that she'd seen in Skirata from time to time. In ordinary civilian clothes—no fatigues or armor that marked him as a standardized product of Kamino—Darman looked like any other being Etain might see on the walkways of Coruscant, and that promised the same possibility for her. "It was me, *Et'ika*. I hit *Kal'buir*."

It was hard to take in. "What?"

"I really hurt him. He didn't even try to defend himself. He just let me go crazy, and kept saying he was sorry."

The thought of Darman even losing his temper seemed utterly alien, let alone doing that much harm to someone he loved—to anyone, in fact. It was a different kind of violence from the kind he was used to in combat.

Is it? Am I so steeped in Jedi belief that violence is acceptable if it's not done from hate or anger that I can't see something fundamental?

"What started it?" she asked.

"He told me everything he kept from us. *Everything*. Ko Sai's research, the new clone army . . . so I called him a liar. I told him I couldn't trust him. And with him not telling me about Kad, I just . . . hated him for a moment. No, not even *him*. I just lost it completely, about everything, just like Scorch did."

It was the first time Etain had realized how broken some of the clone troops were. It was one thing haranguing other Jedi about the clones' inherent humanity; it was another to recognize that it had a negative side, too. Etain had come to see them as invulnerable because she recognized their superior qualities, and forgot that, in time, the intensity with which they fought would shatter them as surely as it would any other being. It just took much longer.

"How can he forgive me, *Et'ika*?" Darman asked.

"Because he loves you—you're his son." It wasn't the punches that would leave the scars on Skirata. She knew that. It was losing Darman's trust. "Have you forgiven *him*?"

Darman glanced at his own hands. The ferocity of his attack showed in the cuts and bruises on his knuckles. "Of course I have. I didn't mean any of it. I was just out of it for a few minutes."

People always claimed they didn't mean the things they said in the heat of the moment, but usually they simply didn't know they thought those things, or would dare say them aloud. "Do you think he's keeping any other secrets from you, Dar?"

"I don't know," he said. "But it doesn't matter now."

Love and trust weren't necessarily the same thing. Etain decided to change the subject. "Let's see if Kad's awake."

He wasn't; he was sleeping peacefully, and they stood watching him for a while, mesmerized, until Etain picked him up and handed him to Darman. Kad woke and looked up at Darman with endearing wide-eyed surprise. Could he tell this wasn't Ordo or Mereel? Maybe he could. He grinned— he grinned at everyone, of course—but this seemed different somehow. Maybe she was imagining it. He'd reacted strongly to Darman when he held him before.

"That's Da-da," Etain said. "Say *Da-da,* sweetie."

Darman just burst into tears. Etain did, too.

There wasn't a lot to say, just a lot to feel, so neither of them tried to rationalize it. They spent the rest of the late afternoon and evening playing with Kad and pretending that there wasn't a war outside waiting for them, that they were just any ordinary young family. They even recorded a family holoimage for the years to come. It was an exotic, heady fantasy for people who were anything but ordinary, and wouldn't be allowed to be ordinary without a fight. Etain pondered the irony of desperately wanting *not* to be special.

"I'm glad you called him Kad," Darman said at last.

"Are you happy that he's growing up as a little Mandalorian?"

"Will he be able to use the Force?"

"Jusik and I are starting to show him how to control it. Well, to hide it, really. I don't want the Jedi Order taking him."

Darman's expression hardened a little. "Would they do that?"

"With a benign smile, but yes. They would."

"It's not all nice, the Jedi Order, is it? It's not quite the image we were given on Kamino."

"Not all Jedi are the same."

"I still want Kad to be Mandalorian."

"So do I."

Etain held Kad's hands and walked him to Darman, but he pulled away and tottered toward his father with a big adoring grin on his face. Darman let him clamber over him, looking equally besotted.

"He looks like you," Darman said, ignoring the fact that Kad was the spitting image of himself. Kad had wide dark eyes and black hair, like Darman and all his brothers. But his nose was narrow and slightly upturned, like Etain's. "I should have been there when he was born, shouldn't I? I've seen it in the holodramas."

"Real life isn't as tidy as that," Etain said. "And I'm glad you weren't there, in a way. It wasn't my finest hour."

"Did it hurt?"

"Like you wouldn't believe."

It was funny how physical pain could be completely forgotten. As Etain watched Darman coming to terms with a baby son when he was no more than a kid himself in so many ways, she was struck by how much he reminded her of Skirata as he handled Kad and talked to him, even down to the faces he pulled to make him laugh. Humans did some things instinctively, and not even cloning and the heartless regime on Kamino could suppress that, but the rest of parenting—they had to learn the hard way.

She'd never known Jango Fett, but his genome hadn't dictated everything in Darman. Skirata's influence was plain. In every sense of the word, Skirata was Dar's father, and had laid down the foundations for the kind of father that Darman would be.

Aliit ori'shya tal'din. Family was definitely more than bloodline—and more than midi-chlorians.

11

*The Mandalorian language has more terms of insult than
any of the more widely spoken galactic tongues.
But whereas most species choose insults that are based on
parentage or appearance, the majority of Mandalorian
pejoratives are concerned with cowardice, stupidity,
laziness, dull conversation, or a lack of hygiene.
It reveals the preoccupations of a nomadic warrior culture
where bloodline matters less than personal qualities,
faces are largely masked, and a clean,
efficient camp is crucial to survival.*
—Mandalorians: Identity and Language, *published by the
Galactic Institute of Anthropology*

Besany Wennen's apartment, Coruscant, 999 days ABG

"I can't carry on like this, Ordo."

Besany hadn't slept well. She'd woken and started tidying
her apartment in the middle of night. Ordo had no idea what
was normal for a human female, but it made sense to him
that if you couldn't sleep, you used the time productively.
Tidiness was essential to good discipline.

She was very upset, and she seemed more upset that he'd
carried on sleeping while she couldn't.

"I know it must be very stressful," he said, watching her
scrubbing frantically at the breakfast dishes. "But I don't
think you should stay here. It's too dangerous."

She whipped around so hard that her hair flew. "I meant
Jilka. She's under arrest, and terrible things might be hap-

pening to her, and it's *my fault*. Ordo, *sweetheart,* I know this is daily routine in your job, but it's not everyday in *mine.*"

Ordo was still unsure what evidence might link Jilka to Besany. The woman had no idea what was going on. However hard RDS tried, they couldn't beat out of her what wasn't in there to be revealed, although beings said all kinds of things under torture just to get it to stop. He poured himself another cup of caf, and wondered where Mereel and Jaing had got to. Watching his brothers come and go reminded him how tied to Coruscant he was most days.

"Ordo, are you listening?"

"Yes, it's a pity about Jilka."

"Pity? *Pity?*" Besany was strikingly beautiful, with a bone structure so perfect that it seemed manufactured; but when she got angry, it all turned to ice, tight-lipped and unforgiving. "*I'm* the guilty party. My friend's in some RDS prison cell *in my place.* I can't let that happen. I just can't."

"So what do you plan on doing?" Ordo didn't think the two women were that close, but Besany seemed to have no friends at all other than Jilka. "Turn yourself in, and tell Palpatine's minions the whole story? Implicate *Kal'buir*? Bring down the escape plan?"

"But she's *innocent.*"

Besany wasn't a soldier, and she wasn't used to the idea of expendability. Ordo wasn't completely inured to it, either, but he accepted there was sometimes a call to be made between doing the right thing in the short term, and making a bigger difference in the longer run. It was a call he hadn't had to make at that level of personal involvement—yet.

And there was the small matter that he was besotted with Besany, and didn't know Jilka at all.

He tried hard to experience his beloved's anxiety for her friend, but he knew he was like *Kal'buir:* there was a circle of those he would sacrifice everything to save, and anyone outside that had to save themselves.

"It happens all the time," Ordo said. "We had to let a company of troopers get creamed because we couldn't alert them to an attack without letting the Separatists know that we'd cracked their encryption."

"*We?* Personally?"

"No." *Would I have done that?* Ordo didn't know.

"Then you don't know what it's like to be in my shoes."

Besany's problem was that she was very moral. He liked that about her. It was why she refused to turn a blind eye to the exploitation of clones; it was why she put her own safety on the line. But it was also why she couldn't handle seeing Jilka arrested in her place. And, apart from rescuing Jilka, there was no way of easing Besany's conscience.

Ordo was more worried about what Jilka might feel forced to say to the RDS interrogators. Skirata was supposed to have done something about that, if it wasn't already too late, and now Ordo had his own moral dilemma: should he tell Besany that Jilka might be silenced for good by the very people Besany had taken the crazy risk for in the first place?

He needed to say something tactful. He racked his brain for the kind of words Skirata would use in these circumstances.

"This might sound harsh," he said carefully, "but you wanted to do your bit in a war. This is what war is like. The consequences cost lives, our friends might suffer unfairly, and it's not like any other job. It's as extreme as life gets. There are no rules, and you don't go home at the end of the day with your life set back to normal for another day in the office tomorrow."

It was all true. Ordo was quite pleased that he had managed *not* to say it was tough luck, and that in the time that Jilka had been detained, thousands of clone troopers had been maimed or killed, also without deserving it.

"Yes." Besany let out a breath through her nose, a resigned sigh. "But if it was *me* in there, I'd want to think someone was going to try to do something to help me."

"Maybe they *will,*" Ordo said. "And if they do, we won't know the result until later."

She could make what she wanted of that. If he lied to her, though, could he live with it any more than she could? Would she hate him when she found out?

There was a knock at the door, and Besany jumped.

"I'll handle it," he said, and drew his sidearm.

Any routine callers—she didn't have many, mostly delivery droids with groceries—would use the door-comm from the ground level. To knock on the door, they had to be in the building already, and Besany wasn't someone who mixed with the neighbors.

Ordo motioned her to stay away from the window, then moved silently down the short hallway to the front door. He checked the security cam, but could see nothing except the smooth velvet pile of the carpet stretching down the corridor to the turbolift, and the spotless cream walls. That was what he expected. He flicked the power setting on his blaster to maximum, and then something caught his eye.

For a split second, his mind said *oil leak,* but the black tarry liquid issuing from the ventilation panel just above the floor level was one he'd seen before. He held his blaster on it anyway while it settled in a pool with an odd, almost domed meniscus.

"At least you knock now," he said.

The pool re-formed itself into a large predator like a dire-cat, with a glossy black coat and long double-tipped fangs. It blinked orange eyes at him.

"That's so you don't get agitated and shoot again," it said in a rich, liquid, male voice. "But that was Jinart who you shot last time. I am Valaqil."

Besany appeared in the doorway. She should have stayed put until Ordo had told her the apartment was secure. "I thought you said you were leaving the last time we met."

"I've come back," Valaqil said. "Not that we owe your kind anything, but Qiilura is now recovering from the human occupation, and your nasty little sergeant has kept his word to leave us in peace. So I keep my side of the bargain. Run while you still can."

"Could you be more specific?" Ordo didn't like Gurlanins all that much, although he accepted it was as an irrational prejudice. He had no reason to distrust them, because they did exactly what they said they would, but shapeshifters made him uneasy. "We've got a lot of things to run from at the moment."

"Very soon, Palpatine will unleash a huge clone army, the one he's been building on Centax Two."

"We worked that out," Besany said.

"He's not preparing to use it against the Separatists."

Now that was a fascinating twist. "What makes you say that?" asked Ordo.

"Because I have been to Centax Two, and I have seen deployment plans, to ensure that Qiilura wasn't on the list."

A shapeshifter was the most feared spy of all. Gurlanins could assume any shape, stow away on any ship, and infiltrate anywhere. They communicated telepathically with one another. They might not have had a civilization with weapons and technology, but they were very bad enemies to make.

"Want to expand on that?"

"Soldier, you can't even see what's in front of you, can you?"

Ordo wasn't used to being told he wasn't smart enough to understand. He wasn't so much offended as shocked. "So what troop strengths are we talking about? What targets?"

"Enough to occupy thousands of worlds."

"Separatist worlds?" Ordo was thinking hard. If Palpatine wasn't planning a massive assault on the Seps, which worlds would he be targeting? Ordo decided to look for some economic angle when the Gurlanin left. "I know this war has been engineered carefully for some other ends, and many wars are, but what does he want out of it? *Which worlds?*"

"*Lots* of worlds. That's all you need to know. I think I know what your plans are, more or less, and so I advise you to put them into effect sooner rather than later. Agent Wennen will be the next Treasury employee who vanishes into RDS cells, and then it's only a matter of time before Palpatine hunts you all down. Go now."

"You know about Jilka, then," Besany said.

"Of course I do," said Valaqil. "That's how we bought you time."

Ordo got there a moment before Besany did. "You set her up, then?" He put his arm out instinctively to block Besany's line of fire before she did something rash, but he also registered the word *we*. "That wasn't very helpful, actually. She's a little too close to us for comfort."

The meaning had now sunk in with Besany. She was white-faced with anger. "You—you—" She didn't seem to have a term of abuse for a predator. "I *trusted* you! You've been prowling around my office? How could you *do* that? Why Jilka?"

"Why anybody?" said Valaqil. "Why us? She ran record searches on that bogus company you were looking for, and that was recorded on the system, and so it was a short step for us to print flimsi copies of information that pointed to an interest in Centax Two."

"She's innocent. Do you know what they're probably doing to her now?"

"Would you rather they were doing it to you?" Valaqil turned in an elegant circle as if he was going to settle down, but he was simply heading for the ventilation grille. He sat down on his haunches, gazing at the plate as if some prey might emerge from it. "You should have been more discreet about your affair with the gallant captain here. It's a very short step to connect you with excessive curiosity about Centax."

Besany turned to Ordo. "You said there was nothing on file about me."

"He was right, there isn't," said Valaqil, "but there are too many beings now who have come into contact with Skirata's gang, and there comes a time when you can no longer operate covertly because too many know you, and you have crossed too many. That time is very close. You'd better hope that your enemies spend more time with Jilka before they realize she's useless to them and start looking again."

The Gurlanin blinked a couple of times as if waiting for thanks or at least a reaction. He hadn't been wrong the last time; Ordo, cautious as he was, believed Valaqil now. The creature became a slick of black liquid before flowing back through the ventilation plate, and then vanished forever.

Laseema's apartment, Coruscant, *Cuy'val Dar*
emergency planning session

"You *can't* slot her," Skirata said, putting his comlink back in his pocket. "That was Ordo. The Gurlanin framed the woman to throw RDS off the scent."

"Then that's her very bad luck." Vau was getting annoyed. Mird whined at his feet, gazing up at him, always sensitive to its master's moods. "This isn't like rescuing one of our own. Get Jilka out alive, and we have to find somewhere to stash her. She won't just say, 'Thanks for saving me, I'll just forget all that happened, and vanish of my own accord.' She'll be a liability for as long as she lives."

"Then we hide her," Tay'haai said. "I'll find some way of getting her off the planet if you can't."

"If she's been framed and has nothing to reveal," Vau said, "then the urgency to shut her up recedes somewhat, except for the fact that she knows Besany's boyfriend is called Ordo. Do I have to draw you a picture, Kal?"

"And we've already got two retrievals to do." Gilamar sounded resigned, and that worried Skirata. He didn't usually agree with Vau even about the time of day. "All the intel says we don't have much time left, and we just can't wander around collecting waifs and strays forever."

"Is this to spare Besany's conscience?" Vau asked. "Because if it is, let me remind you that it's one more problem caused by sentimental attachment, all because your lads don't *think* before they drop their plates for the first girl who smiles at them."

"You *chakaar*." Skirata tolerated no slight against his boys or their womenfolk. "Besany's *earned* the right to be one of us. And there's the small matter of this being the right thing to do."

Vau raised an eyebrow. "I hate it when you get moral."

"This whole operation is about *being moral*. We're in it to save those who've been screwed over by the Republic." *And we were getting on so well.* But Vau was right. If they thought Jilka was going to bring down the weight of the Chancellor's personal police on Besany—and that would mean on them all—then she had to be silenced, kindly or unkindly. He'd been ready to do it himself until he faced up to the effect it would have on Besany, and so on Ordo. It was also hard to forget the look on Niner's face when he worked out what Skirata was considering. "We get her out. We get Uthan out. And we get my daughter out."

"Jilka may already have given up Ordo and Besany without even knowing she's done any damage. Let's just grab Uthan and bang out now."

Vau *always* had a point. Omega and Etain were still on Coruscant, Besany was on her way to the safe house—Laseema's apartment—and Jusik was due to land at any time with the two ARCs, even if he might get tied up keeping an eye on Fi. They had their trillion-credit haul, and more cloning data than even Arkanian Micro could dream of. Now was a good time to go. Jilka could tell RDS everything, but it would be too late to stop them getting away.

Somehow, though, Skirata had to try for Jilka. He hated himself for not automatically putting Ruu at the top of the list.

"We spring Jilka," Skirata said. "And we get her to Mandalore."

"Oh, and you think she'll be grateful to be stuck at the *shebs* end of the Rim for the rest of her life?" Vau said. "Now I know why Omega make a habit of abducting prisoners and not slotting them like they should."

"Walon, let's at least try. We're not savages."

"Exactly, we're *soldiers,* Kal. And we've forgotten this is a war."

The four *Cuy'val Dar* stood pondering the holoschematic of the Republic security building and the service delivery schedules. They had a portfolio of bogus ID chips and could walk in with the catering, the sanitation crew, or even the droid that maintained the office machinery. It was just a case of finding the fastest route, and locating Jilka. It wasn't a huge prison. There were just twenty cells.

The doors opened; Ordo ushered Besany inside. She was clutching a large holdall, and her face was grim. The conversation about Jilka's fate stopped abruptly.

"*Bes'ika* can't go back to her apartment," Ordo said. "No telling who'll show up next."

Skirata's choices had narrowed to one. "We're just discussing how to extract Jilka."

Vau raised one eyebrow. The others said nothing.

"We can't extract her from the RDS facility by force, because it'll get all kinds of unfortunate attention too early in the game." Ordo took out his datapad. "We get them to take her out of the cell, and snatch her in transit."

"You've got a plan," Gilamar said.

"Of course. I've got access to Republic Intel codes. If we time this right, then I simply generate a bogus request for a rendition to the Rep Intel detention facilities. Then we hit the transport en route."

Skirata gestured at Vau. "Yes, but Brain of Galactic City here has already told Zey we're going to extract her."

"Double-bluff," Vau said. "When he hears it happened, he won't wonder if we're involved for some dubious reason and start digging. He thinks I'm spying on you anyway. He'll nod and say, 'Oh, that's Vau doing the decent thing for me, and thwarting those Intel and RDS jokers.' Won't he?"

Skirata just raked his fingers through his hair. "Well, what's done's done, and now we just have to clean up as best we can."

"Okay, let's *triple*-bluff," Ordo said. "Sergeant Vau, you and I will intercept the transport."

"*If* they buy the request."

"Get changed. We'll do it within the hour. Try to look Separatist."

Vau's face didn't move a muscle. "I'll put on my best Jabiimi accent."

Besany looked numb now. She seemed to be acclimatizing to a permanent high level of insane risk. Given another month, Skirata thought, she'd be as bad as the rest of them.

"Come on, *daughter*," he said, taking the bag from her hands with as reassuring a smile as he could manage. "Let's get you settled in. Is this everything?"

She nodded. "Yes. I can't think what to do with the apartment at the moment—"

"Leave things as they are," he said. "If you vanish completely, then it just draws attention. Might be a good idea if you resigned from your job, though."

That seemed to hurt. A little frown creased the corners of her eyes for a fleeting moment. "I'll cite personal problems with my partner," she said, taking it like a trouper. "They don't tend to want to pry into domestic stuff, and it's been noticed that I'm not exactly the woman I was."

Skirata wasn't sure how to take that. When Besany opened her bag and laid the contents on the cabinet in the room kept for Ordo, it told Skirata what really mattered to her. Her subconscious had told her what she couldn't live without, and it wasn't trinkets and comforts she'd crammed into the holdall with a few changes of clothes, but images, information, and her blaster.

She set the holoimage projector on the side table.

"It pays to travel light," Skirata said.

"Well, I understand Mandalorians a great deal better after today." She opened the projector and activated it. "If you can't carry it, it's a burden, and if it can be easily replaced, it's not worth regret."

"You married a Mandalorian. What do you think that makes you?"

At least it made her laugh, and that lit up her face. "I've got to wear armor, haven't I?"

"Nothing but top-grade *beskar*, too. Only the very best for my girls."

Some cultures preserved images on sheets of flimsi, static and silent. Skirata once thought that was a poor substitute for the walking, talking, three-dimensional holoimages, but he found them easier to deal with on the bad days. A static picture was firmly anchored in the past, making the subject untouchable, announcing clearly that those days, those moments, were long gone. But a holoimage brought a special kind of pain; it was the presence of people as they really had been, as if they would answer if spoken to or respond to a touch. It was a cruel illusion. Static two-dimensional images reminded you clearly that it was all over. Holoimages just dragged the untouchable past into the present and tormented you with it.

"Want to see my father?" she asked. "My first one?"

"I'm honored to be the second," Skirata said. "Yes, I'd love to see your dad."

Her father, Norlin Wennen, lived again in the moving holoimage for a few moments. "Are you coming, Bes?" The figure smiled and beckoned, as if he had something wonderful he wanted to show her. "You've never seen anything like this, I'll bet . . ."

Besany smiled, distracted. "It was the jewel-caves of Birsingrial, and we were on vacation," she said to Skirata. "I was ten, I think."

And she could answer her father a hundred times, but he'd never hear, never reply. She watched her ten-year-old self run after him, giggling with excitement as she vanished into the shafts of ruby and emerald light.

"I do that, too," Skirata said softly.

"That was our last trip together before my mother left."

"Did she have a reason?"

"Yes, but I can't recall his name."

Skirata didn't comment. "Want to see mine?" He handed her the small projector he kept in his belt at all times and flicked the controls. A grid of small images hovered in the air for her to select and enlarge. He pointed out detail. "The guy in green armor—Jusik's armor—is my adopted father, Munin. And here's all my *vode* from previous missions. My kids—all of them, clone and nonclone—and Kamino. Walon recorded a lot of this. He reckoned I'd need evidence for the defense if I ever filleted another Kaminoan." He gestured at the images of himself surrounded by a group of six grim-faced identical little boys while he stripped down a large blaster rifle on a table in front of them. "I only ever had to show them once. And here's some of my commandos in training . . . yeah, that's Theta, Dar's first squad. Poor little *shabuire*—all dead now, bar him."

"Why does Ordo always sleep with the covers over his head?" Besany asked.

Skirata stared in slight defocus at the holoimages, then put the projector on the cabinet. "Live ordnance tests. To see how little kids coped with the noise and shock. He couldn't stand the night storms on Kamino after that, and he always buried his head under the covers. Funny, none of his brothers did."

She gave him a long look that he couldn't quite read, and for a moment he wondered if she thought he was reminding her that her own woes were nothing compared with those that Ordo and his brothers endured. Then again, she might just have been trying to imagine the closed world of Kamino, a small group of marginal Mandalorians cooped up together for years whether they liked one another or not, re-creating a small but distorted outpost of their society a long way from home, just to stay sane.

Who saved who? Who needed the teaching of the Mandalorian ethic more—our boys, or us?

Besany's fine-boned face broke into a sad smile again. "Don't let him get himself killed."

"He's Ordo," Skirata said. "He decided he was never going to let that happen to him when he was two years old."

Yes, the Nulls—and all his clones—had come a long way. And they had a lot farther still to go.

Sector L-32, Galactic City, an hour later

Ordo had to hand it to Vau: he looked utterly convincing.

With a ferociously short haircut, as near to shaven as he could get without a shine on his scalp, and a lightly tinted mini HUD visor of the kind favored by the security community, he looked like the real deal. The severe black business tunic set it all off. It said *do not mess with me.* He looked like a Republic enforcer of the most dreaded kind, quiet and implacable.

"Fortunately, my hair grows back fast." Vau sat in the passenger seat of the unmarked black official speeder and passed his palm discreetly across the top of his scalp as if feeling naked. "This is *not* my style."

The speeder wasn't actually one they'd liberated from the GAR command pool, but Enacca's contacts seemed to be able to summon up a facsimile of anything on a drive and repulsors. Ordo contented himself with the ubiquitous helmet and visor common to most enforcement and rescue agencies across the planet. Mereel might have enjoyed disguising himself by altering his hair and eye color, but Ordo wanted to keep it simple.

He checked his chrono. Five minutes until the shift changeover at both the Rep Intel facility and the RDS; it would then be another eight hours until anyone checked the custody sheets again at either end. But Ordo and Vau wouldn't be waiting that long.

"I hope Mird is okay," Vau said, staring out of the tinted viewscreen at the flicker of passing vessels zipping by in the skylane at the end of the alley.

"Is a strill safe around a small child?"

"Being hermaphroditic, all strills have a maternal streak, Ordo. Hence the endless nest building when it sees the baby."

"If it takes my clothing to make nests one more time, I shall be very displeased."

Vau snorted. "Come on. It's charming."

Ordo could recall the time he was terrified of Mird and pulled a blaster on it; the animal seemed bigger than him at that age, a savage thing. Now it had become a comrade in this war. It even played with babies. All things were possible.

The chrono showed 1400.

"Okay, let's do it," he said, opening his comlink. "Wad'e, are you ready for nerf herding?"

Tay'haai grunted. "I hurt my neck last time I did this. Let's try to avoid collisions."

Vau opened his comlink, transmitting a false origin code to appear on the RDS system as Republic Intel. Ordo readied the bogus authority codes, slicing into the Intel system to generate a handover request from a genuine Intel officer who happened to be on a lunch break. It was just a matter of looking down a list of terminals grouped by the appropriate department, and finding those machines that were on standby. It would take hours to show up as an anomaly.

"RDS Custody Desk, please . . ." Vau had a rich, resonant, upper-class voice that he could polish or roughen at will. It oozed authority. He was hard to disbelieve. "Hello . . . yes, this is Republic Intelligence . . . We're requesting a prisoner transfer. We require a female human, Zan Zentis, initial J . . . Would you like me to spell that? No? Very well. Apologies for the short notice, but it's to minimize the risk of a rescue attempt. We have reason to believe that her associates might attempt to extract her. Now, we can collect her, or you can transfer her to our secure unit, but we'd like this done immediately for the reasons I've given."

Vau stared ahead as if in a trance, listening. Ordo both dreaded these gambles and relished the adrenaline rush of taking them. If the RDS bought the story and opted to ship her over, then it would be a physical intervention. If they were lazy, and said to come and get her, it would be a tidy taxi job.

"Yes, I do have authorization . . . stand by . . . transmitting now."

They waited. It was a long thirty seconds.

"Thank you . . . yes, that would be kind. Do transfer her. May I have your transport identity, please, for the security gate?" Vau rolled his eyes, his voice unchanged. "Got that. Thank you."

Ordo kicked the speeder into life and shot off at top speed toward the RDS landing platform. It was secured, but they could hang around and wait for the RDS transport to emerge.

Vau tapped the transponder code into the onboard sensors so that they could identify the right vessel. They were never marked. *"Shab."* He sighed, laying a fearsome sawn-off Verpine slugthrower across his lap. "I hate it when they're conscientious. Why can't they be lazy *di'kute* like every other government department, and get us to do the work?"

Tay'haai, a few blocks away, sounded as if he was tightening all his speeder restraints. On the comlink, metal chinked and fabric rustled. "Can we synchronize holocharts, please?"

Ordo concentrated on the anxious chill in his gut and used it to keep him sharp, just as Skirata had shown him. It was almost the first lesson he'd ever taught Ordo and his brothers: to use their fear. It was their alarm system, he said. They had to heed it, and realize the adrenaline was getting them ready to run faster, fight harder, and notice only the things they needed to stay alive.

Ordo slowed the speeder and brought it to a standing hover at the end of the spur skylane leading to the main route. Government vehicles could bypass the automated nav system that controlled skylane traffic, just like taxis. They could take any route. But in broad daylight, they had limited options for intercepting another vessel without getting a prime-time slot on HNE.

"So where's the best place to take them out?" Vau asked, flashing the sector skylane holochart onto the inside of the viewscreen like a HUD. "Got that, Wad'e?"

"I'm synced in. Thanks. If they take the direct route, I'll try to force a stop at the underpass between the spaceport and Core Plaza. That way we don't get picked up by surveillance sats."

CSF ran the sat system, which was simply a crime prevention tool, and all awkward things could be made to vanish if CSF was approached the right way. The archive was only stored for ten days anyway. Ordo checked the underpass layout. There were service bays to allow delivery repulsortrucks and maintenance vessels to pull in. That looked like the best option.

"Now, what if they don't take that route?" Ordo asked.

"Usual ploy," Tay'haai said. "Force 'em down the levels, the lower the better. But jam their comms first, before they know they're being hijacked. We don't want a full-scale fleet battle in front of the good citizens."

"This is why I prefer the lower levels," Vau said. "You can have a decent shoot-out and an armed misunderstanding down there, and nobody pokes their nose in. Very civilized."

Ordo watched the RDS entrance. After a few minutes, the gates parted and a nondescript white windowless speeder edged out, looking exactly like a million other service vessels cruising the skylanes at that moment, with no livery indicating prison duties. The sensor blipped; it recognized the transponder code. A red pulsing light appeared on the head-up holochart.

"Got it," Tay'haai said. "Watch my trace, please. Running parallel to you."

"Good luck, gentlemen." Vau seemed to love these operations. He came alive. He and Mird responded to the same stimuli: the chase. "*Oya!* Let's hunt."

Ordo kept a sensible five vessels' distance behind the prison transport. The pilot didn't seem to like crowded skylanes and diverted to a side route, probably wanting to spend as little time in transit as possible to minimize the risks. He looked as if he wasn't going to take the spaceport route.

"Okay, I'm looking for service bays." Vau followed the holochart, leaning forward a little and adjusting the display to a larger scale. "I'll call them as we come within a quarter klick of them."

"Left," Ordo said.

The holochart traces shifted, and Tay'haai pulled a block ahead of them in readiness. He was running on a chronocounter that would time his intercept run to cut across the prison speeder's path at precisely the right moment to slow it, stop it, or force it to divert. The idea was to avoid a crash. It didn't always work out that way.

"He's moving down to the repulsortruck lane," Ordo said. "Naughty. That's freight only."

"Rep Intel don't heed transit regs . . ."

"Wad'e, if he carries on that course, can you take him at the intersection with the Gimmut sewage tunnel?"

"*At,* not *in*? Please, Ordo?"

"*At.*"

"Lots of service bays there," Vau said happily. "Droid drivers. Nice and quiet."

The Gimmut was just a huge enclosed tunnel that shunted sewage from millions of buildings into the main waste processing plant that was known to Mandalorians on Coruscant as Osik Ocean. Every species here had a similar name for it. The Gimmut betrayed no external signs of its unsavory traffic except for methane-consuming fungi that clustered around the gas vents and small cracks, but folks were still keen to avoid living within five klicks of it. It plied a lonely trade.

"I think it's now or never," Vau said. "Big service bay, under cover, half a klick."

"Got it," said Tay'haai. "Step on it, Ordo. I'm coming in from the right."

Ordo closed the gap. If the pilot didn't check his six now and wonder why a shiny black speeder was tailing him down here, he never would. Ordo hit the jamming device and made sure the guy never shared his concerns with his control room. It must have produced a failure signal in the cockpit; the prison speeder accelerated suddenly, streaking ahead. Ordo matched its speed. From then on, he was flying by instinct.

Jusik would have done this better. Ordo had to admit that.

The prison speeder veered left, with no exit in sight, as if it was slowing to try an evasive U-turn. Ordo nearly rammed its tail. Tay'haai's intercept speeder appeared out of nowhere and flashed across its nose, pulling up hard right and just above it to block it in. It lost control, and Ordo sideswiped it into the permacrete walls of the freight lane, more by accident than design. It could have lifted free, but he pinned it, and the two speeders screamed along the wall, locked in a shower of sparks, sending 'trucks swerving past them sounding their klaxons. When the service bay suddenly appeared on the left like an open mouth, Ordo forced the prison speeder left while Tay'haai blocked it from lifting. It skidded across the floor of the bay and came to rest against the far wall.

Vau was hanging out of the speeder before Ordo even landed, and jumped down to race across to the battered white vessel. He didn't stop to take names; he fired horizontally point-blank into the cab through the side viewscreen. Whether he was shooting to kill or to keep the pilot from getting out, Ordo had no time to check. He ran to the rear hatch of the vehicle and blew the hinges out with close-range blasterfire, pulled it open, and reached in to grab Jilka.

"Stay down, *stay down*!" he yelled. "Don't move." Vau kept firing. Ordo had to climb inside before he realized Jilka was strapped into a seat. He shot out the restraint anchors and hauled her bodily out of vessel, then bundled her into his speeder. Vau backed away from the prison vessel, still firing sporadic shots while Tay'haai covered the exit, and then jumped into the pilot's seat. Ordo shut the hatch behind him, hammering his fist on the bulkhead to signal Vau to bang out. The speeder rocketed out of the service bay at a sharp angle, into the traffic and away.

"Are you hurt?" Ordo asked. He took off his helmet and tried to stay upright while Vau drove like a Weequay after a heavy drinking session. "Did you hit your head?"

Jilka looked up at him. He hoped it was Jilka, anyway: if they'd snatched the wrong prisoner somehow, he didn't like the idea of what he might have to do next, but he could always dump her in the lower levels with a big credit chip. All prisoners wanted out.

"Are you going to kill me now?" she asked. Her voice was shaky. "Or just maim me a bit?"

"No, I'm Ordo."

Her face—sharp-featured, fresh bruises, scared eyes—changed instantly. "Do you always pick up women this way?"

"No, I shot Besany."

"He's not very good with pickup lines," Vau chimed in from the front. "Actually, Etain shot her, Jilka. Ordo *almost* slotted her. Things were a little *chaotic* that day."

"You can take the macho thing too far, Captain," Jilka said, fixing Ordo with a baleful stare. "Try flowers next time. Maybe dinner and a show."

She shuffled along the bulkhead and sat up on the curve of the repulsor housing. She wasn't exactly screaming in terror. But then Besany had said she was a tax investigator, and she was used to Hutt levels of violent objection to her carrying out her duties. It would have taken more than a hijack to really rattle her.

"Tell me this is a rescue," she said.

Ordo nodded. So she'd worked out the other possibility, then. "It is."

"My life's screwed forever now, right?"

" 'Fraid so. But it beats whatever Rep Intel or the RDS would have done to you."

"We'll see," she said.

Vau seemed very pleased with himself. "It's okay, my dear," he said. "You can join our little bandit gang as a tax avoidance consultant. The hours are terrible, but you get to see the galaxy on expenses."

That was about her only choice now. Everything dug her—and them—in deeper. She held out her hands to indicate that she wanted the cuffs removed, but Ordo decided she could wait until they got to the safe house before he uncuffed her. There was no point taking chances.

Her eyes narrowed a little. "And you're not Separatists . . ."

"We're not on anyone's side but our own," Ordo said. "Sometimes I can't tell the difference between the Republic and the Seps anyway."

As soon as he said it, it struck him as being more profound than he intended. Maybe there was no difference at all; the Republic now had as much reason to treat him as a hostile as the Separatists did. The speeder vanished into the lower levels via a flood conduit, plunging the cabin into darkness lit only by the faint green glow from the cockpit panel.

"Good point." Jilka's disembodied voice was weary. "I can't see the difference, either."

12

*You worry too much, Clonemaster. I only require your
clones to be fit for purpose, and that means they have no
need to meet the same exacting standards as the army bred
on Kamino. The Grand Army has to be the very best in the
galaxy for one single special operation ahead of them.
This is the culmination of my strategy—
two armies with two quite separate tasks.*
—Chancellor Palpatine, to the Spaarti lead clonemaster
supervising the production of a new army on Centax 2

Arca Barracks, Coruscant, one month later

Etain had teetered on the brink of following Jusik into the
state of limbo outside the Jedi Order, yet the final leap still
proved too hard.

Zey tried to press the right buttons. But she couldn't resent
him for it.

"I want you on Kashyyyk with Delta," he said. "You did
fine work on Qiilura organizing the local population to resist
the Separatists. The same job needs doing there."

Zey knew exactly how things had been on Qiilura. He'd
been there with her, keeping the insurrection going; in the
days before he became chained to a command desk, he was
a fighting man, a good Jedi, a good officer. It wasn't that she
didn't respect him now. It was just that they were too far
down different paths, and unable to step off.

"I'm happy to go, Master Zey," she lied, wanting a few
more days with Kad and Darman. "But we're talking about

Wookiees and Delta here. Neither need my feeble hand-holding. However, if I can make a difference . . ."

"Kashyyyk is going to be critical in the war."

"Then I'll give it my best shot, as ever."

"I know what you do, Etain."

She didn't sense any accusation or disapproval in him. Her first thought, though, was that he knew her secret. "What *do* I do?"

"You treat your men as equals."

"Well, they are. At the very least."

"I meant that I approved. As soon as I can get this discussed by the Council, I intend to improve our command style with our troops—I know we're sadly lacking in too many areas. A little respect and kindness go a very long way."

Well, you're a little late to the party, General. But she had never seen Zey treat any clone as less than fully human. He'd been Jusik's Master; the two would never have lasted in that relationship as long as they did if there had been a fundamental difference in their outlooks.

"Better late than never, General," she said.

Captain Maze walked in with a pile of datapads for Zey to check. It seemed a waste of a highly trained ARC trooper to have him in a post like this with a staff officer—there were fewer than a hundred of these men left—but that was the way the Chancellor wanted it: a senior clone trooper for every key Jedi, expert military advice on hand as well as close personal protection. Etain thought Maze was probably frustrated by the role, knowing ARCs as she now did.

"Would you like a cup of caf, Captain?" Zey asked absently. He got up and poured from the jug on the side table. "It's fresh this time."

"That's very kind of you, sir. Thank you."

Maze took his cup and left. Zey stared at the closed doors for a few seconds afterward.

"What do you think is going to happen to a man like that after the war ends?" he asked.

"*Will* happen, or *should* happen?"

"Either."

Was Zey working up to confronting her, or did he know—
or feel—that she had a better insight into the psychology of
clone troops than most Jedi?

"They'll be more alienated the longer this goes on," she
said. There was no point pulling her punches now. "We're
storing up trouble for the future. You can't take an optimized
human being—very intelligent, very resourceful, very
dedicated—and then restrict his life. It's not just morally
wrong—it's dangerous for all concerned. Once they see their
full potential, they won't forget it, or go back quietly to their
barracks. We *must* plan to give them full lives, General. Freedom, in other words. *Choice.*"

Zey was silent for a long time. Etain didn't feel inclined to
interrupt his thoughts. She could see him standing up at the
Jedi Council to make that point, and she didn't want to imagine their reaction. It was one depressing thought too many.

"It's so easy to become accustomed to the abnormal and
unacceptable simply by being exposed to it for too long," he
said. "We get used to doing terrible things. That's why I need
the Skiratas of this world. He lives his compassion, even if
he has no idea what it is philosophically. But so many of us
cherish it as a theory, without application."

Etain took that as a confession. She wondered how Skirata
would take it.

"Well, let's both apply it now, shall we, sir?" she said. "I'll
see you on my return."

As she felt the whisper of air from the doors closing behind her, Etain had the feeling that she was abandoning Zey
in the throes of a quiet crisis, and that he might have needed
to talk to her for much longer. But Darman and Kad needed
her more. She packed her small bag in her cabin at the barracks—she hadn't stayed at the Temple in a very long time—
and took an air taxi to the Kragget, to say her good-byes at
Laseema's apartment.

She was getting practiced at it now. It still hurt every time,
but the more she left, the more she knew she would come
back. The Force had made her certain about Kad and his
destiny—that he would affect many lives—and now it made

her sure she would come home, and that the war was in its final days.

Darman was already at the apartment, playing with Kad. He sat on the floor with the baby, letting him explore the workings of his helmet. Every time the tactical spot-lamp activated or the HUD flashed icons, Kad squealed in delight and giggled. Darman seemed utterly at ease with his son.

"I hope you've deactivated the uplink," Etain said, kneeling down beside them. "Or else he's just committed five battalions to attack Corellia."

Darman laughed. "So you got us shipped to Fostin Nine to twiddle our thumbs."

"There's work to do there . . . ," she said. Kad plucked a wire connector from the helmet and offered it to her, grinning. "Why, thank you, sweetie! I think Da-da needs that to talk to his boss. Shall we put it back?"

"Not much," Darman said. "It's a recce job."

"Commandos do recces. It's in your job description. Besides, my son's father has to come home safe, and there must still be five females in the Outer Rim that Corr hasn't dated yet. I don't want to stop him short of the galactic record."

Kad had now found a marker stylus in Darman's belt pouch, the type he used to mark an unconscious Atin's forehead when he'd given him medication on the battlefield. *Oh, Qiilura. That was horrible. I'd never have survived if Darman hadn't shown up.* The baby scrawled on the lining of the helmet's chin section, and Darman admired his efforts.

"Now I'll have something to remind me of you when I'm away, *Kad'ika.*" He lowered his voice and gave Etain a dubious look. "Can we have another kid one day?"

This was what she wanted to hear. This made her feel solid. They were a *family,* no mistake about it. Things were going to be all right. "I'd love that. With more painkillers, though."

"I really want out of the army, *Et'ika.* Not long to go."

"You *feel* that?"

"*Kal'buir* still thinks all the logistics add up to a big push soon, and he wants us out. It's just a matter of waiting for him to call endex."

Etain knew all this; she knew Skirata's plans, and she was part of them. But the end was now acquiring a solidity of its own, becoming a separate entity that wouldn't tolerate any prevarication or delay on her part.

Fine. It can't come too soon.

She felt guilt for all the men she could never help—men like Corr, who had blossomed at the first opportunity to explore a wider life—but she had to save those she could. The underground escape route beckoned; she would be good at making that work, using her Force skills for something tangible. And maybe she'd influenced Zey into pursuing a more humane approach to the army.

Stop bargaining with yourself.

The chrono ate away at the remaining hours. Kad was in a giving mood today and kept handing her one of his toys, a small fluffy four-legged thing that was supposed to be a nerf. She got ready to leave, dreading the moment Laseema returned because it meant that her time was up. But it wasn't Laseema who walked through the doors next. It was Enacca, the Wookiee.

Kad was transfixed. He'd never seen a Wookiee before. Etain lifted him up so Enacca could hold him, and to his credit he didn't burst into tears. He tugged at her fur as if he couldn't believe she was real.

Enacca made a purring noise, and Kad squealed with delight.

"What brings you here, Enacca?" Etain asked. "Has Kal trashed more vehicles and left you to round up the wrecks?"

Enacca yowled that she was going back to Kashyyyk to help drive out the Separatists who were despoiling her homeworld.

"I'm headed there, too," Etain said. She didn't believe in coincidences. "What made up your mind?"

Enacca jerked her head in silence, a Wookiee shrug. Etain could guess. Eventually Skirata arrived with Laseema, wearing his it's-nothing-to-do-with-me expression. Etain just raised an eyebrow.

"You need all the Wookiees you can get," he said.

Etain couldn't bring herself to berate him for leaning on

Enacca to play minder to her. The Wookiee probably *did* want to do her bit for her homeworld. It was good to know he was looking out for them all. It felt a lot better than being the object of his anger.

"You look after yourself, *at'ika,*" he said. "And that's an order."

"I will, *Kal'buir.*"

He left her to take her leave of Darman and Kad, and she walked away from the apartment clutching her son's nerf, feeling that it didn't look out of place at all with a concussion rifle and two lightsabers.

Kragget restaurant, lower levels, Coruscant, later that day

"Forgiveness is a wonderful thing, Kal." Gilamar ignored every health warning that his former profession had issued, and tucked into a plate of assorted fried meats and werris eggs, moistened with extra melted roba fat that soaked into a breadroot patty. He'd been away for a few weeks and seemed to want to make up for lost time. "All that aggravation about the baby's been forgotten. If only the rest of the galaxy could agree to shake hands and move on."

Skirata was treading water now, waiting for a window for the next stage of the withdrawal. At least Jilka had shut up pretty fast. He hadn't told Besany how close he'd come to slotting her, and Besany hadn't yet told her how she'd come to be in the frame for something she hadn't done. He just hoped Besany wouldn't give in too soon to her honest urges and confess all. It wouldn't be pretty.

Jilka was a fugitive now, anyway, whether she liked it or not. It had a remarkably sobering effect on anyone.

"Guess who's joining us for refreshments upstairs," Skirata said.

"Palps?"

"No, he had another engagement. Someone we haven't seen for a few years."

Gilamar contemplated the translucent yellow glaze of egg

yolk on the white patty. "If it's Dred Priest, let me get my special rusty scalpel first."

"Nothing like that. Come on, eat up. Jaing's dropping in with a handy contact, too. Plans to make, work to do, *Mij'ika*."

Skirata had never quite worked out how Alpha-02 had managed to escape from Tipoca before the war, but he was content that he had. Gilamar bolted down his meal and followed Skirata back to Laseema's apartment. It was going to be a big shock for him.

"Surprise!" said Skirata, opening the doors.

Three clones sat around the table with Besany and Laseema, playing sabacc: Fi, Sull, and Spar.

"Look at Fi, good as new." Skirata wondered if Fi was ready to return to even easy duties yet, but morale and feeling part of a squad again would do him more good than half the fancy medics in Coruscant. "Mij, remember that lad? It's—"

Gilamar walked up to Spar and slapped him on the back. Spar—not usually the most cheerful of men—stared at him for a moment, and then his face split into a knowing grin.

"How you doing, Spar?" Gilamar started laughing. "How's the headaches?"

"Ooh, it's me back, Doc, I can't move . . . and the voices . . . the *voices*!"

Both men burst into peals of laughter and embraced each other. "You *chakaar*. You made my day, you know that?" said Gilamar. "So you've done all right for yourself. Busy?"

"Oh, bit of this, bit of that. I even turned down a job. *Mand'alor* or something."

"You don't want to do all that Mandaloring stuff, *ad'ika*. Look what happened to the last two. Terrible promotion prospects."

Skirata heard every cough and spit in Tipoca City, every scam and scandal in the claustrophobic *Cuy'val Dar* community, but Gilamar had a few cards he kept close to his chest. It was only now that Skirata saw Spar and the medic laughing that he put two and two together, and wondered why he hadn't ever managed to make it add up to four.

"So you're the one who got Spar off Kamino," he said.

Gilamar bowed theatrically, armor creaking. "You saved your favorite sons, I saved mine."

"You never told me."

"You never told me what Jaing was doing to the banking system . . ."

"Good for you, *Mij'ika*." Skirata meant it. "But you can tell me now, can't you?"

"Jango came and went as he pleased, even if we were stranded. You got your supplies of *tihaar* and uj cake, didn't you? There were outbound parcels, too, if you know what I mean. Jango knew when to turn a blind eye to the cargo in *Slave*'s hold. He owed me one."

Skirata wanted to ask what reciprocal deal had taken place, but it could wait until they were both well away from Coruscant and a bottle or two of *tihaar* had been consumed.

"So you're going to join the team, Spar?" Gilamar asked.

Spar reverted to his usual unsmiling self. "I don't want pay. I want a chance at that cure when you lot find it. I want to live as long as the next man."

Skirata cut in. "Son, no clone ever has to ask for what's his by right. I keep telling you that. You don't have to bargain for it. You sure you want in on this mission? You're not obliged."

Spar seemed taken aback. "No, I *am* obliged. And Sull. Him, too."

Sull nodded. "I'm in."

"I'll take all the aberrants I can get," Skirata said. "Good lads."

The Kaminoans were proud of their low rate of *aberrance*. They had a behavioral norm for clones, and any clone who didn't fit it—any clone who didn't have the sense or self-control to keep his opinions to himself—was classed as deviant, and *reconditioned*. They were full of euphemisms, the Kaminoans; it was the language of purity and cleansing. But it was destruction—of will, of hope, and even of life. Clones who survived reconditioning were a psychological mess, Skirata knew, but they met the Kaminoans' standards of not talking back, and that was all they wanted.

Skirata had never worked out if the aiwha-bait genuinely

believed that clones who didn't toe the line were defective, or if they were just cynically callous, the handful of prison camp guards holding down millions simply by terror, wielding the fear of who would disappear next and never return, making terrible examples of a few to deter the rest.

The prison camp analogy bothered him more now in his quiet moments.

We had enough clone troops and arms on Kamino to revolt and wipe out every Kaminoan. Hard men. Best troops the galaxy's ever seen. And yet we stuck to the rules, pretty much. If I'd been half a man, I'd have organized them, led them, overthrown the regime. Force knows I had the years to do it, but I didn't.

Nobody did. Seventy-five out of the hundred *Cuy'val Dar* were Mandalorians, experienced special forces troops, more than enough to take down Kamino and turn it into a wasteland. From the inside? A stroll. Why didn't they rise up? Kamino swallowed them, and Skirata now hated himself for being swallowed. They got used to the prison rules a slice at a time, still *Mando,* still freethinking, but as prey to institutionalization as anyone. They slid into making a difference on the margins, looking after their boys, and never saw the bigger picture or the doors they could simply kick open.

Never again. Never.

"Okay," Skirata said. "I need a hand springing a couple of people. One's a scientist called Uthan. She might be your passport to a ripe old age. The other's my daughter, who's banged up in a POW camp for getting caught in Sep colors."

"Your real daughter?" Fi asked.

"What does that make you, my unreal son? My *biological* daughter, yes."

Fi didn't ask awkward questions, but Skirata could see them forming in his eyes already. "I go where sent, *Kal'buir.*"

They sat down to resume the sabacc game in hushed tones so that they didn't wake Kad. Skirata had never been much of a player, more a drinking observer at the table, and Fi seemed much more interested in talking to Besany. He hadn't seen her—or at least he couldn't recall seeing her—

since he'd been in various stages of coma, and now that he was back on Coruscant, he kept patting her hand, as if he really wanted to give her a big hug but was afraid to. Skirata found it unbearably touching. He hadn't stopped thanking her since the day he landed.

"You saved my life," Fi told her. "You *saved* me."

Besany helped him play his hand. Skirata hadn't realized that she was pretty sharp at cards. "Fi, you were just too good to throw away," she said at last, eliciting a big grin. "I believe in never wasting a good man."

The holoplans of the detention center on Pols Anaxes were projected onto the wall while they chatted and speculated on the quickest way in and out. The best options were always those that required no shooting and heroics, just a cool head. And Enacca wasn't around to sweep up the transport situation—it now fell to Tay'haai. They were still debating the merits of bogus ID—slipping into predictable methods of entry made them vulnerable—versus infiltration via the drainage system when Jaing arrived with a guest.

Sull looked up. "Well, I never. You again."

The woman was short, graying, and swamped by her pilot's overalls. She looked like Skirata felt: wrung out and despairing of the galaxy, but still ready to give it a kick where it hurt most. She met his gaze. He saw a kindred spirit in her eyes that he could do business with.

"Sull, you bad boy," she said, grabbing the ARC in a playful headlock. "I bust my butt getting you out of the Republic's clutches, and you come straight back. Did they get you from the dumb box of clones, or what?"

Sull actually laughed, submitting to the mock attack. That told Skirata a lot.

"This is Ny Vollen," Jaing said. "One of A'den's buddies. And when she's not helping us with removals, she flies freight. Ny, this is Kal Skirata. My father. Sergeant Skirata."

"Us short folk got to stick together." She studied Skirata unself-consciously and held out her hand for shaking. "Want to look at my schedule? I'll show you mine if you show me yours."

"Is it worth seeing?" Skirata asked, feeling unaccountably bashful.

"It'll hold your interest, *Mando* boy. Kuat's nice this time of year." Ny held out her datapad. "Can't seem to stay away from the place."

"I was born on Kuat." Skirata was no longer in control of this conversation, and not even of his own mouth. *Why did I ever volunteer that information?* Ny Vollen unsettled him. "My, you do visit the old place a lot."

Skirata didn't have Ordo's ability to do a quick visual scan of a document and analyze it immediately, but he knew a lot of components in transit when he saw them. It was enough for thousands of vessels.

"Shipyards are extra-busy, then," he said.

"Working-up busy." Ny seemed to be testing him. She probably had a good idea that he wasn't exactly the Chancellor's trusted adviser on procurement issues. "This is all replacement parts for battleships, not small stuff, so they're either delivering a lot of combat-ready hulls or anticipating a big need for replacement parts all at once."

"You ever worked in shipbuilding?"

"No, but I know how to hang around in cantinas waiting for my cargo, listening to folks who do."

"And?"

"Lots of new vessels and transports rolling out now—hundreds a week—and some big panic to be ready in a few weeks' time."

Skirata looked at Jaing for confirmation. The Null had access to the KDY system. He nodded.

"I'm grateful," Skirata said. He pulled a ten-thousand-credit chip from his belt and put it on the table beside her. Placing it in her hand seemed an act of charity, like giving a child spending money. Ny looked at the chip, then tossed it back in his lap.

"I've been getting treble pay and on-time bonuses, thanks. I'm just trading information. It's tax-free."

"So what do you want from us, Ny?"

"A'den's got that sorted. My old man's ship was lost a couple of years ago, and I know he isn't going to be alive, but I want to know the how and the where. That's all."

That shut Skirata up. "Sorry to hear that."

"I'll let you know when I find out more, okay?"

"We're grateful, Ny, we really are."

"And you better hang on to those creds, *Mando* boy. You look in need of it."

"I'm a trillionaire," Skirata said, deadpan.

"If you're worth that much, you can afford some better armor. Look at the state of you. All scrapes."

"We *Mando boys* like to show we've been in action. Anyway, this is top-grade *beskar*—full density, two percent ciridium, no fancy lamination or carbon-alloy."

"Does all that mean it's heavy?"

"Yeah. Very heavy. Heavy is best."

"Explains why you're so short, then."

He watched her go, dumbfounded.

Jaing gave him a prod in the shoulder. "I think she likes you."

"I think she's just trying to joke her way out of being in limbo about her husband," Skirata said, and found himself hoping Jaing was right, then scolding himself because he didn't have time for that foolishness. "Okay, date set. We bang out on . . ." He calculated. "One thousand and ninety days ABG."

"Copy that," Sull said, mimicking the regular troopers.

He had a sense of humor after all. He was going to need it.

Sep-controlled area near Kachirho, Kashyyyk,
one month later, 1,070 days after Geonosis

"You *sure* you saw Grievous leave?"

Scorch aimed an anti-armor round at the wall of battle droids, ducking as dagger-like chunks of tree and fizzing metal shrapnel hammered on his armor. "You *saw,* Fixer, so what else do you think that was?"

"Why, though? Is it a retreat?"

Blasterfire poured down on them from the Trandoshan positions. Every time Scorch raised his head, he was looking at another wave of Trandos and battle droids. "Does this *look* like a retreat to you?"

Scorch couldn't have given a mott's hairy backside about the bigger picture at that moment. It was the first time he thought they might have been in real danger of getting overrun and slaughtered. The Sep presence was putting up a bigger fight than he'd expected.

"Incoming!" Boss smacked his head down again, and his field of vision was full of the crawling debris on the floor. Scorch could hear the drives of a ship. When he knelt up to look again, a supply vessel was dropping down onto the landing pad in the clearing. Trandos rushed to unload it; Sev popped up from the cover of a pile of SB droids and began hosing the pad with blasterfire.

"Can you put an anti-armor round or two in there, Boss?"

"Just getting the range now . . ."

Boss fired once, twice, three times. It was hard to see how accurate his shot was, just a split-second wake of vapor and turbulent hot air, and then everything was one vast sheet of burning gold with a white-hot heart. The explosion shook the ground under Scorch's knees. The blinding light gave way instantly to roiling black smoke, and as the wind parted it Scorch saw nothing left on the pad except burning, twisted wreckage.

"I think he was hauling detonite," Sev said. "I wish they all blew like that."

"We've got to stop them moving around this kriffing forest so easily." Boss looked around, waiting for the next wave of droids, then crouched down in the lee of the barricade, getting his breath. "Okay, the Wookiees can keep picking 'em off, but we need a bigger hydrospanner to sling in their works or this is going to be a running battle for the next five years." He clicked his helmet comlink. "General, can we shortcut this?"

Etain took a few seconds to respond. Scorch could hear the blasterfire in the background, and the roars and barks of furious Wookiees. "How hard do you want that shortcut to be?"

"We'll take a ten, ma'am. We're feeling lucky."

"Enacca says if you can take the bridge at Kachirho, or sever it, you'll cut off their supply line completely." Etain paused as if listening to a running commentary. "It'll cut ours off, too, but Wookiees can rebuild smaller bridges around it in days. Seps can't."

"I like the odds," Boss said. "Let's go, Delta."

Etain's voice was breaking up on the link. "And we've got Geonosians swarming everywhere here—you'll need to be way up in the trees to take Kachirho."

"Bugs!" Sev said cheerfully. "Save a few for me, ma'am. I love their pretty wings, especially when I shoot them off."

Boss reoriented their HUD positioning, and the squad worked its way through the forest, too pumped on adrenaline to worry about what predators might be waiting. Then a hairy arm waved from overhanging branches: Wookiees. They were showing them a route higher up into the trees, a fast track to Kachirho. Scorch shot a rappel line into the branches and winched himself up, then ran up a section of tree trunk that made him feel Jawa-sized to emerge in a tree-house village on a huge mat of branches and vines. It took him a second to spot the Wookiees; he saw the Trandos first. The Wookiees were emptying bowcasters at them with apparently slow, leisurely, but lethal accuracy, seeming oblivious to the incoming Trando fire.

Then they charged.

Wookiees really *did* dismember enemies. Ripping off arms wasn't a cantina joke after all.

Scorch paused for a moment, almost disbelieving, as a Wookiee patriarch nearly three meters tall grabbed a Trando one-handed and tore him limb from limb, then simply plucked a Geonosian from the air and dismantled it like a mechanical toy he'd grown bored with. Even Sev froze.

"Uh," he said. *"Uh . . ."*

The Wookiees were defending their homes, and that made them doubly lethal. They were berserk with rage. Scorch wasn't about to offer them tips on house clearance techniques. The sheer shocking brutality had an instant impact on the will of the Seps to fight. Trandos ran, apparently forgetting they could keep their nerve and fire into the Wookiee ranks, some just diving off the tree platforms to an uncertain death beneath, some just running blindly. One or two did hold the line and keep firing, but dropping big, enraged attackers that were maybe three times a Trando's weight took more stopping power, and the Trandos didn't have it. The Sep defense fragmented. Wookiees poured out of the higher branches, and Delta fell in with them, joining a fast-moving torrent of brown fur and granite-hard muscle. Scorch collided with one, just a glancing blow, and even in his Katarn armor he *felt* its sheer power and mass. Wookiees were sentient and smart, yes, but the primal warrior in them took little unleashing.

The Seps were falling back.

Sev, being Sev, managed to run through the Wookiees, stopping every few meters to pick off Geonosians. He'd said he was going for 4,982 kills, one for every commando lost at Geonosis, and he wasn't joking. He never was. He never said "five thousand," either, and even Skirata rounded up the figure. No, Sev was *exact* about it. War was personal for him.

Scorch kept an eye on him. *Stone-cold, my* shebs.

It was the spider droid that told them they were getting near the bridge. It scuttled down a walkway, cannon aimed, but it wasn't best suited for a close-quarters battle like this one. Scorch leapt on its back and fired a whole clip into it with his DC-17's muzzle rammed into the weak point of a weld. The Wookiees were roaring now, gesturing below, and the big male—the really big one—started ripping apart the branches to get a clear line of sight with the target.

"There's the bridge," Fixer called. "Check your HUDs, people."

Metal bridges were a lot easier to pick out with sensors than living plant material against a background of the same. Only the density variation gave its position away. Scorch didn't need to see it.

"Can I borrow this, ma'am?" He wrestled a grenade launcher from a female Wookiee near him. She obviously wasn't trying too hard to hang on to it. "Won't be long."

The big male Wookiee had opened up a window for

Scorch. The bridge ten meters beneath was now a sitting target, big and juicy, and laden with moving Sep transports.
Scorch decided to play it safe and aim for the span itself, not
the narrow living cables that supported it, and just fired
round after round, blowing apart the close-woven roots and
branches until there was more daylight than bridge. The
structure could no longer hold either its own weight or the
traffic on it. The span creaked and tore into two dangling sections, sending bodies, repulsors, and small transports crashing into the green abyss beneath.

Kachirho was no longer open for Sep traffic. The Wookiees roared in triumph, shaking their fists and weapons at the
canopy above.

"Scorch," said Etain's voice in his helmet. "Enacca says
you're doing okay for a short, pink, hairless creature."

It was impossible to get a big picture of any battle, and
even working out if you'd won or not was, Vau said, something the historians had to decide many years later. But
Scorch felt the destruction of the bridge was a turning point,
and Delta Squad were still alive, so whatever history decided
in the end—he'd won.

They'd won. This time, anyway.

13

*I just thought you needed to know, Chancellor. I understand
how strategically important the Kamino clone facility is to
the Republic's survival, and as a patriot, I thought it was
my duty to hand over this material, which is clearly from
that source. It's limited, and it may be of no importance,
but these Mandalorians acquired it, and I doubt they came
by it by honest scientific means. I have my reputation for
integrity to consider, too. I would not like the tainted origin
of this data to compromise any nomination for the
Republic Science Accolade.*
—Last-known message sent by Dr. Reye Nenilin from his
office before his disappearance, contacting Chancellor
Palpatine to hand over data given to him by a
Mandalorian known only as Falin

Lower levels, Coruscant, 1,080 days ABG

Skirata should have known that something had gone badly
wrong when he arrived at the Kragget.

"Hi, handsome," Soronna said, balancing plates in both
hands. "You haven't seen Laseema, have you? She never
showed for her shift."

His stomach filled with ice. Laseema was punctual to a
fault; she had Kad to look after, and she ran that schedule
better than the GAR.

"I'll go check," he said, striding for the kitchen exit.

"I tried the apartment," Soronna called after him. "No answer."

Skirata broke into a fast walk and then sprinted through

the connecting alley; sixty or not, he could cover a hundred meters almost as fast as one of his young commandos when adrenaline was fueling him. He got to the apartment doors, drew his blaster, and readied his knife. When he keyed the doors open, the apartment was more than deserted. It looked as if it had been stripped.

Skirata wasn't a panicking man, but he was now minus both Laseema and his grandson. He ran from room to room, somehow managing to remember clearance procedure in case someone from his past had come back to settle a grudge, close to vomiting with fear for his family. The apartment was definitely empty. Everything personal *had* been stripped from it. There were no clothes, none of Jusik's paraphernalia, no toys, no crib, nothing. He didn't own much himself, but all that was gone, too—a holdall with a few changes of clothes, his bantha-hide jacket, and some of his weapons, including two of his very expensive custom Verpine sniper rifles.

He would have thought of plain burglary if he hadn't known how well he'd concealed this place, and if Laseema and Kad hadn't been missing, too.

And he'd received no messages. All this had happened in the time it had taken him to leave Arca Barracks, get the shoroni sapphires converted to cash credits, and visit the bank—two hours, tops. If it had been earlier, someone would have commed him.

"*Shab,*" he spat. "*Shab, shab, shab.*"

He secured the place again, planning to come back to sweep for evidence. But first he had to check where everyone was, and his natural reaction, honed by decades of running for his life or chasing someone with the intent of ending theirs, was to assume no comlinks were now secure. He slipped out the emergency exit and onto the roof, where his green speeder—now kitted out as a taxi to bypass the automated skylane controls—was parked under cover. The Aratech speeder bike was too exposed if anyone was coming after him, heavy *beskar* armor or not. He lifted clear to head for the *Aay'han* RV point. If the *osik* really hit the fan, and all comms were down, that was the emergency plan.

He got as far as the next intersection when he heard a police klaxon. A CSF patrol vessel dipped in front of him,
flashing at him to pull over to the nearest landing platform.
CSF were as good as family; he had no reason not to comply.

He set down the speeder, and the patrol vessel settled in
front. The lower levels weren't somewhere you waited on a
platform for a taxi, not if you valued your life, so it was deserted. Skirata had his knife and blaster ready just in case.

But it was Jaller Obrim who jumped down from the crew
bay. Even when the man's face was obscured by a uniform
helmet, Skirata recognized his build and his walk.

He gestured at Skirata to open the side viewplate, flipping
up his visor.

"They're safe," Obrim said, not giving Skirata a chance to
draw breath. He didn't even have to explain who he meant.
"But you're a dead man. Follow me. No comms, okay?"

Well, it was wasn't the first time Skirata had been dead.
The wild fear for Laseema and Kad was replaced instantly
by a dull ache in his guts that told him he'd pushed his luck
too far yet again.

And it was going relatively well. It really was.

Whatever he'd done, his priority was to get his boys out. If
he died doing it, that was fine by him.

And he had nine million credits on him, cash creds at that.
It was just as well that Obrim was the kind of cop who knew
what his real priorities were, and would never search him.

The patrol vessel slipped into a grimy alley, gun turrets almost shaving the walls, and came to rest on a rubble-strewn
patch of permacrete where a building had been demolished.
Two borrats, one a buck with impressive tusks, the other a
smaller doe, lifted their heads from a small, anonymous car-
cass and watched the proceedings as still as statues, noses
twitching. Skirata got out of the speeder, keeping one eye on
them, and swung himself up into the open crew bay of the
patrol ship.

"Okay," he said. "I've blown it, haven't I?"

Obrim took off his helmet. "Yes, my friend."

He held out his datapad for Skirata to read. It was a war-

rant for Skirata's arrest, dead or alive. It was only the authorization seal that made him more concerned than usual.

"If I count the fact that this is from the Chancellor, then
it's a first for me," Skirata said. "But I've still got death warrants out on me on five or six planets. Maybe seven. I forget."

"I know," Obrim said. "I've intercepted this at the CSF
end, and I can only sit on it for a little longer before I have to
distribute it, but other agencies have it, and you have to get
out, Kal. All my boys will somehow draw a complete and in-
explicable blank in finding you, you know that. But I can't
speak for the other enforcement agencies."

"Any special reason I've ticked off Palpatine?"

"My source says some scientist called Nenilin turned in
some Kaminoan cloning data."

Nenilin would be doing some research into how to breathe
without a windpipe, but that would have to wait. And Skirata
could be a patient man. "How did the Chancellor connect it
to me? Only GAR spec ops knew about Ko Sai."

"You'd know better than me who's your weak link there."

"Yeah. Now, where's my grandson, and Laseema?"

"I took them and cleared out the apartment, just in case,
because I know the kid's a bit *special*. Let me know where
and when you want them moved, and I'll do it."

"I owe you, Jaller."

"No, I'm your friend. You'd do the same for me."

Yes, Skirata knew that he would. The two men looked at
each other in silence, and Skirata knew this was the end of
the line for them.

"I don't think I'm going to see you for a long while, Kal,"
Obrim said. "But whatever I *can* do, I'll do it."

Skirata grabbed his hand. "You're a hero and a gentleman,
Jaller. If things go bad for you here, ever, there's a safe haven
for you and the family. It's—"

"Don't tell me where. You know why."

Skirata scribbled a code on the flimsi pad on his forearm
plate. "Okay, but take this. It's a go-between. If you ever need
anything, anything at all, comm this code and they'll find
me."

Skirata hated good-byes. He embraced Obrim in silence,

and then walked back to the speeder without a backward glance. Even when he lifted off, he didn't look down.

Now he was back where he'd been so many times in his life: in a stolen vessel, with just the armor he stood up in and enough weapons to make a stand. But he had nine million creds on him, too, and he was far from finished.

So comms might be compromised. He wasn't going to lead anyone to *Aay'han* by accident. He fell back on the kind of technology that had always left the *aruetiise* flat-footed, and disappeared into an ancient storm-water conduit that had been built and abandoned long before Coruscant had climate management. He switched to an unencrypted GAR channel in his helmet comm, and simply transmitted static.

It was a special kind of static, of course; long and short bursts, carefully interspersed in sequences. To a casual listener, it was just random noise and interference, but to a Mandalorian trained in an ancient message code called *dadita,* it spelled out words. It could even transmit code.

There weren't that many in the GAR with even that basic knowledge; only the Nulls, the commandos, and the last of the *Cuy'val Dar.*

Skirata kept transmitting a coded message, waiting for someone to sift it from the white noise.

Republic Detention Center, Pols Anaxes

"It's handy being a clone," Fi said. "Your uniform always fits."

"I haven't worn this meat-can for years." Spar adjusted his belly plate again. "I'd forgotten about all the interesting places it pinches."

The three clones—Spar, Sull, and Fi—marched into RDC PolAx, as it was called in GAR signals, looking exactly like every other trooper on duty at the prisoner-of-war camp. Jusik played detainee. Fi made sure he held on to Jusik as if keeping a firm grip on him, to disguise the fact that his gait wasn't the paragon of military precision that it had once been.

The camp was chaotic. Fi had expected something grim

and desperate, but it was just crowded. There were gun turrets on the walls that obviously meant business, but once
they passed through the security gate with their counterfeit
armor tallies and prisoner transfer authorizations, they found
themselves in something that resembled a migrants' transit
camp, a ragbag of species, uniforms, and lots of prisoners
waiting in lines for one thing or another.

"Why take prisoners?" Spar asked. "Why not just shoot
them?"

Jusik could hear the conversation going on inside the helmets because he had a concealed comlink bead deep in his
ear, but he couldn't reply. He just cleared his throat meaningfully.

"I mean it," Spar said. "They tie up resources. What use
are they? Let them go, or slot them."

"I think you must have missed the lecture on rules of engagement and lawful orders," Fi said. "It was probably after
you went AWOL."

Jusik stifled a grin. Fi saw his lips twitch.

"You're back," he said, barely audible.

Fi was still more conscious of what he couldn't do than
what he could, but his verbal skills were definitely on the
mend. If he had to choose, he thought, he would trade marksmanship for fluent speech.

Jusik looked a lot older than he'd been at the start of the
healing process eighteen months ago. Fi decided he'd rely on
his own recovery efforts from now on. The effect on his
brother—he saw Jusik as true kin now—was visible. It was
draining the life out of him.

"Okay, Jedi," Sull said. "Here comes the nice camp commander. Look sullen and recalcitrant."

"Call me *Jedi* again," Jusik said quietly, "and I'll show you
my Force kick in the backside."

"How very serene," Sull said.

Fi couldn't let it pass unchallenged. "Sull, why don't you
shut it?"

"Just getting Bardan in character . . . mean, moody Sep
rabble."

The camp commander was a lieutenant from the 55th

Mechanized Brigade, which struck Fi as a waste of skills until he realized how stiffly the man was walking. He'd clearly been wounded. Fi fought down the urge to ask him what had happened and how he'd recovered. He was proof of a soldiering life after injury. There was hope.

"Permission to interview one of your detainees, sir," Sull said, shoving a GAR-issue datapad at him.

The lieutenant looked at the 'pad and nodded. "This is for ID purposes, is it?"

"Yes, sir." Sull was actually pretty good at sounding like an ordinary trooper, but then ARCs were trained to be resourceful. "This prisoner claims he can identify a female human we're looking for. She might be using the alias *Ruusaan Skirata.* If it's the right woman, this is our authorization to transfer her to Coruscant for questioning."

"Oh, her," said the lieutenant wearily. "Very aggressive female, detained on Khemerion. She's in confinement. Not for her own safety—for the rest of the prisoners' welfare."

"Thanks for the heads-up, sir. We'll exercise caution."

"Hut Eight Bravo," the lieutenant said, gesturing to his left. "Show your ID to the droid."

Fi had heard no mention of Skirata's daughter having the slightest interest in her father's culture. Maybe his sons didn't know. Fi shared Ordo's mistrust of their motives; if they found out their dad was sitting on a trillion-credit fortune that was growing rapidly just by being in the bank, they'd probably want to readopt him. Fi hoped his daughter was more grateful for the effort her father had gone to. If she wasn't, he'd dump her out the nearest air lock.

"I think poor old Skirata was under the impression that his little girl was banged up in some disease-ridden death camp," Spar said. "This actually looks quite civilized. Look at that smashball court—they've got better sports facilities than we ever had."

"This used to belong to the old naval training branch," Jusik said.

"Stay in character, Jedi . . ."

The guard droid whirred into their path at the entrance to Hut Eight Bravo to check codes and authorizations, then led

them down a long passage flanked by cells. The place looked
like a mobile medcenter.

"Stay there," the droid said, placing a manipulator arm on
the door. "I must check that the prisoner is secure first."

Fi switched to helmet-only audio. "Ready, *Bard'ika*? Remember, when you recognize her—she's betrayed your people, you want to rip her head off, she stole your lunch creds,
and so on."

"Uh-huh."

"Then she protests she's never seen you before in her life,
and we haul her away." Spar's shoulders looked braced. "By
the time they work out she never reached the Coruscant facility, she'll be light-years away. And if she thinks she really
recognizes you—we'll just wing it."

Fi was still worried. "We can't keep using the trooper
armor as a cover. Someone's going to work out it's an inside
job."

"Fi, do you know how much white plastoid's been scavenged from battlefields in the last few years?" Sull asked.
"We ended up fighting Seps who had more armor than we
did. That's why we have to keep changing the comlink and
data protocols."

A stream of abuse interrupted them, a woman's voice; the
droid reversed out of the cell at high speed.

"You may speak to the prisoner while I observe," it said.
"Exercise caution."

It wasn't joking.

Ruu Skirata—no armor, just prison fatigues—was pacing
the cell, or as much of it as she could in the tiny space available to her. A restraining bulkhead, a sheet of durasteel mesh
that could be moved back and forth to pin the prisoner, had
cornered her. It reminded Fi of the kind of cage veterinarians
used to subdue an animal so they could administer a hy-
pospray without getting ripped to shreds. It created a small
open space inside the cell door. Fi hauled Jusik into it to confront Ruu.

Osik, she was so much like *Kal'buir* that it was scary.

It wasn't just the piercing pale blue stare and the promi-
nent cheekbones that told Fi this was the genuine fruit of his

adopted father's loins; it was the look of a rabid schutta about to run up his leg and sink its teeth in his throat.

"Is this the woman?" Fi said.

He had to hand it to *Bard'ika*. The guy could act. Jusik fixed Ruu with a look that changed from scrutiny to dawning realization to utter hatred.

"Traitor . . ." His voice was a low rumble. It rose to a convincing crescendo. "Traitor! You got us killed! And now I'm going to kill *you*!"

Fi grabbed him in a restraining hold, equally convincing.

"Who the stang are you?" Ruu demanded. Fi hoped the droid couldn't analyze human biosigns well enough to tell that the woman was genuinely taken aback. Her angry-schutta expression gave way to blank bemusement for a moment. "I've never seen you before, because if I had, I'd have punched your face in."

"Liar! Traitor!"

Fi jerked Jusik back by the neck. "You're being transferred to Coruscant, Skirata," he said to Ruu. "Come quietly, and we won't need to use force."

"Look, chum, I'm a prisoner of war and I've got *rights*. I demand legal representation. You can't just take me without due process."

Spar reached past Fi to flash the datapad at her. "Here's your due process. Personally, I'd rather use force, so carry on as you are, ma'am, and give me a good excuse to smack you one."

It was now or never. "Guard, lift the bulkhead," Sull said.

Schutta was an even better description than Fi had imagined. She fought like a maniac, and Sull and Spar had a job on their hands restraining her without breaking anything. As they hauled her down the corridor, she was spitting abuse that made *Kal'buir*'s cussing sound like a Jedi Master's learned discourse.

There was a crowd of inmates gathering outside now. Fi could see them clustering around the door, and his fear was that this would spark a riot. It was supposed to be a low-key extraction. As things were panning out, it was turning into a circus, and that wasn't good.

"You can't do this to me, you carbon-flush," Ruu bellowed. "I know what happens on Coruscant to—"

Spar tightened his grip on her collar and got a good kick in the ankle, which probably still hurt even in armor. It was a weak point. He diverted to his internal audio link. "We *really* need to shut her up . . ."

Jusik coughed and pressed Fi's arm. *Leave it to me.*

"Spar, leave her to *Bard'ika*," Fi said, loosening his grip.

Fi had no idea what was coming next, but he trusted Jusik to pull off something timely. Jusik pulled free from Fi, yelled "Scumbag!" and threw a punch. Fi could have sworn it didn't land—there was no sickening crack of bone, no connecting recoil—but Ruu Skirata slumped to the ground, unconscious, and Spar and Sull scooped her up between them with an audible sigh of irritation. Fi seized Jusik and bundled him toward the main gates.

The crowd of inmates were making restless noises, milling around. Droid guards moved in with a couple of clone troopers to break it up.

"They don't know how to run a prison," Sull said. They were nearly out now. Fi could see the comm masts of the GAR high-speed gunship they'd borrowed for the occasion. There was a lot to be said for a military bureaucracy that kept poor tabs on its assets. "Crowd control. You can't allow inmates out to mass like that. You can't—"

"If they were good at it," Spar interrupted, "we'd have had to fight our way in and out. Be grateful."

The security gates closed behind them. Fi maintained a grip on Jusik until they were out of range of the detention center; Ruu was already coming out of her daze.

"I'm going to kill you . . . ," she mumbled.

"No you're not," Fi said. "Because we're the good guys."

He helped Sull cuff and shackle her anyway, having calculated the damage she might do before they managed to convince her. Fi and Jusik sat watching her in the small cargo bay while Sull prepared for takeoff. It wasn't until the sky beyond the small viewport was densely black and speckled with white-hot stars that Fi felt relaxed. Actually, he felt exhausted. He definitely wasn't as fit as he'd been. He'd have to start a serious training regime again.

"You did great, Fi," Jusik said. "If I hadn't known what had happened to you, I'd have had a hard job spotting there was anything wrong."

"I can get by the way I am now." As soon as Fi heard himself say it, he knew he'd passed a watershed. "Any more improvement is a bonus."

"Good man." Jusik patted him on the back. "Let's see what our guest has to say for herself."

"That was fascinating, *Bard'ika,*" Spar said, removing his helmet. "Some . . . *punch.*"

Jusik was sixty kilos wringing wet, if that. He smiled to himself, miming a quick right hook. "I've got the weight and reach," he said. "Could have turned professional."

"How'd you do it?"

"Force stun."

"Yeah . . . of course . . ." Spar still seemed wary of Jusik. "I thought you'd given up all that spooky stuff."

"Not in an emergency."

Ruu's eyes were fully open, and the bravado had ebbed: she was scared now. She looked from face to face, then settled on Jusik.

"My jaw ought to hurt," she said. "But it doesn't. And I *really* don't know who you are. What do you want? I'm nobody worth kidnapping."

"Your father sent us to get you out, *Ruus'ika.*"

"Father?" She squirmed to sit up. *"Father?"*

Fi braced for a stream of invective about abandonment, all kinds of *osik* that he wasn't going to let her say about *Kal'buir.* Instead, she just blinked a few times.

"You mean Kal Skirata?" she said.

"You got another one?" Spar asked.

"Yes, Mama remarried."

Fi decided it was probably safe to untie her. The mention of her father had subdued her better than any whack on the head. "And that makes me your stepbrother, Ruu. My name's Fi."

"How kriffing heartwarming," Spar said, exasperated. "There won't be a dry eye in the house."

"Dad came for me." Her face was pure stunned joy. "He really did."

"Well, *we* did, because he's a bit busy at the moment." Fi savored the bizarre moment of epiphany; he had a sister, of sorts. And he had a wife, too, and a father, a *legal* one, and he had brothers. He was like any other man. The out-of-reach normal life that had tormented him was now fully his. It was wonderful, even if very few beings had a family as strife-prone, heavily armed, and bizarre as this. "But he *never* forgets his kids."

"I always knew he'd come back. I *knew* it. How did he find me?"

"Your brothers got in touch . . . eventually."

"Has he forgiven me?"

"For what?"

"Never contacting him."

It was hard to know what to say. Fi glanced at Jusik, who gave him a look that said to leave it for later. Spar rolled his eyes and slipped into the cockpit to join Sull, probably driven back by the threat of a tidal wave of sentimentality.

"You're back now," Fi said. "And that's all he'll care about."

Chances were, Fi thought, that *Kal'buir* was busy running for his life. They'd all had the message from Ordo: *Buir* now had a warrant on his head.

But Ruu didn't need to know that yet.

Coruscant underground emergency reservoir

"Nearly there," Skirata said. *"Nearly there."* He loaded his belt pouch with ammo clips from *Aay'han's* armory and shoved an extra blaster in each boot. "Can't lose our nerve now."

Ordo had come to find Skirata hoping that his father would stay put, wait for the rest of the team to come to them, and then bang out in *Aay'han.* But he was Skirata, and sitting on his *shebs* wasn't how he did things.

"As soon as Jusik's back and Ruusaan's secure here, I suggest we grab Uthan and get it over with, *Kal'buir.*"

"Omega's not due back for a week," Skirata said. "I can't leave without them."

"They might have to RV with us elsewhere."

"Son, I know they can hijack anything with an ion drive or a bantha hauling it, but I don't want to rely on that. The more stragglers you have, the more routes you have to secure."

"And assembling in one place can make us more vulnerable."

"On balance, it's still safer. Minimize time and distance spent separated. Regroup."

"Then *I'll* retrieve them. But all the intel I'm getting is of a big fleet buildup, and we can't delay."

"Actually, we *could*. We could have left anytime *before*. We can leave anytime *now*."

"*Buir,* from the shipyard end, you can't hide it. And Centax shipping movements are ten times what they've been before now. Something's going down, and soon."

"Isn't anyone asking where all this extra activity is *going*?"

"Nobody's checking in that direction, *Kal'buir.* Only us. I can't find any overlap—there's no comm traffic between Centax Two and GAR command, and nothing that indicates any tasking of the second wave of vessels."

It seemed staggering. But then nobody had spotted the Grand Army in preparation for ten years, and even if Kamino was cloistered and off the charts, Kuat was *not*. Ordo marveled at the fact that a vast war machine—a whole fleet, weapons, and equipment for millions of troops—had been manufactured and stored without anyone leaking information or wondering what Rothana or its parent company KDY was doing.

He'd thought that it was just because three million was a small army in galactic terms. And then he realized that it was actually because most beings weren't very good at putting pieces of a puzzle together and seeing the bigger picture. Palpatine could hide *anything* that way. He hid his secret in plain sight, mixed into the sheer mundane business of the galaxy.

"I've got to get back to HQ," Ordo said. "*Kal'buir,* please don't take risks, okay?"

It was a feeble thing to say to a mercenary, and Ordo knew it. "I'm going to retrieve *Kad'ika* and the ladies, and then we grab Uthan," Skirata said. "Can you find a way to recall Omega?"

"Have they said they're willing to desert?"

"Not in so many words. Sometimes you have to give folks a nudge to save themselves."

Skirata had learned nothing about giving others choices. He'd kicked straight back into father-knows-best mode, despite the fight with Darman; but that blind reflex had saved Ordo and his brothers, and it was impossible to condemn it. When it went right, it was salvation.

"Where are you going?" Ordo asked.

"As soon as Jusik's back, I'll go with him and spring Uthan."

"And you've got a plan."

"We will have, by the time we get there."

"You taught me planning was everything, *Kal'buir.*"

"I also taught you that you have to seize opportunities." Ordo held up an admonishing finger. "You will *not* put yourself at risk. Your luck's run out. Take a rest. Or you'll never live to see another grandchild."

Skirata paused. "You telling me something, son? Is Besany . . . ?"

"No. No, not at all." Ordo was taken aback to think *Kal'buir* might have believed he planned things so haphazardly. "I'm just increasingly worried by the risks you take."

"Big risks for big gains." Skirata went back to loading himself with weapons. Ordo could have sworn the adrenaline had taken ten years off him. It was fascinating to see what crushed him and what put him back on his feet again. "Don't worry, I've got too much to live for."

"I'd better report in to Zey," Ordo said, "and give him the illusion that he commands me. Stay in contact, but don't take any risks on comms."

"Yes, son." Skirata grinned. "And I promise I won't stay out after midnight."

Ordo slipped through the deserted tunnels and automated pumping rooms that controlled the underwater lake's levels, then made his way back to HQ, reversing his security measures: change out of civilian clothing, then into overalls, then stop again to change into his armor and collect his speeder bike. An ARC captain in his showy scarlet pauldron and red-trimmed *kama* was conspicuous even on Coruscant, where wild variety was the wardrobe order of the day.

Or at least he *thought* he would still stand out from the crowd. Now there seemed to be a lot more clone troopers on the walkways, regular security patrols, red or blue markings on their white armor. He'd watched the numbers grow discreetly over the last few weeks.

The ones with blue markings were 501st Legion, just one more designation in a complex army that preferred numbers to names. He decided to seize the moment, and swooped onto a convenient landing platform to speak to them. He looked like any other ARC captain; they couldn't even tell he was a Null ARC by scanning him, unless he chose to present his real number, N-11, on his armor's electronic tally.

"Sergeant," he said, approaching one of them. "How long will you be on patrol here?"

"Until twenty hundred, Captain."

Ordo listened for the subtleties of the accent, and knew this man hadn't been trained on Kamino. There were overtones of Coruscanti accent that few would spot, but Ordo did. And he'd watched the 501st, and the other troopers in the red livery, the shock troopers, noting their level of precise discipline.

"Very good, Sergeant," Ordo said. "Carry on."

These weren't the economy-model clones from Centax 2. These had to be the direct Fett clones from the Coruscant facility that the Nulls hadn't yet located. It hadn't seemed as urgent a task as finding what had to be a huge production line on Centax 2.

The few Centax clones that had been detected—well, no wonder they didn't know what Kamino was like. Ordo had no doubt they'd been told Centax *was* Kamino, so that they didn't make any gaffes about their origin and expose the army-in-waiting. In a closed world, you had no reason or way to disbelieve what you were told.

They'd passed the test—most of the time.

Ordo landed the Aratech outside Arca Barracks' main entrance in the row of dispatch speeder bikes and went in search of Zey, mainly to report to him now that Skirata was officially suspended. Maze passed him in the corridor, helmeted; that was unusual these days. It meant he was engrossed in a lot of comm traffic.

"How's Skirata?" Maze asked.

"I have no idea," Ordo said to his retreating back. "He's vanished, as the general is fully aware."

"Of course he has," said Maze, walking into the refreshers.

Ordo was working out what stunt he could stage to get Omega recalled when the alarm klaxon sounded. It stopped him in his tracks; he'd only ever heard it tested for routine maintenance, and he'd never really expected to hear it used for real.

It was the incoming attack alert.

Air assault. Invasion.

Ordo paused to check the nearest building control panel, expecting to see a red flashing light indicating a short, and that the alarm was a false one.

The panel was operating normally. An incongruously serene droid voice drifted over the open comm system. "This is not a drill. Repeat, this is not a drill. Inbound enemy ships have been detected. Report to muster stations. Execute emergency procedures."

There were suddenly droids, civilian staff, and even the occasional trooper issuing from every doorway. The insistent two-tone noise was so deafening that the audio buffers in Ordo's helmet kicked in. Maze came running back down the corridor at full tilt, adjusting his armor.

"It's a whole stanging *fleet*," he snapped, tapping his helmet to indicate he was patched into the tactical display. "Great timing."

Ordo agreed, but he meant it, and for wholly different reasons. Opportunity, *Kal'buir* said: opportunities were also threats. It just depended on how you handled them. "You get Zey to the command bunker, and I'll start locking down the system."

An ARC trooper's role on the ground if Coruscant was compromised was protecting the command center and strategic targets if the enemy managed to land. If the enemy got a foothold, then his task was sabotage, assassination, and eventually organizing the populace to wage total guerrilla war. Maze sprinted in search of Zey. Ordo decided that if he had to trash Zey's personal data to protect it, he'd take a fast download of it first.

"Sir!" A commando from Yayax Squad jogged up to him, still fastening his belt. He was one of Bralor's—Cov, if memory served. "I'm rounding up the new intake. They might as well learn on the job. Orders?"

Ordo didn't have enough intel yet to know where to concentrate his men, and that was Zey's role anyway. He had his own ideas in the meantime. He defaulted to the main contingency plan. "Get everyone as tooled up as you can—strip the armory if need be, and get as many vessels as possible in the air." The commandos weren't pilots, but they could fly well enough to shift a LAAT/i or any transports hanging around. "Then deploy to HNE headquarters. Keep them on air to transmit emergency public broadcasts—GAR artillery is supposed to take up position there. Give them support."

"Yes, sir. And Sergeant Vau's on his way—I just saw him."

Ordo did a quick mental check of who was where before he took another step. Fi, Jusik, Spar, and Sull were inbound; Mereel and A'den were still in the city. Jaing and Kom'rk were on their way back to Utapau, and Prudii—if he was on schedule—was causing a reactor on Sep-controlled Birix to go critical about now. Why hadn't anyone seen this fleet coming? It wasn't as if they hadn't been keeping tabs on General Grievous.

Someone knew he was coming, though.

It was all very convenient timing. Was this all part of some elaborate ambush by the Republic, luring the Seps to a relatively sparsely defended capital only to smash them with a hidden army? If that was Palpatine's plan all along, Ordo felt he owed him an apology, grudging as it was.

Clever boy, Chancellor. Maybe I misjudged you.

Ordo slipped into the nearest control room to activate its holochart projector, then keyed in the code to display the real-time battle chart being generated from the main GAR HQ three kilometers away. It was the first time he'd felt on the margins of events. He wasn't in control of this. He could only react, or take orders. This wasn't how he liked to fight.

ARC-170s were already airborne and streaming out to meet the Separatist starfighters that were sweeping ahead of the main fleet. Switching to the ground chart, he could see armored units being moved into skylanes and surrounding key buildings. Now the planetary defense shield had been activated—why so late, what took so long?—and hundreds of enemy vessels, including capital ships, had now been caught within it.

Like being locked up with a rancor. It's going to get messy.

The GAR's overstretch was now painfully visible. Too many assets were spread elsewhere in the galaxy. They'd have to recall units immediately.

But it was not his decision to make.

He was watching a fragment of the war, like any other soldier, and even a better idea of the bigger picture didn't help.

Boots and claws clattered down the corridor. Vau skidded into the office, Mird at his side.

"Palpatine knew this was coming," Ordo said. "Is he going to get that shiny new fleet here in time?"

"Maybe. Get your *beskar* on, *Ord'ika*." Vau placed his black helmet over his head with an almost ceremonial air. It transformed him instantly into a faceless warrior, age and species and gender indeterminate. He was an archetype of war. "We're going to end up fighting droids on the ground, and not for the *shabla* Republic, either. And we need to grab Uthan. There's no better time. Perfect cover to move— everyone's too busy to worry about us."

"No time to pick up my armor," Ordo said. "I'll fight in this rig. It's served me well so far."

Mird, frantic but silent, thrashed its tail and darted around, occasionally letting a tightly suppressed whine of excitement escape. Ordo sprinted for the entrance, abandoning the *dadita* code to talk to Skirata on the comlink while he ran. Nobody was going to worry about hunting him now that the planet was being invaded.

"Stay put, *Kal'buir*," he said. "Do you hear me? I need you in *Aay'han* to act as a forward operating base."

"HNE's just repeating the stay-calm message," Skirata said. "I've got the GAR tactical displays in front of me now. I need to get Laseema, Besany, and Kad down here."

Vau's voice cut in on the comlink. He was right behind Ordo. "Kal, they're now with Mij and Wad'e in another safe house, lower levels—code coming to you now. *Don't* move them unless the area comes under attack. The Seps are going to be after the high-value targets first, not slums."

"Gosh, I'd never have worked that out, Walon . . ."

"I'll RV with Fi—Sull's still trying to land. He's coming in a long way south of the GAR landing platform. The fighting's too heavy above the center of the city."

Ordo's instinct was to go to Skirata, but another urge told him he had Seps to kill, and yet another said this was—as Vau observed—the best time to grab Uthan. Then his helmet comm kicked into life again, but it wasn't *Kal'buir*.

"Zey to all Special Ops personnel, Inner Rim. Code Five, Code Five. Repeat, Code Five, Code Five. Any way you can, people. Keep comlink overrides open. May the Force be with you."

Every Republic commando on SOB strength, wherever they were in the galaxy, had heard that signal. It was one of a long list of worst scenarios; it was immediate recall to Coruscant for any squads deployed in the Inner Rim to defend the capital.

Their generals—in those few places where Jedi officers accompanied them—would have heard it, too. If the situation deteriorated, the recall net would be cast wider.

"First things first," Vau said. "Let's find Fi's ship, and then Mereel and A'den."

"Agreed," said Ordo. He started his speeder bike's drive. "Is Mird okay on a bike?"

Vau hot-wired the speeder bike standing next to Ordo's. He was good at appropriating transport. "Loves it," he said, swinging onto the seat. Mird scrambled up behind him and seized the pillion seat and Vau's back plate with his claws. "Six legs give you a good grip."

It was only when they lifted off and headed south that they saw the scale of the fighting. The ARC-170 squadrons were still holding off Separatist fighters high in the atmosphere, but the aerial bombardment had begun, and there were already palls of smoke rising from the business quarter near the Senate.

"This is where we choose sides, Ordo," Vau said, a disembodied voice in his helmet. "We fight for the Republic, or we fight for the survival of our own. We can't do both, except by accident."

"*Aliit,* then," said Ordo, thinking about the RC squads who would do their duty to the end, and feeling wretched at his choice. "Our clan."

14

Okay, I admit it now. Palpatine's strategically and tactically
brilliant. He's spread the GAR so thin that the Seps thought
Coruscant was here for the taking, and so they roll in—and
bang, *he unleashes his second force behind them. He gets*
them to come to him. Well, at least we know now what he
was building that second clone army and all the ships for.
Now all we have to do is get out in one piece.
Nice one, Chancellor, you slimeball.
—Kal Skirata, interpreting Palpatine's motives in a logical
military light—and getting it completely wrong

GAR rapid assault vessel, inbound for Coruscant,
five hours into the Battle of Coruscant, 1,080 days ABG

Omega Squad dropped out of hyperspace and stared in disbelief as they reoriented themselves.

"*Osik . . . ,*" said Niner. "Now we're screwed."

A seething mass of warships spread in a massive formation, converging on Coruscant. There must have been a couple of thousand, and that was just the ones they could see
with the Mark One Eyeball from the viewplate. *Big* ships.

"Hold the *osik*," Atin said. "They're *ours*."

Niner tapped keys and the cockpit scans rolled a long list
of Republic transponder and pennant codes. Darman leaned
over Niner's shoulder.

"I didn't think we had that many hulls to deploy," he said.
"Anyone recognize any of these crates?"

Atin shook his head. "I don't know half of these."

"Right pennant code, right transponder, right drive signature." Niner hit the key again, and again, and the same confirmations flashed on the cockpit display: a cycle of Republic codes and ship names, *new* names. This fleet was the good guys. "We seem to have acquired a new box of warships. Maybe it's our birthday and we forgot."

Darman flipped from sinking dread to elation to resentment in seconds. He thought the timing was pretty sick, given the last three miserable, fruitless, futile years of sweating blood and seeing no real progress, of taking a planet and then moving on only to see it fall again. They could have done with an injection of ships and men like this a long, long time ago.

"Home, my good man," Corr said, tapping Niner's shoulder. "And don't spare the drives."

As the assault vessel headed at top speed for Coruscant, threading between carriers, destroyers, and cruisers, it was becoming clear that they were looking at a turning point of the war.

"Sergeant Kal was right," Atin said. "Palps really *did* have a secret army and fleet up his sleeve."

"Better late than never," Niner said, fists tight on the vessel's yoke. He was a competent pilot, but not a confident one. "Let's check in with Zey. Dar, ping the old man for us, will you?"

It took a few moments to get Zey to respond. While Darman waited anxious seconds, the assault ship—designed for thirty troops, the first asset they could grab—skimmed inside the safety zone of a massive cruiser, so close that Darman could see the markings on the hull. There were no scorch marks, gouges, or even widespread pocking from space debris. This ship was *new*.

"Omega," Zey said, shimmering into life as a blue hologram. "Niner, what's your estimate?"

"Half an hour to Arca Barracks, sir, if we don't run into trouble."

"Divert to these coordinates, Omega." Numbers flashed up on the nav display. "We've got mobile anti-air batteries at all the main utility stations around Galactic City, but it's only a matter of time before the Seps get a foothold on the ground. If we lose power over large sectors, then we've got a major civilian safety problem, and we don't need a few billion citizens stranded without pumped water and comms on top our current woes. Keep that generating station running, Omega."

"Copy that, sir." Niner was *never* mocking Zey when he said that, unlike some. "Mind my asking where our extra assets came from?"

"You tell *me*," Zey said sourly. "The additions to the fleet have come as something of a surprise to us *all,* Sergeant. But now is not the time for the Jedi Council to ask the Chancellor *why.*"

The holoimage shivered and vanished.

"If only it was just a nice simple war," Corr said. "Still, mustn't grumble."

"That's the trouble with fighting in a place like Coruscant." Niner kept tapping vectors into the nav computer, looking for a clear run in through the vast maze of ships. "Complex, crowded infrastructure that's easily disrupted— billions of scared folk fleeing in speeders, clogging the skylanes because the autonav is down—fires, collapsed buildings, ruptured water mains—you name it. Look at it as keeping the civvies out of our lads' hair while they get on with the job of killing Seps."

Darman hoped someone planetside would remember to drop the shields for a moment to let the assault ship land. It was a terrifying picture of a city under attack. There was a certain simplicity to warfare, the act of trying to kill the other guy before he killed you. Once civvies were added, though, it all became much messier.

And once you knew you had a baby son down there on Coruscant, it made it messier still.

"Kad better be safe," Darman said.

"And Laseema." Atin nodded to himself. "All of 'em, in fact."

It was all he needed to say. The squad fell silent. This wasn't just a mission. They all had a very personal stake in saving Coruscant. Darman was pretty sure that none of them felt *stone-cold* now, like an HNE news droid had once said commandos always were.

"At least Etain's offplanet," Corr said. "If the Seps are piling in here, Kashyyyk might be quiet for a while."

Niner huffed. "Well, lucky her, because it's not quiet *here*."

He brought the AV around in loop to clear two vessels exchanging cannon rounds. Omega were past the single mass of Republic ships now, and into a mixed chaos with enemy vessels, fighters, and even random friendlies. An armed Mon Cal freighter caught in the melee was pouring fire from its small cannon onto a Sep gunship with magnificent abandon. The AV streaked past it before Darman saw the outcome of the skirmish.

Corr leaned forward in his seat to look at the screens. The whole squad was crammed into the cockpit, watching the status screens. "*Shab,* Niner, look at the shield level."

"Yeah, we've managed to trap a lot of stingflies down there. That'll be fun . . ."

Cannon fire was ripping hulls apart all around him, and starfighters were ending their sorties in balls of silent blinding white light. Atin looked at the sensor screens. "Some *shabuir* on our *shebs*." It looked like a fighter on the scan. "If he's not targeting us, he's worked out we're going in."

"He's tailgating," Niner said, pushing the drive to the limits. "Hang on to your frillies. Sixty seconds to shield."

Corr tightened his restraints. "Knock-knock, let us in . . ."

"Remember to brake if they don't," Atin said.

"They can *always* open an intersection for us." Niner was dead serious. He always was at times like this. "They only have to drop one generator node for five or six seconds."

But Darman's thoughts strayed. He was thinking ahead, to when the Seps would be beaten back, and maybe—maybe—the war would be over or in its dying days. There was a topic they hadn't mentioned since Skirata had broken the news to them in the barracks refreshers, but Darman knew they'd all thought about it a lot.

"I'm going over the wall," he said gravely. "When this is done, I'm deserting to Mandalore. Who's with me?"

Corr raised a finger. "Me."

"Yep," Atin grunted, patting the DC-17 on his lap.

Niner didn't answer. Darman waited.

"Okay, I don't want to be the last nerf steak left in the shop," Niner said. Darman never expected to hear that. "I'd better come, too."

The relief was palpable, even though they were hurtling toward a defense shield still firmly in place.

"Omega Squad to Shield Control, we need entry."

Silence. The checkered field of Triple Zero's towers seen from the air rushed up to meet them.

Five, four . . .

"Omega to Shield Control, let us in . . ."

Three, two . . .

"Shield Control, to Omega, you're clear."

A flash of light showed that a short-lived portal had opened, and the AV plunged through.

"Omega, *on your six!*" Shield Control snapped.

The Sep fighter had made it through behind them. It was a stupid thing to do, seeing as the *di'kut* was now stuck in Corrie airspace, but some pilots got that red mist in front of their eyes and only thought a second ahead.

Misted or not, he could still shoot.

The cockpit sensors throbbed with red light and a frantic rasping alarm. The Sep had a lock on them. The AV bucked and spun 180 degrees, turning into its own smoke and flames, and that was the only way Darman knew the crazy pilot had fired.

"Shabuir," Niner said, and—even in this chaos, even with the towers of Coruscant spiraling up to meet them—he let loose a couple of Firaxa heat-seekers. "Brace for impact."

"Dumbest way to die," said Corr.

The ball of flame might have been theirs, or it might have been their pursuer's. They had no way of knowing until they hit the ground.

Darman felt his teeth smack down into his lip about the same time as he heard a loud crunch in his helmet, and then he was upended in a gray hot fog.

Something shook the cockpit. The sudden rush of air was as loud as a scream, although he couldn't feel it. Something caught his leg. He was still sharply aware of needing to get the *shab* out of there as fast as he could, because his brain said *fire* even though he couldn't see or feel it, and he kicked at what he thought was a cable snagging his boot.

"Dar, it's *me*!" A fist hit his leg plate. "Stop kicking!"

It was Niner. The next thing Darman knew he'd fallen onto something hard that wasn't moving. Someone grabbed both arms and hauled him away so fast that his boots dragged and he fell. He was *sure* he fell before the explosion behind him knocked him down.

Vhoooooom.

He could see now. It was all yellow light and sharp shadows. When he sat up, trying to get to his feet, he saw burning wreckage and the gaping cockpit of the AV with its viewport split into sections.

"You got jammed under the instrument panel by the impact," Atin said. "Niner blew the viewport's emergency bolts to drag you clear. And your Deece."

"Thanks, Sarge." *Thanks?* It was pitifully inadequate. "Save me one more time, and you get to keep me."

"We'll all need saving if we don't get a move on. Come on. Let's orient ourselves and crack on. Work to do, bad guys to slot."

The smoke from the burning wreckage gave them cover for a moment. Niner turned and ran for the protection of an office building. All the lights were on, but nothing was moving inside. When Darman dropped into the doorway and squatted to check his Deece and sight up, he was looking back on a mass of twisted metal and shattered permacrete. The fighter pursuing them seemed to have exploded before it hit the ground and had scattered debris everywhere. A drive housing with protruding shafts had embedded itself in a wall. Niner crouched with his glove to one side of his helmet, trying to raise HQ on the comm.

"Where's everyone gone?" Corr asked.

"Shelters, I hope," said Atin.

Niner stood up, making quietly exasperated noises. "It's chaos back there. They don't want us at H-6 now. They want us to report to tactical control at GAR HQ. That's ten klicks."

"A stroll," Corr said. "Nice evening for it, too."

Darman could see a strobing light reflecting off the transparisteel. He peered out from the doorway, ready to blow the next thing he saw to *haran,* but it was a CSF assault ship hovering close to the wreckage. He signaled to it and ran out to beckon the pilot to land.

The side hatch opened. "You can't park there, soldier," the cop said. "Not on even-numbered days."

"What are you doing out here?" Darman pointed at the aerial light show. Debris—metal, fuel, flame—was raining down just half a klick away. "Haven't you looked up yet?"

The cop shrugged, smoke-stained and looking weary. "Been herding civvies. Why do they not understand *stay indoors and don't block the skylanes*? There were so many trying to enter the grid that the skylane nav system fell over. Anyway, I saw the smoke here and decided to take a look."

"We bounced." Darman thought of Kad. "How many civvy casualties?"

"Thousands. I couldn't give you a definite figure. It's the debris. When you get a Sep cruiser to fall on you, you know all about it. Area medcenters can't cope."

"Can you give us a ride to GAR HQ?"

"Sure. Might have to divert if we get a call, but hop in. You commandos?"

Darman beckoned the squad. "Yeah. RCs."

"You'd know Fi, then. Top man, that."

Darman had to smile. Even in this direst of circumstances Fi was a legend, at least among the cops of Coruscant. He'd find that funny. Omega Squad piled into the crew compartment of the cop ship, and it lifted clear.

"Didn't know we had that big a fleet," the officer said. "The news said there were more coming in. Where have they been?"

"Waiting," Niner said. "It'll all be over soon. The whole war."

It would. Darman could almost feel it. He checked his comlink for a sitrep from Etain, but there was nothing yet.

He could wait, too.

Manufacturing district, Coruscant

Zey would probably have forgiven him and welcomed his help about now, but Skirata decided there was no point pushing his luck.

Right then, he didn't give a mott's backside about Palpatine, or Zey, or the whole Jedi Council; he just didn't want them getting in his way when he had his clan scattered across a city under siege. He paused the airspeeder at an intersection well in the cover of tall buildings and looked down, and then looked up.

Coruscant had never seemed bigger. Without the vessels packed into the skylanes at the heart of Galactic City, he could see a lot farther, and the full scale of the artificial canyons hit home. There were thousands of meters of empty skylane above him, and thousands below.

The view left unimpeded by citizens who'd fled the center was a spectacular pyrotechnic show. The dusk was alight with explosions high in the atmosphere. One instant ball of white light faded to yellow right above his head, then red, and then seemed to be getting bigger very fast—and then he realized it was a massive chunk of burning debris plummeting to the ground. He hit the speeder's accelerator just in time to hear the *whuuush* and crackle in the air behind him. Smaller fragments fizzed past the hatches and bounced like hail off the viewscreen.

It was a reminder to move under cover. He opened his comlink, and if the Chancellor had time to chase him now, it was too bad. "*Ord'ika,* Walon, are you receiving?"

"Bad signal, *Kal'buir,* but I hear you."

"Where are you, son?"

"I've linked up with Fi, Jusik, and the ARC double act. And Omega's just had a hard landing."

Thank all the forgotten gods of Mandalore: at least they were back, although it was a spectacularly bad time and place for a rendezvous. "How hard?"

"They ended up with a Sep fighter up their *shebs.* But it's okay—they're heading for GAR HQ."

Skirata formed a mental map of the city and placed his

priority people on it again. *Get them all down to* Aay'han, *get Uthan, and go.* "Is *Bard'ika* with you now? Is Ruu giving him a hard time?"

"He didn't say. She's safe. That's all. What now?"

"I'm going for Uthan." Skirata paused; he could see med runners and a firespeeder streaking along an empty skylane far beneath him. Somewhere close—above him, it seemed— an anti-air battery was pumping ion rounds into the sky at something he couldn't see, and the rhythmic *whump-whump-whump* shook his chest like a second heartbeat. "We walk in and we take her. And we do it now, in case they evacuate the patients. I need *Bard'ika* in a suit, and two lads to act as clones."

"We *are* clones."

"I mean white jobs. You and Sull, preferably."

"Fi. We take Fi."

Ordo was very fond of Fi, and when a Null had formed a close bond, nothing short of detonite would break it.

"Okay, son. But is he up to it?"

"He got your daughter out of prison."

"Okay. We RV at the lower-levels landing platform directly beneath the Valorum Center. From there—well, we grab the breaks we can get."

It took Skirata ten minutes to get to the RV point. On a normal day, it would have taken four times as long. He landed the speeder, realized that he'd have to abandon it on Coruscant sooner rather than later, and stood watching the ongoing aerial battle with a sense of disbelief that he could wander around a battened-down city under fire and not feel part of it, as if it were some holodrama. Eventually, he got back into the speeder and watched the HNE coverage. The media had dispatched cam droids, and the images from right among the ships were astonishing.

It's real. Boys like Ordo are dying up there—fighter pilots, ship's crew. Not just Seps. Stop watching it like a show.

It was too voyeuristic for Skirata. He switched off the images and just kept the audio running for information, with one ear on his helmet comlink listening to chatter from the GAR command center. When he heard the throb of drives approaching—it was eerily quiet, even with the distant noise of the battle—he ducked down until he confirmed it was a GAR-liveried LAAT/i gunship, showing no navigation lights.

"*Ord'ika,*" he said on his comlink, "is that you approaching the RV point?"

"It's Fi." The landing lights blipped briefly. "How you doing, *Kal'buir*?"

When the gunship set down, Fi was first out, and Skirata rushed to slap his back and hug him. He found himself looking over Fi's shoulder—a stretch, given how much taller clones were—to stare at a short, scruffy-looking, thirty-something woman in brown prison overalls.

She stared back. "Dad?"

Skirata didn't need to ask. Thirty years' separation just compressed into nothing. She was his little girl, his *Ruus'ika*. There was nothing he could say, so he just hugged her, unable to even marshal his thoughts.

"Sorry about the timing, Ruu," he said at last. "And the location."

"Dad . . . I've waited such a long time . . ."

"When we're done here, we can take you back to Drall, or you can come with us."

Ruu just prodded him in the chest with her forefinger, eyes brimming. She didn't seem able to speak now.

"You'll like Mandalore," Skirata said.

"Kal, get a move on." Vau stuck his head out of the LAAT/i. "I've got your *aruetyc* clothes here. You might want to change before we do our house calls."

"Okay, we do a front-door job, then." It was an effort to switch back to being the bad old *Mando* merc, because he wanted to be an indulgent dad right then. It struck him that Ruu had probably never known precisely what he did for a living. This was a shocking way to find out. "Jusik and me—we go in as suits. Fi and Ordo—meat-can armor, our armed escorts."

"Whose authorization are we claiming?" Vau asked. "I need to fix the ID chips."

"Oh, Chancellor's Office. Might as well tick him off completely. I hate doing half a job."

"It's good to be back in the field, *Kal'buir,*" Fi said, grinning.

"Good to have you back, son."

It was good to have *everybody* back. There was only Omega Squad and Etain to gather in now. The plan was nearly complete.

Valorum Center, Coruscant

The explosions and screaming of fighters overhead had stopped bothering Jusik now, although he still ducked instinctively. His Force sense told him the danger wasn't close enough to warrant running for his life. It still helped to react like a regular being when he pressed the security intercom at the main gates, though.

"Security," said a voice.

"Here's my identichip and authorization," Jusik said, playing Denel Herris again and slapping the chips into the slot with the air of a man in a big, annoyed hurry. "Herris, Coruscant Health. Have you evacuated the inmates yet?"

There was a crackling pause. "We haven't been instructed to, sir."

"Do you not have an evacuation plan for civil emergencies?" Jusik glanced at Skirata, who looked remarkably urbane in his bantha jacket. He could be dapper, and he could be so low-key that he was invisible, but he would never pass for a psychiatrist. His hard life was etched in his face. "Apart from the welfare of the patients, is your director aware that you have an inmate the Separatists would like to release, and who could do immense damage to the Republic's defense effort? I do believe he is."

Jusik could hear mumbling and shuffling at the other end of the comlink. Eventually, the security gates parted with a metallic grinding sound. Jusik strode in, flanked by Skirata, Ordo, and Fi. When he got to the inner doors, they were met by an anxious-looking woman in a medical tunic.

"We've not been told to evacuate yet, Master Herris." She was in a hurry to get them inside, and kept looking up at the sky even though the height of the buildings around the center obscured the view of the fighting. "There's an emergency shelter below, but the patients here need escorts and supervision, and we don't have the staff or the droids."

"Where's your director?"

"He went home to check on his family when the fighting broke out. He hasn't come back or commed us. I'm just the duty nursing officer . . . and I'm in charge, I suppose."

It was perfect. The top man had run away, and this poor woman had an unfair responsibility dumped in her lap. Jusik didn't have to feign sympathy.

"Then at least I can solve one problem for you," he said. He indicated Fi and Ordo with a tilt of his head: *It's okay. I've got the army with me, and you can trust us.* "We have authorization to remove one of your inmates, Dr. Qail Uthan, to a secure place in case the city falls and she's taken by the Separatists. Can you take us to her, please?"

Jusik proffered the bogus clearance from the Chancellor's office. The woman took it. She didn't seem to have any idea how to verify it anyway.

"This way," she said, picking up a datapad. She looked at Skirata. "Have you got restraints, then?"

She seemed to think he was the hired muscle. Jusik didn't meet Skirata's eyes.

"We might not need to use them, ma'am," Skirata said in his best sergeant's voice. "But we'll need details of any medication she's on, obviously."

The doors parted, and Jusik made a conscious effort not to feel what was happening around him. He'd never managed to fully shake off the memory of the first visit. Recalling the unquiet souls he'd brushed against in the Force here had felt like opening an old wound each time, fresh with pain. And they were still here. He struggled to close his mind to them.

As he walked through the carpeted corridors, he felt that mind again, the one that wasn't detached from reality and shouldn't have been there, locked up for reasons he would never know. And knew he could *not* stop to intervene.

I should. How can I walk on by?

But he did. He had a duty to his brothers, and at that moment the needs of clone troopers came first. Jusik didn't rationalize it on a scale of necessary evils and forgive himself. He simply accepted that he had done a shameful thing, and that he would have to live with it.

"Nice place," Skirata said, almost to himself. "Must cost a packet to run."

Jusik could hear voices. There was crying coming from one direction, and occasional shouts to be let out, probably because the inmates could hear the bombardment going on. He could have sworn he heard that language again, the one that had made him think someone was speaking *Mando'a*. Skirata didn't react to it. But Skirata's hearing had been damaged by years on the battlcficld, so maybe he didn't pick it up.

"This is Dr. Uthan's room," the nurse said, unlocking the doors and taking a few steps back. "She's all yours."

Skirata flexed his shoulders, making the bantha-hide jacket creak. Uthan wouldn't know either of them from a Hutt; she knew what clones looked like, though, and Fi had helped abduct her. There would be some explaining to do when the helmets came off. But by then it would be too late to argue.

Uthan was sitting at her desk, making notes on a 'pad as if she had no cares beyond a pressing schedule. She glanced up at Jusik.

"Oh, *you* again," she said. She indicated the world above her ceiling with a jerk of her head. "I do hope they reduce your corrupt little planet to rubble."

Jusik smiled and clasped his hands in front of him, then dropped his voice to a whisper.

"I said I'd get right on it when you asked to be released, Dr. Uthan," he said. "And I did. But I don't work for the Republic. Would you like to leave?"

The look of permanent disdain on her face vanished gradually like melting frost. "And who *are* you?"

"Just Mandalorians doing a job, ma'am."

She'd had a Mandalorian minder on Qiilura, Ghez Hokan. She might not have thought much of him, but the *M* word said *friendly forces* to her.

"I hope you're more effective than the last one," she said quietly. "Have I got time to collect my research material? Because if I haven't—"

"Of course," said Jusik. "That's why we're here."

It was all completely true.

There was a bit of Jusik—a bit he didn't like to look at—that relished the game, enjoying the bluff and feint like a sabacc player. *I'm capable of terrible things. I must never forget that.* He watched her gather up datapads and piles of flimsi, and pack them in a bag.

"Nurse," she called. "Nurse, can you let the soka flies free in the morning? They kept me sane. It's the least I owe them."

Jusik revised his view of Uthan just a little. She picked up her bag and walked out through the doors of her cell as if she'd been expecting this rescue all the time.

Skirata didn't look at Jusik, maintaining his act of bored sidekick, but he radiated satisfaction and relief in the Force. Jusik found himself wondering what other scams *Kal'buir* had pulled over the years. He accepted that Skirata was a criminal and a killer, *and* still loved him dearly. There were no *buts* in that thought. Skirata was, from most perspectives, a complete *shabuir;* but his one saving grace was so vast, so all-encompassing, that it dwarfed any wrongdoing into insignificance. He could love unconditionally. He could love those who couldn't possibly be of any use to him, the marginalized and dispossessed, and even those who hurt him; and when he loved, he would give his life doing it, and ask no questions.

Jusik could forgive Skirata anything for that painfully rare quality.

"Nicely done, son," Skirata murmured.

They were now on the final leg of the mission. It was going fine, all things considered, right up to the point when Jusik heard that voice again; that one tantalizing, half-familiar sound that made him listen.

"Nurse," he said. "I need to check something." He held up

a forefinger for silence. "Hear that voice?" It was the female one that sounded almost as if she was speaking Mandalorian. Something insisted, begged, *demanded* that he at least go and look. Leaving the Jedi hadn't severed his connection to the Force. "May I see that inmate? She may be on our list."

When the nurse's back was turned, Skirata shot Jusik a glance. *What are you playing at?*

Jusik just raised his finger a fraction farther. *Bear with me.*

"I'm afraid she's very uneasy around males," said the nurse. "And she has a history of violence against them."

Jusik peered into the room. The woman was maybe forty, forty-five, a little older, and didn't look as if she could mete out even a harsh word. She huddled in the corner, rocking for comfort, and when her eyes met his, he knew she was very troubled indeed.

"Can I talk to her?" Jusik asked.

"Just be careful." The nurse slid the 'pad in front of him. "She's on a five-hundred dose of zaloxipine, just to manage her, but she's been detained indefinitely for three homicides. I can't take responsibility for her."

Jusik squatted down and resorted to a little mind influence, the most benign, to make her realize he meant her no harm. It was worth trying even if he was stretching their luck. Something told him he had to, and maybe it was simply that he'd walked by one inmate too many.

"Ner gai Bard'ika," he said. *"Tion gar gai? Gar aliit?"* He'd told her his name was Bardan, and asked her name and her clan name.

She stared at him. It was as if she didn't believe what she was seeing, or hearing.

"Arla," she said. She glanced at the nurse as if the woman was eavesdropping. *"Neyar gain Arla Vhett."*

It wasn't *Mando'a,* but it was close enough for any Mandalorian to understand. Jusik turned slowly, still squatting, to look at Skirata. The old sergeant's face was a study in suppressed shock.

"I think this patient should be on our special care list," Jusik said. He beckoned to her. He knew he didn't look remotely threatening. *"Arla, mhi'alor at'morut'yc taap."*

He told her they would take her somewhere safe. He knew it was what she needed to hear. Somehow, he persuaded her to stand up and walk out the front doors with them, and into the ship waiting a few meters away.

Jusik heard Skirata let out a long breath that he seemed to have been holding for months.

"I'm dying to hear the explanation," Uthan said as the hatch closed. She looked around at the helmeted Mandalorians, troopers, and Ruu, and edged away a little from Mird, who sniffed her leg enthusiastically. Arla cowered in a recess by the weapons locker at the sight of the armor, and would *not* be coaxed out. "But thank you, gentlemen. Where to now?"

"We'll wait somewhere safe until the fighting dies down," Skirata said.

The LAAT/i lifted. Vau indicated Arla with a gracious gesture.

"Did we plan this, Kal?" he asked. "Why do we have an extra passenger?"

Skirata rubbed his face wearily with both hands. "I think I agree with *Bard'ika* that we couldn't leave her behind."

"But what was she *in* there for? It's important, Kal, given the business the Valorum Center is in . . ."

"She murders people," Skirata said mildly. "Like that makes her not good enough for *us*?"

"Oh, *shab* . . ."

Ordo said nothing, but Jusik could see Fi's shoulders shaking slightly, and knew that even in this terrible, bizarre, potentially deadly situation, he was laughing uncontrollably.

"I thought *I* was a chancer," Skirata said, "but *Bard'ika,* you make me look like a Neimoidian accountant. You know who that is, don't you? If she *is* who she thinks she is, anyway. Because she's supposed to be *dead.*"

"Oh, I know," Jusik said. In the last few years, he'd absorbed all he could about Mandalore and its people, both from *Mando'ade* themselves and from *aruetiise* who knew them all too well—like certain Jedi. "And that's why she deserves our help."

"So who is it?" Vau asked, plainly irritated. Mird watched the woman with head cocked, tail slapping. "We'd better have a good reason for taking a psychotic killer with us tonight."

"We have," said Jusik. "That's Arla Fett—Jango's missing sister."

15

I didn't realize they had names. What do they think about?
They don't know what life is really like, and all they
know is war, so they're probably perfectly happy.
I'm glad they don't suffer.
—Jedi Padawan Simi Noor, discussing clone troopers

Kashyyyk, three days into the Battle of Coruscant, 1,083 days ABG

Sev sat with one hand to the side of his helmet as if he was having trouble hearing his comlink. Fifty meters beneath the thick cables of living vine that formed the walkways from tree to tree, Scorch could see the beaten track of crushed vegetation. Battle droids couldn't climb trees.

"What's happening?" Scorch whispered, even though he knew sound couldn't be heard outside his helmet. "Have they Code-Fived us yet?"

Sev shook his head. "Inner Rim only. Anyway, aren't we busy enough? Listen for yourself. I'm trying to concentrate."

"I'm eavesdropping on the Sep comm band."

"Well, Corrie's taking a pounding."

"*Shab.* Have they landed ground forces yet?"

"Yeah, it's hotting up down there. But that's okay, because we have a nice big fleet now."

"Allies? How kind of them to remember us."

"*Ours.* Looks like Palps kept his spare war machine down the back of the sofa for a rainy day."

Scorch didn't take his eyes off the route below as he

switched channels to pick up the command frequencies at HQ. He knew the battle droid patrol was coming, and Boss was keeping visual observation from the ground. It wasn't as if Delta didn't have a job to do here, but the sheer helplessness of hearing the comm traffic—he switched out of the pilots' circuit because it was actually distressing him—was painful. They were light-years away. There was nothing he could do. Even with the massively reinforced fleet outside the shield, it was a desperate battle to stave off the destruction beneath it.

And he was waiting to ruin a Sep patrol's entire day himself. It was a rare moment of quiet; the Wookiees were reestablishing a bridge network higher in the trees to replace the one at Kachirho, much narrower and more fragile spans that wouldn't take enemy traffic. If the Seps wanted to use these borrat-runs of aerial pathways, they'd have to be on foot.

"Fixer, this is Scorch—you receiving?"

"I'm ready." The vine walkway vibrated under Scorch's boots as Fixer emerged from a mass of foliage and padded along the aerial pathway. Scorch thought it was a lot of vibration for an eighty-five-kilo man to generate until he saw Enacca ambling behind him. Skirata's Wookiee buddy usually fixed his transport and safe houses for him, and Scorch wondered how he was coping without her. "Enacca says the Seps have been moving triple-A parts. They're reinforcing the battery position west of here."

Enacca rumbled in her throat and gestured with a long, hairy arm.

"Good idea, we'll go recce that battery first," Sev said. "Let's see what the general has to say, though. Is she wearing her earpiece?"

"She is," said a voice on the channel, but Etain didn't sound annoyed. If anything, she sounded as if she'd had a disagreement with Command. "I listen to the experts, which in this case is the Wookiees—and you."

"Flattered, ma'am," Sev said. "But do I get a droid to play with later? I like to see how they come apart."

"Do you think they're sentient, Sev? Droids, I mean?"

It was a weird question to ask when they were getting ready to destroy yet more enemy personnel, a bit too philosophical for the mood of the moment. Sev was still hyped up despite few hours' sleep. It was killing Geonosians, not droids, that had become a focus for him. Scorch knew he was itching to get at some more. He kept his head tilted up as if waiting for the bugs to come back, and from the shared HUD icon, Scorch could see he still kept a tally of Geonosian kills. His sensors were set to detect their specific flight pattern.

"Yeah," Sev said casually, which didn't match what Scorch could see happening in his HUD. "Tinnies think, act, and they don't want to be destroyed. And they're smarter than a lot of wets we meet."

"Just asking because of the way *wets* don't think of *you* as being real beings."

Scorch made a winding gesture to the side of his helmet. *Humor her, Sev.* But Sev carried on.

"I don't kill 'em because I think they're inferior to me, ma'am," he said. "I kill 'em because they're trying to kill *us*."

"We'd all be best buddies," Fixer said. "It's just our wicked masters who set us against each other. Otherwise we'd be having an ale together."

Etain went quiet. Scorch wondered if she was feeling the pressure, too. He had an understanding with her now. She didn't tell him to get a grip or buck his ideas up when he lost control. She just made him feel better—not that he was any more comfortable about the Jedi mind trick, but she'd asked his permission first—and let him know he wasn't crazy; it was the situation he was forced into that was insane and wrong.

Jedi or not, she had to be feeling it as well.

"You okay, General?" he asked.

There was a crackle in the circuit as if she'd switched off her audio for a moment.

"I'm worried about Coruscant," she said. "I have friends and . . . family there."

Well, at least she was honest enough to admit she had a bit of a thing going with Darman, in not so many words. Scorch found he could shut the doors on feelings like that. Getting that close to anyone caused pain; Vau had told them so, when they were wide-eyed kids drinking in his wisdom and he was the most important figure in their limited world. Letting anyone get under your skin, trusting anyone who said they loved you, was a recipe for being hurt and betrayed. So they had to protect themselves by keeping the world at arm's length. It was good advice for the life they led.

"Darman will be fine." Scorch took the risk of acknowledging her open secret. "He's a survivor, like all the Omegas. *Shab,* they couldn't even kill Fi permanently, and he was *dead.*"

"Yeah, *nobody* could shut Fi's mouth for good," Sev said. "It's a force of nature in its own right."

That was another cover story nobody bought but that everyone accepted. Etain swallowed loudly. Boy, was she in a weird mood today . . .

"I have a child," she said.

Scorch really didn't have a comeback for that. It even shut Sev up. Nobody said a word, except Enacca, but it was very soft; and they didn't understand every word of Shyriiwook.

"That's kriffing *awkward* for you, ma'am," Boss said at last. They knew the Jedi rules, although they also knew there was now some weird Jedi sect that had shown up to fight alongside the Temple boys, and they were okay about having families. "We didn't even hear you tell us that. We know nothing."

"Thank you, Boss," Etain said. "Now let's see what our Sep friends are up to."

Scorch had no idea where Etain was until she swung onto an almost horizontal branch above them that was thicker than she was tall. She dropped down and hardly made the vine walkway shiver.

"If only we'd known Grievous was on his way to Coruscant from here," she said.

"Not much we could have done about it, except warn Zey." Scorch was trying *not* to dwell on the idea that Darman was the father of Etain's kid. It was another thing Delta knew that they would never discuss outside the squad, if they discussed it at all. "And the new fleet caught them in the end."

That wasn't much comfort if your child was on Coruscant. Scorch switched off the distracting thoughts and concentrated on what he could control and understand best.

"Let's go," Boss said.

Scorch topped up his impromptu camouflage by smearing handfuls of gritty moss across the bright yellow and white flashes on his armor, and decided that there really were times when stealth did matter. Those camo-coatings that the 41st Elite wore had their place.

Enacca let out a very low rumble, right on the threshold of Scorch's hearing. It showed up on his HUD sensors as a jagged and short-lived trace on the 'scope. A patrol was approaching. He lay flat, looking down on the forest floor below. Sev and Fixer followed suit.

A familiar sound grew louder: the *chunk-chunk-chunk* of battle droids. Their gait was slower and less regular than usual. They were negotiating uneven ground, branches, vegetation.

Crash.

And pits. Wookiees were good at digging deep, *deep* pits.

Scorch heard loud metallic crashing and the creaking of green wood. The droids clattered to re-form, leaving two behind to retrieve their fallen—very fallen—comrade.

"Mind your step, clanker," Sev said.

They weren't making fast progress. Delta, Etain, and Enacca moved along the network of vine paths above the patrol, unseen and unheard through the dense foliage and chattering wildlife. Eventually, they ran out of path, and the droids clanked off to the right deeper into the trees. Scorch swung his rappel line—firing it would produce a sound clearly not of the forest—and hooked the next tree, swinging across to the nearest branch like the locals. Sev and Fixer followed him. Boss and the others were somewhere behind now, out of sight in the sun-dappled branches.

Enacca growled.

"She says that if you were a meter taller and covered in hair, Scorch, she might think you were attractive," Boss said. "You swing like a Wookiee."

Sev snorted. "That's the best offer he's had all year."

"Any idea when the Council plans to take a crack at Kashyyyk, General?" Fixer asked.

"As soon as Master Vos finishes up at Boz Pity," Etain said. "Which could be anytime now."

"I'm *so* going to enjoy serving alongside him . . ."

"If I run into him, I promise I'll give him a quick lesson in courtesy."

"Good for you, ma'am, it's—" Scorch stopped dead. His HUD sensor picked it up first, an abrupt change in density and a shift from organic to metallic compounds, but then he saw it; it was like a warehouse that had been airlifted and dumped in the heart of the forest. "My, the Seps have been *busy* bad boys."

They'd built structures that soared into the tree canopy, soaring charcoal-gray metal insults to the landscape. Scorch had to check his sensors again.

"Turbolaser battery," said Boss. "Decisions, decisions. Take it now, or come back with a few hairy reinforcements?"

"Come back later, after I've rigged some of my special-recipe ordnance," Scorch said. "And I'll take it offline the loud, enjoyable way."

"You get all the fun." Sev studied the structure as if he was going to bite a chunk out of it to test it. "Can I pick off the Trandos as they run away screaming?"

"Knock yourself out," said Boss. "It'll give you a treat to look forward to."

They lingered for another quarter hour, carrying out passive scans of the tower to get a better idea of the layout, and then made their way back to the aerial walkway. Scorch was already calculating blast radii and optimum placement in his head when Enacca stopped dead and waved them down. The vine path was still shivering as if there was traffic coming the other way.

Droids couldn't climb trees. But Trandoshans could.

There were two of them walking gingerly down the vine path, looking as if they had just discovered the route and were scoping it out.

"Mine," Sev said. "All *mine.*" He stepped off the path into

the branches, slung his rifle, and hauled himself farther up
into the tree canopy. Scorch and the others melted into the
side branches.

Nobody needed to speak. Scorch wondered if he should
explain the procedure to Etain, but from the way she moved,
she'd done this kind of ambush before. He realized now exactly how dirty things had become on Qiilura when she was
organizing the resistance there with Zey, back in the days before they ended up doing more desk work than either of them
wanted. It seemed so long ago.

It wasn't even three years. But when you were coming up
thirteen *and* twenty-six years old at the same time, that was
a big chunk of your life.

I hope you find that cure for us, Kal.

They waited. The Trandoshans edged forward, not as confident up in the trees now since they'd encountered Wookiee
hand-to-hand, limb-from-limb fighting. Scorch would never
get that image out of his mind, however much he wanted to.

They were right under Sev now. He dropped like a silent
stone onto one of them, forcing an *oof* from the Trando's
lungs and slapping a gauntlet over the barve's mouth before
he could draw a breath to yell. Etain knocked the other
Trando flat without laying a finger on him. Sev's vibroblade
silenced the first Trando; Fixer pounced on his comrade,
seized his head, and snapped his neck with a sharp twist.
Enacca picked up both bodies by the belts like groceries,
strode along until she found the two-meter gullet-like bloom
of a carnivorous plant within throwing distance, and lobbed
them in. The bloom shuddered with the impact. The last
thing Scorch saw was four legs vanishing slowly, boots in the
air, as if sinking into quicksand.

"Pays to keep the houseplants fed." Scorch watched
Etain's reaction, reminding himself that he should have been
surprised that Jedi could kill and maim so easily. "Potassium
encourages flowering. So they say."

Etain studied the carnivorous plant before moving on, as if
she was considering its merits for a flower arrangement. "Do
you ever look at the enemy and wonder just what the difference is between us?"

"Only after I've slotted them."

"But you don't hate Trandoshans. We don't even know them."

"No," said Scorch, "but I'm human, and the only way you psych yourself up to killing something that's similar to yourself is to be scared of it, or to pretend it's not a person like you are."

"But I hate Geonosians," Sev said sourly. "And we *do* know plenty about them. Only three thousand, four hundred and twenty to kill, and we'll be even. Then I'll start on the rest."

Sev overtook Scorch, scraping plates as he edged around him. A gray worm-like creature longer than Scorch's arm extended itself from the bark of a tree as Sev passed and tried to grab his wrist. Sev yanked it out of its lair in an indignant fist. He held its head up to his visor in a one-handed, strangling grip.

"Don't even *think* about it," he growled, and dropped it over the side into the leaves below.

Enacca, who'd been listening patiently to the debate, yowled softly. Etain might not have hated Trandoshans, she said, but they looked very different to a Wookiee. No slaver or slave owner could ever be *likable,* she said, even if they tried to be nice, which Trandos didn't. That was why they got their arms ripped out of their sockets. All slave owners deserved their fate.

Scorch waited for Etain to continue the debate. But she just glanced at her comlink, tapped it impatiently, and put it back in her pocket.

Yeah, Wookiees were very eloquent, if you knew how to listen.

HNE HQ, Galactic City, day four of the Battle of Coruscant, 1,084 days ABG

The ARC trooper stood on top of the pile of rubble looking down at Darman.

"Are we keeping you awake, Shiny Boy?" He had twin blasters, just like Ordo's, but he was a lieutenant; Lieutenant

Aven. "Look sharp. The tinnies are going to be back again." He jumped down from the vantage point and strode among the commandos who were the last line of defense for the HNE building—Omega and Yayax squads. "Got to keep the voice of freedom and democracy on the air."

Darman had now been awake for the better part of forty-eight hours, snatching a few minutes' sleep between waves of battle droid attacks. He was hungry; not the usual peckishness of a clone fueling a fast metabolism, but a gnawing sick hunger that demanded satisfaction.

"Yeah . . ." His head buzzed with fatigue. It took conscious effort to move his muscles. As he reloaded his Deece with another clip, his arms felt like they belonged to someone else, directed by strings he was holding. "We blew up one on Gaftikar. Or it blew us up. One or the other."

"What?"

"Holonews station. Where's *At'ika*?"

"You're rambling, lad. Take a stim. Got to stay alert."

"Here, Dar." Atin ran at a crouch toward him with something in a large flimsi bag. "Been on a replenishment run." He opened the wrapping and revealed a treasure trove of round, sugar-crusted cakes, wafers filled with something brown and gooey, and containers of an unnaturally bright red liquid. "Guess what? From the news grunts in the HNE building."

Darman had to take his helmet off to eat. He popped the seal; at that moment, he didn't care if some tinnie blew his head off. He *had* to eat and drink. Atin reached into his belt pouches and rummaged, pulling out a stim-sharp. Darman didn't even have the energy to flinch as Atin jabbed it into his neck. Every fiber of his body was dedicated to getting one of those cakes in his mouth, and when he finally bit down—it was *exquisite*. He grabbed a container of the red stuff to wash the cake down.

It was intensely sweet—calorie-laden, nutritional junk, but pure instant energy. *Bliss.* He felt it flood his muscles with renewed life. "I'm never going to shoot an HNE hovercam on a job again," he said hoarsely. "This is *really* nice of them."

Corr's helmet popped up out of nowhere. He grabbed a cake. "Well, seeing as we're getting our *shebse* shot off so they can keep broadcasting, sharing their *skraan* is the least they can do for us."

Niner was curled in a ball on a slab of permacrete, grabbing some sleep. It really was possible to sleep anywhere if you were exhausted enough.

Cov, Yayax's sergeant, redistributed ammo—plasma rounds and grenades—among the eight men. "Where's their food supply, then?"

Corr rolled over on his back and pointed up at the tower. There was a big hole in it, about three-quarters of the way up its height. "The other side of that."

"They're crawling along a girder to transfer the supplies out of the office canteen," Atin said. "I have to admire folks who care about their stomachs just as much as we do. They've got this weird siege mind-set going. I swear they're enjoying it."

"Well, if they like it that much, they can grab a rifle and come down here and enjoy it with us." Cov took a swig from the bottle of red-whatever-it-was. "Still, we need 'em talking to the citizens now, so . . ."

"Have they got that mobile transmitter ready to roll yet?" Aven didn't help himself to the food. "Sooner we get that out of the building and move it somewhere secure, the better." He was already thinking in terms of encouraging resistance and setting up a guerrilla network if the worst happened. Darman wondered how many Coruscanti would fight to overthrow a Separatist occupation. "Cov, take one of your boys. Haul it down with service droids if the turbolift is shot on those floors."

Cov jogged away. Yayax all wore gray-and-brown dazzle-pattern camo armor, and they merged remarkably well with the debris of permacrete and transparisteel. Aven looked up suddenly.

"Here come the tinnies," he said. "Okay, my lads, time to make shrapnel."

Buoyed up on a wave of sugar, Darman now felt fine. Omega and two Yayax men, Dev and Jind, took up positions.

Tinnies were predictable; they just kept coming in dumb waves, so it was largely a matter of who ran out of bodies first. One thing was for sure, though—there might have been a lot of them, a torrent, but there weren't quadrillions or anything close. Skirata was right: if the Seps really had those numbers, they'd have poured them all into Triple Zero by now, and the war would have been over. But they hadn't, and it wasn't.

It only took one tinnie to ruin your entire day, though. Darman wasn't going to celebrate yet.

He edged over the makeshift parapet of permacrete and sighted up. A quick hello from an anti-armor grenade would bring down the front rank, and the second as well if you pitched it right, and then their own debris would slow them down enough to let you hose them with everything else you had.

The tidy, synchronized ranks marched toward them down an avenue that the sapper droids had swept clear of chunks of ships and buildings. The Seps definitely wanted the heart of the Republic's broadcasting capacity in one piece; they could have reduced it to rubble by now. Darman noted that the line of droids was wider this time, requiring more fire along its length to drop them. That was how they overran positions. They encircled them by sheer force of numbers.

"Fire!" Aven barked.

Once Darman squeezed the trigger, things somehow fell into a natural rhythm. It was almost as if he didn't have to think, like singing a song and hearing his own voice before even thinking what note came next. Droids dropped, metal fragments fizzed and hissed as their shrapnel rained down, and flying debris took out their comrades as surely as a GAR-issue grenade; but the others still advanced.

Niner and Atin took a section of the line each, bringing down a dozen tinnies, and in the rank behind, six droids literally shattered like crystal without a direct hit, smashed by the overpressure alone.

"Well done, Prudii," Atin said. "Nobbled at the factory . . ."

The super battle droids behind them weren't from the same sabotaged batch of durasteel, though. They started running, weapon arms held out straight in front of them, and even though Corr and Jind were laying into them with an E-Web repeater, the SBDs kept coming. Now they were meters away. They were so close that Darman's rounds threw shrapnel back at his visor. The next thing he knew, one of the things was nearly on top of him.

Fine; *that* was the way to kill them.

It was pure reflex. Darman ran into its arms, inside the range of its weapon, and brought his vibroblade up into its left armpit where the material was flexible and thinner, slicing through the servos. Its arm fell limp. All it had now, as long as he clung to it, was its weight, and Katarn armor was crush-resistant even under that bulk. The SBD flailed wildly, unable to target its blaster arm or dislodge him. He hung on for grim death while he pulled a micro-sized thermal det from his belt and crammed it into the gaping hole in the SBD's casing. Then he let it throw him clear in its wild attempt to shake him off. He landed meters away as the blast— directed down inside its casing—blew out its chest plate.

Events were, as always, in a distorted time frame. Darman, flat on the ground and trying to get up, saw a ragged disc of metal just miss the E-Web. Corr flung himself sideways. Dev leapt on the SBD coming up behind it while Aven rammed both muzzles of his twin blasters up under its arm joints, and fired.

SBDs were vulnerable if you engaged them very, *very* close.

Nothing came over that rubble ridge for a few more seconds.

Darman got back on his feet. All he could hear was his own gasping breath and his heart pounding. He didn't hear the noise of drives until after Aven yelled "Air support incoming!" and the rapid *clunk-clunk-clunk* of droid feet at a run began again.

Darman ducked as the shadow of two LAAT/i gunships blotted out the sun. Staccato plumes of pulverized ferrocrete fountained into the air high above the parapet line as the larties opened fire on the droid ranks.

"Pull back!" Aven grabbed Darman's shoulder and half dragged him until he got his balance back and ran for the cover of HNE's colonnaded entrance. "Get down!"

The oddest things got your attention in combat. Darman found himself looking up at a sky that was full of dark clouds—not natural ones, but the smoke and windborne debris of the aerial battle that still raged overhead, joined by the rising smoke from a burning, bombed city. He wondered how he would have reacted if the dots in the sky suddenly enlarged and resolved into Mandalorian troops with jetpacks.

Weird. Stims, fatigue, and too many food additives.

"You're a psycho, Dar," Atin said, patting his shoulder. "Classy."

Niner, Corr, Jind, and Dev flopped down next to them in a clatter of armor plates. "Just heard on the comm," Niner said. "Another thousand ships have joined the fleet."

"Whoopee," Atin said. "Can they pop down here and give us a hand?"

One larty landed in front of their position nose-forward, and a couple of troopers jumped down from the open hatch. The droids had withdrawn again. Darman twisted to look over his shoulder, and saw Cov, a civilian, and the remaining member of Yayax Squad—Yover—hauling three crates on a repulsor trolley from the side door of the building.

It was the equipment they needed to broadcast on HNE bandwidth from anywhere on the planet. Whatever happened to the network's headquarters, Coruscant and the Republic would not be silenced now. Darman watched the equipment being loaded into the larty, followed by a dozen HNE staff—humans and two Twi'leks—and then the gunship lifted clear and vanished.

Aven lowered his head as if receiving a message in his helmet comlink. Then he ambled back over to the exhausted pile of commandos.

"Two-hour watches, okay? Move into the foyer and get some sleep. I'll take the first watch."

It was late afternoon again, judging by the sun. Darman was losing count of the days. "Sir," he said, "do you know if comms to Kashyyyk are operational yet?"

"I've heard it's patchy. Why—waiting for a call from a Wookiee?"

Darman shrugged. "Something like that."

"They've bypassed Sep blocking, but the system must have overloaded by now. The fleet's grown by thousands of ships almost overnight. Knowing those useless barves in Procurement, they probably didn't add enough extra nodes to the network. Another thing they forgot to tell us about."

Aven squatted down a few meters from them in silence, cleaning his blasters in the lull.

It was now or maybe never. Darman risked opening his comlink. Etain was probably worrying her guts out. She didn't answer the comm, of course; he tried again, but there was no telling what she was doing, and he decided to send via the uplink while he still could. The message would at least sit there and wait for her to reconnect. The comms' routers could go down at any time, and he might not—

No. I'm staying alive. I refuse to die now.

He scribbled with his stylus. He hated tapping out long messages.

MHI SOLUS TOME, MHI SOLUS DAR'TOME, MHI ME'DINUI AN, MHI BA'JURI VERDE. TRANSLATE AND RESPOND. RC-1136.

Darman was still coming down off the adrenal high of fighting, but those words gave him a delicious feeling of contentment that made him smile. Etain knew enough *Mando'a* to understand what it meant. All she had to do was resend the words to him. A pledge was a pledge, a deal was a deal, a vow was a vow; you didn't have to be in the same room to accept a marriage contract. Once she replied, it was legal for Mandalore.

And he didn't care about Coruscant law now.

"I can hear you smiling," Atin said. "What's so funny?"

"Not funny," said Darman. The slight click of teeth and the faintest of breaths was enough for Atin to gauge his brother's reaction behind the helmet. "Just my half of the marriage contract, while I still can. No point hanging about now."

"Don't be so morbid," Niner snapped. "We'll all be fine."

"I meant losing comms . . ."

"Awwww . . . ," Corr murmured. Darman wasn't sure if he was teasing to take the edge off Niner's seriousness. The guy could get *very* tense. "You next, *At'ika*. Me, I'm keeping my options open out of generosity to all the lovely females who haven't had a chance to meet me yet. It's only fair."

Atin made a huffing noise. Darman heard the click of his teeth and a slight rustle as he switched to another comm circuit. He was comming Laseema privately, Darman was sure of it. He watched Atin's shoulders tense and then relax, and his head nodded a little, as if he was talking. After a few moments, he leaned back and punched one fist into his palm in mute triumph.

Corr nudged him. "She said yes, then . . ."

"There's no privacy in this *shabla* squad." But Atin sounded happy. "And she said Kad's babbling 'Da-da' all the time. Just thought you needed to know that."

Darman did. In the debris-strewn, deserted foyer of the HNE building, with the prospect of enemy droids swarming back at any time, he now felt he could handle anything again.

He dozed despite the stims, leaning against Atin. It was the faint blipping noise of a message arriving in his HUD that woke him rather than the barrage going on outside. It wasn't Etain, though; it was Ordo.

SO YOU'RE STILL ALIVE, OMEGA. REPORT IN WHEN YOU CAN.

That was how Mandalorians greeted each other—*Su'cuy gar,* You're still alive—but it was also quite funny for Ordo, who wasn't exactly a comedian. Skirata was obviously fretting.

One day, Darman would have fine stories to tell Kad about the days when he wrestled with battle droids. He shut his eyes and resumed a brief and precious sleep.

Safe house, lower levels, Coruscant, day five,
1,085 days ABG

In the bowels of Galactic City, the desperate battle was a distant thunderstorm that raged day and night.

Skirata thought it was probably the first time in millennia

that it was safer to walk the streets of Triple Zero's sleazy un-
derbelly than it was to venture out in the respectable skylanes and walkways up above. He stared at the door to
Uthan's room and rehearsed how he was going to tell her that
she was now a prisoner again. He didn't want to sound tri-
umphant and depress the woman. He needed her cooperation, although he didn't think she was the suicidal kind.

I didn't think Ko Sai would hang herself, either . . .

"Okay." Vau put his finger behind the blind and eased it
away from the grimy window to check the walkway outside.
It was surprisingly busy. Plenty of people from the upper
levels had fled down here. The pickpockets were having a
field day. "Let's take stock. We're in the middle of a Separatist invasion. We're holding a death-dealing Sep scientist
who doesn't realize she's been kidnapped, your stroppy long-
lost daughter, a tax inspector whose life we've managed to
trash, and Jango Fett's lunatic homicidal sister. Have you
warned Rav that this happy crew is heading her way, provided we don't all die horribly in the current unpleasantness?"

Skirata felt his heart skipping beats, making him want to
thump his own chest to stop it. Rav Bralor was twice the man
that most men were, which was quite something for a good-
looking woman. She'd take it all in stride. "I think we need to
start transferring people to *Aay'han.*"

"Kal, we have a total of twenty-one *personnel,* for want of
a better word. Plus the baby. Etain, Kom'rk, Jaing, and Prudii
are offworld, and we'll have to arrange another RV point for
them—they can't come back here now. *Aay'han* has sixteen
berths, plus the cargo space, which would take another fifteen bunks if we hadn't filled half of that with emergency
supplies and Mereel's *shabla* toy."

Skirata had a trillion credits. They could leave the *Gi'ka*
behind and Mereel could buy another dozen of the things
when they got out of here. "*Bard'ika*'s got the Aggressor laid
up, and that can accommodate eight plus a pilot," he said.
"It's got a secure hold—it's a bounty vessel. I say we get
Ruu, Fett's sister, and Uthan out in that first, with Sull, Spar,
and Mereel. Then we follow in *Aay'han.*"

"Well, when a few thousand warships have finished pounding ten shades of *osik* out of each other, and the planetary shields are lifted."

"Walon, it was always going to be a case of winging it."

"Yes, I know."

"If you want out—"

"*Shab,* no, Kal. I've come this far."

"Look," Skirata said. "That's the easy bit. The hard bit is getting Omega out now. And Etain. The Nulls can come and go because Zey and his cronies are used to that, but the others are pretty visible. Have you spoken to Delta?"

"No. They'll get to hear, and then they can make their own choice. What about your other squads? I know Omega's your pride and joy, but when are you going to put the word out that there's a haven for the others, too?"

"When we're sure Kyrimorut is secure and everyone's settled."

"Okay."

"Walon, I know I've bitten off more than I can chew. But I had to try. And I think we're as close to pulling it off as ever."

Vau sighed. "Okay." He slapped his thigh plate. "Mird? *Mird'ika,* come on. Let's go round up the stray nerfs."

At least everyone was on the lower levels, except Kad, Laseema, and Besany. The Seps were after the strategic targets: government buildings, the spaceports, military installations, and infrastructure. It didn't make it any easier if yours was the district that lost its power supply, and the misery from above was slowly trickling down in the form of refugees, but at least it was possible to move around the streets and skylanes down here without getting killed by stray ordnance.

Skirata decided to collect the ladies and his grandson sooner rather than later. *Aay'han* wasn't so bad as temporary accommodation, and it was in as safe a location as any on Coruscant now. He threaded his way across the city along the lowest skylane he could navigate in the speeder, then climbed to the upper levels almost vertically when he reached Obrim's neighborhood, Rampart Town. It was a modest, quiet part of Galactic City; Obrim had made dangerous enemies, as cops did, and he preferred to keep a low profile in a sprawling multilevel apartment that looked unremarkable from the outside. Only the elaborate security precautions revealed how difficult his job could get.

It was a ghost town. There was nowhere to run on a crowded planet, so anyone with a grain of sense had battened down the hatches and waited. Telti Obrim took a full five minutes to open the doors.

"Jaller's still stuck at HQ," she said. "Haven't seen him for two days, but that's normal for Jaller. Is everyone okay?"

"Fine," Skirata said. "It's weird how I can move around some parts of the city and not others. Look, I know I'm putting Jaller at risk by calling, but I need to move the ladies." He took the nine million creds out of his belt; it seemed such a small stack of chips for a huge sum. The figures he dealt with these days had just numbed him now. "I want you to do something for me, Telti. Take this. You and Jaller deduct what you need to stay safe, and if there's anything left, give it to that crazy Senator Skeenah to fund his care home for clone troopers."

Telti stared at the chips, mouth slightly open. Skirata now realized it was probably very hard for a cop to take a sum like that without leaving himself open to some unhealthy attention, but times were changing, and none of them knew what the next day would bring. Telti was still staring at the fortune, muttering "Oh . . . oh, Kal . . ." when Besany came out into the lobby and put her arms around him. He felt dwarfed. She was as tall as Ordo.

"Don't scare me like that again, *Kal'buir*," she said.

"Time to run, *ad'ika*."

"You're not going to try to beat the blockade, are you?"

"No. This is a standby, and we'll wait for the battle to die down."

"I'll get Laseema." She winked at him, but the fear was etched on her face now. She was still putting on a defiant show, though, still *mandokarla*. "Excellent use for the sapphires."

Kad was silent, very alert, not at all like a baby today. He didn't fret or grizzle; he just sat on Besany's lap, both hands flat on the transparisteel sidescreen, staring at the world streaking by as Skirata took the fastest route down through the layers of the city to reach the reservoir entrance. The speeder eased through the service tunnel, with just enough clearance to avoid scraping the bodywork.

"Oh, this is wonderful!" Laseema seemed genuinely impressed by *Aay'han*. She patted the bunk in her tiny cabin. "I've never been in a ship like this. What do you think of this, then, *Kad'ika*?"

"Ma!" He tottered across the deck and tried to clamber onto the lower bunk. It was a valiant attempt, and he failed, but he kept trying in grim silence until Laseema gave him a leg up. *"Mama!"*

Mama. "Have you commed her?" Besany asked.

"I'm going to recall her now." Skirata knew he should have spent more time worrying about Etain. "She might have to go straight to Mandalore, if she can get transport. But I'm not happy about that. I'll see where that Vollen woman is. Maybe ask her to retrieve *Et'ika*. Or Jaing can do it."

Besany took his hand and squeezed it. Then she gestured to the blaster on her belt. It hadn't been so long ago that she didn't even want to handle one. "We'll maintain proper security, Kal. We'll be fine here. I'll keep the hatch closed."

"You won't be on your own long. The rest of the *aliit* will be along soon. The whole clan."

She gave him a dazzling smile that radiated trust. "It's all coming together, Kal. You're going to pull this off. You're a hero, you know that?"

No, he wasn't, even if Munin and Besany and a handful of other people had told him that over the years. He was what most thought he was: a chancer, a killer, a marginal man, a thug. But he knew he was also a man who sometimes did the right thing for the most deserving people. He could live with himself, most days.

Skirata pondered loose ends as he headed back to the safe house to clear out what few things remained. He knew where everyone was; he knew, more or less, how they were getting to *Manda'yaim*. And yes, they were *aliit*—they were a clan, however odd a mix of personalities and backgrounds they were.

He commed Gilamar without fear of being picked up by the Chancellor's minions now, marveling at this incongruous protection afforded by being at war. "*Mij'ika?* Doctor stuff. About Fett's sister—I've been thinking about where we ought to—"

Gilamar cut him off. "Kal, have you been monitoring the GAR or SOB channels?"

Shab, could *nobody* find time to comm him? "Not for the last hour or so."

"Palpatine's been kidnapped by the Seps and taken off the planet. Big flap on. Zey's language is very un-Jedi-like at the moment."

All Skirata could think then was that it was weird to abduct the Chancellor, and that it might mean a chance of getting through the planetary shield. If anything told him he didn't see the Republic's welfare as his own, it was that.

"Does that change our plans?" he asked. "Other than that it might force a surrender or cease-fire?"

"They're recalling various Jedi—maybe time to get Etain out."

"Opportunities and threats, Mij. One and the same."

Skirata didn't have to worry about getting arrested now. He could call Enacca. It was great that she was a Wookiee patriot, but it was also handy that she was keeping an eye on Etain.

He owed the furball. He'd make sure she was set up for life when the current *unpleasantness* was over.

16

*There are two reasons why we have to wear armor. One is
so that we don't get killed too easily. The other is so that we
all look Mandalorian, however different we may be
from our brothers and sisters.*
—Mandalorian mother, explaining one of the *Resol'nare*—
the six obligations of Mandalorian identity—
to her daughter

Emergency reservoir, Galactic City, day five of the
Battle of Coruscant, 1,085 days ABG

Skirata waited, his personal comlink in one hand and his
helmet comm channel set to the GAR command network.

On the underground quayside, Jusik was keeping Fi busy
by teaching him to use a lightsaber. It was, Jusik said, an easier weapon to handle until—it was always *until,* never *if*—Fi
got back full motor control.

No matter who was swinging the *shabla* thing, Skirata still
didn't like that humming sound. It had a soulless, relentless
quality, almost like a droid casting about for victims with a
sensor scan, implacable, not caring who it killed or why.

"How's it looking, *Mer'ika*?" Skirata asked. "What transponder are you using?"

Mereel was in the Aggressor, waiting on a deserted public
landing platform in the midlevels, with a camo net over the
airframe. From the air, the fighter looked like another casualty of the battle, but it wasn't the kind of vessel the Republic used, so it was vital that it wasn't taken for a moving Sep

target. Fake transponder signal or not, there was always the chance that a smart clone would eyeball the *shabla* thing, trust his judgment over the computer's, and open fire.

"Small sports yacht," he said. "Rich civvy making a run for it. We might have a window soon—they've recalled Kenobi, for a start."

"They'll need to bring the shields down to get his ego and red carpet in . . ."

"Fine by me. I'm ready to jettison the net and bang out the moment I see a gap."

"Everyone okay?"

"Medicated where necessary, in separate cells—and Uthan hasn't spotted yet that three of us are clones. I *love* my *buy'ce*. It lets me keep some mystery in a relationship."

"I think a few Mandos on board can keep her quiet if she works it out before she gets to Mandalore. Now, how about the data duplicates? Contingency RV points?"

"All sorted, *Kal'buir*. Stop worrying."

"I can't."

"It's okay, Papa. It's all on schedule." Mereel rarely used the word *papa;* it was always *buir*. "Rav's waiting with her clan at Kyrimorut, so nothing's going to go wrong at that end, either. We're ready to run."

"K'oyacyi, Mer'ika," Skirata said quietly. *Stay safe, stay alive, hang in there.* "Next time we see you, it'll be on *Manda'yaim*."

Jusik and Fi could obviously hear him. The *vzzzmmm* of the lightsaber had stopped.

"Uthan's going to go *nuts* when she finds out who's nabbed her," Fi said. "I wonder if she'll recognize me and Omega?"

"Got a lot more work to do before we worry about that, *ad'ika*."

Skirata really *hated* waiting. He was getting too old for this game, at least for the slow grind of it, all the snatched sleep and the missed meals. He paced, he wandered, and he went down below in the ship a dozen times. Besany rocked Kad, one finger held to her lips. Jilka sat looking as if her life was over, which could so easily have been the case by now.

Skirata paused to pat her head. "You won't want to be on Coruscant when this war ends, anyway," he said. "I'm sorry. I really am."

"It's been an education." Jilka had the voice of a woman who didn't suffer fools gladly. She didn't thank him for his generosity, or tell him what a kind and generous *buir* he was. "Seems I didn't know Besany kriffing Wennen at all."

Besany didn't react. Skirata made a mental note to keep an eye on that tension, but they hadn't slugged each other so far. What Mandalorians took for granted in the ups and downs of a day's work, a civilized office worker in the galactic capital—even one with a risky job—saw as a trauma.

"Kal'buir," said Mereel's voice. "Shields are coming down. Grievous has withdrawn—I think the battle's turned. I have to go. *K'oyacyi."*

"K'oyacyi. I love you, son."

Skirata went up top and jumped from *Aay'han's* casing onto the quayside. He couldn't see the sky from down here, but the urge to go up and watch the Aggressor leave was more than his body could resist. It wasn't even near here; he'd never see the ship anyway. But he did it blindly, and then stood facing the wall, helmet resting against the permacrete, counting the long minutes out a second at a time. Someone put their hand on his back and stood there with him. He didn't turn around.

Mandalorians had dispensed with their gods long ago. Masters—whether divinities or Mandalores—were only tolerated as long as they pulled their weight. It left Skirata with no higher authority to bargain with for Mereel's safety.

Six minutes, seven . . . ten . . .

"Kal'buir, we're clear of Coruscant now."

"Mer'ika!"

"You should see the traffic around the place. The debris's more of a danger in orbit than the live ships."

"Don't hang about, son, *go."*

"We're gone."

The comlink closed. Mereel had jumped to hyperspace. Skirata straightened up and put his hands to his helmet, sweat prickling on his upper lip. When he turned around, it wasn't Fi or Jusik behind him, but Vau.

"You worry too much," he said. "Grievous has banged out. Palpatine's back in one piece."

"I know. Where's Mird?"

"In my speeder. Well, *someone's* speeder. It was abandoned up top, so I liberated it for a while. I'm going to play nerf herder again until we pull out. There's still pockets of fighting going on, and HNE's saying there's a fair few home-grown anti-Republic elements still causing trouble, so it's not safe on the ground yet even if the fleet engagement's done and dusted."

Skirata switched back to the GAR comm circuit, listening for Kashyyyk traffic. They weren't discussing the Wookiee resistance, but Masters Vos and Yoda appeared to be ready to start the big assault inside forty-eight hours. Etain had to be out before that kicked off. Enacca had her orders.

Skirata commed Omega. He'd kept an eye on the squad's status via the GAR links, but now he needed to talk to them personally. Atin answered first.

"What's it like up there, *At'ika*?" Skirata asked.

"We're still mopping up, Sarge."

"Who's tasking you at the moment? Zey?"

"Yeah, direct or via Lieutenant Aven."

"Keep me posted on every move, okay? I can get into the GAR system, but I want to be doubly sure you *are* where it says you are over the next couple of days. We're going very soon, son, and you better be ready."

"I'm ready," Atin said. "We all are. Is Vau there?"

"Yeah . . ." It was still thin ice, even if hostilities between the two men had been shelved for the duration. "Want to talk to him?"

"No, just tell him that the war's over between us. It really is. Back home, we start anew. *Cin vhetin.*"

Vau heard anyway. Skirata put the link back in his belt.

"I only ever did it to make sure they survived, whatever happened," Vau said. "I'm not a sadistic man."

"Yeah." Skirata didn't want to restart that fight. But he knew he'd take his knife to Vau, just like old times, if he so

much as raised his hand to those lads again, and yet somehow that coexisted with a respect and . . . yes, *affection*. Vau
was family, too. "I've got to catch up with the rest of my
boys. Go keep an eye on the ladies. I'll even trust you with
my grandson now."

"Oh, I'll build a nest, then," said Vau, and stepped off the
quay onto the hull.

Skirata watched Jusik teaching Fi the art of being an un-
Jedi for a few minutes, and then went to collect his speeder,
the one that had been his temporary pride and joy when he
stole it from a dead Jabiimi dissident.

He was going to miss that crate.

Core Plaza, late afternoon, two days after
the flight of Grievous from Coruscant, 1,087 days ABG

"He's back, *Ord'ika*."

Jaing's voice popped in Ordo's earpiece as he patrolled the
devastated retail district with a CSF unit, flushing out looters. "Grievous?"

"He misses Utapau, obviously. I got a tip-off."

"You're not *there*, then."

"No, we're just tidying up a few loose ends on the Rim."

"Time we told Zey?"

"Yeah." Jaing sounded tired. "There's still something not
right about this, but I'm past caring, and so is *Kom'ika*.
Where's Grievous's massive droid army now, eh? Quadrillions, my *shebs*. Maybe they all booked the same week's
vacation and couldn't make Coruscant."

"Pull out, then, *ner vod*. You're now officially missing in
action, and Kom'rk, too. Go straight back to Mandalore."

"We were supposed to RV on Triple Zero."

"Yes, but Bralor needs a hand wrangling the menagerie
that *Kal'buir* dropped in her lap. I'll square it with him."

Jaing laughed. "I'm going have to dump my ARC armor.
Shame. I looked *great* in that. Still, my *beskar'gam* matches
my lovely *special* hide gloves."

"*K'oyacyi, ner vod*."

"You too, *Ord'ika*."

Ordo checked his chrono. He'd give this a little longer, and then swing by Arca Barracks to hand Zey the location to find Grievous. He leaned out of the patrol ship's bay as it banked over the heart of the sector, marveling at the opportunism of all species, that they could venture out to steal when fighting was still going on in places. A gang of Rodians and humans was busy removing the contents of a fashion store. The police pilot wheeled around to bring the ship level with the walkway, and the marksman sighted up.

The CSF sergeant didn't even get the chance to warn them off; the looters scattered at the sound of the drives, vanishing into bombed buildings and down stairwells.

"I'm amazed they even try," said the sergeant. "There's so many of your boys around now."

"Not enough to guard every store."

"Oh, I wouldn't say that." The sergeant leaned out even farther than Ordo. "They're *everywhere*. I've never seen so many troopers. They all seemed to show up in the last few days. Is there anyone still fighting out there in the rest of the galaxy?"

"Plenty," said Ordo. "The big push on Kashyyyk's just started. It's business as usual in the Grand Army."

It wasn't, but the sergeant didn't need to know that. Ordo had checked the fleet deployments that morning, and staggering numbers of vessels were in play now, although not many showed up where he expected them to be. They were out there somewhere, though: an army and a navy of millions upon millions, making the core of the GAR, the three million Kamino clones, look insignificant.

"We suddenly got reinforcements." Ordo checked his chrono again. "Hurrah for the Chancellor."

The sergeant smiled ruefully. "Yeah, *we* say it like that, too . . ."

The patrol ship dropped Ordo off near the barracks and he made his way across the square, surprised by the numbers of ordinary citizens who were now venturing out. The presence of so many clone troopers on the ground seemed to have

given them confidence to leave their homes and come out of
the public shelters.

It didn't matter anymore. This would no longer be his
world in a matter of days. He was going *home*.

*With my wife. With my father. With my brothers, and their
wives. Even if we never get to live a long life, we now have a
real one.*

There were troopers guarding the barracks now—they
never had before—and they even asked to see Ordo's ID.
They clearly hadn't been up close to an ARC trooper before.
He wanted to ask one of them to lift his helmet so he could
look him in the eye and see if he was exactly like his Null
and commando brothers, but it was demeaning, and it was no
longer his business. If he connected to these new clones in
any way, he'd end up like *Kal'buir,* feeling that each man was
his personal responsibility to rescue.

Inside Arca Barracks, his boots echoed in the empty corridors, so little had changed for the Republic commandos.
Maybe the GAR would start cross-training more men.

"Good shopping trip?" Maze said. "Shoot any looters?"

Ordo took off his helmet and clipped it to his belt. "Mongrels bewilder me. If I were going to steal in a crisis, I'd take
weapons and food. Not garments. Is Zey around?"

"He's in his office. It's back to normal—too many fronts to
cover, too few men, Jedi generals spread all over the place."

"Ironic, given our sudden expansion."

The two ARCs strode down to see Zey. Ordo tossed the
datachip to the general. "Intel on Grievous's whereabouts."

Zey looked at Ordo with a completely blank expression.
Ordo sometimes came close to liking the man. He almost felt
sorry for him.

"Grievous," Ordo repeated. "Jaing and Kom'rk tracked
him to Utapau—he's still there now. There's the layout of the
camp from the areas they could access remotely. Who are
you going to send after him—that windbag Kenobi? General
Yoda's your best bet, if he wasn't occupied elsewhere."

Zey's corrugated brow suggested that he found it *significant* that Jaing and Kom'rk had struck pay dirt at this particular time. "You don't *approve* of General Kenobi, then."

"Cody might think the sun shines out of his ear, General, but I think he's a glory seeker who wastes too many men."

"As he's fond of saying—from a certain point of view." Zey clearly knew better than to debate with Ordo. He was also canny enough to resist asking how long the Nulls had known this information. He put his hand briefly to his chest as if stomach acid was playing him up. "This may well be the beginning of the end, Captain. Thank you."

Ordo half turned for the doors. "I'm not banking on it."

"Captain." Zey put out his hand to beckon Ordo back. It wasn't an attempt to grab his arm. He seemed almost afraid—as if he thought Ordo would swing at him, as if he didn't think his Jedi powers would ward off a blow. That wasn't the Zey that Ordo had come to know. "Captain, you don't like the Jedi Order, do you? Just tell me why."

Ordo almost choked. The naïveté of it genuinely stunned him. Maze stood like a statue, nostrils flaring slightly as he tried to take deep breaths without opening his mouth. Maybe it struck him the same way, because—as Spar and Sull had proven—the Alpha ARCs weren't the unquestioning automata most of their commanders seemed to think.

"Because you can't see what you've degenerated into," Ordo said. "That's what comes of having one leader dominate your organization for *centuries.* You need a big change in command structure. But maybe you don't see anything wrong in creating clones with no choice when you take Force-sensitive children and turn them into Jedi whether they like it or not."

Ordo met Zey's eyes. He didn't want to stare the man down; he just wanted to search his soul. He needed to know what went on in a Jedi's mind, because whatever it was, Jusik was no reliable guide to it. Jusik had his own moral compass. So did Etain. Maybe it was a generational thing, with the younger Jedi starting to ask how things had come to this sorry pass.

All Ordo could see in Zey's face, though, was a man drained of hope, almost too embarrassed to pause and look at his own actions.

"I think the whole Republic needs a change of management," Zey said at last. "The war is wrong. The conduct of it is wrong. Our compliance with it is wrong. And Palpatine has outstayed his welcome."

Maze still didn't move a muscle, but Ordo was hypersensitive to the slightest sound. The Alpha ARC held his breath for a moment. He wasn't happy with that, not at all.

"Don't forget your slave army," Ordo said, then touched two fingers to his temple in a not-quite-salute. "That wasn't the smartest move, either."

Ordo left with Maze close on his heels. In the corridor, he strode ten paces and then halted to spin around. Maze stopped dead behind him. Their eyes locked.

I thought we'd reached an understanding.

"There was a time," Ordo said, testing their comradeship, "when you'd have tried to punch me out for not kissing Zey's Force-using *shebs*." He offered Maze a strip of ruik. "So?"

Maze accepted the proffered snack. "I just wanted to talk. I'm no fan of Palpatine, either, but he was elected, more or less, and the Jedi weren't. Who are they to judge who runs the Republic?"

"My, Jango's little gung-ho pep talks didn't work, did they?"

"Jango's orders were to *serve the Republic.* Not the Jedi. They're like us. Instruments of the state."

"Maze, I'm amazed his orders weren't to *kill* the Jedi, given what happened to him at Galidraan." Ordo felt genuine pity for Jango; first his family, then his surrogate father, and then every last one of his comrades—all were killed by worthless *chakaare.* That didn't excuse prostituting his genetic material for credits and an heir, though. "But it's good to see that you Alphas aren't all Jedi-worshipping planks."

Maze raised an eyebrow. "Orders, you crazy Null boy. Try following them sometime. They're what separates an army as the expression of the electorate's will from an armed rabble out for its own ends."

"You've been reading holobooks."

"You sound like a civvy."

"I should smack you one for that."

"While you're out on the town with your lady friend, what

do you think the likes of me and the white jobs do with our off-duty hours? You think we're put back in stasis, offline for the duration like good little droids? Me, I read. Some guys play limmie. Some watch the kind of holovids that just make you realize what you can't have. But I read."

It was a sobering rebuke. Maze was right; it was too easy to slip into that civilian way of un-thinking, of never wondering how human beings just like them spent their rapidly passing lives.

"You know what your future is, don't you?" Ordo said.

"Body bag, or a couple of rounds to the head. Best scenario—clone instructor. Yeah, I know. Zey offered to *relocate* me, shall we say. He was very upset to find out about the Republic's approach to ARC retirement."

"Let me know if you want relocation, then. I can do a better job than Zey."

"I'll bet." Maze chewed thoughtfully. "But it's nice of him to even offer when other Jedi just snap their fingers at you and call you *clone*."

"Tell me something," Ordo said. "I was raised as a son, not a commodity. I'm fully aware that clones are exploited. Do *you* have a sense of injustice?"

"Too right I do," Maze said quietly. He spat the fiber left from the ruik root into a waste container with impressive force and accuracy, and walked away toward the mess, helmet under one arm, *kama* swinging.

Kashyyyk, three days after the flight of Grievous from Coruscant, 1,088 days ABG

"About time," Fixer said, cramming ammo clips into his belt. "I was getting fed up fighting this war on my own."

Scorch nudged him in the back, indicating Boss and Sev. "What were *we* doing, then, filing our nails?"

"I meant Vos."

General Vos had arrived from Boz Pity with the first wave of troopers the night before; General Yoda was inbound with the 41st Elite and the Wookiee chieftain Delta had extracted from the Seps' prison camp, Chief Tarfful. The Republic was pouring resources into the Kashyyyk theater. Scorch agreed that it was a little overdue, and also that it was remarkably handy that all those extra troops and ships had become available, freeing up the likes of Yoda.

It's a big ambush; Coruscant first. Grievous gets his tin shebs kicked, and runs. Chancellor, you better be right, or we're finished.

"Ready?" Boss said.

"How long have we got?"

"Time on target for Yoda's flagship—thirty standard minutes."

They walked out onto the vine bridge and scanned for visible vessels in the dawn sky. The Seps knew reinforcements were coming, too; their fleet was piling in, and a cruiser had taken up position at coordinates that looked as if it was going to engage Yoda's flagship.

Wookiees were massing, too. Scorch heard them long before he saw them, a random chorus of rumbling, growling, yawling voices, growing louder, and you didn't need to know a word of Shyriiwook to get the gist of the sentiment. They were psyching themselves up—not that they needed it much—to take back their world. They were going to do it with their bare hands, and Scorch believed them, oh yes, he *did*. He'd seen it. He wasn't keen to see it again. The screams would be enough. The Wookiee chieftains were massive, brandishing heavy bowcasters and long-guns as if they were tiny hold-out blasters. They were working their troops up to a fever pitch. They thrashed their fists against their chests, then raised their arms to the sky again, bellowing defiance. The whole Wookiee army joined in. It was a wall of sound that Scorch didn't just hear but felt in his sinuses.

Enacca came up behind them, and even Fixer jumped. She growled and pointed back into the forest.

Boss checked his chrono. "Yeah, I know you're looking forward to pulling off some arms, but I think our best bet is to take control of the turbolaser battery. That cruiser's positioned to stop Yoda from disembarking ground troops, and we need it gone."

Enacca let out a roar of approval. She wanted it gone, too.

Etain came jogging along the platform and stood beside her. It was an image of extremes that Scorch wouldn't forget in a hurry—the two-meter-tall Wookiee with a bowcaster slung across her back like a small accessory, and Etain, so tiny that he was still sure her conc rifle weighed more than she did.

It was nice to see a Jedi general who used more than a lightsaber. Etain knew exactly what it felt like to haul heavy kit for hours on end, so she understood when her troops needed a break. But there was something poking out of her belt, in the shadow of her robe, and Scorch realized after a few baffled seconds that it was a small furry toy, an animal.

"Reckon you can take that battery in eighteen minutes, Delta?" she said, winking. "Omega would try for fifteen."

"We're easily provoked into rash displays of competitive machismo, ma'am," Sev said. "We accept the challenge."

Scorch indicated Etain's mascot. That's what he thought it was, anyway. "Your Wookiee's not very big, ma'am."

"It's my little boy's toy nerf," she said. "He put it in my hand before I left, and right now it's really comforting. It smells of him."

Sev said nothing. Scorch was grateful for that. Boss clapped his gloves hard to get their attention. "Come on, Delta, move it. You can play with the toy later."

Etain gave them a casual fingers-to-brow salute and disappeared with Enacca. They were booby-trapping the walkways so that the 41st Elite could drive the Trandoshans into a trap and pick them off.

"I call dibs on the main cannon," Sev said. "A Sep cruiser is like one big bug. I haven't had my bug-splattering fix today."

But he'd get plenty of chances once they blew their way into the big silo-like emplacement. The Seps had built into the trees, almost sleeving them in metal at some points and driving durasteel shafts clean through the road-wide trunks. The first set of doors Scorch blew unleashed a wave of spider droids, and Fixer picked them off with anti-armor rounds.

Boss checked his HUD chrono, flashing the countdown to

all of them across their readouts. "Fifteen to go, so let's not let the generals down. Grab the first anti-air turret you see and hang on to it. One each. Between the four of us, we should be able to put a dent in that *shabuir.*"

Scorch could hear the voice traffic now in his helmet between the 41st and Vos's forward air control. The Sep cruiser was maneuvering to block the flagship, and Commander Gree was searching for alternative sites to land men. If he was forced too far from the landing zone, they'd have a hard haul back through the forest before they could engage the Sep targets. The cruiser had to *move.*

Two MagnaGuard droids blocked their path to the battery positions. Scorch almost didn't count the Trandoshans who opened up with blasters. He lobbed a grenade their way while Fixer and Sev charged the droids, slicing one of them in two with a burst of plasma bolts and smashing the other to the floor with the butt of a Deece before emptying a clip into it.

Fixer ran on and swung himself into the gunner's seat on the first turbolaser position. He waved Scorch and the other two past him, and started punching the controls. Scorch dropped into the next bay. He found a Trando trying to get a firing solution on the GAR flagship, which was now looking awfully close and in need of a parking space. Scorch brought his vibroblade up under the Trando's chin just as the barve reached for his rifle, waited for him to stop struggling, and dragged the body clear of the seat.

By the time Scorch had taken control of the cannon's targeting system and found the optimum points on the cruiser's hull to do the most damage, Boss and Sev were gone, sprinting on to take control of the last two cannons. Fixer was already opening big vents in the cruiser's hull. But the thing wasn't going to go down easy; now Scorch could see four streams of laserfire playing along the keel of the Sep ship.

"Yeah, feel free, join the party." Scorch thought Fixer was talking to him on the comlink, but when he saw triple-A coming up from the ground in brilliant white staccato lines, he realized Vos's larty units had moved in. "That's our sky, buddy. Move over."

The cruiser was losing height. Its buckled hull plates

shuddered every time it took a hit, and then it started to break up. Flame vented from rips big enough to swallow a gunship.

"We're going to be wearing that thing for a hat if we don't move soon, Boss," Scorch said. "It's as good as dead."

"Job done, Deltas. Bang out."

Scorch swung out of the gunnery seat and ran for the turbolift, Deece ready, but he was running over dead Trandos and shredded metal. Any remaining Seps in the battery had made a run for it, too, possibly because of the imminent fireball from a dying cruiser. Boss, breathless, was calling in a LAAT/i for extraction as he ran.

Then Sev cut in. Scorch looked around. It was the first time he'd noticed that he wasn't with them. When he checked the point-of-view icon in his HUD, Sev still seemed to be looking out from the turbolaser viewport, and then the image broke up into streaks before going black.

Sev's voice carried on. "Boss, I've got a problem here . . ."

"Sev, where are you?"

"Sector . . . multiple hostiles . . ."

Fixer jabbed the comlink reset on his helmet. There was just the wash and crackle of static. "Lost his signal, Boss."

"Well, find it again. Delta, regroup—we're going after Sev."

The forward air controller from Vos's unit cut in. "Negative negative, Three-Eight, new orders came through from the generals—clear the area and evac now."

"I don't care if they came from General Yoda himself." Boss gestured to Fixer and Scorch to make a move after Sev. They could always claim they hadn't heard the message. "Sev—"

"As a matter of fact, they *did,* soldier. Now get your squad out of there."

Explosions shook the ship. The comm circuit was a disjointed mix of half-snatched conversations; it was all going to *haran.* Sep forces were streaming in from the north and east of their position, converging on them. Delta had killed the cruiser and enabled the 41st to land, but the battle had only just begun.

"He's right, Boss," Fixer said. "We've got to get out *now.*"

Scorch grabbed Fixer's arm. "We can't leave Sev. *Nobody* gets left behind. Remember? Remember how Sev blew up when we left Vau on Mygeeto? You want to do that to *our brother*? You want to abandon him? Leave him to die here?"

"He's Sev," Fixer said. "If he's alive, he'll hole up somewhere and we can retrieve him later."

"What if he can't?"

"Then he's *dead* anyway."

"We don't leave without a body, moving or otherwise."

"If we don't evac now, we'll *all* be dead."

"Fine, then we go *together,* not running off to save our own *shebse* while Sev's left here."

Boss said nothing and just watched as if he had nothing better to do, even though they had seconds to make their move. Then he took hold of Scorch's shoulder.

Scorch hadn't wept since he was a kid, but he couldn't see for tears now. "I'm not leaving him, Boss. You go if you want to. Not me."

"This is an *order.*"

"Screw orders. Omega wouldn't leave a man."

"Scorch . . ."

"You'll have to shoot me."

Boss put his hand on his sidearm. "Losing one guy is bad enough. I'm not losing two. Don't let me down now." He shoved Scorch hard in the back and nearly knocked him over. The larty was hovering level with the exit hatch of the turbolift. "Shift it, Six-Two."

"I'll never forgive you for this, Boss. Or you, Fixer. We're *brothers,* for fierfek's sake. I'd never leave *you.*"

But he did. He left. They *all* left.

"Sorry, Sev." Boss's voice was suddenly husky. He wasn't the weepy type, either, but he sounded like he was struggling. And maybe Sev could hear them, and maybe he couldn't, but if his end of the comlink was still live, Scorch could imagine what he was going through now as he listened to his brothers leaving him to die, or worse.

"Delta . . . move out."

Sev was as hard as they came. Vau had made survivors of them all. Fixer was probably right: if Sev was still alive, he'd probably stay alive for a long time, and they could always go back.

But they didn't know.

No, you didn't pull out all the stops for Sev.

Skirata would have told Yoda to shove his orders, cut the comm, and gone looking for him.

As they jumped into the larty's crew bay for the evac, Boss put his hand on Scorch's shoulder, but Scorch shrugged it off. He longed for a cannon round and instant oblivion, some way of stopping the guilt of *not* being dead, *not* staying to search, *not* making a final stand and defying Boss and CIC and even *shabla* General Yoda. He wanted to die of shame. He could only imagine how much worse it would feel in years to come when he had to face himself every morning.

It was just as well that a clone's life span was limited.

17

*You have to know the limits of your physical and mental
endurance, so you can recognize them and pass beyond
them. This is why I will push you beyond any suffering you
can imagine. You will not give up and die like lesser men;
you will not crack up like lesser men; you will not lose
heart in the direst circumstances like lesser men. You will
carry on beyond your imagined limits. And you will be
the last men standing, when the weaklings have opted
to do the easy thing and die.*
—Sergeant Walon Vau, *Cuy'val Dar,* addressing junior
clone trainees (average biological age: ten years old) on
Kamino, five years before Geonosis

The Battle of Kashyyyk, afternoon, 1,088 days ABG

Enacca picked Etain up bodily and dropped her over the side
of the vine-rope bridge.

"No!" Etain yelled. She landed safely, buffering her fall
with the Force, but she didn't need to: an old male Wookiee,
gray-streaked and battle-scarred, caught her. Her small brown
fabric bag fell after her. "You can't do this! *I* can't do it!"

Enacca swung down from the higher level, yawling warnings that she had her orders, and she *agreed* with those orders, and so she would carry them out with extra enthusiasm.
Etain had to go home. She was *taking* her home.

"But we can't leave Sev!" It was her fault; she'd told them
to take the turbolaser position faster than Omega could, turning a life-or-death mission into some stupid joke because she
thought it was better for morale than warning them about

their chances of surviving. "I can find him, I can get him back—"

She found herself thrown like a sack of tubers from Wookiee to Wookiee along the bridge and across gaping chasms. Her Force powers should have enabled her to at least fight back, even if she was a scrap of nothing compared to these enormous beings, but she would have had to use a lot of damaging force to stop them.

I can't abandon Sev. He'd come back for me.

Etain concentrated, pushing away from the next Wookiee's grasp. It was a big, elderly female; the matriarch tottered and almost fell. Wookiees knew what they were doing up at these heights, and Etain's Force pushes just messed things up. She landed on the next platform on her feet, but was then pinned down by three more Wookiees and warned in no uncertain terms that she was going to get one or more of them killed.

Maybe I want an excuse to run. Maybe they know that and they're sparing me my own shame.

She almost missed the next platform and was grabbed by both arms, hauled inboard, and shoved into a heavily camouflaged shuttle nestling under a trellis of slim branches. Enacca strapped her into the seat, then dropped her bag beside her.

"We can't leave Sev here. We never leave a man behind. We—"

Enacca roared that she would take her to Coruscant, or even Mandalore if she wanted, and then go back to search for Sev with the other Wookiees. If he hadn't been killed immediately, then the best people to search for him were Wookiees, not humans. If Etain hadn't located him with her Jedi powers, Enacca pointed out, then she might never find him anyway. So—she could leave.

Etain tried to find Sev in the Force. She thought she knew him well enough to find the impression he left, that strange blend of focus, confidence, fear, and a child-like need to please, to excel. But she only felt the combined pain and fear of men fighting a battle. Enacca lifted the shuttle clear of the platform and wove between the branches just under the canopy, heading away from Kachirho and the coast and out of the battle zone. Eventually, the vessel's nose lifted at a sharp angle and they were in bright sunlight a long way inland, with the palls of smoke just visible in the distance as the ship looped around and climbed out of the atmosphere.

Etain found herself putting her hands over her ears. She didn't understand the reflex. It was just instinctive.

"He'll think someone's coming for him," she said. She couldn't just forget Sev like a closed topic and move on to the next item on the agenda. "If he realizes he's been abandoned, can you imagine how he'll feel?"

Vau had raised his young clones to be hard, ruthless men. They never got any love from him, Skirata had told her, because he had never had any from his father. Vau had told a different story: that he pushed his boys harder than they ever thought they could endure, because the tougher they were, the longer they'd survive. Atin had tried to run a knife through his old sergeant more than once for the terrible scars—physical for sure, mental almost certainly—that Vau'd given him.

Enacca listened patiently to Etain's outpouring of guilt, then rumbled a placatory response that General Yoda had ordered Delta to pull out, so she had no choice.

"Did he tell them to leave Sev behind?" Etain snapped. "Did he even *know* they had a man missing? Would he have given the same order if he had?" She knew she was on blasphemous ground now, because Master Yoda was the most venerated of living Jedi, the guiding hand of the Council for centuries. He couldn't be criticized. He *was* the Jedi Order. "We sent ARC troopers to rescue Jedi from Hypori. We didn't say, 'Oh, war sure is tough, we're bound to lose a few.' We decided it was worth risking clones' lives to get them out. Why isn't Sev worth that? Why is a Jedi worth more to the war effort than he is? Because we're running the show? Because we *own* them?"

Enacca said nothing for a long time. Etain leaned back in the seat and shut her eyes. She found herself searching in her pockets and bag to find Kad's toy nerf, and pressed it to her cheek so she could lose herself in that very primal, uncomplicated emotion for a moment.

Enacca trilled, asking if she wanted her to let Vau know that Sev was missing.

"No, I'll do it," Etain said. "If he doesn't already know." She took out her comlink. Comms had been very patchy on Kashyyyk; but she had messages waiting, data received while she was fighting and unaware of receiving, and so she read them. Most were operational, not urgent, but one was very special indeed, and she felt intense guilt that she could swing from despair for Sev to selfish elation in a matter of seconds simply because she had a message from her lover.

MHI SOLUS TOME, MHI SOLUS DAR'TOME, MHI ME'DINUI AN, MHI BA'JURI VERDE. TRANSLATE AND RESPOND. RC-1136.

Her *Mando'a* wasn't even close to fluent, but she was learning. She knew what that meant, though. If she just repeated that pledge, that vow, it was an agreement in Mandalorian law, which managed to be simple, informal, and binding at the same time.

"Of course I will," she said to herself. Enacca glanced back at her from the cockpit. She copied the marriage vow carefully, then stored the reply so that it would transmit as soon as the ship was back in realspace.

DAR'IKA, I'M SORRY I'M SO FAR FROM YOU. *MHI SOLUS TOME, MHI SOLUS DAR'TOME, MHI ME'DINUI AN, MHI BA'JURI VERDE.* I LOVE YOU, DAR. I'LL BE BACK BEFORE YOU KNOW IT.

And it was as simple as that; as soon as the vow was transmitted, she would be married.

She should have been happy. She was now going back to the first place she could ever really call home, to live with her husband and their son. No matter how many years they had left to share, it would be enough. It was a magically ordinary situation that neither of them had been raised to expect, in a galaxy where almost every other being took it for granted.

But she was also leaving a comrade behind, a man she was responsible for as commanding officer. Sev wasn't a friend, but his life mattered as much as anyone's. She couldn't stop herself from veering between those two extremes of emotion.

She wasn't even sure she wanted to.

Enacca caught up with the last sitrep received before the hyperspace jump, and told her that Coruscant was now

largely peaceful, with most of the Separatist forces driven
out. Only one or two pockets of fighting remained, involving
citizens of CIS planets already living on Coruscant who had
rallied to Grievous during the attempted invasion. Things
would be back to normal soon; General Kenobi had been
sent after Grievous.

"We might as well go straight to Coruscant," Etain said.
"That was the original plan, and if you drop me there, you
can be back on Kashyyyk sooner. And I need to pick up
some clothing."

Enacca yowled that it was very thoughtful. She had a war
to fight, she said, and she was keen to get back in the fray,
however kind and generous Skirata had been to her.

"And it's best that I tell Vau in person why I left Sev," Etain
said.

Even if it was acceptable to exchange marriage pledges by
comlink, bad news deserved to be delivered face-to-face.

It wasn't the only message she had to deliver personally,
though. She had one more. She read the message on the
small screen, satisfied herself that it was dignified and final,
and stored it to be transmitted.

It was to General Arligan Zey, Director of Special Forces.
It was notification that she had renounced her status as a
Jedi, and wanted a brief meeting with him to explain—
without mention of her son or her clone husband—why she
had decided to leave the Jedi Order, and begin a new life as
an ordinary human being.

Arca Barracks, Coruscant, 0600 hours, four days after
the Battle of Coruscant, 1,089 days ABG

Darman passed Ordo in the corridor leading from the accommodation block. The captain gave the impression of still
being utterly dedicated to his GAR duties, or as much as a
Null had ever been. Ordo could act.

"Make sure you're ready," he said, pausing to clasp Darman's arm, *Mando*-style. "*Any*time now. Etain's on her way
back."

Over the last few days, Darman's mood had lurched from fear to elation to being so tired that he would have been content to drop dead. It was the roller coaster he lived with in this job. Now his gut settled on excitement. Things were happening.

Etain's coming back.

"I thought she might go straight to . . . you know." He was afraid to say it aloud, just in case the walls had ears. "But I suppose it's safe here now."

"Yes. Still a few stragglers and basic criminals around, but the clearing-up is under way."

"Where are your brothers?"

"Mereel's . . . *home,* and the others are heading that way."

"How's the . . . doctor?" He meant Uthan. "Has the reality dawned on her yet?"

"She's been locked up in seclusion for more than two years. She's used to not knowing what's outside her door." Ordo pointed in the direction of the briefing rooms, then walked away. "You'll be late. Go keep Zey quiet."

Yayax, Aquila, and Manka squads were already getting their briefings from Maze when Darman caught up with the rest of Omega. It was all domestic security tasking with CSF.

"Are we just the home guard now, sir?" Cov asked. "Parking duties, maybe? Haven't they got enough meat-cans on every walkway already?"

Maze gave him that watch-my-eyebrow-show-disapproval look that seemed common to all ARC troopers. "Civil order must be maintained, Private. We have looting of damaged property, and any number of malcontent Separatist sympathizers still on our turf. Just because the enemy fleet's gone, it doesn't mean that all the dangers have passed."

"Permission to go after the malcontents, then, sir?"

"If you're volunteering for public order patrol, be my guest." Maze looked at Omega. "Unless you sensitive artists have got any special requests, you're deployed with Aquila and Manka—two men riding with each CSF assault ship. Okay?"

"Yes, sir."

"Get to it. The cop ships are picking up from the parade ground."

It was fine by Darman. There was a time when he would have bridled at confinement to the capital, and wanted to be out doing real soldiering, as Skirata called it, but not now.

Corr seemed in very high spirits. "Atin, you and me?"

"Fine."

"Come on, then, *Dar'ika*," Niner said. "Corr, don't you lead our old married buddy astray. I know what you're like."

Atin hadn't seen Laseema since the start of the siege, and just chatted with her in snatched moments by comlink. Darman couldn't even talk to Etain until she dropped out of hyperspace; Enacca was taking her time. He checked his comlink, found no message, and reminded himself that Etain was fine.

"Heard about Sev?" Cov said, brushing past them. "MIA. They pulled out of Kashyyyk without him. Vau's going to go off the deep end. I assume he knows."

Niner moved in as if to quash any defeatist talk. "Come on, the battle's still ongoing. Delta might have been pulled out, but we've still got troops there. They'll look for him."

It was true, in theory, but Darman already knew what Sev's chances were. Special forces were the ones who were supposed to do the extracting, not the ones who needed it. It didn't bode well.

Atin looked uncomfortable. "We ought to volunteer to search."

"I don't think they're asking for volunteers," Cov said. "You were one of Vau's, weren't you?"

"Yeah. I was."

It took just one flicker of the eye, one breath held for a fraction too long, and suddenly they all felt bad about not grabbing the nearest ship that wasn't secured and inserting into Kashyyyk to bring back one of their own. There were plenty of beings in theater who could do it, and who should have been doing it, but somehow even *thinking* that made Darman feel like he'd walked away and personally left Sev to die.

"I'm disgusted with Delta." Cov was angry. Bralor's squads had a reputation for being all-or-nothing. "They're still in the gun battery complex, and they see he's not with them, and they don't go back? Just because they lost comms? The general could have kissed my *shebs,* because *I'd* have gone back. *All* of us, or *none* of us. That's the way this game is. What a bunch of *chakaare.*"

He stalked off. Darman felt suitably chastened. He'd been that man stuck behind enemy lines.

"No, Dar," Niner said, able to read his mind pretty accurately now. "That's one step too far. It's not your problem."

Atin gave him a friendly shove with his shoulder as they walked out onto the parade ground to wait for the CSF ships to land.

"I voted to carry on the Qiilura mission without you, *ner vod,*" he said quietly. "So if I ever get stuck, you don't owe me. Vau raised us *different* when it came to survival."

Darman hadn't known that. The whole squad had risked their necks looking for him. "Would you vote the same way now?"

" 'Course not. You're my *vod'ika.* Your life matters more than mine, because if I had to stare at your empty seat every day, I wouldn't have much of a life, would I?"

Darman understood that perfectly. When everyone thought that way, everyone came home alive. *Tion'ad hukaat'kama?* It was the phrase they all used: Who's watching your back? If they didn't look after one another, nobody else would.

It was a nice day for a trip out, but even in the capital, even with the threat level reduced, Darman still watched Niner's back, and Niner watched his.

Arca Barracks, 2100 hours

Ordo estimated that he had less than four hours left to spend on Coruscant. He decided to use some of them shaving and making himself presentable.

He laid his helmet on the windowsill in the 'freshers and inspected the state of his reflection, feeling for stubble. *Long day. Soon, it'll be over.* Only A'den and Etain still had to report in at the RV point. Omega were on patrol again after a six-hour break, and he knew exactly where they were to

within a block at any given time. Mereel had reached Kyrimorut.

Everyone else was waiting in *Aay'han*, or at least on the
underground quayside.

Ordo took out his razor-edged knife and shaved the
Mando way, drawing the blade carefully across his skin. No
lubricating foam, no fancy depilatory chemicals; the kind of
shave you could have anywhere, anytime, and leave no telltale scent of toiletries to betray your presence to an enemy.
He noted that it was time to get his hair cut, and that he now
had a few gray hairs at his temples.

The doors parted. Maze walked in to relieve himself.

"Tell your two brothers," Maze said, staring straight ahead
at the tiles, "that Grievous was indeed at home when General
Kenobi came to call. Now he's *dead*."

"I know." Ordo concentrated on not drawing blood. Besany always fussed over cuts. "They give good intel."

"Eventually . . ."

"Uh-huh."

"Are we the last two ARCs left on the planet?"

"Looks like it, *ner vod*. Is this how you saw your glorious
service career when Jango was honing you into a perfectly
formed killing machine?"

"Not really." Maze shook his hands under the steri-dryer.
"But who knows where I'll be deployed next, now that the
army's changed shape so dramatically?"

Ordo wasn't sure if Maze was being literal, or if he was
making an oblique opening gambit to discuss an unofficial
early retirement. It was hard to tell if Maze was the deserting
kind.

Ordo patted his face dry with a cloth and then dried his
knife. "Those Five-oh-first lads are a little keen for my tastes.
They'll replace us, you know."

"And what about you, Ordo?"

"What *about* me?"

"Career plans? No, don't answer. I'm not sure I need to
know." Maze headed for the doors. "Zey's over at the Jedi
Temple—I think it's the news on Grievous. He'll be back
soon, he says, but I'm rostering off for the night."

It would probably be the last time Ordo saw Maze, but a hearty farewell seemed asking for trouble. He listened to the ARC's footsteps fading down the corridor, and went on tidying himself. Jaing was right; it was good armor, even if it was a little too *aruetyc* in places. He'd have to leave it behind, even the *buy'ce*. All the data in it had been downloaded and duplicated, and all he had to do now to make it safe to discard—safe in the sense of having too much data stored—was to break out the memory modules and pocket them. He'd leave the kit here, and walk out of the building in his black bodysuit and a jacket to pick up his *beskar'gam* from a locker at the anonymous public storage facility on the way to the reservoir.

No . . . he'd take the Aratech bike to save time, and dump it. They'd realize he'd deserted sooner or later.

Ordo was about to brush his teeth when he heard the comm warning in his helmet blipping. He slid it into place, annoyed at the interruption, and wondered if it was A'den checking in, or Etain dropping out of hyperspace.

It was a voice message.

And it was neither A'den nor Etain.

"Execute Order Sixty-six."

It was the Chancellor, the source verified by security encryption.

Ordo had perfect recall. Memorizing all 150 contingency orders for the worst scenarios had taken him no time at all, but every ARC, Republic commando, and clone commander had learned and repeated those orders from childhood until they knew every syllable and comma. Some of them found it a slog, but it was part of the job. CSF officers had their own set of emergency orders, covering their different responsibilities; every Republic service and department had a handbook of procedures like that, to be put into action when things went badly wrong.

Even so, Ordo froze.

It was the order to execute his Jedi commanders.

"Yes, sir," he said.

18

Hemli Tower Boulevard, Galactic City, 2120 hours,
1,089 days ABG

"**Y**ou okay?" said the CSF akk handler, patting his animal.
The patrol ship cruised slowly down the skylane, keeping an
eye on crowds that had ventured out to sample the nightlife
for the first time since the invasion. Galactic City wanted
to boast that it was open for business again. "Something
wrong?"

Darman hardly knew where to start. He'd been sure he'd
misremembered the contingency orders, and that Order 66
was the command code for shutting down the banking system to avert an enemy computer attack, but it was wishful
thinking. It was *desperate* thinking.

"Change of tasking," he said, stomach knotted. "They
can't make their minds up."

"Yeah, we've just had an emergency comm." Niner backed

him up. "Can you set us down somewhere? We need to call in our own unit."

It was sheer *osik,* of course, born of panic. What they needed to do, what they were *required* and *obliged* to do, was to seize and execute any Jedi they met. If they were serving alongside Jedi, that meant killing them on the spot. If they were operating alone—it was a case of assassination if a Jedi crossed their path.

"Sure, no problem." The officer leaned through the cockpit bulkhead. "Vil, can you set down the lads, please?"

Niner switched to the private helmet link. "Dar, don't worry. Don't think about it. We'll get Etain out. Jusik—well, he's out already. *Don't worry.*"

How would Etain find out there were death warrants out on every Jedi? She was in transit. She wouldn't be able to receive a comm until her ship dropped out of hyperspace. How could he warn her?

Darman opened his secure link to Skirata. *Kal'buir* responded instantly as if he'd been waiting.

"Dar?"

"Sarge, have you heard—"

"Yes, I heard. Order Sixty-six. Now, *don't worry.* Get yourselves down here, all of you, and we'll take care of Etain. Okay?"

"How are we going to *warn* her?"

"Leave it to us. Jusik and Ordo are on the case already. We've got it covered."

Skirata would have said that if the galaxy was ending. He thought he could take care of everything and everybody.

Darman was now aware of some anxious conversation taking place between the two CSF officers. The akk handler tapped Niner's back plate.

"Sergeant, we've just had our compliance order rescinded," he said. The cop ship came to rest on a landing platform. "Is this anything to do with your retasking?"

"What?"

"Jedi. Our standing order is to comply with any Jedi request. We've just been told to ditch that and to report in if we have any contact with Jedi."

Niner looked glacial from the outside. Only a brother would have known what was going on under the helmet.

"Of course," Niner said calmly. He sounded like a stranger. "I forgot that CSF would also be affected by any change in their status. I've got no intel about this other than my orders. What's happened?"

Vil, the pilot, squeezed out of the cockpit into the crew cabin. "Attempted coup. The Jedi bigwigs walked into the Chancellor's office and tried to take control of the state. Can you believe it?"

"Violence?" Darman asked, wondering why he wasn't more shocked at the news.

"At least one Jedi Master dead. Come and have a listen to the comm traffic. It's chaos around the Jedi Temple sector. Troopers called in, the place is on fire, everything."

"Burning the incriminating evidence, I reckon." The akk handler patted his animal fondly. "Who'd have thought it, eh, Jossie? Bad Jedi!"

"Bummer," Niner said mildly. "Okay, Dar, this is where we get out." He turned to the cops and touched his fingers to his helmet. "Thanks for the heads-up. You go careful, okay?"

The CSF patrol lifted clear, and Darman and Niner were left standing in a vastly altered world.

"Oh *shab.*"

"Dar, she's going to be fine. Just treat this like a mission. We're Republic commandos. Extracting Jedi when they get into scrapes is part of the job description."

"But she's not *any* Jedi. She's my girl. She's my *wife,* when she responds to that vow. She gave me a son."

Niner let out a long sigh, and looked around as if he was searching for something.

"What do we do if we run into other Jedi?" Darman asked.

"Turn blind," Niner said. "Someone else can deal with them. It's not like we haven't got enough troopers on the ground now."

"You were always so *proper.* You haven't changed your mind about deserting, have you?"

Darman thought about a conversation they'd had back on Gaftikar, discussing whether they'd leave their brothers be-

hind for a new life if the opportunity arose. Niner had been
as upset by the idea as Darman had ever seen him.

"No," said Niner. "You guys—you're all I've got. I can't
face being alone, not again. I won't be parted from you. I
don't feel comfortable running away, but *Kal'buir*'s right
when he says we never took an oath to serve, and I just can't
hack it on my own here."

Darman took his arm and squeezed it hard. "We're all in
this together, *ner vod.*"

"I'll commandeer some transport," Niner said, and strode
toward a young Osarian male who was sitting in the saddle
of a large speeder bike, minding his own business. "*Kal'buir*
and Ordo have enough on their plate at the moment. Hey, citizen! I need your bike. Emergency Republic business."

It was hard to ignore a Republic commando, especially at
night. The blue-lit T-shaped visor proved very intimidating,
especially set against matte-black stealth armor. The Osarian, startled, looked at Niner, then at his DC-17 rifle, and
then past his shoulder as if he'd seen something on the sky-
line. Darman turned.

There was a fire, a big one. The night sky, which was always a dense mass of illuminated signs and light pollution
that blotted out the stars, was now showing a distinct, smoky
orange ellipse. The Jedi Temple was being engulfed in
flames.

"Er . . . okay, Officer," said the Osarian, and handed over
his keypass. "Will I get it back?"

"At the address shown on your permit," Niner said, clearly
lying. He turned to Darman. "Mount up, Private."

They took off, leaving the bright-lit entertainment area beneath them, but neither of them knew where to go yet. Niner
found a quiet vantage point high up on an office block. The
two commandos sat perched there on the bike like a couple
of armored raptors.

"What do we do when we know Etain's landed?" Darman
asked. "It's not like we can collect her on this thing. Only two
seats."

"We'll do what we always do—dynamic risk assessment."

"Wing it."

"Yeah."

Darman almost didn't want to know what was going on elsewhere in the city. He had his HUD on default, receiving only emergency data and set to night ops. His comlink to Skirata and the others was kept open. Then he risked patching into the GAR comm chatter just to listen to things he knew he didn't want to hear.

It was surprisingly calm.

There was the ebb and flow of reports from across the galaxy, most of them about casualties, requirements for supplies, and—almost incidental, this—occasional voice traffic reporting the completion of Order 66 in a given location, and that Jedi General this, or Jedi Commander that, had been terminated.

Darman heard only one comment about it on the open comm net, and that was a clone trooper reporting in from an Acclamator: "I still can't believe they'd try to seize power like that," he was saying to an ops room somewhere. "We never saw it coming. How could the Jedi betray us like this?"

"Ke narir haar'ke'gyce rol'eta resol," Darman said, more to himself than Niner. *Execute Order 66.*

It was an unremarkable order among many others in the days when they first learned the list. Nobody thought the Jedi would actually turn bad; but if the worst happened, and they did, simply detaining a being with prodigious Force powers wasn't an option. It *had* to be lethal force. It was the same for a number of other species and organizations on the contingency list, who were great allies but who would need a *lot* more stopping power than a simple arrest if they turned into enemies.

An order was an order. And orders had to be followed, or else society fell apart. It wasn't blind obedience, Skirata told his commandos, but a conscious suppression of individual choice that every soldier made in a democracy. The soldier was the instrument of the state, not its master, and the state was the citizens. The citizens made their choice of civil government, and that government tasked the army. The army couldn't pick and choose which lawful orders it obeyed. An army that took those decisions upon itself undermined democracy, and ended up overthrowing the government.

And orders—followed instantly—kept you alive; *take cover, cease fire, fall back.* Orders came from those who had the bigger picture when you didn't; *move that battalion, withdraw from that sector, press forward on the enemy's flank.* If you stood around arguing the toss about them, you got yourself and others killed.

Darman had no problems with orders. He just wasn't ready to kill his wife. He hadn't signed up to do that.

He hadn't signed up at all, in fact. None of them had.

Etain wasn't part of whatever the Jedi Council had tried to do. Neither was Jusik. Those who really *had* tried to depose Palpatine—well, they should have known better. The Grand Army's purpose was to defend the Republic—even against Jedi.

19

I bet they wish they'd asked a few more questions before accepting command of a slave army now.
—Spar, formerly ARC Trooper A-02, first deserter from the Grand Army of the Republic, now a bounty hunter specializing in live retrieval

Private vessel landing corridor, Galactic City airspace,
2220 hours, 1,089 days ABG

Enacca threw back her head and yawled in protest.

"It's too late," Etain said. "We're committed to landing now. Just take us in as planned, and drop me at the Kragget. It's okay."

Enacca didn't agree. She wanted to land, refuel, and take off again. She could always land near Skirata's secret mooring, and then Etain could—

"*No*, because if anyone's tracking us, we'll lead them straight to Jusik, to Fi, to the Nulls, to Dar, to . . ." She trailed off. "And anyway, I'm not even a Jedi now. I'm not in danger. Just land. Please."

Enacca's roar of warning filled the small cabin, but she did as she was asked. She set the shuttle down on a rooftop above the Kragget, and insisted on delivering Etain personally to the doors. They stopped short in the shadows of the doorway of a derelict cantina nearby.

"Enacca—look, I—"

The Wookiee grabbed Etain's hand and slapped a blaster into it. She was going to need that, Enacca said, and there was no time for long good-byes. She'd see her around one day. Then Enacca loped away, vanishing into the turbolift shaft. Etain ripped off her brown robe, the one that marked her so clearly as a Jedi, and dropped it off the walkway into the urban abyss below. Then she walked calmly into the Kragget in her light beige tunic and pants. She still needed to change into plain civilian clothes.

"Hi, sweetheart," Soronna said softly. It was a restaurant full of cops, most of whom knew exactly who Etain was; and they all knew the Jedi were on the wanted list now. "Why have you come back here?"

"I need a change of clothing, fast."

Soronna bundled her into the kitchens. She grabbed the first garments she could find, stuff that the cooks had left lying around, plus her own coat and boots, and Etain swapped her rough-spun ascetic uniform for a motley outfit that made her look like a girl who didn't have the credits to be fashionable but did her best. An ordinary young woman; an average human female of her age from this poor part of town.

"Perfect," she said, and gave Soronna a kiss on the cheek. "I don't know how I'll ever repay you."

"Oh, come back and wash the dishes sometime . . ." Soronna opened the trash incinerator and threw in Etain's old clothing and boots. "Is there anything in your bag that'll give you away if you're stopped?"

"I've got two lightsabers, a blaster, my comlink, my datapad, and Kad's toy."

"You're crazy. Ditch the lightsabers."

One of them was her own. But one was Master Fulier's, her old Master, the Master who was killed because he stood up for what he thought was right, in a very un-Jedi way by current standards. Fulier would never have come to this point. Fulier would have refused to lead clone troops, would have kicked up a stink, would have called Master Yoda any number of unflattering names and demanded to know why they'd all gone down this path with barely a whimper.

She couldn't leave his lightsaber behind. *See, you'd be proud of me now, Master, and I'm not even a Jedi any longer.*

And if she carried his weapon, then she might as well keep her own. She'd just be careful.

"Good-bye, Soronna," Etain said, and walked out through the kitchen doors into the restaurant again. She had never felt more calm, more certain, and more *safe* than she had right now. The terrible ripping sensation in her chest that had stopped her breathing even while the ship was still in hyperspace had faded, its place taken by an animal determination to *live*.

I have plenty to live for now, and not just an ideal.

As she reached the entrance, one of the CSF cops stood up and blocked her path, with his back to the transparisteel frontage that overlooked the skylane. Her stomach knotted. This man *wasn't* going to stop her leaving. But in the split second that it took for her to choose which way she was going to make him move, he glanced over his shoulder at the skylane, and then back again as a GAR patrol gunship swept by.

"All clear, kid," he said. "They're just running general security patrols with our boys. Off you go. Good luck."

The galaxy was full of good folks. She needed to remember that.

From the walkway, she could see a pall of orange-lit smoke rising from the Jedi Temple. It was visible clear across the city; flames leapt to the peak of the four corner towers every so often, then dropped again below the tumbling smoke. She caught a speeder taxi to the upper levels and got out at the Boreali Holotheater, where the mass of crowds was the best camouflage.

The line waiting outside was facing away from the theater doors as the patrons watched the fire. It was as if they thought the war was over, and this disaster was a distant entertainment. On every walkway, there were clone troops. Etain flipped open her datapad to check for new messages again in case she'd missed one.

They'd come through in a flurry as soon as Enacca had brought the shuttle out of hyperspace and the comlink had picked up the local node. The one from Skirata had come through first: GAR HAS ORDERS TO KILL JEDI ON SIGHT— ATTEMPTED COUP. WINDU DEAD. SEND LOCATION AND WE'LL EXTRACT YOU. DON'T TAKE RISK. There was another from

Darman: DID YOU GET MY MESSAGE? And now Jusik had tried to reach her. TELL ME WHERE TO FIND YOU.

She tapped out a message to Darman—I GOT YOURS, DID YOU GET MINE?—but she got a relay warning back saying that the node was inoperative.

Stang. Maybe they'd changed the GAR comm protocols in the last twenty-four hours. They did it occasionally because helmet links fell into enemy hands, and they needed to keep one step ahead on comm security. She'd try again later. Jusik and Skirata were off the GAR network most of the time.

Etain was aware of the scrutiny of a couple of troopers with blue armor flashes, the 501st, men she would normally have sought out and befriended as she did every clone she met. Now all she could think was that they knew she was a Jedi.

I'm not. I'm no longer a Jedi. They can't tell me from a non-Force-user.

The Chancellor's office probably wouldn't quibble over that fine distinction, though. She swallowed hard a few times, trying not to look as if she was panicking, and tapped in a reply to Jusik.

IN CIVILIAN CLOTHES. I'M OKAY. I'M HEADING FOR THE RV POINT. DON'T LEAVE THE OTHERS.

She slipped the comlink back in her pocket and decided the only way to get past the patrol was to behave like a regular civilian—scared, confused, or both. She'd been in battle, and all she had to do was focus on that feeling, on negotiating a battlefield.

A coup. What was the Jedi Council thinking? Had they sanctioned it, or did Windu take it on himself to act?

Other pedestrians were trying to hail air taxis, but most were zipping past already occupied. There was a definite movement of traffic away from the Temple sector. Etain approached a trooper and decided that if he saw her disorientation, he'd think that was absolutely normal on a night like this.

"Captain," she said. He was a lieutenant, and that was clear from the subtle rank insignia on his chest plate, but her knowledge might have raised suspicion. "Captain, I need to get to Quadrant J-Twelve." She didn't, but it was close enough without giving her destination away. "Are the sky-lanes closed? What's happening?"

The trooper looked down at her. She felt him in the Force; he gave her that same impression of *child* that Darman had exuded when she first sensed him. He was new to this.

"Nothing to worry about, ma'am," he said. "Some trouble at the Temple. There's been an attempted coup, but it's under control now. You're free to go anywhere, but the skylanes around the Temple are closed for the time being because of drifting smoke."

His accent was different. He was *almost* like the men she knew and served with, but not quite. Now she was as sensitive to tiny variations as any clone.

"Thank you, Captain," she said.

Her comlink blipped again. She checked it, and it was Jusik: I SAY AGAIN, WAIT UNTIL I COLLECT YOU.

Etain was getting annoyed. She didn't have time to stop and send messages now. She didn't have far to go—five or six klicks, no more. She tapped a reply. I'M FINE. STAY THERE. WHERE'S DAR? TELL HIM TO GO. CAN'T REACH HIM.

She started walking toward the reservoir sector. It would take her ten minutes to cover the walkways to the speeder bus terminal. If she stayed among crowds, she'd be fine. The only uncertain part of the journey was when she had to descend to the lower levels, and that was because of the low-life scum she'd encounter, not because she'd be hunted for having been a Jedi.

She strode out across the paved plaza, feeling awkward because Soronna's borrowed shoes were a little too big for her and she was sliding around in them. As she rested her hand in the bag slung over her shoulder, and felt the silky fur of the toy nerf, she realized that her jumble of emotions didn't include shock at the fact that Master Windu had tried to oust the Chancellor.

Skirata obviously had good intel, but she was more surprised that someone had managed to kill Windu during the attempt.

Aay'han, emergency reservoir, 2235 hours

"No," Skirata said firmly into the comlink in his fist. "I'm not having everyone running around this *shabla* city like maniacs. Get your *shebs* down here, Corr. And drag Atin by his ears if necessary. It's under control. We're *dealing,* okay?"

"Yes, Sarge, but—"

"I love you, son, but I need you to do exactly what I tell you. Okay?"

"Yes, Sarge."

Skirata understood completely how Corr felt, because his own instinct was to get up top and haul people in. He'd never been good at securing the hatches and leaving, even when it was the most sensible option that would save the most lives. He stared up at *Aay'han*'s deckhead as if he could see through it if only he concentrated hard enough, and kept checking the chrono readout on the bulkhead. Eventually, he heard familiar voices through the open outer hatch. He breathed easy again, at least for a moment.

Atin gave him a playful punch in the shoulder.

"I said to dump the armor," Skirata scolded.

"I know, but we looked more conspicuous in bodysuits."

Corr looked around the crew cabin, thumbs hooked in his belt. "It's cramped, but I'll take it."

Fi stuck his head out of the galley. "You think you're funny, but I'll show you how it's done *properly.*"

Nerves were frayed. The banter, the sharp and strained humor, had started. Skirata could hear the edge in their voices, even Fi's. He paced up and down the deck.

"Okay, we're still short Etain, Niner, Dar, and A'den. Etain's on her way, and won't behave and let us collect her—Dar and Niner haven't called in for fifteen minutes—and A'den, as far as I know, is—"

"Where's Ordo?" Fi asked.

"At the barracks, doing a final check to make sure we haven't forgotten anything."

It was crowded in the small submarine. They all had cabins or bunk space, and Skirata wanted everyone to keep clear of the main crew deck, mainly because he was getting agitated with folks trying to keep out of his way. But also because he was worried about Vau. The old *chakaar* had taken the news about Sev in complete silence, not a twitch on his face, and that usually meant things within him were fermenting at an unhealthy rate. Vau stood leaning with one hand flat on the bulkhead, the other tucked in his belt while he gazed down at his boots. Mird sat at his feet, staring intently into his face. Vau obviously wasn't looking at the strill.

"Walon," Skirata said, "can I do anything?"

"I understand," Vau said quietly. "I actually get it. *Shab,* why didn't I see this coming?"

His tone was so un-Vau-like that it got instant silence on the deck. "You want to talk?" Skirata asked. It was a lousy time. "What's the problem?"

"Jango . . . Jango had *patience.* Jango could wait for eternity if he had to. And, *wayii,* it seems he could wait after death, too."

Skirata glanced around the deck at everyone standing idle. *"Bard'ika,"* he said, "come here. Everyone else—into your cabins, and get some rest if you can. There's still a hard night ahead."

It was an order, however softly it was phrased, and they all got the picture pretty fast. The deck emptied. Jusik stood between the two men, silent.

"Get it off your chest, Walon," Skirata said. "Come on, *ner vod.*"

Vau straightened up. "You never liked Jango, did you?"

"I liked him enough. What I *didn't* like was how he ended up. Jango never gave a toss about anyone but himself. Some Mandalore he turned out to be—he was always away in the latter years, and he was as bad as the Jedi when it came to turning a blind eye to what was happening to his clones. No, Shysa's a fool if he thinks a Fett dynasty is good for *Manda'yaim.* We're better off without him."

"You reckon?"

"I do. Sorry, but I do. You suddenly his best mate or something?"

Vau suddenly grabbed Skirata by the collar. *Shab,* he was strong; he almost lifted Skirata bodily as he shoved him against the bulkhead. They'd brawled many times, drawn blood, come close to killing each other, but Skirata had never seen Vau lose his temper, not once. And that was enough to stun him into silence.

"Now do you see? *Do you?*" Vau hissed the sibilant like escaping steam. Mird cowered on the floor, whining softly. "I'm sick to death of your sentimental twaddle about Jango betraying us by letting Kamino use his genes. *He did it to stop the Jedi.* He did it to create an army strong enough to bring them down. You drone on about the injustice of un-elected elites, my little working-class hero—well, now they're *gone.* Yes, it cost our boys' lives, but the Jedi are gone, gone, *gone.* And they won't be killing Mandalorians again, not for a long time. Maybe *never.*"

Vau was white-faced and trembling. Then he seemed to shake himself out of whatever alien persona had taken hold of him, adjusted his collar, and tugged down the sleeves of his flight suit. He was the ice-cold patrician again. Skirata still couldn't summon up any love or guilt about Jango, but suddenly *it made sense,* and he knew in his guts that it had been about a lot more than five million creds.

I should have known. Why demand a son as part of the fee? Jango lost everyone he ever loved or cared about, time after time.

And the Jedi had still killed him in the end. If Boba was anything like his father in more than looks, then he'd have a monstrous sense of vengeance boiling up in him now, and no Jedi to take it out on.

"You never told me what you got up to on Kamino in the time before the rest of the *Cuy'val Dar* showed up," Skirata said, trying to look as if he'd taken the outburst in stride. "So what else are you going to tell me?" *Shab,* they might not have been best buddies from birth, but they were as close as two *Mando'ade* could get. Vau owed him some honesty. "You were the galactic freestyle dancing champion, too?"

Vau didn't meet Skirata's eyes for a moment, but he glanced at Jusik. "I could have been at Galidraan, but I wasn't, and I never forgot that. Not my fight. *Should* have been my fight."

"And you could have been dead, now, too. *Bard'ika,* if you don't know—"

"Oh, I know what happened at Galidraan," Jusik said. "I know Jedi wiped out Jango's entire army." He paused. "And I know Jango killed Jedi with his bare hands, too, because I once talked to a Jedi who was *there.*"

Vau nodded approvingly. "See, if you want to take out Jedi," he said, "only the likes of Jango could really do it. Only his clones, trained by him, and by men and women like him. That's why he knew it *had* to be done. He couldn't take them all down alone, but he knew an entire *army* of Jangos could."

Skirata thought of the abuse he'd heaped on Jango. He knew the man; he'd fought with him, in every sense of the word, and he'd also had comradely moments with him. The thought that he might have done him a disservice was one burden of guilt too many. He shut it out. If Jango had been playing the long game, Skirata had never caught a whiff of it. He knew it wasn't all about the credits. He'd seen Jango cradling Boba in the early days, and that man wanted a son as much as any man ever had. So Skirata hadn't looked for any motive beyond that. It was the only motive Skirata would have had.

"I stand corrected," said Skirata. *How do I apologize? Where do I even start, with the* osik *I have to deal with now?*

"So I was wrong about Jango."

And now I know why Shysa wants Jango's legacy to live on at any cost.

Vau shrugged. "I let him down once." Vau would never shake off that feeling of having failed, the legacy of his vile father. He'd instilled it into his clones, despite himself. "But I never let him down again."

"Don't beat yourself up. I should have been at Galidraan, too."

"I know," said Vau. "That's why I chose you for the *Cuy'val Dar.*"

Skirata grappled with the stomach-knotting realization that he really didn't know Vau half as well as he thought he did.

He chose me. Shab, *he chose me.*

"Okay, Walon, answer me this, will you? No *osik.* Did Jango want me on the team?"

"We discussed all personnel fully."

"Don't talk like some *shabla* administrator to me. *Did he want me?*"

Vau wavered for a moment. Outbursts and wavering in one night; it was all revelations. "You know Jango. He could get his downs on people, and then he'd see sense. Does it matter a *shab* now?"

"No, Walon, it doesn't." Skirata knew he was everything Vau said—thug, thief, killer, uncultured oaf, and way too emotional. But he knew how to fight—anything, anytime— and he knew how to love. It was as much a survival skill as using his blade or knowing how to construct a *vheh'yaim* for shelter in the field. *That's the gift. That's what both my fathers taught me.* He held out his hand to Vau. "Walon, whatever we've said or done to each other before this moment, it doesn't matter. *Cin vhetin.* A fresh field of snow."

Vau looked at him blankly for a moment. Maybe he knew how precariously Skirata balanced on the edge of his resources right then, but that craggy humorless face softened for a few telling seconds.

"Cin vhetin." Vau grasped Skirata's arm in a vise-like grip. *"Mhi vode an, ner vod."*

Vau seemed purged. He slapped his thigh plate, and Mird trotted after him into the galley.

"Sorry about that, *Bard'ika,*" Skirata said. It couldn't have been easy for the kid to hear all that bad blood about Jedi on this particular night. He might have turned his back on them and put on the *beskar'gam,* but they'd been his family, and some of those killed must have been his friends. Jedi were living beings, too; some might have got what was coming to them, but others were probably decent like Etain and Jusik. "We're tired old men, with tired old grudges."

Jusik looked at his chrono and then checked his comlink. "Had to be said." He shook his head slowly. "I'll make sense of this later . . . maybe. But . . . okay, I understand Fett's vengeance. But if the whole Grand Army was planned just to take out the Jedi Order, then Fett alone couldn't have done this or even hijacked it. Why is nobody asking *this* question? Who planned the army in the first place? Who bankrolled it? And what's Fett got to do with the second wave, the Centax clones, the massive new fleet? What's the link between the Chancellor and the Jedi plan?"

It was a *shabla* good question.

It would also have to wait.

Skirata opened the comlink. "Dar? Niner? Wrap up whatever it is you're doing, and make your way to the RV point. It's endex. It's over."

Arca Barracks, Special Operations Brigade HQ,
2240 hours

Ordo finished his sweep of the accommodation block, satisfied that Omega hadn't left anything foolish or accidentally incriminating in their quarters.

They were smart men, but the smallest thing might be a link in a trail that would lead eventually to Kyrimorut, or—worse—to the discovery that Etain and Darman had a child. *Kal'buir* was already on Palpatine's list for stealing Ko Sai's data from under him. It wouldn't take a genius to guess that Mandalore was a likely bolt-hole.

But *Manda'yaim* was a big empty planet, mostly wild and unspoiled, and nobody could disappear quite as well as *Mando'ade* when they put their minds to it.

Ordo changed into his red Mandalorian armor, his *beskar'gam*. It was the final act of severance from the Grand Army of the Republic, which had never asked him if he wanted to sign up anyway. He left his fine white ARC trooper's armor in a tidy pile on the bunk that he rarely used, then relented and scooped up the helmet in the red-trimmed, gray leather *kama*. It was a sentimental act; he thought he was less tied to his memories than that.

There was one place left to clean up, just in case. That was Arligan Zey's office. Ordo came down in the turbolift with his ARC bucket tied in the *kama* like a sack of booty, his red

Mando buy'ce in his other hand, to find himself in an echoing emptiness. The faint disembodied voices of comm traffic drifted down the corridor from the ops room. All command and control had been switched to the GAR HQ, but nobody had shut down the room. It was as if SO Brigade had suddenly ceased to exist.

Special Operations had been a Jedi project. Now the Jedi were dead and gone, from the Temple a few kilometers away to the besieged worlds of the Outer Rim, shot where they stood.

Fine. No interruptions.

Ordo activated Zey's computer and bypassed all the security lockouts, then began stripping out the data onto his own 'pad as he erased it irretrievably from the Republic's system. It didn't matter what it was. If there was anything in there that would compromise Kyrimorut, then it was safer to trash the lot.

Five minutes. Kal'buir, you haven't called in. I'll call you when—

The sound of someone lurching along the pleekwood floor outside, boots scuffing, caught him unawares.

He hadn't expected to see General Zey tonight. Zey, it seemed, definitely hadn't expected to find a Mandalorian rifling through his desk. The general filled the doorway, disheveled and smoke-stained. Blood had dried in a thin trickle from his forehead down to his chin. His left arm hung limp at his side. Someone had nearly killed him.

Ordo tried to feel some compassion. But Zey was outside the small group of beings that Ordo had bonded with, and he accepted that he couldn't convert that intellectual understanding of Zey's human failings and virtues into the sensation in his gut that told him that this was someone he loved and cared about. It would be enough not to kill him.

"General," Ordo said. "I'll be gone in a moment. Do you think it's wise to be here?"

"Ordo?"

Ordo took off his helmet, wondering if it made any difference in helping the Jedi recognize him. But he always seemed to. "Hide while you still can."

"They killed us . . . They killed us all . . . *Why?*"

Ordo stood up and pocketed the datachips, then tucked his helmet under one arm. Power was a strange, shifting thing. Ko Sai had been the arbiter of life and death for him as a small child, and then the Jedi had become his masters—or so they thought—and now both were dead. It was best to be your own master, and lord it over nobody, because, sooner or later, the beings you trod down always came to get you.

"Orders," Ordo said. "You never read the GAR's contingency orders? They're on the mainframe. I suppose nobody thinks contingency orders will ever be needed."

Zey leaned panting against the door frame as if he was about to collapse. "But *why?*"

"Because," said Maze's voice from outside the doors, "it's neither your right nor your position to decide who runs the Republic. Who elected *you?*"

Ordo heard the click and whir of a sidearm. It was time to go. This wasn't his war or his world any longer. He picked up his belongings and took a few paces toward the doors, wondering what would happen when he had to shift Zey out of his way.

"Maze, what are you going to do now?" Ordo asked.

"I've never disobeyed an order," said the ARC captain. Zey didn't seem to have the strength to turn and look at his former aide, just shutting his eyes as if he was waiting for the coup de grâce. "What am I supposed to do? Pick and choose? That's the irony. The Jedi thought we were excellent troops because we're so disciplined and we obey orders, but when we obey *all* orders—and they're lawful orders, remember—then we've *betrayed* them. Can't have it both ways, General."

Zey summoned up some effort and stumbled toward his desk to slump over it. Ordo put down his two helmets and slid the man into the chair. Maze walked in. He was holding his blaster at his side, not aiming it. He wasn't the one who'd shot Zey; there was no smell of discharged weapon clinging to him.

"I really must be going, General," Ordo said. But he had to know. "Just tell me, is it *true* that Windu tried to depose the Chancellor?"

Zey raised his head, all anguish and agony. "He's a *Sith*. Can't you see? A *Sith*! He's taking over the government, he's occupying the galaxy with his new clones, he's *evil* . . ."

"I said, is it true?"

"Yes! It was our duty as Jedi to *stop* him."

"What's a Sith?" Maze asked.

Jango Fett hadn't been very thorough in the education of his Alpha ARCs, or maybe he didn't want to muddy the waters with sectarian trivia.

"Like Jedi," Ordo said, "only on the other side. Mandalorians fought for them thousands of years ago, and we got stiffed by them in the end. We got stiffed by the Jedi, too. So, all in all, it's a moot point for us."

"Palpatine's probably the one who had you created," Zey said. He was lucky he was still breathing. Ordo wasn't sure why Maze hadn't just slotted him. "Why couldn't you see what he was?"

"Why couldn't *you* sniff him out with your Force powers?" Ordo asked. "And why the *shab* did you never ask where *we* came from?"

Ordo had had enough. He walked away. He was halfway down the corridor, and he could still hear Maze asking Zey to come quietly, because he was *arresting* him, because maybe he might get a trial.

Poor Maze; he really believed that political *osik* he read on his off-duty hours. The world didn't work that way.

"I'm dead already," said Zey. His voice was getting fainter. Ordo had expected him to fight to the death. "Please, do it. I know you have no malice in you. End it for me. I know what'll happen if he gets me."

Ordo's forefinger hit the keypad on the main doors to open them for the last time. He could just about hear the end of the conversation in the deathly quiet.

"I'm really sorry, sir," Maze said. "But if that's an order . . ."

A single blaster shot cracked the air. Poor Zey, and poor Maze. Everyone got used in the end.

Except us, Ordo thought. *Except us.*

20

*I hesitated for a moment when I received Order Sixty-six—
because the last thing I expected was a Jedi coup. Did I feel
betrayed? You bet I did. I thought of all my men who'd died
under Ki-Adi-Mundi's command, and if I'd known then that
he and his buddies were gearing up to do the Separatists'
work for them and overthrow the government,
I'd have shot him as a traitor a lot earlier.
He betrayed the trust of every one of us.*
—Clone Commander Bacara,
formerly of the Galactic Marines

Galactic City, 2250 hours, 1,089 days ABG

"**D**ar, she's not here," Niner said. They cruised up and down
the main skylane from the holotheater, but Darman couldn't
see Etain anywhere. "She was here some time ago. You know
how much ground she can cover. Give it up."

"I can't," Darman said.

He kept checking his comlink. He'd received her messages now, and he worked out the rough location of transmission based on what Jusik had said—that she'd come from the
Kragget. The comm traffic on the CSF channels was scaring
him. He listened, mouth dry, heart pounding, to the control
room supervisors juggling incoming reports and tasking patrols.

". . . All units, look out for Jedi, *young* Jedi, possibly
disguised now . . . Do not approach, I say again do *not* approach, armed and dangerous, call for military backup im-

mediately . . . May not have braids, repeat, may have removed identifying marks . . . Copy that, Five-Seven . . . No, numbers unknown . . . Yes, confirm that, arson *is* suspected, fire investigation team is seeking access, requires military escort, please advise . . . Confidential material *has* been destroyed . . . Jedi may be trying to escape with highly sensitive security data, so this is top priority . . . Chancellor's office . . . Military has orders to shoot on sight . . . Person of special interest, male, Teevan Veld, first name Tru, do *not* approach, call for Five-oh-first backup immediately . . ."

Jaller Obrim had called Skirata to let him know that one of his men had spoken to Etain when she left. If she was following a direct route on foot, she'd probably have come this way. If she'd taken a taxi, she would have been at the RV by now, and Skirata still hadn't seen her.

"Why doesn't she just *call in*?" Niner sounded exasperated. "Doesn't she know we're going to come out and look for her?"

"She's like *Kal'buir*. She thinks that if she says not to do it, then we won't."

Darman was now desperate. He knew Skirata would wait for her until Mustafar froze over, but the longer she was out there, the more likely she was to run into problems.

"She's in civvies," Niner said. "She doesn't *look* like a Jedi. As long as she doesn't start waving the shiny stick around right under some trooper's nose, she'll be fine."

"She accepted."

"What? What did she accept?"

"We exchanged marriage vows. It still counts over a comlink, you know. It's legal."

Niner didn't seem to know what to say. He swung the bike around and headed for the reservoir.

"What are you doing?"

"Time's up, Dar. All we're doing is worrying *Kal'buir*." Niner clicked his helmet comlink. "Sarge? It's Niner. We're heading in."

Skirata responded instantly. "I've got Ordo looking for her. She's okay. She's just staying off the radar. Jusik says he can sense her. *Shab,* I'm going to kick her *shebs* when I get hold of her for scaring us like this."

"There, Dar," Niner said. "Told you not to worry."

"Humor me. When we get to the RV point, can we wait up top, so I can see her coming?"

Niner accelerated toward the reservoir. "Of course."

It wasn't hard to spot the location, even without global positioning in their HUDs. The emergency reservoir might have been an invisible and forgotten facility for most Coruscanti, but there was a large slab-like tower on top of it—part of the pumping system—and when the bike got within a hundred meters of it, Darman saw an intermittent infrared pulse on his HUD. It was very regular; it was being emitted to attract someone's attention. As they approached it cautiously, it resolved into a CSF speeder parked on top of the tower.

"Osik." CSF had been the clones' staunchest friends for a few years. Darman wasn't sure why he now felt uneasy when he saw them. It was the compliance order. CSF had been told the Jedi were now the bad guys, and not everyone worked within the wide influence of Captain Obrim.

"Dar, let me do the talking." Niner brought the bike to a stop, facing in the opposite direction to the police speeder. "It's okay."

The speeder's sidescreen opened.

"Come on," said Jaller Obrim, hanging one arm over the edge. He indicated with a cutting motion across his throat to switch off their comms. "I can't sit here all night. Get below."

"Captain, you gave us a start . . ."

"I'm here to see you all get away, okay? Don't let Kal know I'm here. You're not on his frequency, are you? I said I'd keep out of his way now that Palps is after him. Now where's that woman of yours? Haven't you told her to keep her comlink open?"

Darman could hear a LAAT/i drive nearby. There was a GAR patrol coming. It was a sound every clone could pick out at a zillion klicks, because it was the sound of a gunship coming to give welcome air support, or extraction under fire. He couldn't work out why the gunship would be out here and not patrolling the main thoroughfares.

"CSF's working with GAR patrols," Darman said. "You should know—why are they around here?"

Obrim jerked his thumb over his shoulder. "What's behind me?"

Darman checked his HUD holochart. "Monit Town, the Tibanna storage depot, and Chance Palp Spaceport."

"Correct. And where's the Jedi Temple in relation to that?"

"Ah." The RV point was almost on the direct route from one to the other. Darman could see the orange glow; the fire still raged. "I see."

Obrim indicated the comlink sitting on his speeder console. "Quite a few of the junior Jedi escaped the Temple before it went up in flames, and logic says that they'll probably try getting off the planet via somewhere crowded like one of the spaceports. So they've got troops covering all the likely routes." He rubbed his eyes with one hand. "I hear they torched the place themselves. Don't know what they were trying to get rid of, but the fire service couldn't save the Archive. The Chancellor's pretty annoyed about that."

Darman knew that anyway. He was shocked that the Jedi had pulled a stunt like this, even though Skirata kept telling him now how corrupt they were. On Kamino, discussion of Jedi had been very neutral, and he'd never spotted any of the strong Mandalorian mistrust of them back then. "What if a patrol picks up Etain?"

"I'll have to talk them out of it, won't I? But there's no *reason* for her to get picked up."

Darman nodded. "Thanks, Captain."

They waited. The larty swooped over them, searchlights playing across the roofs and spires of the pumping station as it tracked toward the spaceport. As far the LAAT/i crew were concerned, it was just a commando patrol pausing to chat to a CSF comrade. Darman hoped they didn't spot that the speeder bike wasn't regulation GAR issue.

Then his helmet comlink clicked.

"Dar?"

"Et'ika!"

"Where are you?"

Darman heard Niner let out a breath. "RV point," Darman said. "Where are *you*?"

"I'm about five minutes' walk from the Shinarcan Bridge Extension. I can see a big crowd at the shopping plaza gates. Any idea what's happening? Because I have to go through there."

"Wait one," Darman said. He turned to Obrim. "She's coming up to the Shinarcan Bridge. What's the crowd problem?"

Obrim's speeder lit up with a head-up viewscreen display showing CSF control room information. He read it carefully, red and yellow light dancing on his face. "It's a security checkpoint. They're channeling all pedestrian traffic in that area through it. CSF and GAR personnel on duty, just routine, so all she has to do is walk through. It's not like we've got a Jedi detector device or anything."

"Are you getting this, *Et'ika*?"

Niner made his impatient noise, an irritated click of the teeth just like Skirata. "I say we wander down there and just make sure she gets through okay."

"I could do that," Obrim said.

"But you're the head of the Anti-Terrorist Unit," Niner said. "Everyone knows you. It'll raise questions."

"My boys don't ask *questions*. They don't see, hear, or know anything unless it's in our interests for them to do so."

"I meant *us* doing it. I meant the GAR." Niner started the bike's drive. "The good thing about being a clone is that we could be any *one* of us."

"*Et'ika,* we're coming to meet you on the other side of the checkpoint," Darman said. "Slow down. Amble or something."

Skirata's voice cut in to the circuit. Darman didn't think he'd picked them up. "What are you two playing at?"

"*Kal'buir,* we're just seeing Etain through the last barrier."

"Didn't I tell you to get down here? Okay—take it nice and casual."

Niner switched to the private helmet link. "He's going to put his boot up our *shebs* when we get back. We've really ticked him off."

It was a small price to pay. In a matter of minutes, they'd be starting *Aay'han*'s drives, and all the complications would be forgotten. As they dropped down over the bridge, they could see the stream of pedestrians milling around the checkpoint, waiting to pass through, and there was a convenient space among the parked patrol vessels. Niner landed as if it was routine. There were no CSF officers visible, but some 501st troopers with their distinctive blue markings were just standing there watching everyone walk through, looking serious and armed. They didn't seem to be doing any stop-and-search.

Niner and Darman stood looking serious, too, and a DC-17 looked like a lot more firepower than the long rifle of the troopers. And nobody seemed to turn a hair about the bike. They were commandos; the rest of the GAR thought they were eccentric at best, and an undisciplined gang of thugs at worst.

"Here she comes," Niner said.

Darman was twenty meters from Etain now. He looked through the sea of strangers and could see just one being out of all of them—*Et'ika*.

She caught sight of him, and glanced away before she gave in to a smile.

On board *Aay'han*, RV point, 2255 hours

"Enough," said Skirata. "I'm going out to see them in. I can't bear this waiting."

Jusik put on his helmet. "Okay, but I'm going to stay on comms and get the drives on idle. Just in case."

"Ordo's piloting."

"I know, but if for any reason he has to come down here at a run, and we're in a *real* hurry to bang out, I'll be there to get us moving."

Jusik was a great little planner. Skirata patted his shoulder. "Good thinking," he said. "Can I have your lightsaber?"

Jusik paused, but handed it to him. "Don't lose it. And what for?"

"Trophy. To look like I'm there to kill Jedi, not escort one to safety. Sorry, *Bard'ika*. This isn't pretty for any of us."

"Mind your hands, then."

Skirata waggled his fingers. "*Beskar*-impregnated fabric . . ."

"We're coming, too," Corr said. "Sarge, we're big strong lads, and you're not, and if it gets hairy, you'll need backup."

Skirata didn't have time to argue again. "Whatever happened to 'Yes, Sergeant. Right away, Sergeant!'? Okay. Come on."

They had to take Vau's speeder because two commandos and a *Mando* in heavy *beskar'gam* wouldn't fit on a bike, even if they had one handy. As Skirata looked down on the bridge, he could see the pedestrians building up into a huge crowd as the choke point of the security cordon started to build a backlog. They set down between two GAR assault ships. The transport wasn't helping the congestion by taking up so much space on the bridge, but it formed a good defensive barrier.

"Coming through," Atin barked, clearing white-armored troopers out of their way. "Mind yer backs."

A couple of the CSF officers gave Skirata an odd look, but either they knew who he was, and so would say nothing, or they saw the lightsaber hanging prominently from his belt and assumed that he was *Mando* bounty-hunting muscle on hand to tackle Jedi. Anyone who knew about *Mando'ade* knew they could—in theory—tackle Force-users. But most Coruscanti who weren't part of what was known euphemistically as the *enforcement community* or those who serviced them didn't know what they were anyway, and just saw them as quaint offworlders in pretty armor. They'd never seen Mandalorians fighting on their home turf.

Skirata looked toward the cordon. It was a dam waiting to burst.

"You better hope this stays calm and orderly," Skirata said to nobody in particular.

"I see her," Corr said.

"Good. Stay calm, folks. Just let the line work through."

A 501st sergeant walked up to him. "I don't have an identity code for you, sir."

Sir. Skirata shuddered inside. He flipped the lightsaber off his belt and spun it in his fingers.

"Here's all the ID you need, Sergeant. I kill Jedi. We like trophies, we Mandos." Skirata rapped his gauntlet against his chest plate. "They might take *your* head off, son, but I'm wearing *beskar.*"

It seemed to satisfy the man. Skirata stood with his weight firmly planted on both boots, one thumb in his belt, and drew his short-barreled Verpine to rest it against his shoulder in the safety position.

The comlink in his helmet clicked. "You look like a bad boy, *Kal'buir.*"

"Dar, is that you?"

"Copy that."

"Don't do anything dumb, *Dar'ika.* Niner—I don't see you."

"We're both behind you."

"Okay, boys, just relax. *Ord'ika,* are you getting this?"

"Standing by."

Skirata had said *calm* and *relax* so often now that he knew he was the one who needed to listen to his own advice. The crowd was relatively good-humored; they'd heard the news, they could see the flames, and after the thwarted invasion, the combined protective might of CSF and the Grand Army was enjoying some popularity.

A female Biravian paused at the checkpoint to open her bag for inspection. "I hope you get them *all,*" she said to the clone trooper. "No wonder the Seps managed to land here. The Jedi were traitors all along. You're doing a *wonderful* job, trooper."

Skirata thought it was a bit late for civvies to feel warm and cuddly about white jobs, but it was better late than never.

It was all going *calmly.* The chatting from the queuing crowd was a steady, loud hum. Etain was getting near the front of the line. Skirata could see her. Darman could, too. Skirata heard him say, *"Cyar'ika."*

And then—

Three young humans, two males and a female, were slow in opening their bags. The clone trooper held out his hand to take them, the girl paused, and then something fell on the floor—a stack of datapads and . . .

"Jedi!" someone yelled. "They're kriffing *Jedi!*"

And the lightsabers came out, blue and humming. Skirata only saw Etain, and then all *haran* broke loose in the melee.

21

Ca'nara ne gotal'u mirjahaal—shi gotal'u haastal.
Time doesn't heal. It only forms a scab.
—Mandalorian proverb

Etain's instincts had long been honed to seize a lightsaber and snap it into action.

The Masters put her first weapon in her hand at four years of age.

But not tonight; *not now.*

Sudden danger did the same thing for her as it did for the clone troopers, for the CSF cops, for any soldier under fire. Time ceased to run its normal course.

Screams echoed. Bodies jostled. She was back on Qiilura, hiding from Hokan's militia, knowing that her lightsaber would mark her out as a Jedi for slaughter, like her Master, and so she *could not* reveal it.

She stood firm in the panicking crowd, in another and somehow buffered universe, making no attempt to draw her lightsaber, knowing it would seal her fate, and watched— stood back and *watched*—as three Jedi she thought she recognized batted away blaster bolts, scattering bystanders. A man fell, trapped by the crowd that couldn't get away fast enough, hit by a blaster ricochet from the lightsabers.

Nobody could safely use a lightsaber in a crowd. But they were kids, just Padawans, terrified and panicking, fighting

for their lives. Innocent pedestrians—packed too close—
were caught by the flashing, humming blades. More bolts
flew. She ducked. Someone else fell. She didn't see who. A
civilian? A trooper?

It was chaos. She *had* to go. She had to walk away, to get
past that barrier, to get out *now.*

Etain—the Jedi didn't sense her, or maybe there were
other Jedi in the crowd, but from behind, she heard the clatter of boots over the screams as more troopers rushed in, and
she looked up, saw Darman on the other side of the barrier—
so *close,* so *very close* to grabbing freedom with him—and
for a moment, torn by instinct to *do* something instead of
save her own skin, she turned back.

A frozen moment; a clone trooper—a man like Darman—
seemed paralyzed in mid-lunge, but it was just the way time
lied in a crisis.

*They put his first weapon in his hand at four years of age.
Like me. Like Dar.*

The young male Jedi spun and raised his lightsaber to the
clone, desperate to get past him, *through* him. Etain snapped.
Pure reflex, animal and instant: she blocked the Jedi, every
bit as fast and Force-agile as he was. Her hand went for her
weapon, unbidden. Her body took over. *"Don't touch him!"*
She felt it was unraveling in slow motion. "Don't!"

Because she knew what a lightsaber could do, because
she'd killed with one, because the trooper was a *man,* a living breathing *man*—she stepped into the clone's path, and
into the downward arc of a lightsaber.

It might have been meant for her.

It might have been meant for him.

The screams were suddenly a long way away. The pain—
it took moments to register on her brain, but she was now
staring up at a smoke-hazed night sky, and every cell in her
body felt on fire. She saw chaotic lights above her, a white
helmet, the T-shaped visor so familiar and so *loved,* and for a
moment . . . for a moment she thought things were going to
be all right.

"Kad! *Dar!*" But it was not Dar, and the clone couldn't

save her, and Kad was out of reach. She couldn't hear her own cries, but she was sure her lips were moving. The pain—she couldn't breathe.

"Dar!"

And then the pain stopped forever.

22

Skirata took off.

Darman's screaming filled his helmet; or maybe it was his own voice. "Etain! No, no, no, no, *no!* Not my girl! *Not my girl!*"

He was aware of another scuffle starting to his left, but he was *targeting,* and he was *running,* and now he had to kill or be killed, *nothing* in between.

He cannoned into the melee, pushing troopers aside, and swung with a vibrobladed left fist. He knew he'd hit a Jedi. The man staggered, turned, and swept the lightsaber across him, but it skidded off his neck plate. The Jedi hesitated, because *that wasn't supposed to happen.*

Skirata's three-sided knife was in his hand already. He brought it up into the Jedi's chest, under the rib cage, in that fraction of a second's pause. It was hate; it was an explosion of loathing and grief. He wanted to destroy the world and every breathing thing in it that wasn't *his.*

The yelling and screaming was outside his helmet as well as inside. A trooper captain shoved him aside and dropped to his knees beside Etain, hands crossed, flat on her chest, trying to pump. It was Ordo. He tried, he really tried, but she was dead, eyes staring, sliced from shoulder to spine, dead, dead, *dead.*

Skirata's brain shut down. Something else seized control. He drew Jusik's lightsaber, snapped it alive, wading into the crowd in pursuit of another Jedi. They seemed to be every-where. He saw six, seven of those *shabla* blades, those filthy cold things, and he saw nothing else. Jedi were still trapped in the press of bodies. People were being trampled. It was a battlefield; he saw only what he needed to kill. And Jedi needed to die. He got one square in the back, kidney level, and those burning blades worked on a Jedi every bit as well as on a *chakaar* like him. One got away. Skirata swung around to chase.

Darman was still screaming names, but it was Niner now—*Niner, Niner, where are you Niner?*—and that was when Skirata saw that Darman was way back behind, looking down over the edge of the bridge, frantic.

Darman saw the Jedi too late, and Niner hadn't even been trying to stop the kid escaping. The Jedi leapt; Niner fell.

If it had been Darman in his way when the barve tried to jump clear, he would have had a vibroblade in his throat now, killing for killing, death for death, because—even though Darman's brain was saying it *couldn't* have happened, that Etain would be coming through the barrier now because she'd been so close, so *very near,* just a few meters and minutes from putting her hand in his and leaving forever—he'd seen the lightsaber strike.

She's dead. No, she can't be.

Even though he was looking down onto the maintenance walkway below the bridge and could see Niner lying at an awkward angle, his vision was filled with that split second of Etain and the lightsaber.

She's gone, she's gone, she's gone—

It wouldn't stop. But his hard-wired training interrupted him and he swung out from his rappel line, on autopilot, dropping down beside his brother.

"*Shab* . . ."

"Can you move? What hurts?" Darman defaulted to being another Darman, RC-1136, because that was what he did under fire, what Skirata had drummed into him to stay alive. "Atin, down here! Man down! *Atin!* Below the bridge, maintenance parapet!"

"Dar . . . Dar, what's happened to Etain?"

"Can you move?"

"Shut up about *me*." Niner's voice was hoarse, a gasp. "Where's Etain?"

She can't be dead. She can't be. She was right there, right in front of me. "Can you—"

"*Dar!* For *shab*'s sake, what's happened to her?"

"Shut up. Can you move?"

Niner lay at an odd angle, legs bent. "I can't feel my feet. *Shab,* Dar, what's up with you? *Etain!* The *shabla* Jedi hit her. What happened? Is she okay?"

"She's dead. She's *dead*." Darman said it, heard it, and hated himself. He'd said it; he'd made it real. How could he be here? How could he be moving, talking, dealing with Niner? Why wasn't he *doing* something about Etain? He didn't know *what*. "It's over. Nothing matters."

"What about Kad? What about your kid? *Go!* Go to him!"

How do I tell him I couldn't save his mother?

"It's my fault." A minute ago, maybe two, Etain had been alive and now she wasn't. It was such a fine, cruel, implacable line. It seemed impossible that he couldn't push it back. He couldn't believe she wasn't there anymore, and that nothing he could do would ever change that. "I should have done this different."

The if-only started right away—if only she hadn't gone to Kashyyyk, if only she'd gone straight to Mandalore, if only she'd told him sooner—and he slapped it down almost before he dared think about it. Another Darman took over. It was the Darman who had been drilled and drilled and *drilled* to keep his head when the very worst happened, to evaluate, and to save who was savable.

There was only one way he was going to get through even the next few minutes, let alone a day or the rest of his life. *Niner.* He couldn't think beyond that. He couldn't even begin to think straight. His hands and eyes were going through the numb motions of checking his brother. The world had ended for him, but he was still moving like a decapitated animal. Something warned him that he'd have to wake up after this crisis was over and live with the reality of life without Etain.

"Dar, run," Niner said. "Get out now. *Kal'buir*'s ready to go. *Run.*"

Darman flashed the priority override in his HUD. He cut across all local comm circuits within his unencrypted frequency range. "We need a casevac right now, people—spinal trauma, bridge parapet—look for the kriffing rappel line, I've got my spot-lamp on. *Medic!*"

"Look, get out now. Get to the RV point. Leave me."

"I'm *not* leaving you. They'll do to you what they did to Fi."

"She's dead. They *killed* her. Kad needs you."

"I know, *I know,* shut up—"

"If you don't get out now, Dar, you'll be stuck here."

Darman could hear Atin yelling over the edge of the bridge. It was all in their helmets, no external sound, and inside the confines of his bucket, Darman was on a screaming, shouting, confused battlefield.

"Dar! Can you move him? Can you get Niner moving? We've got to get out—now."

"He's broken his spine. I can't."

"*Shab. Shab.* Wait one—"

Kad was his son, all he'd ever have left of Etain. Kad had everyone to look after him; Niner would have nobody if Darman left him now. They'd pulled the plug on Fi when he was hurt, but he didn't die. He lived because Besany wouldn't abandon him to callous scum who saw him as nothing more than a flesh machine. If Darman left Niner this badly hurt, maybe beyond recovery, he'd be leaving him to that fate. He couldn't go.

Kad's okay. Kal'buir's *got him. He'll be safe. Niner won't.*

"Get out, *At'ika.* We'll work out a way to get home when Niner's okay again."

"*Dar!* You're crazy. You can't stay. Niner can't stay."

"Can't move him. Three-six out." Darman cut the comms. He hadn't signed off as Three-six for years. It was his autopilot speaking for him. He could see his call for a medic had been heard, because a LAAT/i gunship was hovering, edging closer, and he could see a clone trooper in the doorway, in the open hatch, getting ready to jump across and give Niner the help he needed. It had always been such a reassuring sight. Now it was also the end of his brief, fragile, shattered, not-meant-to-be dream of family.

Darman had his hand under Niner's head. "You'll be okay, *Ner'ika*," he said. "Look what they did for Corr."

"You *shabuir*," Niner hissed. "Don't you *shabla* well stay with me. Go with Kad. You can't leave him."

"And I can't leave *you*," Darman said, his heart not just broken but utterly destroyed forever. How could he feel so much pain twice? The LAAT/i medic thudded onto the per-macrete beside them and started putting a brace on Niner's neck, immobilizing his spine. The man had no idea what was going on; he couldn't possibly have known they were talking about desertion. "Kad's fine. You'll be fine. One day—we'll all be fine. I can't leave you. You never left me. You came for me on Qiilura. You didn't even know me then."

Niner could still move his arms. He hit Darman hard in the chest. "Go. *Get out.* I don't need you."

Darman watched the medic assembling a metal tubular gurney under Niner and strapping him to it. "Hey, careful with him."

"Get the *shab* out, Dar. You can't leave that kid. What kind of a father are you? What would Etain say if—"

"Don't you dare use her name like that," Darman snarled. He almost lashed out but managed to pull up short. He knew his sanity was temporary, and once the pressure was off and Niner was in the medcenter, he'd fall apart.

That couldn't happen. He had to hold it together. He had to plan. He didn't know what, but he had to have a plan.

"Shabuir," Niner said quietly. "You stupid, stupid *shabuir.* I'm not worth this."

"Too late," Darman said. "It's over. It's all over. But no-body's going to pull the plug on *you*."

"Don't worry," the medic said, almost as if he'd heard him. "Your buddy's going to be fine."

They always said that.

Darman could still see Etain and the lightsaber like a freeze-frame in his HUD when the holoimage emitter had gone haywire. He let it stay, switched off all comms, and screamed Etain's name over and over in his silenced private purgatory until he couldn't scream anymore.

Ordo dragged Atin back from the edge of the bridge by his shoulder.

"He's cut me off," Atin yelled. "He's cut his comm."

There was nothing they could do to extract Niner at that point, unless they wanted to kill him. Could they wait? Did they dare hang about after this night? The LAAT/i lifted into the air, and the last thing Ordo saw was Darman staring out from the open hatch, just a blue-lit T-visor in the darkness, and then he was gone.

Kal'buir was frantic. Corr had him by the arm, almost twisting it up his back, trying to calm him down. It was all silent; the drama was entirely on private comm circuits within the confines of their helmets, and all that onlookers could see of the unfolding private agony was gestures that made no sense, exchanged between a bunch of clones and a kill-crazy *Mando.*

Ordo's chest felt crushed with pain for him, and for Etain, and Darman, and Niner. Like *Kal'buir,* he wanted to destroy everything in his path to stop the agony. But he couldn't, because Skirata needed him to keep his head and get them out.

Jaller Obrim sprinted across the bridge, now a scene of bedlam. There were civilian medics tending to people who'd been crushed in the stampede, hit by deflected bolts, and even clipped by lightsabers. HNE news droids were arriving. Having their images all over the news was the very last thing Skirata's team needed.

"Ordo, you've got to go, *now.*" Obrim stopped to bark at two cops who were trying to move Etain's body. Her face was covered with a CSF jacket. "Hey, you two! *No! Did* I tell you to move her? *I did not!* Leave that body. *Leave it!*" He swung back to Ordo. "Get Kal away from here now. It won't take long for these wooden-tops here to find out she's a Jedi, and then you're all in really deep dwang. I'll keep an eye out for Dar and Niner, but you *have to go.*"

She's a Jedi. Was; she was *gone.* A few minutes, even a second, and she was alive but only in a slip of the tongue.

Skirata managed to pull off his helmet, revealing a face utterly white, all rage, a man you would never want to meet, let alone cross. "Not without Dar and Niner. And not without Etain, *not* without my girl."

"Your cover's as good as blown, Kal—I won't be able to keep them off your back unless you get out now." Obrim shoved him. "Please, buddy, do it for me."

Skirata was proving too much for Corr to subdue. When he was enraged, he was simply an animal, with all the strength and fury that went with it. "I'm not leaving without my boys."

"You *will.*"

"I will *not,* you *shabla* will let me go and I'll get them—"

"Sorry, old friend," Obrim said, "but it has to be this way." He took out a small pistol, pressed it to Skirata's neck, and fired. Skirata dropped like a stone; Corr took his weight. Obrim switched into an obvious show to throw any onlookers off the scent, just a cop yelling at *Mando* heavies who'd got out of hand on his turf. "Get that kriffing crazy *Mando* out of my face, and move that body."

"Yes, Captain," Ordo said. "Stay with the body until A'den comes." He signaled on his link; A'den was cruising around now with Ny Vollen in her transport, looking for stragglers, and they could pick up Etain. "A'den, you getting this? Obrim's going to guard Etain. Get over here now."

Obrim looked down at Corr and the crumpled Skirata. "Tell him I'm sorry I had to do that. Tell him I'll do whatever I can to see Dar and Niner are okay. Now go, and look after yourselves."

"Thank you, Jaller."

"The honor's mine, Ordo." The CSF captain's face was stricken. "And I'm so sorry about Etain."

Ordo put *Kal'buir*'s right arm over his shoulder, and Corr took his left. They bundled him into the speeder with Atin, and then lifted clear in what should have been a moment of relief, of triumph, but that was simply black desolation.

Ordo understood vengeance better than anyone, but there was nobody alive now to take it out on. Some Jedi, though . . . some might have made it.

He'd know what to do when he met them.

23

It's entirely possible that the Jedi's increasingly clouded
vision was the result of their own moral degeneration.
They'd let so many of their principles slip that the reason
they couldn't see the dark side was so close to them was the
lack of sharp contrast with themselves, like trying to see a
gray nerf in fog. They turned off the light themselves.
—Bardan Jusik, former Jedi Knight

Kyrimorut, Mandalore, 1,090 days ABG

It had been the worst night of Fi's life, and he'd had an awful
lot of bad nights in a short career.

But he couldn't imagine what it had done to Skirata—or
Niner, or Dar. As soon as *Aay'han* settled on her dampers, Fi
heard the sound of boots on the hull, and both the top and
port-side cargo hatches popped open from outside.

Mereel jumped down from the top hatch like a medic
hauling casualties from a larty, but even he froze as soon as
he looked around. The sense of defeat that hung in the air
was almost solid enough to bail out like water.

Nobody said anything for a few moments. Then Laseema
stood and scooped up Kad—still awake, still craning his neck
and gazing around as if he was looking for something—
and stepped out through the cargo hatch. Besany got up and
took Kal's left hand.

"Come on, *Kal'buir*." She glanced over her shoulder, then
gestured to the rest of them with her free hand. "Everyone,
into the house. I know none of us feels like it, but the first

thing we do is get a meal inside us, and then try to get some sleep. We won't get far without that."

It was an order, however gently spoken. The females were taking command now, as if this was the second phase of a battle. It was; and it would be far harder than the first. Fi waited for Atin, Corr, Ordo, Vau, and Jusik to exit. Jilka sat with her hands in her lap, staring at Skirata as if she didn't know what came next. But Mird nudged her with its nose, then caught her sleeve carefully between teeth that could crush cranial bone, and led her out. The strill was even more intelligent than Fi had thought. It was *diplomatic*.

"It's okay, Fi, I'll see to Kal," Besany said. "Parja's going to be waiting. Go greet your wife. We'll be along shortly."

Fi didn't expect it to be daylight outside, let alone a sunny afternoon. A thick carpet of snow made the light painfully bright. It was all wrong; it should have been night, and terrible weather, because this was only going to taint all sunny days for him from now on. He stood on the hatch coaming and watched Parja checking the landing gear with stress sensors, giving the huge damper pistons sharp blows with a hydrospanner and listening carefully each time.

"Hi, *cyar'ika*," she said, holding out an oil-smeared hand to him. She didn't have to ask how he was, because she knew. "As soon as everyone's disembarked, we'll roll *Aay'han* into the hangar. I missed you. Welcome home."

His mouth worked, eventually. It wasn't the aftermath of his injuries this time. It was just the enormity of events that he would never have found words for even when he was at his peak.

"You heard what happened."

"Yeah," Parja said. She put her arms around him, and they stood there for a while. "I heard."

It was amazing how silent a place could be even with more than twenty people wandering around in it. Laseema had instantly become some kind of loadmaster, directing operations and assigning rooms with Rav Bralor. Even Jilka, who had no reason to feel positive about this anarchic Mandalorian gang—Fi accepted that was what they were, and felt no shame—was in the kitchen when he walked through it. She was organizing meals with Ruu, as if her own expectation of a relatively peaceful life hadn't just been utterly destroyed out of the blue because she was in the wrong place at the wrong time. Everyone had fallen into a role in an unspoken duty roster, except him. Or at least he thought that until he saw Jusik and Ordo standing in the passageway to the armory, looking way beyond lost. They were both tough men in their individual ways. Now they didn't seem sure what came next.

It was fatigue. When the plug was pulled after a heavy engagement, the sense of hitting a wall was almost unbearable. Fi had been there too often. But a night's sleep, or even a week's, wasn't going to fix what was wrong this time.

"Parja needs to move the ship under cover," Fi said. "Give us a hand, will you?"

Standing around and dwelling on loss didn't help. Fi believed in exhausting himself with frantic activity until his body gave in and sleep like unconsciousness overwhelmed him, and when he woke up he would do it again, and again, until—eventually—things settled down to a tolerable level. He'd coped with losing his first squad that way. He could do it again.

"Yeah, better cover our tracks." Ordo strode out, upright and alert again as if someone had thrown a switch. "What's the Met forecast? Some more snow would be handy to cover the footprints and churning."

Skirata and Besany weren't in *Aay'han* when Fi went outside again. Parja had one of the inspection plates hanging open on the underside of the hull, working on something. She gestured out into the snow. Two figures sat huddled on the highest of four time-polished chunks of granite that jutted up through the soil. "He wanted to wait for A'den. *Bes'ika*'s keeping an eye on him."

Ordo checked the sensors on his forearm plate with a conspicuous flourish. "It's minus eight out here. They'll be hypothermic if they're not careful." He walked toward them, picking an irregular path as if he was stepping on stones, still a commando trying to disguise his presence. Some conversation appeared to take place. Then he walked back again.

"Besany says they're fine," Ordo said. "She'll make him put his helmet on and seal his suit."

Vau wandered out to join the inspection. "He'll go like Jango." Mird tiptoed around them, leaving remarkably misleading footprints. "The first bereavement knocks the guts out of him, and then the next one turns him into something frightening, and all the anger gets swallowed and recycled into long-term retribution. But don't worry. It kept Jango going on a slave ship all those years, and it'll keep Kal alive, too. It's a *Mando* thing—long memory, short fuse, big revenge."

Fi was still coming to terms with the Mandalorian psyche, the contrast between not caring what someone did before they joined, and yet clinging to ancient pasts and feuds. It was in him, too. He was only just starting to find it.

Ordo started up *Aay'han*'s drives and nosed her down into the hangar concealed in the shallow slope to the north of the house, with Fi and Vau playing aircraft directors. With the associated chores of swabbing down the compartments, replenishing stores, and prepping the ship for the next flight, the five of them—Mird insisted on helping—managed to occupy a big chunk of the afternoon.

"Who's going to break the news to Uthan?" Vau asked as they sat on upturned crates in the hangar. "She thinks she's in a safe house awaiting transfer to some nice Sep facility."

"Let her think that," Ordo said. "Until *Kal'buir* decides it's time."

Mird went snuffling around the hangar. Fi found that the strill didn't smell so pungent to him now, maybe because he'd grown used to the animal's strong scent. Then it threw up its big, slobbery head and looked toward the hangar doors with a fixed gold stare, whining. A few moments later, Fi heard the faint *aka-aka-aka* noise of a vessel's drive as it lost height overhead. They went outside to face a sun sitting low on the horizon in a blinding ball of amber, and saw a rusty freighter coming in to land.

"Honor guard," Vau said sharply. "Turn to."

Skirata and Besany were already at the ramp when A'den stepped out of the hatchway. Fi, Ordo, Vau, and Jusik took up position almost without thinking, standing to attention in line with the ramp. They weren't alone in their reaction. From the front doors of the bastion, Bralor, Tay'haai, Gilamar, and the rest of Skirata's clan trooped out and arranged themselves silently so that there were now two ranks facing each other.

"Apologies, *Kal'buir,*" A'den said. "Ny had some stragglers to collect." He waved someone out of the hatch. It was a commando squad, four weary-looking clones minus helmets, but still in dazzle-camo Katarn body armor.

"Wayii!" Bralor said. "Cov?"

"Yayax Squad reporting, ma'am." Cov saluted, puffing clouds into the freezing air. "I can't believe we're doing this."

"Fall in, *ad'ike,*" she said. "*Olarom.* Welcome home."

Ny Vollen stood on the top of the ramp, looking down at Skirata. "Hi, old man," she said softly.

Skirata nodded in acknowledgment. "Thanks for bringing her home."

"I'm so sorry."

"I'm sorry about your husband, too."

"Yeah. Maybe it was better not to know the details." She looked down at her hands for a second. So A'den had found out how her husband had died. "But at least it stops me imagining something even worse."

Skirata nodded. "That's the truth."

"You ready? I've got a repulsor trolley."

Skirata put a boot on the ramp. "No. Too cold. Too *freight.*" He disappeared into the ship, and came out carrying a small body in his arms, wrapped in a blanket, head covered, as if he was just making sure she didn't get too cold. "At least you're home, *Et'ika.* Kad's waiting."

Fi heard the faint, ragged intake of breath.

Everyone—man or woman, soldier or civilian—drew that same breath that he did, as if they'd been punched in the chest. Skirata walked between the two lines and paused.

"*Bard'ika,* it's cremation for a Jedi Knight, yes?"

"It is, *Kal'buir.*"

"Tomorrow, then—a final night in her own home with her

family around her, and then she goes to the Force, or the *manda,* or wherever, like the Jedi she was."

Normally, *Kal'buir* used the word as an insult. It was clear now that *Jedi* could mean something totally different to him. Fi wondered who would crack first, and he wasn't as surprised as he thought he would be when it turned out to be Ordo. He thought the stifled sob was his own for a moment, until he saw Ordo put the back of his gauntlet to his mouth for a count of two, and then recover and stand to attention again.

"Shab," Vau said. "Kal's building up some steam for a real good hate, now. Enough to last for generations."

Skirata disappeared through the doors of the bastion, and the impromptu honor guard fell out. Fi found Parja's hand somehow, not even realizing she'd been next to him, and braced for a long, hard evening.

Kyrimorut bastion, later that day

The dining table at Kyrimorut was, as Gilamar said, the kind you could use as an operating table if you ever had to.

It was cut from a single plank of ancient veshok, a native hardwood that covered much of Mandalore's northern hemisphere almost as far as the polar ice caps. Jusik felt it was a table for life events, huge rambling discussions, and somehow also for dismantling engines. He sat between Mereel and Jaing, while Skirata took a seat at the head of the table in true patriarchal style, more to be heard than to hold court, Jusik suspected.

"You heard the ladies," Skirata said, face still gray and drained. *"Haili cetare.* Fill yer boots. Tuck in."

Enlightened Coruscant society would have tutted at the traditionalist view that the females of the household were valued for their cooking skills, but Jusik was getting used to a subtler *Mando* take on that. The whole clan—even if Jusik couldn't define it, he knew the *feeling* of clan—was a fighting unit. Those who weren't on the front line as teeth were the essential tail, and many happened to be female. Sometimes women fought alongside the men, as Bralor did, and sometimes they didn't. But those who didn't still had a job to do—keeping warriors fed and supplied, and the base or homestead defended. One couldn't operate without the other. And at this moment of crisis for the Skirata clan, the females had taken over and made sure that the front line was fed and rested. There was no weeping into shimmersilk handkerchiefs and waiting by the door. There was just an efficient, robust logistics operation that would still be there when the Nine Hells of Corellia were dust.

Etain was . . .

Etain was *dead*. Jusik said it to himself every few minutes, because he looked at live friends, loved friends, and couldn't reconcile the two states.

Laseema said that Kad had screamed inconsolably for a full five minutes at the moment his mother had died, then had calmed down and regarded the world with grave eyes and contemplation more like an adult's.

He was now eating pureed kaneta with a spoon all on his own, although a lot of it was ending up on the table. He seemed suddenly sober, like a little old man rather than a baby. Something had changed in him. Skirata kept him at his side in an elevated chair, pausing between mouthfuls to help Kad eat and wiping his mouth. Skirata had all the hallmarks of a man who knew his way around raising small kids, and who regarded it as respectable work for a warrior. Jusik imagined him coping with a company of small commandos-to-be.

But Jusik was now wholly responsible for Kad's care in an area that even Skirata's unerring paternal instinct couldn't handle. The child was Force-sensitive, and living in a new era when that probably meant a death warrant. Jusik reached out in the Force and gently touched Kad's awareness. The baby stopped smacking his spoon on the kaneta puree, and turned slowly to stare at Jusik.

You're doing fine, Kad'ika. This is a game that only we can play, and only with our clan around. Jusik visualized the thick, safe walls of the bastion, and gave Kad a clear sensation of being protected within them, but not beyond. He gave him an impression as best he could without words. *It's special. It's not for outsiders. Mama wanted you to be safe from bad people.*

Jusik didn't want to make the baby paranoid, but it wasn't being taken by Jedi Masters that he needed to fear now. It was a Sith who killed Jedi, and would want to control any Force-users he came across. Palpatine knew Skirata had something that he wanted already. Jusik didn't want to give him an extra reason to hunt for Kyrimorut.

"Does my Force-using at the table bother anyone?" Jusik asked. They could see Kad's reaction and work it out. Jusik Force-pushed a bowl of *tiingilar* across the table to Laseema. It was a blisteringly spicy meat-and-vegetable casserole, which had the prized characteristic of *hetikles,* pungent enough to burn the nasal passages, one of the four qualities in *Mando* cooking. "Just teaching Kad some Force-using etiquette."

Corr looked to Fi as if to work out whose turn it was with the wisecracks, or if they were even acceptable right now. Fi nodded.

"Well," Corr said, "officers' mess rules say you shouldn't use the Force until *after* the Bespin port is served, but we're very *relaxed* here."

Jusik wanted to laugh, but it felt wrong and so close to tears he didn't risk opening his mouth. Etain's body was lying in a room next door; and here they were enjoying a meal. But if there was anything that would have gladdened her heart, it would have been seeing Corr transformed from indoctrinated, cloistered slave to a man who was wringing every drop of joy and sensation out of newfound freedom. He seemed to get a faint smile out of poor Jilka and a very bemused-looking Ruu Skirata.

What a time to be reunited with your estranged dad . . .

"*Bard'ika,*" Skirata said suddenly, "what happens to Jedi when they become *one with the Force*? That's the phrase, isn't it?"

It was the hardest question of all; but Jusik didn't realize how much harder it could get until now. "We don't really know," he said. "But I truly believe some Jedi Masters can come back as ghosts in the Force, to interact with the living. Not everyone believes the ancient accounts, and thinks they're a myth—but I think it's real."

The whole table went silent; no chewing, no slurping, no scraping of metal on porceplast. Jusik looked around the faces, clone and nonclone, and felt the shock.

How *could* he have failed to understand the impact that revelation would have on them so soon after losing Etain? And now that they thought there was a possibility of existence after death for Jedi, it had made them all feel . . . excluded. Ordinary beings had no such hope. Jusik wondered whether to emphasize the uncertainty of it, but that would have been a lie. He believed it, and he'd heard convincing cases. So he didn't. He traded off truth and the possible comfort of Etain's consciousness not being completely obliterated against the resentment he might come to face about a Jedi privilege that any bereaved being would envy bitterly.

Jusik squirmed. He tried not to think where it would leave him after his death if he were right about the ghosts.

"Well, I never," Skirata said, bringing him back to the here and now. Jusik wasn't sure if it was sarcasm or weary resignation. "Fancy that."

Jusik had to confront it. Ordo's stare was burning a hole in him. "If you're asking if Etain exists fully in another plane like that, or if anyone else does but can't return, I have absolutely no idea. I wish I did."

Of course it was what they were all wondering. How could it *not* be? Mandalorians had a vague concept of *manda,* but it was very much rooted in the all-embracing continuation of the living culture rather than a literal afterlife.

"It's okay," Skirata said, sounding tired. Kad offered him a sloppy spoonful of vegetables and he took it. "Don't be afraid to say it—dead, death, the dead. It isn't going to go away, and if we don't face it, we'll just make it bigger than it really is. Can't live without death, can't die without life."

He went on eating, head down. Ordo leaned back in his seat to reach for a bottle of *tihaar* spirit and poured a small glass for his father, but Ruu took it carefully from his hand. There was a tense moment as their gazes locked, and she got up to walk to the head of the table and place it in front of *Kal'buir.*

"Thanks, *ad'ika,*" he said. "It's good to have you back again."

Skirata looked as if he was going to weep. The mood around the table stood balanced—as it would for weeks, months, and maybe even years to come—on a knife-edge between crying and laughing.

"Kal, you'll go over it in your head a thousand times," Ny said. She seemed to be able to read Skirata as if she'd known him all her life. "Over and over. I've *done* it. But remember that Etain only died once, and then it was *over.*"

On first take, it sounded harsh, if brutally true; but Jusik recognized the wisdom and comfort in that observation, and actually felt some beginnings of peace. Nobody died as often or as painfully as the living left behind, who kept reliving the moment of death, and speculating on it. There was no end to their dying once they let it drive out everything else. The loved one whose end they repeatedly tried to endure and imagine was now beyond pain. Skirata seemed to chew it over, then gave Ny a sad smile.

"You've got a point there, freight jockey," he said. She seemed to have given him a reserve tank of emotional oxygen to get him out of a suffocating spot. "I should know that by now." He drew himself up with a little cough that got everyone's attention as surely as bringing his fist down on the table. "You want me to make the right kind of speech? We don't need speeches in this *aliit.* We just need reminding. The one thing Etain wanted was for Dar and the clones she cared so much about to have a full life. We've got to grieve, or else we've not loved her enough, but there'll come a stage when the grieving would hurt her, and she'd want to see you all getting pleasure out of every day and every moment, all the little things you thought you'd never have. Relishing life is the best way any of you can make sure she didn't die for nothing. She'll never see her kid grow up. *You* will see it for her. And Dar and Niner *will* be coming home."

"*Oya,*" Prudii said, tilting a small glass of *tihaar.* "*K'oya-cyi.*"

Ordo held a glass only for appearances' sake. "To Etain," he said. "To bringing Dar and Niner home. To getting our life spans back. To seeing Kad grow up as one of *many* of our children. To never being at the mercy of the *aruetiise* again, and to gratitude for the few good ones, like Jaller Obrim and CSF."

"*Oya.*"

"*K'oyacyi.*"

"*Oya manda.*"

Mandalorian sensibilities revolved around those words, all of them from the same root, the word for *life,* and the urge to live it while it remained. Jusik felt embarrassed about his certain and privileged ticket to the hereafter. The meal went on for hours, breaking up into small conversations as if nobody wanted to be the first to face sleep, or to leave Skirata on his own. When his turn came to clear plates, Jusik found Ny in the kitchen, feeding Mird scraps.

"He's an ugly barve," she said. "But he's adorable."

"*It,*" Jusik said. The strill grumbled with delight, happily crunching bones. "Mird's neither, or both, depending on how you look at it. Mind what you feed it, or Vau will fret."

"I meant Skirata."

Jusik almost blushed. "Yeah, I suspected A'den was *engineering* something there . . ." He looked for bashfulness, but Ny didn't flicker. She was still grieving herself. "His sons want him to be happy. He's poured years into them, every drop of sweat. This has just gutted him, the poor old *shabuir.*"

Ny cocked her head to mimic Mird's mute appeal for more tidbits. She gave in fast. The strill had her well trained now. "I got to know Mandos pretty well doing this job," she said. "Okay, you don't want to cross them or fight them, but they're hospitable, and they love their families. But that in there tonight—for all the grief, there's so much love that you could saw a chunk out of it and build a kriffing house. It's a magical thing."

Yes, it was. It had drawn Jusik, and Besany, and Etain, and Etain had paid for it with her life.

But life went on, because it had to. And Kad was living proof.

Besany had no choice but to sleep. Her body demanded it. She thought she would never sleep again for the turmoil in her mind, but her face touched the hard pillow and she fell unprotesting into a black void.

A child's crying woke her.

She opened her eyes, and for a moment she was aware only of straining to hear. It was a thin, distant sound. Then she remembered—Etain dead, Darman and Niner marooned—and she had to put her hand to her mouth to stifle the sob. She was lying on top of the covers, still dressed; the light was still on. Ordo lay curled in a ball, head buried under the blankets as usual.

But it wasn't a baby. It wasn't Kad.

The crying sounded like an older child. Besany slid off the bed, pulled on her boots, and crept out into the passage, picking her way carefully in the darkness. The place smelled of newness, fresh plaster and paint. It was the kind of smell that went with a fresh start and hope for the future, not grief and terrible, unerasable endings.

She couldn't make out where the sound was coming from, and stood still for a moment to try to identify the direction. Was she dreaming? It was faint, and if she could hear it, then others surely could. But as she crept past the various rooms, all the doors were closed, and no light showed. The quiet here, the complete absence of any sound of urban or even village life, was eerie.

The kitchen was deserted. In the chair by the fireplace, a blanket lay crumpled, and the fire looked in need of a few more logs. Skirata's refusal to sleep in a bed was a touchstone, a habit that had grown into a ritual to remind him of all the things he had to put on hold while he made the world right for his boys; if they were deprived, so would he be, too. He seemed to be afraid that if he changed that ritual, he would lose his resolve. Skirata wasn't a superstitious man. But it showed how much the years had ground him down, that he would cling to a daily ritual for strength and focus like a sports player.

The doors leading onto the storage area were closed.

The sound was coming from in there. No, it wasn't Kad.

Besany stood for a moment, almost afraid to enter because she had no idea what she might find. She pressed the controls, and the doors parted silently.

"Kal?" she said.

Skirata was sitting on a crate with his arms folded and his head almost touching his knees. He was weeping like a child crying itself to sleep, stifled sobs punctuating great rattling breaths. It took him awhile to control it long enough to reply.

"Just letting it out," he said at last. "I didn't want to wake anyone."

"Mij left some relaxants. Might be a good idea to take some."

"I've still got to wake up sometime and face it, *Bes'ika*." Skirata stood up. He was always unashamed of his emotions, and Besany found that admirable. "I've got work to do. Lots."

"The . . . cremation. I can do that. Ordo and I can do that."

"Thanks, *ad'ika*. You're a good girl. I've made a mess of your life, haven't I?"

"We all came along willingly for the ride," she said. "Except Jilka and Ruu."

"I'm just shaping up to show Kad his mama's body in the morning. It has to be done."

Besany recoiled. Maybe it was a Mandalorian custom, but it seemed brutal. On the other hand, if the child didn't see Etain, he might regret it later. Mothers were very absent in this clan at the best of times—Skirata never mentioned his, birth or adoptive, and Besany barely thought of hers. It was a world of fathers.

"You need to start leaning on people for support, Kal, or you won't make it," she said. "It's only been a *day*."

"What about Dar? What's that boy going through right now? He needs his family with him. And he's stuck in some trash pit of a GAR barracks right now, if he's lucky, maybe not even with Niner because the lad's in a medbay if he's still alive. We can't even comm them yet, or Jaller. I let all of them down. None of it needed to go that badly wrong."

"Dar made a choice, Kal. A brave one. He really is a grown man. We *all* made choices."

Skirata seemed to be back together again now. He settled down in the kitchen chair and submitted to having her pull the blanket over him. It still surprised her how *Mando'ade* could sleep in armor. She had that education to come.

Niner; maybe that's who I pity most right now. And I know he's alive.

Poor Niner, lonely and serious, trying to play the father to his squad like Skirata had been to him, was probably in torment now for making Darman stay. Besany wasn't sure if Vau had the best of it. He saw his father as a monster, an example to be avoided, while all those who saw Kal Skirata as a paragon of fatherhood were doomed to fall short in emulating him, and berate themselves for it.

Ordo had shifted position when she got back to the room. He'd let the blanket slip down to chin level, and she spent a few minutes propped on one arm beside him, watching. He was starting to go gray at the temples; she hadn't noticed that before. Sometimes—rarely, but sometimes—she forgot how unfairly fast time was passing for him.

"K'oyacyi," she said, and kissed him good night.

24

Gar taldin ni jaonyc; gar sa buir, ori'wadaasla.
*Nobody cares who your father was,
only the father you'll be.*
—Mandalorian saying

Kyrimorut, dawn, next day, 1,091 days ABG

"Is it going to burn properly?" Kom'rk asked. "Do you want some accelerant on the pyre?"

Ordo thought that was a good idea, and wondered how it could be done discreetly. He realized yet again that he lacked some awareness that most human beings had—social blind spots—and knew he didn't react quite the same way as others, so, as long as they were beings whose feelings he cared about, he took care to note what might offend them. Etain's cremation was a ritual, something to soothe the onlooker, not a disposal to be carried out with maximum efficiency.

"If it's subtle," Ordo said carefully. Some pit tar underneath the branches might do the trick; nothing obtrusive, just enough to make the wood burn hotter. "Yes, some tar."

"*Ord'ika*, have you seen any HNE bulletins today?"

"No."

"Palpatine's dissolved the Republic—it's the Empire now, and he's declared himself Emperor."

"How modest."

"I have to wonder where that leaves our brothers still on Coruscant."

"Does it make any difference?"

"Yes." Kom'rk took out his datapad. "Look. I know why we can't get comms."

The small screen showed a portal that Ordo didn't recognize. It should have been the GAR mainframe, which they'd been able to access legitimately—and slice illicitly—up until a couple of days ago. Now it looked very different, with an Imperial symbol and a different interface. Ordo activated a bogus terminal location on Kom'rk's 'pad to disguise the access attempt and began keying his way in.

But he couldn't.

"Shab," he said.

"They've completely overhauled the system overnight, *Ord'ika.*" Kom'rk took back the 'pad. "Data, comms, everything. We can't get in. We can't take stuff out. We can't talk or listen at will. We can't spy."

It was the first time Ordo could recall when he and his brothers had not been able to get at anything they wanted. Nothing had been closed to them; they'd even hacked the Tipoca mainframe as children. The Imperial networks, though, were slammed in their faces. All of them.

"It's more an annoyance," Ordo said at last. The mist that had hung over the quiet white landscape was lifting. It was going to be a sharp, clear day for the funeral. "None of this is beyond you or me to bypass, and Mereel or Jaing can crack this over a cup of caf."

"I'm sure we can, but we're starting over. The whole system's changed. We've been used to being on the inside, exploiting opportunities, but if we want to keep that level of access, we're going to have to start working harder."

"Apart from extracting our brothers, why is this urgent?"

Kom'rk shrugged. "Just in case."

And we hate being shut out. Ordo and his brothers were used to being in control. "We still can't comm Darman or Niner, then?"

"No, and we can't even get a medical sitrep on Niner. Or find out where Darman is. Because it's the Imperial Army now. There *is* no SO Brigade, or Republic command."

"Then we start over. But first things first. You get the tar for the pyre, and I'll see how *Kal'buir* is."

Ordo crunched back through the snow, forgetting his boot prints for the moment. They hadn't tried to contact Darman because they'd been in hyperspace transit, and when they landed they'd been busy licking their emotional wounds. And then—the window of opportunity had closed, at least temporarily. Ordo knew that *Kal'buir* would be upset by that, and that in turn upset him. He'd delay the discussion until after the funeral.

We all decide what those we love should know and not know, and think we're being kind. Isn't this where it all started?

He found Skirata in the room where Etain's body had been laid out. She looked fine. It was an odd thing to say, but she looked at rest, and that upset Ordo because he knew how her life had ended, and that it hadn't been peaceful at all. He could never trust his eyes again to tell him how things had really been. And it wasn't as if he'd led a sheltered life when it came to death and violence.

"Ready, son?"

Skirata held Kad in his arms. The child was gazing at the body, looking not distressed but puzzled. He stretched out a hand, and Skirata dipped a little to let him touch Etain's hair. Bralor had done a tidy job of making her look her best. Kad gripped a lock of hair and seemed reluctant to let go.

"*Ord'ika,* clip a piece of her hair, would you?" Skirata said. "And his. He'll need something of her in years to come. Did you see where her bag went? She had a bag."

Ordo lifted the battered brown fabric sack and looked inside. "Two lightsabers, data and comm kit, and a toy." He checked the datapad and comlink. "No datachips in these . . . no, nothing else in the bag. You want the toy?"

It was the toy that seemed to finish Skirata off. He handed Kad to Ordo in compete silence and walked out, returning a few moments later looking shaken.

"I'm sorted now," he said. "Is everyone ready?"

"Yes."

"Let's do it, then."

This time, Skirata used a repulsor trolley to move Etain's body. It probably felt one step too far to carry her as if she were still alive and then lay her on the pyre. She was now the deceased, and some distance had to be created. Skirata picked up the toy nerf from the bag, and Kad held out his hand for it. He clutched it to him when Skirata passed him to Laseema. Jusik took the lightsabers before Skirata could put them on the pyre. *Kal'buir* wanted to get rid of them, but he'd regret it later, Ordo knew.

"They won't burn completely," Jusik said. "Besides, they both meant a lot to her for various reasons."

"Okay," Skirata said. In the few awful moments between looking at her for the last time and setting fire to the wood, Kad grizzled and squirmed in Laseema's arms, holding out the nerf.

"He wants to give it to her," Laseema said. "He does that. He hands you things. Come on, then, sweetie."

She moved close enough for him to drop the toy next to Etain. Skirata muttered something that Ordo didn't hear because he had his head lowered, but he lifted it again and simply went to the pyre to strike a spark from the metal firestarter that he kept in his belt. The sparks took immediately. Flames began licking the branches, leaping higher until they were level with the body.

"Nu kyr'adyc, shi taab'echaaj'la," he said. Not gone, merely marching far away. It was what *Mando* warriors said of fallen comrades. They were never gone; as long as someone repeated their names daily, and talked about them and the fine times they had, then they *lived*.

Ordo didn't even have to ask. *Kal'buir* had already added Etain's name to the memorial list he whispered to himself daily.

There was a limit to how long anyone could stay watching a cremation. There was too much detail that mourners best avoided seeing. Laseema stepped back to hand Kad to Jusik, and the motley crowd seemed at a loss for any ceremony or ritual to find closure here. Not even Jusik said anything; but he rested his forehead against Kad's, and maybe something passed between them that the likes of Ordo would never grasp.

"I'm never doing this again." Skirata walked back to the

pyre. Ordo saw his lips move, but he didn't hear the words. He watched his father reach into the flames—no gloves, no apparent fear of being burned—to grab something before dropping what looked like the lock of Kad's hair into the fire.

Skirata came back clutching the scorched toy, and turned to the mourners. "*Ori'haat,* I swear—I am never, *ever* going to see one of my children go to the *manda* before their time again."

Skirata had started with just over a hundred commando trainees, and now there were around eighty-five left serving. Yet only Omega seemed to have become this central to his life, however much time he spent talking to the others wherever they were deployed. Ordo wondered if he would now start obsessing about the rest. If he did, that was all right by Ordo.

"You've burned your hand," Ordo said.

Skirata put the toy in his pocket. There was something pitifully tender about that. "No big deal, son."

"You said the *gai bal manda,* didn't you?" It only took a few words to formally adopt. Posthumous adoption counted, too. "You finally adopted her. That's a noble thing you did."

"Being my son's wife wasn't enough," Skirata said. "I want to make amends for the way I yelled at her, and she never knew her parents. Well, she knows her father now." Ordo thought Skirata was going to lose his composure again, but he seemed to have passed a watershed. "When the flames die down, I'll gather the ashes for Darman. Fi? *At'ika?* Come here, lads." He beckoned them to him. "Have a hearty breakfast. And put on your full *beskar'gam,* too. We're going to have a chat with an old friend."

"Uthan?" Fi said hopefully.

"Yes," Skirata said. "We've honored the dead. Now we look after the living."

Skirata was genuinely grateful to have Dr. Ovolot Qail Uthan around.

It was a little more than the potential she represented for giving his boys a full life. She was also useful distraction. She was a task, and he could pour his sharp edges into deal-

ing with her. All those things saved him; they saved him from
drowning in grief, unable to claw his way up the sides, and
from lashing out at those just as deep in grief as he was. He
unlocked the armory door, followed by Atin in his newly acquired purple-brown armor, and Fi in the plates he'd scavenged from Ghez Hokan on Qiilura. They looked totally at
ease, as if they'd been free *Mando'ade* all their lives and
never served the Republic.

"Wait until I call you in," Skirata said.

There was an uncomfortable irony in Hokan's *beskar'gam*,
having just cremated the Jedi who'd decapitated him, but
Etain had probably changed from that first kill. Skirata suspected it was the moment she started drifting away from the
Jedi Order.

"Doctor!" Skirata forced cheerfulness. "How are you?"

Uthan looked up from her papers. Mereel had made her
very comfortable; she had everything except links to the outside world, but then she was used to being in solitary confinement.

"I'm well," she said. "How's the war progressing? Has
Coruscant been taken yet?"

"The war's over," Skirata said.

"Really?" Uthan blinked. *"Really?"*

"See for yourself."

Skirata placed the HoloNet receiver and screen on the
table. It was a high-quality set. She was going to be a guest
here for a long time, so there was no point skimping; when
he switched it on, it was already tuned to HNE's news output.
Uthan watched, her face a picture of amazement. She hadn't
seen a news program in nearly three years, and all she knew
of the war after Omega had snatched her from Qiilura was
what her captors had told her.

Shock was an interesting expression, Skirata thought. It
unfolded in stages. It was almost too slow for the person
doing the shocking. Uthan was trying to process a gap of
three years, the end of the war, the end of both the CIS and
the Republic, and now she was going to get the crushed nuts
and syrup on her Neuvian ice sundae.

"Doesn't time fly?" Skirata said, and leaned around the open door. "*Ad'ike?* In you come."

Atin and Fi walked in. Atin didn't get her attention—he looked like any other *Mando* minder she expected to have guarding her—but Fi . . . Fi wore Ghez Hokan's red and gray rig, and she'd known Hokan pretty well on Qiilura.

She stared at Fi. She'd probably forgotten how tall Hokan was—not very—and she just fixed on the armor.

"So you're still alive, Ghez," she said.

She would have no idea how funny that sounded to a Mandalorian; it was the direct translation of the universal greeting, *Su cuy'gar.* Fi chuckled, and then lifted off his helmet.

Skirata smiled. "An image is worth a thousand words, they say."

"Surprise!" Fi said. "Miss me, ma'am?"

Uthan just put both palms slowly to her cheeks and stared. It was an oddly genteel reaction, not the gesture Skirata expected from her.

"You've not rescued me so I can continue with my unique research into neutralizing Fett clones, have you?" she said at last. "Just a woman's intuition."

Fi sat down opposite her. He really was coming on in leaps and bounds; he still had that unsteadiness and hesitation, but his confidence was sky-high. It was clear that he felt like a competent soldier again.

"We've got names," Fi said. "And wives, and nice clothes, and bank accounts, and *everything.*"

Skirata still couldn't tell when Fi was putting on an act and when he was being distressingly literal, but it sounded good either way.

"Is this revenge?" Uthan asked.

Skirata respected someone who didn't go to pieces when they found they'd been totally scammed. "So, do you really want to kill clones, or were you just trying to solve a puzzle, Doctor?"

"Why do you ask?"

"Because I can't imagine why any intelligent being would genuinely want to kill strangers for no reason. So either you're a sad, sick *shabuir,* or you're a typical scientist who just wants to make something work without thinking too hard about the consequences."

"Or," said Uthan, "I could be a patriot who doesn't . . . didn't want my planet to be run by a Coruscanticentric dictatorship, and so used her skills to target its army."

"Big word, that. Mind if I write it down?"

"Would you be giving me this moral lecture if I was just making blasters to *shoot* your clones?"

"Maybe." Skirata tried to visualize what this woman loved and cared about, but it was almost as hard as working out what made a Kaminoan tick. He opted for the basics. "Do you have children, Doctor?"

"No."

He might have been imagining it, but he was sure she'd hesitated for a split second. She might have been lying; or it could have been a touchy subject. He concentrated on her eyes, searching for pupil dilation or any flickering movement that would betray emotion.

"Did you *want* kids?"

Again, the slightest pause. She blinked. "Once. But then life got in the way, and the next time I thought about it, it was too late."

Gotcha.

"Well, these clones are my sons." Skirata's tone was soft and conspiratorial. He knew the buttons to press now. "Not figuratively—literally. I adopted them. They're my kids and I love them, and they were my second chance at getting a family right. I want them out of the army and I don't give a *shab* if Coruscant disappears up its own trash compactor as long as nothing happens to my boys."

"Are we doing a deal here?"

"No."

"Ah."

"I just want you to understand my motive, Doctor. I didn't care for the Republic, because I'm a Mandalorian, and Mandalorians don't like being herded. The Republic wanted to force its brand of democracy on everyone, and the Jedi strong-armed for them because they always know what's best for grunts like us. No, I'd rather have been fighting for the

Separatists, but I had sons on the front line. I still have. And there's something you can help me do."

"Why would I want to?"

"You haven't heard what I want yet." Skirata ruffled Fi's hair, and gestured to Atin to take off his helmet. "These charming lads age twice as fast as you or I do. I want that unfortunate state of affairs to stop."

"You want them to have a normal life span."

"Yes."

Uthan stared at him for a few moments and then looked out of the slit-like window. Maybe it was the unbroken whiteness outside that unsettled her. Kyrimorut seemed as far from civilization as anyone could get, a wilderness that reminded folks how utterly alone and insignificant they were in the greater scheme of the galaxy. Uthan might have coped in her fancy secret laboratory on a backwater planet like Qiilura, but she was no longer on her own turf among allies with a guaranteed flight home.

"What's in it for me?" she asked.

"Spoken like a *Mando'ad*." Skirata smiled. "What do you think?"

"Knowing your kind, I get to live."

"Doc, no good playing the ice queen with me. I've lived with Kaminoans. I *know* ice. Just cut the *osik* and tell me what you want. You're already free of the Republic, the Seps, and even our new Emperor."

"I want to go home. I lost nearly three years of my life in that cell."

Skirata thought she would want credits, or at least to walk away with the research—she would want *that,* he was sure—but her reflex was to ask to go home.

Could he ever let her go?

No, not as long as there were clone troops vulnerable to her bioweapons. She hadn't had the chance to perfect the nanovirus before Omega Squad had seized her on Qiilura, but it was now viable as far as he knew, and the army was still full of Fett clones.

"Put it another way," Skirata said. "What do you want to

do with your life? Be rich? Famous? Academically respected? Save the galaxy from disease and pain?"

"If I didn't know better, I'd say that smacked of desperation."

"I'm trying to work out how much data I can safely give
you without turning you into a threat."

"If you had data, you wouldn't need me."

Skirata knew that tone. Uthan had the same need to solve
puzzles—at best amoral, at worst malevolent—as Ko Sai,
Nenilin, and all the others. She coveted knowledge, and that
was her power. Well, *he* had knowledge, too. He switched on
the data screen on the table.

"See for yourself," he said.

Uthan hesitated for a moment and stared him straight in
the eye, defiant, but then curiosity got the better of her and
she turned her head slowly to look at the screen. Skirata took
a few casual steps back, pulling out a few strips of ruik root
to chew.

"Go on, Doc. Take a look."

She did. And she wasn't a sabacc player; her face betrayed
her. It was like watching a hungry kid let loose at a banquet.
She scrolled through the screens slowly at first, then at increasing speed until she stopped, drew back, and looked at
him with an expression of breathless excitement.

"You've got *everything* here."

Skirata did his I'm-just-a-simple-mercenary shrug. "Yeah,
we have."

"How did you acquire all this?"

"We mined the lot in the last couple of years. Kamino,
Arkanian Micro, GeneSculpt, TheraGene, the Republic
Livestock and Agriculture Administration, Khomm Central
Population Planning, Columus Institute of Health, Lur, research still in progress at the Republic's top universities—
there's not much cloning and genome data for sentients or
nonsentients left in the galaxy that we haven't ripped off."
Skirata paused for effect before mentioning Uthan's former
employer. "Even the Gibadan Academy of Life Sciences. We
just aren't completely sure how to put it together to achieve
the result we want."

Uthan looked torn between gorging herself on the research and looking for the catch. "Nobody's ever assembled this much in one database."

"My boys are obsessive. And thorough."

"And all you want is for these clones to have normal life spans."

"Yes."

"Really . . . ?"

"Really."

"Skirata, this is worth billions. You could turn this over to any one of the companies and be a very, very rich man indeed. They'd kill to see their competitors' data."

Billions? He had a trillion creds, and the sum grew daily. "We only stole it for one reason. Now, are you in?"

Uthan stood staring at him.

"I said, *are you in,* Doctor? Do we have a deal?"

"What's the catch?"

"If you try to stiff me, I'll personally cut your throat—unless one of my boys gets to you first, of course. Either way, it won't be quick. If you play nice and do the job, and don't use any of this data or your own to harm Fett clones, then you can stroll off with it."

Uthan appeared to do some calculation. "That could be many years away."

"The faster you work, the sooner you leave," Skirata said. "Trust me on that."

Uthan didn't really have any other options anyway. "I'll do it," she said.

"Good." Skirata picked up his helmet. "Give Fi your shopping list and we'll get any kit you need."

"So what did happen to Ko Sai?"

"I'd like to say I killed her, to focus your enthusiasm," Skirata said. "I certainly dreamed of it often enough. But she took her own life. I suppose it can get pretty grim here for a Kaminoan. Or maybe that's how all supremacists like her prefer to go—anything rather than let an inferior species do it for them."

Despite himself, Skirata almost liked Uthan. There was something in her, some spark of passion that Ko Sai and her

vile kind didn't have. It wasn't as if they were even on opposite sides, politically speaking; it was just that her job had
been to wipe out clones. If only they could have ironed out
that difference, then they might have had a great business relationship.

Jaing and Mereel were waiting outside the doors a little
way down the corridor. They straightened up when they saw
Skirata coming and ambled toward him. Jaing was wearing
those gray leather gloves with his gray *beskar'gam.* He was
very attached to the gloves now. Skirata wondered how else
Ko Sai had been immortalized after he sent her head to General Zey.

I never took trophies. Funny, that. Not my style, I suppose.

"Well, *Kal'buir*?"

"She's playing ball," Skirata said. "I do believe the tide is
turning."

He walked through the Kyrimorut bastion and found himself singing under his breath. It was a shame Etain hadn't
lived to see this. Jusik had given him some hope, though; if
Jedi had this deal with the Force, and Etain was somehow in
a Jedi *manda,* then maybe she knew, and maybe she'd passed
beyond missing those she'd had to leave.

And if that was the deal—no, Skirata didn't resent Jedi
privilege at all.

25

Rejorhaa'ruetiise meg'oyacyi jorcu mhi r'asham.
Tell the aruetiise *that they live because we died.*
—Inscription on a Mandalorian memorial to fallen
mercenaries, Kyrimorut

Kyrimorut, 1,095 days ABG

Mandalorians didn't have memorials. Nomadic warriors
never stayed anywhere long enough to tend cemeteries, let
alone create public expressions of commemoration. But
Mandalore was home now, and Skirata had other ideas.

He hadn't planned it that well. It just happened when he
stopped sobbing about Etain during the night, and found it
was nearly sunrise, so he walked out into the frosted grass
around the lake and waited for the dawn. As he stared at the
horizon, seeing shapes and memories, he reached into his
pocket and found a few pieces of hard plastoid.

They were armor tallies, the last remains of dead clone
troops. He was absolutely determined they wouldn't be forgotten. The little tags with their ID circuitry needed to be
commemorated, like any piece of armor from a fallen comrade.

*We're your clan, your family. So we'll keep your memory
alive.*

Most of the tallies he had were from men he didn't even
know. It didn't matter. He had their names—just numbers,
mainly—on his list, every one of them up to the moment
Mereel last linked to the GAR network.

It was going to be a lot of work. But that was okay. He had time. He began pacing out a large rectangle in the grass, crunching his way in straight lines through the hard-frosted blades until he could see the outline. A memorial would stand here to make sure that these men were *not* invisible, *not* anonymous, *not* forgotten.

Even the *aruetiise* would know the size of the army's sacrifice when—if—they ever saw it.

Skirata walked back to the outbuildings to get a shovel. Mird, snuffling around the yard, stopped and looked up at him with an expression that was painfully human.

"You want to keep me company, stinker?" It was unusual to see the animal without Vau, but it had established its territory around Kyrimorut now and seemed content to leave its master sleeping while it patrolled. Maybe it didn't see Vau as a master; maybe it saw him as a father, and the strill was no more subservient and enslaved than Skirata's clone sons. "Come on, *Mird'ika*. You're a soldier, too."

He could have sworn the strill nodded at him. It fell in behind him and sat watching like a sentry while he turned the first soil for the foundations. In his mind's eye, he saw a broad-based obelisk, polished smooth, with the tallies inlaid or names and numbers inscribed. Perhaps that was both too ambitious and too at odds with the unspoiled beauty around it. It would also be a landmark in a place where he needed to stay hidden. One day, though; one day.

He'd think about that. He thought while he hacked into the rock-hard soil.

Mird jerked its head around, whining softly. Someone was coming, and Mird knew who it was. Skirata went on digging.

"Only Mandalores have graves," said Vau.

"I'm being an iconoclast." Skirata braced for a sarcastic comment on his expanding vocabulary but none came. "It's not enough for us to remember them. It has to be something the whole galaxy can understand. However trumped-up the war was, they still did their duty and died."

Vau squatted down as if he was checking Skirata's construction lines for true. "Agreed. You reckon we can build something big enough to take that many names?"

"Die trying."

Vau turned to Mird. "Shovel," he said. "Fetch, *Mird'ika*. Shovel."

Mird wheeled around and raced toward the homestead. Skirata was glad he hadn't shot it. It was a remarkable creature, and there were few of them left. They were all in this together: clone deserters, ragtag civvies with nowhere else to run, disillusioned Jedi—and a strill.

"Do you think he knew, Kal?"

Skirata went on digging. Vau totally upended him when he showed his decent side, and made him ashamed of all the years they'd spent hating and fighting. "Who?"

"Sev. I never told him I was proud of him, and I was. Did he know I loved him every bit as much as you love your boys?"

Skirata knew that pain well. Did Etain know? Had he ever made up for the things he'd called her when she first told him she was pregnant?

"I know he did, Walon," Skirata said. Vau had never had a father worthy of the name; all things considered, he'd done his best to be one himself. "I know he *does*. He's missing. Missing men often get found. Our missing men *will* be found."

Vau nodded, silent. He was the picture of regret, but whether that was for his relationship with his trainees or his life in general, Skirata had no idea, and thought it was a bad time to ask.

"So, Walon, materials? Shape? Dimensions?"

Vau looked distracted. "Something that can expand to three million in time. Something that looks like a natural formation from the air."

Skirata almost asked about the many millions more that Palpatine had produced on Centax and Coruscant, but that task was beyond him whether they were clones of Fett or not. *Do what you can.* What he'd done seemed pitifully inadequate, just a handful of men out of so many.

But it was still early days. Maybe more would follow.

The sun was climbing from the horizon, thawing the frost between the shadows. Skirata put his hand in his pocket again and took out the tallies. There were more in his quarters, in a box under the bed he still hadn't used, and in which he wouldn't sleep until he'd completed his mission to stop the clones' accelerated aging. In his belt pouch, his fingers closed around something soft, small, and heartbreaking.

"What are you going to do with that?" Vau asked.

Skirata turned the toy over in his hands. "Give it back to *Kad'ika* when he's older, of course. In the meantime, it's comforting me. Crazy, isn't it? The hard old *Mando* merc and his cuddly toy."

He felt he'd done pretty well to get this far without breaking down again. He'd had enough of crying. It wore him out; it pounced on him when he least expected it. It was the kind of sobbing that was dry and painful, just convulsions in his chest and a terrible pain behind his eyes and in his throat.

Part of the ongoing pain was not being with Darman to comfort him. The poor kid didn't have the experience to deal with that kind of bereavement, even if he was with Niner.

Who am I kidding? I still can't deal with it, and I've been watching people I love die all my life.

Skirata struggled to get his breath. "I've got to go back for them. The longer we leave it, the harder it'll be for everyone. I can't even comm him now."

"I know," Vau said. "You'll understand why I need to go visit some Wookiees for a while, then. Study trees."

"Oh, I understand. Need any help?"

"If I know I can call on you, that's enough."

"I've got some creds I owe Enacca. Maybe you'd hand them over personally."

"My pleasure."

Skirata scraped the soil off his shovel and headed back to the house to sit down with his family, have a solid breakfast with them, and make plans.

Etain had always said the Force told her things about the future. Skirata wondered if it had told her that her name would be on a memorial to the fallen of the Clone Wars, the only nonclone he would ever allow to be honored there, apart from Bardan Jusik when his time came.

The kitchen was full of good comforting smells, and the

general noise level was high. *That* was what a clan home should have been like: the bustle of existence. Skirata summoned everyone to the table, and they ate. Ruu picked at her breakfast, looking as if she was studying him whenever he wasn't looking. He felt he'd picked up where he left off with her, and in the worst way—leaving her to fend for herself while he got on with more important business. Eventually, he got up and moved next to her, putting one arm around her shoulders.

"You okay, *ad'ika*?"

"Just taking stock, Dad."

"I'm sorry." Skirata didn't specify what he was apologizing for. She had a long list to pick from. "I'm neglecting you all over again."

Ruu shook her head. "You're into some dangerous stuff, Dad. And things must be pretty bad for you at the moment. It's okay."

It wasn't. The last thing he wanted now was sympathy from her. If she'd raged at him, he'd have felt better.

"What are you going to do with Arla?" Besany asked. "Poor woman's been stuck in her room for days now. It's no improvement on the Valorum Center."

"I'm going to visit Concord Dawn, and see if there's any distant relatives around. I don't expect them to look after her, but it might help her get her cogs back in gear." Skirata thought about it; he had use of a fortune, maybe more than Fett ever amassed. Some of it would be well spent on Arla. Even if she didn't ever get better, she'd at least have some comfort. "I don't imagine Boba's going to want to see his long-lost aunt, if we ever find him."

"Are you looking for him?"

"Not really."

There was no hurry this morning. It was a bitter winter, so even if the farm had been up and running, there'd have been no work to do. It was another project on the list. In the meantime they could afford to sit and plan while they waited for Uthan to come up with some results.

A'den came in and helped himself to a bowl of boiled grain. He liked his meals to have the sticking power of gasket compound. "The Empire's looking for mercs and bounty hunters," he said. "I've been down to Enceri, and there's a lot of talk about opportunities."

"You thinking about it?"

"I'd have to be very bored," A'den said. "And I'm not, not yet. But I'm worried about some other business heading our way. I hear the Empire's offered a lot of creds to lease land for a garrison here, so they've got a base for operations in the quadrant."

Ordo just *looked*. He had eloquent eyebrows.

"I don't like the sound of that," Besany said.

"It's a lot of creds, and there's a lot of folk here who don't have our assets and liquidity," A'den said. "Can't blame 'em."

Skirata didn't need the Empire in his backyard, even if the base was a long way south nearer Keldabe. The planet wasn't big enough as far as he was concerned.

"So who are they putting the offer to, in the absence of a *Mand'alor*?" Laseema asked. She was a bright girl. She was getting more confident every day, and becoming a shrewd businesswoman. There'd been very few Twi'lek Mandalorians, so she was going to have to be discreet about her location and circumstances whenever she ventured into town. She'd be noticeable; there was no anonymity under a helmet for a being with head-tails. "Does it even count as foreign policy?"

"Chances are it's a simple lease deal with the guy who owns the land, wherever that is."

"Sounds crazy to me," Laseema said.

"Sounds dangerous," said Ordo. "And that's a good reason to anoint a Mandalore soon."

"Sounds messy," Fi said. "Does it involve ointment?"

It *was* messy, in the other sense. Skirata didn't want to be conspicuous, and he didn't want to get involved in the politics of Mandalore as long as he was trying to run an escape network for clone deserters. But he needed to get things straight.

Maybe it was time he saw Fenn Shysa. If there was anyone capable of steering the clans away from short-term thinking and long-term disaster, it was him.

And that wasn't saying much.

Skirata sat Kad on his knee and helped him tackle a small plate of shirred eggs. He was at the age when little clones had played games designed solely to improve their coordination, visuospatial ability, and reasoning skills. Skirata tried to put that out of his mind now.

"Lots of protein makes you big and strong, *Kad'ika,*" he said. "Like your daddy. He'll come home one day, and he'll be so proud of you, won't he? And then all the *Mando'ade* will stay at home, and never have empires, and never fight *aruetiise*'s wars for them. So they'll have to find some other silly people to do the dying, won't they?"

Kad looked into his grandfather's face with grave, serious eyes. He didn't smile at everyone like he used to. Jusik said he sensed that his mother was gone, and probably had an awareness of death that ordinary children of that age didn't. Skirata liked to think that Etain's Force certainty that Kad would change many lives was actually true, and that he might grow up into someone who could put Mandalore on its feet again.

"You're politicizing him young," Ordo said. "What if he wants to be a waster, hunt a few bounties, and drink *ne'tra gal* to excess?"

"He's the son of a Jedi and an elite commando," Skirata said. "He'll choose his path without career advice from me."

"I'll take some, then," said Ruu. "Got time?"

Skirata took the hint. "Of course I have, sweetheart."

After breakfast, he walked her around the lake to the north of the bastion and showed her the memorial site. It felt like amnesia. It was as if he'd simply forgotten all the years between but somehow knew exactly who she was, everything that mattered. She wasn't a stranger at all; there was simply a lot to find out about her. A sheet of ice spread from the shoreline toward the center of the lake like a pier. *Vhe'viine*—small rodents that robbed the grain fields in packs—popped up from their burrows to watch warily, almost invisible in their white winter coats.

"Where do you want me to start?" Skirata said. "My side of the story? Yours?"

"No, let's hit the reset button." Ruu puffed clouds of vapor into the icy air. "What's the phrase? *Cin vhetin.* We begin again."

Life needed a reset button. It would have solved a lot of problems. Skirata suspected he'd make the same mistakes again anyway, and settled for putting right the ones he'd already made instead.

"Tell me what your life's been like, *ad'ika,*" he said, linking his arm through hers. "I want to hear it all."

26

"**B**oba's out there somewhere," Shysa said. He had a habit of putting his boots up on the nearest chair, which was poor etiquette even in a bantha's backside of a joint like the *Oyu'baat*. "He might be his father's son, or the poor wee lad might be so shook up that he's lost his guts, but if he's a true Fett—Mandalore needs him."

"Maybe so." Skirata wished he hadn't come to Keldabe now, because Shysa was a very persuasive man, and part of Skirata—the part that didn't want to shut himself away from the *aruetyc* world, the part that wanted to keep tabs on it so he knew how to kill it when it next threatened all he held dear—needed to stay on top of events. He found himself mired in a discussion. "But Boba's not here, and he's barely come of age anyway, so what are we going to do for a bit of direction while we wait for the savior to show and lead us to glory?"

"Ah, you're mocking me now, so you are."

"Yeah, maybe I am." Skirata indicated an empty mug. "I get less mocking with a few mugs of *ne'tra gal* inside me. I'm told I get sentimental and sloppy, in fact."

Shysa let out a long sigh. "Spar was right. Touting him as the son and heir was a canny public relations exercise, but it's no substitute for a real *Mand'alor.*"

"I nominate you, Fenn."

"I was worried you'd say that."

"*Everyone's* saying it."

"The clans are reassured to see Palpatine offering paid work now, with no hard feelings, so they'd cheer for a bantha wearin' a *buy'ce* these days."

"Talking of which, why is anyone seriously considering leasing a base to the Empire?"

"They've offered a good price."

"Who did they offer it to? The individual clan, or Mandalore?"

"The clans met, and it's just a temporary land deal."

Skirata didn't hold it against Palpatine for being a Sith. It wasn't a big deal for *Mando'ade;* they'd worked for Sith in the past, and they'd fared better with the Sith than they had with the Jedi. No, Skirata didn't trust Palpatine because he was a *politician,* and just as the slimeball had wanted to impose the Republic's nice shiny democracy on the galaxy, he now had a new name for his megalomania, *Empire.* Only the branding had changed, really.

"Palpatine never did anything temporary in his life, Fenn." Skirata huddled over his mug of ale. "I *know.* He's just spent thirteen years—at least—building a galactic war and two armies purely to get rid of the Jedi. I'm not complaining, but you can't have failed to notice that he's occupying the galaxy a system at a time, so what part of the phrase *Do not let this man camp in your backyard* do we not understand?"

"Which part of *We haven't had a credible army since Galidraan* do *you* not understand?"

"So the only option is to roll over and become an outpost?" Skirata couldn't believe that the Galidraan losses were still irreplaceable. This was Mandalore: the raw material of fighting men and women was all around them. "Look at the holochart. What are we a convenient base *for*? I can only think of Roche, and if Palps really likes Verpine kit that much, he can walk in. He doesn't need a garrison here."

"You're a suspicious man, so you are."

"I'm a man who worked for the Republic's army for more than ten years. The one that wiped out the Jedi. And I didn't see *that* coming."

"What would Palpatine want here, anyway? It's not like we've got prettier views than Naboo."

"We've got two things here—*beroyase bal beskar.* Men and metal. Although now that he's removed the Jedi, he might not need so much Mandalorian iron. But there's nothing else of value here, except us."

Shysa was smarter than he liked to let on. The amiable rogue image didn't fool many. It was probably why he didn't want to be pushed into being *Mand'alor.* "Look," he said. "If we said no to the base, the garrison, whatever you want to call it, then we might get his attention the wrong way, clans would lose creds, and he might well show up with his great big hairy new army anyway, and there'd be sweet *naas* we could do about it. We've got four million people here. He's probably got armored divisions bigger than that."

This is not my problem. My problem is to bring home my boys, cure them all, save more clones, look after my own. Nothing else.

Skirata repeated that to himself, because the temptation to grab Shysa by the collar and warn him that things would go to *osik* almost got the better of him. He needed to operate covertly; he couldn't do that if he got involved with clan politics.

"See, if we can't say no, and if we can't raise the kind of conventional army that can show unwelcome visitors the door," Shysa said, "then our only option is to be ready to do the kind of sneaky fightin' that your good selves are so fine at."

Selves? "Me and Vau, we're too old."

"Ah, sure, you're the cutest age for training young soldiers."

"I came here to talk you into being *Mand'alor* and putting some common sense back into how we do things. Don't sidestep the issue."

"I don't want power."

"You'd be *Mand'alor*. Power's not the word. Focus. Direction, maybe. Despite the scruffy hair, Fenn, you've got focus, and you're young enough, too. Yeah, get your hair cut, you scruffy *shabuir,* and we'll make a *Mand'alor* of you yet."

"Ah, I love me hair, me crownin' glory . . ." Shysa still had a reassuringly dull sense of responsibility under that smooth-talking ladies'-man patter. "Okay, if the garrison looks like it might turn ugly, I'll step up and keep the seat warm until Boba shows up."

Shysa was making an awfully big assumption about Boba's willingness to take over where his dad left off.

"Fett's got an older sister, you know. Arla."

"No, Vizsla killed them all."

"Not all."

"Now you tell me. Are you having me on, Kal?"

"No, *ori'haat.* I swear. Jango thought they all died, but the girl survived somehow—at least, what was left of her when Vizsla's latrine dregs were done using her. She showed up on Triple Zero some years ago."

"If Vizsla wasn't dead, I'd be wanting to kill him again a few times myself." Shysa shook his head. "How did she get from Concord to Corrie? Why didn't Jango know?"

"She wasn't in any state to make contact with him. We don't know what happened to her between the time the Fetts were killed and when she . . . well, I brought her nearer home, anyway. She's had a bad time."

"Here? Oh, that's fine news."

"Don't get your hopes up."

"High time we had a female *Mand'alor* again. The ladies know how to keep us fellas in line." Shysa wasn't joking; he seemed to clutch at the idea of a real live adult Fett. It smacked of hereditary royalty, and that was very un-Mandalorian. "We could give her plenty of support. She'd be a fighting girl, no mistake."

"She's not Mandalorian, *Fen'ika.* Only Jango joined us."

"She could *become* Mandalorian."

"Yeah. She *could.* But she sits rocking herself in a corner for most of the day, and she's never quite sure where she is even when her meds wear off, so I don't think she's the woman for the job, do you?"

"Ah." Shysa closed his eyes for a moment at the brutal slap-down. But the man had to be told. "So why'd you bring the poor lass back?"

"Because she was rotting in a lunatic asylum, and I can't walk away from a locked door when someone's inside being treated worse than an animal."

Skirata surprised himself. He heard his voice as a stranger might, and felt like a hypocrite. *You're such a great guy that you let Etain fend for herself, and she's dead because of you.* Shysa grabbed his shoulder and squeezed it so hard that it hurt.

"You're a good decent *buir,* Kal, so you are."

"Maybe I just like thieving so much that I steal people, too."

Shysa screwed up his eyes for a moment, caught out by memory. "I'm sorry, Kal. I shouldn't be leaning on you at a time like this. I'm sorry about your wee girl. Terrible, it is."

Mandalorians didn't distinguish between daughters and daughters-in-law, or even between daughters and sons. All were *ad'ike.* If Shysa had any inkling that Etain had been a Jedi, he didn't let on. Skirata fought an urge to tell him because he was so proud of her—so proud, too late—but any surviving Jedi were on a death list now, and the son of a Jedi wouldn't get the benefit of the doubt. Kad was doubly at risk.

"We cremated her." Skirata found he needed to keep saying that to convince himself she was dead. He still expected her to walk through the doors at any moment. "She was from . . ." He didn't know. For the first time, Skirata realized he had no idea on which world Etain had been born. It was sudden and terrible; he would never know. "*Shab,* I don't know. She married one of my boys."

"Ah, the baby's a soldier's son . . . I'll bet he won't be the only one. Big strong healthy lads."

Skirata hoped so, too. He gave Shysa a friendly shove, anxious now to leave the *Oyu'baat* and shut himself away with his family to do some healing. "I've got diapers to change. You go be a leader, Fenn Shysa. You'll be a great one. I know it."

Skirata got up to go. The barkeep jerked his thumb at a holo-display on the back wall. It was the current bounty-hunting list, images and details of miscreants and other unfortunates with a price on their heads and therefore of interest to whichever of the *Oyu'baat*'s patrons were looking for work.

"You're a popular man," said the barkeep, indicating a frame that said SKIRATA, K, PREFERABLY ALIVE. There was no image, and he didn't check the size of the bounty in case it was insultingly low. "The Emperor obviously took a real shine to you."

No *Mando* would come after him, Skirata knew. It wasn't the done thing. But there was an image of Jilka, and nobody here knew she was off-limits yet. They'd have to be careful.

"I'll send him a holocard," Skirata said.

Skirata's pace picked up as he walked toward the speeder, and he broke into a run for the last few meters. His ankle was fine, like it had never been shattered at all. Now it was his chest, his heart, that hurt. Once the hatch closed and he stared up through the transparisteel canopy at the brilliant turquoise sky, he wept again. *Better out than in, but am I ever going to stop? The clan needs me in control.* It still took a few minutes for his vision to clear enough to steer.

Dar, if I miss her this bad, what are you going through? You should be here with us, ad'ika, *home with your son.*

Darman's comlink was still down. Obrim's was down, too, and there was no word of Niner. Mereel said they were up-grading the comm kit to be compatible with the vast new Im-perial Army, but he'd find a way to contact Dar and Niner even if it meant going back to Coruscant and walking into the barracks.

You're coming home, lads. One day, soon.

The new speeder had been worth the creds, as if he had to worry about that now with a massive fortune getting fatter by the end of each banking day. It was fast, and cut the transit time to Kyrimorut by an hour. As he brought the speeder low through the treetops to avoid detection—he was starting as he meant to go on—he was reassured by how hard it was to spot Kyrimorut from the air, and how the clearing caught him by surprise.

Someone was waiting for him when he landed. Arms folded, Ny stood like a loadmaster waiting for cargo, glancing at something in her hand.

"Ny," he said, jumping out. Her transport was still ticking over, as if she'd just landed. "You okay? I thought you were working out of Fondor now."

She held out her hand to offer him something. It was a tiny piece of glittering plastoid.

"Found it," she said. "It was stuck between the layers of soundproofing in the crew bay. Ordo said Etain's datachip was missing from her 'pad, so I checked where I'd laid her body."

It was a datachip, all right, and Skirata found himself promising the Force some grudging respect if only it was Etain's. He looked at it for a few long minutes. It took a little while longer before he could speak.

"Thanks, Ny. I'll add it to the list of a million things I owe you."

"Debt paid."

"Sorry it wasn't better news about your husband." Skirata still didn't know the details, and didn't want to pry. "I'll shut up about it if you want."

"Nobody's getting much good news at the moment, Kal. I'll settle for closure. Some widows don't even get that."

She turned to leave, but he caught her arm. "Have they fed you, that bunch of mine?" He turned the datachip over and over in his hand. What was on it? It might have been nothing. If he didn't look, he'd never know.

And he *had* to know.

Ny hovered, almost telepathic. "I can look at it for you if it's going to be too upsetting."

"No, I have to do this. Thanks anyway."

"It's no trouble."

He took a breath and slid the chip into his datapad. Ny had the right stuff. She was *mandokarla*. "This isn't going to be easy either way."

Skirata expected the chip to be full of heartbreaking images of Etain with Kad, and he wasn't disappointed. Mothers did that; they kept pictures of their kids, especially if they knew their time with them would be limited.

You told her you'd take her son from her.

But it wasn't just her and the baby; it was Darman, too, all three of them in some of the holos. The pain in Skirata's throat was sudden and intense, enough to make him open his mouth. His own sobbing caught him by surprise. Ny put her hand on his shoulder.

"I could have done something . . . ," he said.

"No, Kal."

"I could have let them be together. I broke every rule in the book, so why not that one? Why didn't I do it from the start?"

"Regret gets you nowhere." It was hard to square her forbidding exterior with the obviously kind woman within. "By the way, I took a chance. Got room for some more?" She popped the hatch on her shuttle. "Can't resist strays, me."

A clone in a pair of gray pilot's coveralls, the sort any freight jockey wore, walked down the path toward them. For a terrible moment, Skirata's heart leapt and something in his mind said *Darman,* but it wasn't Dar. A fleeting thought like that could crush Skirata for days.

The clone looked embarrassed. Skirata had expected anything from relief to fear, but not embarrassment. And this wasn't any of his boys. He was a stranger. Any clone was welcome here, though, and the man was instantly family. That was his *right.* They were all brothers, *vode an.*

"Levet," said the clone. "I served under General Tur-Mukan."

Ah, this was the commander who'd known Etain was pregnant and kept his mouth shut. Levet held out his hand to Skirata for shaking.

"So, you're the one Ordo calls Commander Tactful."

Levet raised an eyebrow. "I try to be. Thank you for the refuge, Sergeant. I'm not proud of myself, but something snapped."

"Nothing to be ashamed of, either, *ad'ika.*" Skirata beckoned toward the house. "You more than did your duty. Now it's your time to do what *you* want."

"A farm," said Levet. He looked around him, taking in the farmhouse with an expression like a lost child checking the darkness for monsters. "I don't know the first thing about farming, but I can learn to do just about anything. And General Tur-Mukan . . . I'm very sorry indeed."

"Her son's doing fine." Skirata patted him on the back. This lad had nothing, just the clothes he stood up in. "Go inside, and Ordo will get you settled in. Get some food down you." Skirata looked at Ny. "You staying for a meal? Least we can do for you."

Ny considered the invitation slowly. "That would be nice. Can I raise a delicate topic?"

Skirata felt a little hope, but he knew he'd feel guilty if he thought of his own needs before all his boys' needs were met—and that included finding a method for stopping their headlong rush to old age.

"I'm all ears," he said.

She waited for Levet to go. "Jedi."

"Where are we going with this?"

"You didn't hate them all. You loved Etain and you love Jusik. They're not all bad, are they? Whatever the Jedi Order turned into, they can't all be guilty."

"No." It was common sense. The fact that they'd killed Etain and used his clones like droids didn't change the fact that he knew there had to be good ones for the likes of Jusik to exist at all. "They're not. And Jusik isn't a Jedi."

"What if I came across some nice folk whose only fault was that the Force dumped midi-chlorians in their system? How would you feel about them?"

"What do you mean, *came across*?"

"It's an occupational hazard if you haul freight. You find stowaways and illegals in your hold, and you hear their stories, and sometimes you don't feel right dumping them out the air lock, and pretty soon you start trying to do the decent thing in a nasty galaxy."

Skirata fixed her with his best don't-even-think-about-it look. "Hypothetically . . ."

"Mandos don't care about your roots. Only what you do. Right? Pretty tolerant for a bunch like you."

"Yeah."

"I might have two Jedi who escaped."

"If one's Quinlan Vos, bring him on. I've got a knife that's lonely."

"Kal . . . come on . . ."

"Okay, who are they?"

"One's a kid." Ny's face was still pitiless detachment personified, but there was a silky note in her voice that was almost like being stroked. "I *mean* a kid—maybe only fourteen. Name's Esterhazy or something. She helps grow things, and says they thought she was a useless Jedi, more mundane talent than Force skills, and that sounds like poor Etain to a *T.* No decapitating. The other's . . . a Kaminoan."

Skirata actually gasped. It wasn't loud, more a slow inhalation, but he had no idea that Kaminoans ever produced Force-users. *Aiwha-bait and saber jockeys.* His two favorite objects of hate right then; and here was one who scored on both counts. His knife whispered to him.

So why did Ko Sai get so excited about Kad? If the gray freaks had their own Force-users, why didn't they tinker with their own midi-chlorians to create Force-using clones?

Because they were the master race, and everyone else was just meat. He could see that now. They'd never use their precious, perfect genome to create a *product.* Ko Sai had told Mereel that after he said hello to her with an electroshocker. She was *really* offended when he asked if she was the clone "mother"—whether their somatic cloning method had used Kaminoan ova for the Fett DNA.

"I'll confess I'm not crazy about the idea," Skirata said, having the weirdest feeling that this was *very* important. "I can just imagine what a lovely, caring, modest being a Kaminoan Jedi is . . ."

"She's called Kina Ha. She didn't strike me as a monster—"

Skirata remembered his first day on Kamino. *Such gentle voices.* "They never do, at first."

"—but she's from a special line of very long-lived Kaminoans. They genetically engineered her bloodline for long space missions."

Skirata almost collapsed.

He had to repeat those words in his head a few times before he believed what he'd heard, and his hammering pulse slowed enough for him to get a grip.

So . . . they can *extend life, too, as well as shorten it. No wonder Palps went crazy trying to get hold of Ko Sai before I did. No wonder he thought she could make him immortal. She could probably do something pretty close.*

And that means . . . Dr. Uthan will be very *interested in her genome. And so, my dear sweet aiwha-bait, am I. I am so very, very interested in that . . . for my boys.*

"Kal, I know this is hard," Ny said, frowning. "And maybe the wrong thing to ask after what happened to Etain."

"You're right." He struggled with his conscience—not about the plans that sprang fully formed into his mind, because a Kaminoan deserved no consideration, but because he didn't like the fact that he was taking advantage of Ny's good nature.

But this is for my boys. They come first. Before me and my needs. Before Ny Vollen's opinion of me, too.

"No, it's fine."

"I can bring them back here?"

I must be insane. But what an opportunity. "When were you thinking of doing it?"

"I'll be passing their location in a week or two."

"Okay. But be careful. Full security. First sign of trouble—I'll personally make them one with the *shabla* Force."

Ny smiled. She *could* smile, and it was a nice one. "You're a good man, Kal."

"No," he said. He'd level with her sooner or later. She'd probably hate him for it, and that was a pity, because he liked her more every time he saw her. But he had a duty. "I'm not good at all. But I do love my boys."

Imperial Army Training Center, Centax 2, Coruscant

Darman had been trained to survive against all odds behind enemy lines, and that was what he was doing now.

Strength of will: that determined who lived, and who didn't.

"Dar?"

He knew when he was plunging into the abyss. Kal Skirata had taught him to spot the signs of despair and weakness, so he would know when he needed to get a grip. It wasn't lack of water, or food, or even being shot that really killed you in these circumstances; it was letting despair eat you alive. It was giving up.

"Dar, can you hear me?"

If you take control of pain, fear, and loss, then you take control of your situation. Make it work for you.

He could hear Kal Skirata's words as clearly now as he ever could. He chose to hear the man as he first knew him when he loomed over Darman as a training sergeant, and not as the father he'd come to love as the years wore on, because that dredged up too much raw pain. He needed to be a different Darman for as long as it took to escape; the Darman who'd come to think he had a right to a life beyond the army, who'd loved a girl and married her, seen her die, and held a son for far too short a time before it was all snatched away from him—that Darman was too fragile to survive an indefinite period in this alien environment. That man would have to wait in suspension until the time was right for him to come alive again, if that time ever came at all.

"Darman!"

Someone shoved him hard in the chest. He shook himself out of his near-meditative state and found he was looking at Niner, walking awkwardly on cybernetic braces to demonstrate that he was up and about again.

"You seem very chipper, Sarge," he said.

"I'll be back on duty in a couple of weeks."

"That's great."

"Dar, you want to go somewhere quiet and talk?"

"Why?"

Niner was looking hard at him. "Take your helmet off, Dar. Please? Talk to me."

Darman lifted off his bucket and set it on the table. He preferred his old Katarn rig, but if he was going to change one thing, it didn't matter if everything familiar went down the sewer. It made it easier to be a different Darman. Niner lowered himself into the seat next to him, supporting his body weight on muscular arms, and took a firm grip of Darman's hand.

"Dar, it's okay to go a bit nuts after what's happened," he whispered. "But I'm your brother. Do what you like in front of these *di'kute,* but you can be yourself with me. Okay?"

The 501st troops were pretty sharp, but some of the other new boys weren't up to scratch for commando training. It wasn't so much the mediocre performance on initial testing that got to him—what else did they expect from clones grown in a year or two?—but that they seemed to think Centax 2 was Kamino. Some *di'kut* had told them this before the war ended, and they would *not* believe Darman's stories about endless oceans and cloud-locked skies until he made them study the Kamino system database.

They had to, anyway. There was a contingency plan to deal with Kamino, which wasn't exactly best buddies with the Empire now. Darman was keen to refresh his relationship with the aiwha-bait. If they were looking for volunteers to bring Kamino into line, he'd be first in the queue.

"I'm fine, Niner," Darman said. This was the worst he could imagine, the lowest ebb. But he was surviving, and if he could hold himself together at rock bottom, then he would eventually live his life again, because no pain he would ever encounter again could be worse than this. "I'm coping."

"Dar, I know you well enough to see what's happening now."

"What, then? What *is* happening now?"

"Okay, *ner vod.* It's okay. I'm not pushing you."

Darman wanted to tell Niner that if he tried to get the old Darman to come out, the pain would destroy him. And the things that other Darman knew had to remain under wraps. The best way to do that was to forget that he knew them, and lock them down for another day. What he consciously shut out of his mind could become habit—he had a technique for that—and then he wouldn't let anything slip, or incriminate those he loved.

So it was for the best. He put the old Darman away, and with it the unbearable pain of being so very close to an idyllic happiness and having it snatched from him. That Darman couldn't survive here, not even with his brother Niner supporting him.

But he could hide, and come out when it was over.

"You could have left me," Niner said. "But you didn't, and I'll owe you for the rest of my life."

"We never leave a brother behind," Darman said. "How could I?"

And he wouldn't be left behind, either. He knew that. Someone would come for him. While he waited for that day to come, though—he'd do whatever he had to, the way that Kal Skirata had taught him.

Barracks block, Imperial Army Training Center,
one standard hour after lights-out

Scorch had finally forced himself to stop replaying the events of the Kashyyyk operation in his mind to work out what he could have done to save Sev.

There was plenty.

But that was in the past, a moment gone forever, and now he could do nothing except drive himself crazy with self-recrimination. And he had a new job to get on with that wasn't going to wait around while he grieved. There were no Skiratas or Vaus in the Imperial Army to let the remnant of Delta Squad do as they pleased, or to care how they felt. This was a new world, much more like the restricted one of Kamino than the independence they'd grown used to. Even the new barracks had that white antiseptic feel of Tipoca City.

"Have you seen him, then?" Boss asked, voice barely audible. He leaned over the edge of the upper bunk and prodded Scorch. "He's here. Him and Niner."

Scorch was grateful for the momentary distraction. He broke off from his perpetual guilt about Sev's fate to wonder if Etain had survived the purge. Jusik had: Scorch knew because he'd seen the death warrant on the list of missing Jedi that was being circulated. Palpatine had put a bounty on Skirata's head, too.

But if Darman was still here—it didn't look like Etain had made it. Scorch was certain he'd have got her away to safety if he could.

"No sign of Corr or Atin," he whispered.

"I heard they're on the deserters' list, with the Nulls and a few others . . ."

Scorch didn't reply. He could hear Fixer snoring mechanically in the next bunk, and the noise now seemed reassuring rather than something that exasperated him enough to pour a jug of water over his brother while he slept. The rest of the commandos in the dormitory area were men he didn't know. A little familiarity was precious right then.

"Would you shoot them if ordered?" Boss asked.

Sev had once asked Scorch a similar question. "I don't know." But Scorch wanted to say no, he wouldn't; and good luck to them. "Would you have shot Etain if she'd still been with us when Order Sixty-six went down?"

"Academic," said Boss, evading the issue. "She wasn't."

"Did you get a chance to ask Dar why he's still here?"

Boss paused. "Yeah."

"And?" Scorch expected news of Etain. His stomach clenched. "What, then?"

Boss swallowed. Scorch heard it. "All he said," Boss whispered, "was that he couldn't leave Niner behind."

Scorch knew Boss well enough not to ask him how *that* made him feel.

He felt the same way.

27

I didn't accept that he was gone until I saw his name on the war memorial. Then it had a finality to it. He wasn't mine any longer. He was absorbed into the ranks of the dead, untouchable, separate, frozen in stone.
—Widow of Lieutenant Commander Ussin Fajinak, first officer of Republic warship *Aurodia*

Keldabe, Mandalore, next day, 1,097 days ABG

Kad was restless today. He'd whimpered through most of the night and everyone had stood their watch with him, trying to soothe him to sleep. Fi bounced him on his lap.

"Nice day out, *Kad'ika*!" He loved that kid. Maybe he was putting too much pressure on Parja to have one just like him. "See all the funny *Mando'ade* playing with knives and blasters, and singing rude songs?"

Kad clung to his scorched toy nerf with both hands and refused all attempts to distract him. He gazed out of the speeder window as if he was looking for something. Fi was sure he was watching in the hope of seeing his mother or father, whatever Jusik said about the kid understanding death better than ordinary babies.

"I think *you* get more excited about a day out in Keldabe than he does," Skirata said, hands relaxed on the steering yoke. "It's good to see you happy again, son. You heal an old man's heart. Etain would be so pleased."

"When we go back for Dar and Niner, I'm in, okay? I want to do that mission."

"You will be."

Skirata seemed to be in a mood that Ordo called *contemplative*. Something was up, and his willingness to go to Keldabe made Fi wonder if it had anything to do with Shysa. But *Kal'buir* insisted he was just going to buy some stuff to keep Uthan happy—holozines, toiletries, maybe even a bottle of fancy wine. It was too much of a risk to get goods delivered to Kyrimorut from outside the area. And Skirata seemed to need to get out and stretch his legs occasionally.

"Kad, want to try my *buy'ce*?" Fi held his helmet over the child's head like a Basani high priest performing a coronation. "Lots of funny noises. Lots of colors."

Kad looked up at him with big, wary, dark eyes. Then his lips flattened into a thin, tight line and he frowned, tears wobbling on his eyelashes. But he was silent. He was very good at not crying aloud. Fi reckoned that every baby had the right to bawl its eyes out, Kad more than any of them.

Fi lowered the helmet anyway. "Here it comes, *Kad'ika* . . . look at the pretty colors. Buckets on! There, you're a soldier now."

Kad accepted the crown for a moment, with Fi's hands taking the weight. Then he squirmed away. "Dada," he said. "Dada?"

"Can't start the kid too soon," said Skirata. "We'll have Beviin Verhayc make him a nice little *buy'ce* of his own. No expense spared. Even a little flight suit. Mirgo Ruus makes good ones. Only the best for my *bu'ad'ika*."

"Is Bardan going to teach him to use the lightsaber?"

"No reason why it's a weapon only for *jetiise*." Skirata was worried, Fi could tell. There was always that carefully controlled note in his voice that cut off some of the higher registers. "Discreetly, of course."

Fi watched Kad like a Fleet Met storm forecast. He was sure the kid could sense his father in the Force, and if anything happened to Darman, Kad would know first.

Keldabe was busy today. It wasn't Coruscant by a long chalk, but Fi had given up on his ambition to rappel from the highest tower in Galactic City. Keldabe was on a scale he could handle, and he was more confident with every passing day that—eventually—he would remember his way home without ever needing a datapad prompt. The two men wandered through the alleys for the morning, Skirata carrying Kad on his hip in typical proudly paternal *Mando* fashion.

They stood in the square outside the *Oyu'baat* tapcaf, looking over the edge of the rail into the Kelita River to amuse Kad. He was still more interested in the sky for some reason. He was looking for something.

It was then they first saw the ships.

Overhead, assault vessels and transports swept in a loose formation toward the east of the river. They'd once been a welcome sight on the battlefield, but now they were a threat of dark days to come. The Imperial garrison was moving in, and they hadn't wasted any time. They were obviously in a big hurry. Skirata looked up and sighed.

"I've got what I came for, *ad'ika*," he said. "I think it's time we disappeared."

"I'm glad I didn't take the *Mand'alor* job," said Fi. "I bet Spar is, too."

So that was what Kad had sensed and fretted about: Jusik could sense trouble in the Force, so Kad probably could, too. That was what he'd been watching for. Fi preferred to think so rather than imagine him pining for poor Etain.

They headed back to the speeder. A man in amber armor paused to touch Skirata's arm as he passed. "Have you heard?"

"What, that we're going to rue the day we let Palpatine in?"

The man shook his head. "No, Shysa. Fenn Shysa's just accepted the *kyr'bes*. He's our new *Mand'alor*. The ale's flowing in the *Oyu'baat*."

The man walked on, apparently happy that the three-year interregnum without a *Mand'alor* since Fett's death was now over. Maybe he didn't know what Fi knew: that Shysa had told Skirata he'd take the top job if he didn't like the look of his Imperial guests. Shysa had obviously made up his mind right away.

"I don't think I'm thirsty." Skirata glanced at Fi. "Are you, son?"

"I'm the designated driver," Fi said.

A gunship—not quite the beloved LAAT/i, but close, clad in the new Imperial livery—swooped low over the center of the city, looking as if it was going to clip the MandalMotors tower.

Fi put a finger to his lips. *Stay quiet.* Kad mimicked the gesture in complete silence. It was a good habit to get the boy into. Kad looked up with his fist in his mouth, eyes wide, brow puckering with the start of tears. He already knew that he'd need to be unseen and unheard to survive the years to come.

Skirata watched the sky until there were no more ships, and Fi had seen that look before: wary but not cowed down, wary—but with something up his sleeve, something more than his three-sided knife. Kad whimpered quietly.

"It's okay," Skirata said, stroking the boy's head. "I'm here, son. I'm here."

Read on for an excerpt from
STAR WARS
The Clone Wars: No Prisoners
By Karen Traviss

Published by Del Rey Books

General Skywalker *could* have made it an order, of course. But he hadn't; it was just a *request*. A mere *suggestion*.

Clone Captain Rex added reading between the lines to the list of things they'd never actually taught him on Kamino.

Okay, sir, I get it. Understood. You want your Padawan out of your hair for a few days. Done.

Orders were orders, and orders given subtly seemed to have even more weight. They did if they came from Anakin Skywalker, anyway.

"Am I getting on his nerves?" Ahsoka asked.

"As if." Rex could see a little frown wrinkling her nose. "Now, why would he *ever* think that?"

She gave him a narrow-eyed stare for a moment, almost theatrical, searching the T-shaped visor as if she was trying to look him in the eye, and then grinned.

"You're hard to read, sometimes."

"Everyone needs a break from combat, littl'un. Even Jedi. And even if it's spent training. That's all."

It was true. Rex believed that—well, *generally*, anyway—so if Ahsoka wanted to test how he felt about it in the Force, she wouldn't sense it as a lie. But he'd decided *he* didn't need to know why Skywalker wanted her out of the way for a while, and if *she* wanted to know—well, it was time for her to learn about need-to-know. She was going to have a little trouble mastering that skill.

He was more concerned with the six new clone troopers assigned to Torrent Company.

They were *very* new indeed.

While Ahsoka gazed out of the viewport, they sat on the two bench seats, three men on each side, facing one another in still, studied silence. Sergeant Coric, one of only six men from the original Torrent Company who'd survived the assault on Teth, sat to one side, seeming engrossed in his datapad.

In theory, the new boys had learned all they needed to about every class of warship; in practice, they'd had only Kaminoan flash training, which was thorough but no substitute for hands-on experience. And anyone fresh out of Tipoca City could never be fully prepared for the real world beyond that cloistered training existence, the untidy galaxy of thousands of new species that had nothing in common with humans or Kaminoans.

I wonder how much they'll see of it before they get killed.

It was a thought that had become quietly insistent at the back of his mind, not enough to eat away at him, but an uncomfortable feeling he tried to brush away.

Rex considered them carefully, listening for the telltale clicks and faint breaths that would tell him what was going on inside their helmets. He could see what they appeared to see; their point-of-view icons in his head-up display all showed the man sitting opposite.

Well, that was where their helmets were facing, anyway.

Takes a long time to rebuild a company from five survivors. Takes a lot more than training, too. What do Kaminoans know about bonding? Less than they thought, I reckon. A lot less.

Ahsoka interrupted his thoughts. "What's so special

about *Leveler*?" She gazed out the viewscreen as the shuttle came alongside the warship. "Looks like all the others of her class."

"All ships have their own peculiarities." Rex called up the schematic of *Leveler* on his HUD with a couple of rapid blinks. "Even ones that look the same. But *Leveler*'s just had a refit, so she's got some experimental toys for us to try out."

"*Destructive* toys?"

"Concussion missiles. Prototypes. So if they're not destructive, Pellaeon better ask for a refund."

The six new clones—Ross, Boro, Joc, Hil, Vere, and Ince—didn't move a muscle. Rex switched to his internal helmet comlink so Ahsoka couldn't hear him.

"Gentlemen, show me some life signs before I resort to CPR . . ."

"Receiving, sir," Ince said. "Just . . . awaiting orders."

"You can move, you know. And talk."

"Yes, sir."

Rex decided he'd have to factor some *social* time into the training. His new boys needed to loosen up. Maybe they were nervous about being 501st Legion now, because a certain cachet—a certain *responsibility*—came with that cap-badge.

And if they didn't start talking and giving him all the little clues of individuality that helped one clone trooper recognize another in a sea of near-identical faces and armor, then he'd have to resort to checking who was who with his tally sensor. That was somehow discourteous like having to read an officer's name tag every time—and an admission that, as a commander, Rex didn't *know* his men.

"Permission to engage in witty banter—in your own time, go on."

"Witty banter commencing, sir . . . stand by."

So Ince had a sense of humor after all. Rex smiled to

himself and let them mull over the fact that they weren't on Kamino any longer.

The shuttle aligned with the aft bay and settled on its dampers with a slight shudder. As the ramp went down, Ahsoka bounced out first, ahead of Rex. As he put his boot on the deck, Gil Pellaeon walked across the durasteel plating in his gray working rig and came to a halt a few meters away. His stance said that this was his world, his ship; and the captain was the law.

He looked down his nose at the tiny Togruta Jedi, not unkindly, but out of necessity. Ahsoka was short. She might have acted as if she were Wookiee-sized, but nothing could change the fact that she was *small*—and a kid. A few crew paused to watch, some clones, some nonclones. Rex hovered on the brink of intervention.

"Ma'am." Pellaeon nodded formally, clicking the heels of his polished boots. "Welcome aboard. First thing we do is get you kitted out in proper rig." He glanced over his shoulder. "Chief? Chief, get Padawan Tano some fireproof fatigues and safety boots. Smallest size the stores can find. Cut off the length if you need to."

Rex hadn't actually thought to warn Ahsoka about suitable attire for the acquaint. It was sensitive stuff, telling a female what to wear, especially a Jedi, even if she was a fourteen-year-old. Besides, Pellaeon was so much more *gracious* with the ladies. The captain kept his eyes fixed on hers.

"I didn't have to wear fatigues on any *other* ship," Ahsoka said stiffly.

"You're not suitably attired, my dear." His tone was very paternal for a moment. "We do *not* expose flesh in this ship, not only because it's unbecoming, undisciplined, and *distracting,* but because a ship is a dangerous place. Sharp edges, noxious chemicals, hot exhausts, weapons flash. Safety first, Padawan. Cover up."

"But I *fight* like this." Suddenly Ahsoka was any youngster defending her choice of fashion to a stuffy parent, not a Jedi at all. She looked down at her bare legs and midriff as if she'd suddenly realized she had them. "And I never get hurt. Admiral Yularen let—"

"Admiral Yularen may do as he wishes in his own ship. This vessel is *my* domain. You'll cover up, please, Padawan Tano."

"But I always—"

"Not in *my* navy."

Rex had no choice but to stand at attention and wait for the battle of wills to end. The new troopers were commendably unmoving in a neat line to his left; Coric rocked back and forth on his heels very discreetly, movement almost unseen, boots creaking a little. Pellaeon waited, and then extended one arm out to his side as the Fleet Chief came striding toward him with a pair of solid boots and folded dark blue coveralls.

Pellaeon took the items without even looking around and handed them to Ahsoka.

"Thank you," she said, chin down. Then she trotted back up the ramp.

Pellaeon's shoulders relaxed visibly. "Good grief, Rex, doesn't Skywalker tell his underlings to put some clothes on? What does he think this is, a cruise liner?"

It was at times like this that Rex savored the true value of his bucket. He silenced his helmet audio for a moment with a quick eye movement, roared with laughter, and then switched the speaker back on.

"Would you like me to ask him, sir?"

"Rex, you're enjoying this . . ."

"Me, sir? Never, sir."

"We're both captains, Rex . . . it's Gil. Drop the *sir.*"

"Navy captain outranks army captain, sir. Strictly speaking."

"Shut up, for goodness' sake, man, and come have a drink."

Good old Pellaeon. He didn't give a bantha's backside about protocol. They worked in silence. Eventually, Ahsoka strode back down the ramp of the shuttle, blue fatigues belted tightly at the waist, over-long sleeves rolled up to her wrists, and presented herself to Pellaeon.

"Will this do?" Poor kid; she looked embarrassed. The brightly colored stripes on her three head-tails looked more vivid than ever—a blush, Rex had learned, sometimes one of discomfort, sometimes anger. He guessed it was a little of both this time. "I just want you to know that it's so baggy that I'm going to trip over it and break my neck, that's all. Not very *safe*."

"You'll grow into it, my dear," Pellaeon said, looking satisfied. "And Jedi are too spatially aware to trip, yes? Chief Massin will show you to your cabin."

Pellaeon waited for Ahsoka to vanish through the bay doors behind the Chief, then turned to Rex. "How long a respite do you need?"

"I'm told two to three days."

"Ah, not *your* request for downtime for your men, then."

"No." Rex trod carefully. "General Skywalker has his reasons for wanting to operate alone, whatever they might be, and his Padawan is still at the over-curious stage. I really appreciate your help, Captain."

"My pleasure." Pellaeon beckoned to the troopers; Coric followed them up like a herd dog. "Besides, you might be able to help me knock some of my crew into shape. Ah, for the days when a commanding officer could dump a useless minion out the air lock without having to worry about filling in *forms* . . ."

"Very unsporting, sir," Coric said. "Unless you give them a fifty-meter start."

Pellaeon laughed. But like all humor in this war, it was a thinly worn veneer over permanent anxiety, and the crew *did* end up dying in hard vacuum, and the only way most personnel seemed able to cope was to joke in ways that seemed inappropriate ways to beings cocooned in peace and safety.

Rex took his laughs where he could. This was as near to downtime as he might ever get: among others who understood him, far from civilians on Coruscant who never would, a safe limbo between the two extremes.

"It's going to be boring, sir," Coric said to him as they walked down the passage to the mess deck. "And in a *good* way."

"Make the most of it," Rex said. "Catch up on some sleep. All of you."

Two or three days of relative idling was just what they needed. All he had to do was to keep Ahsoka occupied. And how hard could that be?

A tiny figure came striding down the passage toward them, coping remarkably well with a pair of durasteel-capped safety boots. Ahsoka's head-tails bounced like braids.

"I'm ready, Rex." She beamed. "Show me the conc missile bay."

Athar: next morning

"You!" yelled the overseer at the factory gates. He was strikingly pale, and for a moment Hallena thought he was an albino. But he was just very blond, an oddity in Athar. "You, with the red scarf! You want some machine shop work?"

She realized he was pointing at her. She stood in the ragged line of laborers outside the munitions factory, just one of a crowd waiting for work assigned by the day.

Great way to miss security checks. Some dictatorships are so wonderfully dumb.

"No, sir." That was always the hardest act for her: pretending to be deferential. "Just sweeping up. You got any jobs?"

The gray dust had drifted everywhere like fine, grubby snow. At least the wind had dropped.

"We've always got sweeping jobs," the overseer said, kicking a pile of dust into the air by way of demonstration. "Especially now. Get in here. Where's your ID?"

Hallena edged her way to the front of the line, drawing surly and envious glances as if she were being accorded some kind of privilege. As she turned sideways to edge between two men—*remember, mind your body language, think passive, think humble*—she caught the eye of one of them, and it was a moment of reminder, of revelation. She looked into the eyes of a starving man; not literally, because he seemed solidly built, but a man desperate to find a day's work, and perhaps she had snatched it from him. The man stared back. It was just a heartbeat, not even a second.

She had never seen that look on Coruscant, not up close. Suddenly she understood the heart of the enemy she was facing; and it scared her more than warships and invasions, because it could not be shot down, bombed, or brought to a negotiating table. It was the face of desperation, of a fear and need so primal that it could be mobilized to do *anything.*

We've picked a loser here.

This place is ripe for revolution. No wonder the Seps want to move in. One push, one coup—

"What are you kriffing well waiting for, then?" the overseer yelled. "You want this job or not? I got a hundred ready to take your place, sweetheart."

"Sorry, sir." *Arrogant barve. I hope I have cause to drop you* . . . "Right away, sir."

Hallena jerked her eyes away and pushed through the line. She hadn't realized it had been that obvious. It was just a split second's glance. She'd have to be much more careful in a society where everyone was clearly geared up to watching and denouncing their neighbor to survive.

She held out her fake identichip to the overseer. He took it, slipped it into a chip reader, and stared at the display. It wasn't the first time that she'd stood on that knife-edge between life and death, hoping that her cover wasn't blown, but—

Hey, I'm not behind enemy lines yet. I'm here with the Regent's consent and knowledge. Why am I feeling like this?

The overseer smirked as he glanced at the readout. It must have shown him her prison record. "Learned your lesson, then, troublemaker?"

"I just want to keep my head down and put food on the table," she said.

"If I get a single *sniff* of you stirring up the rabble in here, I'll personally cut your throat."

Yes, *this* was the hardest part of undercover work. Not staring down the muzzle of a blaster; not dreading discovery and a lonely, anonymous death, undiscovered and a long way from home. The most unbearable moment for Hallena Devis was biting her lip while a piece of scum like this insulted her intelligence, and *not* dispensing the instant justice he richly deserved.

But she could find a few moments for that in her busy schedule later, she was sure.

"Like I said," she murmured, eyes lowered, hating herself for even being able to *feign* submission, "I want to eat. That's all."

The supervisor seemed to feel that he'd made his point. "Report to the personnel office," he said, and stepped back to let her pass into the compound. The rusty main doors parted to let her in, and the clanging, hissing, throbbing noise of a busy factory spilled out in a deafening wave. It hurt her ears as she walked with her head lowered through the cavernous hangar, past assembly lines where

scores of workers were sealing small canisters or checking durasteel components against measuring rods, but nobody took much notice of her. One man glanced up,
smiled, then went back to riveting a durasteel sheet
around the curve of what looked like an exhaust. By the
time Hallena got to the personnel office—a shabby cubicle at the far end of the factory floor—a scruffy droid that
looked in worse shape than the metal being hammered all
around her was watching intently.

While one arm continued shuffling flimsi and the other
tapped on an accounting pad, it reached out behind itself
with a manipulator mounted on its back. A broom arced
around in that third hand and almost smacked her in the
legs. If anyone was doing an efficiency study, the droid
scored a clean hundred every time. Hallena wondered
what it was doing with its legs under the desk. No limb
was idle, that was for sure.

"One broom," the droid said. "You break it or lose it,
you pay for it. You sweep the entire production area floor
plus the refreshers and the corridors. Ten-minute meal
break when the klaxon sounds. You go home when the
place is inspected and approved by the overseer. If he ap-
proves, you get paid and come back again in the morning.
If he doesn't, you get nothing, and don't come back. Any
questions?"

Hallena was tempted, but her discipline had kicked in
fully now. She didn't even *think* a sharp retort.

"No," she said, and took the broom in both hands,
quarterstaff-style. "I don't need a floor plan to find my
way around, do I?"

The droid was incapable of sneering, but it managed to
convey its disdain pretty well simply by pauses that would
have made an actor envious.

"What's to find?" it said at last. "Eyes down, find the
dust, push the broom. Stop when you can see the original
color of the tiles."

So Hallena had managed to disappear instantly into the shrouded existence of the workforce. So far, so good. She headed for the refreshers and concentrated on looking authentic.

Stang, they stank. If she needed any excuse to hide away from the factory floor, a pail of disinfectant and a brush would be the perfect cover to retreat out here. She got to work. A quick and discreet sweep with the bug sensor set in her wrist chrono showed there was no surveillance cam making sure the workers didn't linger too long in here with a copy of a holozine.

Is the rest of the planet as vile as this?

Republic Intel said it was. But it wasn't the Republic's problem. All that mattered was stopping the Separatists from overthrowing the Regent and invading the planet.

Maybe they can overthrow the regime when the war's over. This isn't an ally I like very much . . .

The one good thing about living in a dictatorship like JanFathal, though, was that the information underground, the exchange of whispered news and gossip, was a lot faster and sharper than in the complacent walkways of Coruscant, where they were more worried about smashball scores and scandalous holovid actresses. That was democracies for you: They didn't know what they had until they lost it. Here, information was precious. Secrets mattered. And within an hour, Hallena backed out of a refresher cubicle to find the path of her broom blocked by two workers in dark gray coveralls.

Their working clothes had probably been another color once, but that gray dust got everywhere.

Hallena paused and leaned on her broom.

"My mama used to say to lift your feet when a lady was doing the cleaning . . ."

The two were familiar. They should have been. She'd studied their holoimages for long enough.

"Sister Taman," she said, holding out her hand. "I think

you're among friends again. I'm Merish Hath, and this is my comrade Shil Kaval. We're *union*."

"*Union*," Hallena said slowly, "got me a few years in jail."

"Times are changing," said Shil. "But not fast enough."

Hallena went back to sweeping. "Don't expect me to help you speed 'em up . . ."

Merish had effectively blocked the exit. It was all working better than Hallena had hoped. "They say you were a committed activist in Nuth before the Regent had the town razed to the ground."

Oh, great briefing, Intel. What? Razed when? "Don't want to talk about it."

"And we've got more *supportive* friends to call on now the war's kicked off."

Hallena paused, straightened up, and maintained a skeptical face. Desperate people did indeed do desperate things. This was, just as Intel had said, the route to the Separatist infiltration here. It was going to be a more straightforward job than she thought.

Maybe just a few weeks. Maybe—I can find some time with Gil.

Maybe I won't feel bad at all when I look back at how I stopped these people from putting their Regent's head on a well-deserved spike.

"This had better be good," she said. "I'm not doing any more time inside."

"You won't need to," said Merish. "All that's going to change."

Hallena managed one more careful moment of hesitation and then shook the woman's hand. Shil patted her on the back.

Now—*now* she was behind enemy lines.